"MAKE LOVE
TO ME, MIN

Brad's voice was like an intoxicating potion.

For a moment Minta hesitated. Loving Brad would not be simple. There would be nothing purely physical about it. Caring about another human being meant sharing his triumphs and his trials, and today she'd sensed that Brad was in trouble.

As his mouth settled upon hers with a seductive gentleness, her misgivings were swept aside. With slow deliberation she began unbuttoning his shirt, slipping her fingers inside to tangle in the hairs on his chest. She continued to undress him until they were touching, clinging, caressing in a lovers' tight embrace. When his hard masculinity began straining against her, she silently led the way to the bed.

She forgot all the questions she was planning to ask him—for tonight was the only answer she needed.

DEBORAH JOYCE
is also the author
of this title in
SuperRomance

A QUESTING HEART

Beryl had no intention of joining the Everest expedition when, in place of her ailing brother, she flew to Nepal with supplies for his team.

Then fate and Rock Rawlings' dark magnetism conspired, compelling her to stay. Though their longing for each other was unmistakable, Rock made it clear nothing would distract him from reaching his goal.

Long ago, disillusioned by love, Beryl had vowed she would never fall for a man like Rock. But he tapped a primitive current within her, piercing her defences. She found she could not resist even this . . . a love so transient it could last only as long as the climb.

SILVER HORIZONS

Deborah Joyce

A SuperRomance from

HARLEQUIN

London · Toronto · New York · Sydney

First published in Great Britain in 1985 by Harlequin, 15–16 Brook's Mews, London W1A 1DR

© Deborah Joyce 1984

ISBN 0 373 70142 X

11–1085

Printed and bound in Great Britain by Cox & Wyman Ltd, Reading

CHAPTER ONE

MINTA WAS A FEW PACES behind the tall man, admiring his lean hips and long strides, when someone jostled his elbow. A leather case he held under his arm plunged to the floor. She paused, watching as a sheaf of papers scattered across her path. One fluttered to a stop directly atop the toe of her suede boot.

She bent over automatically. "I'll get this one."

"Don't." The sharp command came from a masculine voice overhead.

She ignored the order, holding on to the paper as she straightened. The owner of the case had dropped to one knee, grasping for the papers. She couldn't help but be amused by the stubborn resistance of the thin sheets as they slithered just out of his reach.

The man she surveyed had first caught her attention in the airport in Miami. She hadn't realized until now that they'd taken the same flight.

As he gathered his papers she had time to study him closer, and she liked what she saw. The straight nose, the deep crease in his blunt chin, the full curve of his mouth. His coppery bronze skin fascinated her. Either he'd acquired it by lying in the sun for hours, or it was natural, like her own. The only way to be certain would be to catch a glimpse under his dark business suit.

He rose and faced her. His eyes were brown with amber flecks and his expression was intent. She moistened her lips and smiled, wondering what he'd think if he could read her mind. Holding out the paper she still held, she said, "This one got away from you."

He reached out and grasped it with a swift motion. "Thanks," he said roughly and impatiently. As he shoved the last papers into his case she started to move past him. It was one thing to be preoccupied and another to be uncivil, she decided.

"Sorry if I seemed abrupt," he added from behind her. There was a hint of humor in the deep voice now. "I'm not used to having an attractive woman picking up after me."

She stopped, adjusting the canvas garment bag slung over her shoulders. Several strands of her long black hair were entangled in the wide straps, and it took time to unwind them. Acutely aware of his gaze, her fingers were stiff and clumsy. Finished at last she glanced up and met admiration in his tawny eyes.

"Now we're equal," she said huskily. "I don't make a habit of picking up after an attractive man, either." With that parting comment, she turned and walked away.

His low laugh was still rumbling pleasantly in her ears when she rounded a corner and spotted a bank of wall phones. She paused, watching as he continued down the corridor. Grand Cayman was a small island, she reminded herself. With any kind of luck, they'd meet again.

The first pay phone she tried worked, more than she could say for the majority of the ones in Washington, D.C. Her call went through smoothly, but no one answered in her office. An unseasonable April snowstorm had been threatening when she'd left D.C. earlier that day. Probably workers on the Hill had been advised to leave early to avoid the massive traffic jams. She replaced the receiver, deciding the call had been unnecessary anyway.

Across the hall she spotted a small gift shop and went inside. After selecting a magazine and several thick novels, she began searching a rack of postcards for the sunniest scenes. Without thinking she added a newspaper to her purchases at the cash register.

She was back in the hall before she realized what she'd done. Habit. Like most people, she read the constant barrage of bad news, never realizing how much damage it did to her mind. For the length of this vacation she'd vowed to remove herself from other people's troubles. It was the only way she could sort out her own. Folding the newspaper with a snap, she glanced around for a trash barrel.

She still hadn't found one when she saw the car-rental agency. A uniformed young woman with sandy hair stood behind the desk as she approached. "Minta Cordero. I have a reservation for a compact," Minta said.

"Just one moment." The accent was clipped, very British. "Yes, here's the card. Which color do you prefer? We have red or tan left."

"Red." Minta's own car was a bright-red Austin-Healey, but it spent most of its time stored in an expensive garage in D.C.

Before leaving the desk she remembered something else. "My travel agency said I could pick up keys here for the cottage where I'll be staying. Surfside Realty is handling the details."

There was a brief pause as the woman's clear blue eyes studied her. "I'm afraid I've already given the keys to a man...."

"No, Diane." A lean black man in his early thirties emerged from the back office. "Richard left another envelope when you were on your break. Look in the top drawer." He turned to Minta. "Busy tourist season. Good thing you made reservations."

She smiled as she accepted the envelope from Diane. "Could you give me directions to my cottage?"

"There should be a map inside the envelope," said Diane.

Minta ripped it open and pulled out the slip of paper. "Great. Looks like I'm all set." She glanced down at her brown wool blazer, red blouse and softly gathered chamois skirt. "At least I'll be all set when I can change into something cooler."

Outside she matched the license number with the receipt and was unlocking the door of the red compact when she realized what was wrong. Damn, she hadn't thought about the Caymans being British. Driving on the left side would be a new experience. *Think backward,* she told herself. *Remember to glance the opposite direction of what seems normal before pulling out of the parking lot.*

Traffic was light with more bicycles than cars on the narrow road. She rolled down the windows and got her first whiff of the salt-scented breezes. The soft wind tangled the silky blue-black strands of her hair and cooled the back of her neck. The flow of the gentle air fingered into the cleavage of her blouse, and she removed one hand from the wheel long enough to unfasten several buttons.

Within moments her tense shoulder muscles relaxed. She began searching the radio dial to locate a music station. A harsh voice invaded the intimate space, stating, "Police announced today the kidnapping of an Italian businessman...." With an irritated gesture she flipped off the sound.

Vacation, Cordero, she reminded herself grimly. Or at least that was what she had insisted on calling this month of enforced rest. Al Slessor, her immediate superior, had wanted it to be labeled medical leave. Reason: Overwork leading to impaired judgment on the job. She'd refused, and Jerry Richards, one of the top men in the agency, had intervened on her behalf. She owed him one for that.

She turned her attention to the lushly green scenery on both sides. Oleander bushes with delicate pink flower clusters spread in confused splendor along the road. Here and there magenta hibiscus dotted the landscape. Trailing vines of orange and scarlet bougainvillea covered fences and walls. Clashing colors were mysteriously blended into a pleasing harmony by some secret of the plant world. Already she was falling in love with this island paradise.

As the road curved she caught a glimpse of the sea. Sun sparkled on the blue waters tinted with cobalt and turquoise. A shining wave rose and fell, and she watched as another formed in the distance. At the water's edge lay a limitless expanse of sand. Sand so white it glistened with blinding intensity, reminding her she needed to buy sunglasses tomorrow.

Delighted with the scene before her, she pulled over to the side of the road for a few moments. Inhaling deeply she delighted in the perfumed breezes. *Alone.* The word seemed almost magical. *Alone but not lonely,* she thought. There was a difference, one she knew well.

After checking her map once more she drove on, turning at the next cross street onto a hard-packed marl road. Here there were even more bicyclists, and she had to maneuver her way around several colorfully dressed throngs.

A car sped past her, and she caught a glimpse of red. The car was identical with the one she was driving. She was still tailing close behind it when she turned onto a road skirting the beach. A small cluster of beach cottages dotted the shoreline.

Their pastel shades of pale pink, baby blue and mint green were ethereal, dreamlike. The puffy white clouds overhead and Victorian gingerbread trim on the wide porches of the cottages reminded her of a spun-sugar village.

She visualized herself swaying gently in one of the porch swings, watching the hypnotic waves. Indulgence. Pure indulgence. And memories to be stored for those times when her life was a constant fight against violence and ugliness.

She caught sight of the number on a wooden hanging sign. Three. Her own cabin was number ten. In the distance she saw one cottage set far apart from the others. It had to be her own. She'd asked for isolation.

When she came to the end of the road, she braked to a stop and then noticed the car that had passed her earlier had stopped also. The realtor, she decided instantly. Her travel agent must have alerted him to her arrival time.

"Hi," she called out her window, smoothing her hair into a semblance of order before getting out.

"Hello."

Minta glanced up in surprise at the familiar voice and found herself staring at the man she'd encountered in the airport. She was even more aware of his broad cheekbones, strong chin and sensual lips in the strong sunlight. Six feet of compactly built masculinity, she summarized as he swung out of his car. She pointed to her own car, laughing. "I'm really not following you."

Golden lights twinkled in his brown eyes. "This *is* a pleasant surprise. Are you with Surfside Realty?"

"No. Aren't you?" He had removed his suit jacket since she'd last seen him. Trying not to be obvious, she observed the immaculate fit of his white shirt and the way he had loosened the maroon tie at his throat. If a vacation fling had been on her agenda, this was undoubtedly the man she would have picked to enjoy it with.

"I've rented cottage nine," he explained, holding up his envelope.

"I'm sure this is ten," she said gently. There was no reason to embarrass the man over making a mistake. "It's the last one along the beach."

"That one is eight," he said with amusement, as if he'd guessed what her thoughts were. She followed his gaze to a sign near the house behind them, verifying the number. For a moment she was taken aback.

"Since there doesn't seem to be a number on this one, there's only one way to find out," she said finally. Holding up her key, she itched to dispel some of his smug confidence.

She strode ahead of him, becoming more waspish with each step as the heels of her boots sank into the soft, deep sand.

"Here, let me help you," he said, moving up beside her and grasping her elbow. "I don't think those shoes...."

"Are suitable," she snapped, pulling her arm away. She hated being at a disadvantage. Leaning over, she unzipped first one boot and then the other.

He paused beside her, watching as she struggled to maintain her balance.

The humidity in the air made the soft suede leather cling tenaciously to the length of her legs. Realizing she was close to making a fool out of herself, she bent her knee and held her foot out. "How about a tug?"

"Glad to." He grasped her foot firmly, adding, "Grab hold of my arms."

She reached out tentatively, intending only to rest her fingertips against him, but his firm movements propelled her toward him. Her hands encountered sinewy muscles beneath the silky fabric of his shirt, and at such close range she had no choice but to stare into his eyes. She shifted, suddenly warm.

As one boot fell to the ground, she attempted to stand on her other foot. He steadied her by reaching a hand under her blazer and grasping her waist. It was an intimate gesture, one that took her by surprise. The warmth of his fingers burned through the silky fabric. She glanced up and their gazes met and held. His look was long and personal and her blood seemed to heat, flushing her coppery skin most attractively. The smile he gave her was as potent as it was unexpected.

He was the first to look away. "Why did you wear these to the Caymans?" he asked as his fingers removed the other boot. Leaning over, he picked up the one on the ground and presented both to her.

Minta sought to discipline her voice. "When I left home this morning it was freezing. I had a meeting to attend before my flight." She removed her hands from his forearms and stepped away, wondering how it was possible for such a brief moment with this man to raise her blood pressure to such heights.

As they neared the cottage she could see it was much larger than she had expected. There were two porch swings, one on both ends. And twin front doors with ovals of frosted glass.

"Damn, I think it's a duplex," he muttered.

His total change in manner startled Minta. "You're right. There's a nine on that door and a ten on this one."

"I won't tolerate this. I specifically asked for my own cottage," he said, his tone growing angrier.

"So did I," she returned, equally firm. He ignored her, walking up the steps to thrust his key in the lock of cottage nine. He strode inside without glancing back, slamming the door.

Men didn't usually mutter oaths over the thought of being next door to her, thought Minta dryly. While she was as upset over the mistake as he was, she didn't appreciate his anger. After all, it hadn't been her fault. She opened her own door and went inside.

The clean white walls and sky-blue ceilings blended with antique wicker furnishings. Sheer ruffly white curtains floated gently against the open windows. Hand-crocheted rag rugs dotted the bleached-wood floors. *Homey, old-fashioned, a total contrast with my apartment in D.C.,* Minta concluded immediately. *And exactly the place I need for this vacation.* It had definitely been worth raiding her savings to rent this luxury beach cottage.

She put down her key beside a pearly pink conch shell and made a quick survey of the other rooms. The bathroom was small but sparkly clean with shells embedded randomly in the wall tiles. She fell in love with the glass-doored cabinets in the kitchen and the view over the sink of a sweeping expanse of ocean and sky. On a rear veranda she glimpsed a hammock swaying invitingly.

The last room she inspected was the bedroom. It was a melange of soft pastel shades, like the dishes of sherbet she had loved as a child. The wicker bed was piled high with lace and satin pillows in lime and peach and pineapple pales. She tried to imagine the man next door in a bed like this, his muscular body reclining against the lace pillows, and gave up, laughing at her fantasy. Undoubtedly at this moment he was making arrangements for another place to stay.

If he left, she realized she might need to as well. The realtors would then be free to rent the other half of this duplex to anyone. It would ruin her vacation if a group of merrymakers moved in next door and partied all night. She had come here to rest and engage in some serious decision making. As much as she loved this cottage, she'd have to settle for one of the single ones farther up the beach if her neighbors were annoying. Somehow, the man next door didn't seem the type to make unnecessary noise. Maybe he wouldn't move after all.

Reluctantly she returned to the living room and located the phone. Glancing at the tag on the cottage key, she saw the number for Surfside Realty. The phone was answered on the third ring.

"I'm in cottage ten and. . . ."

"I know," said the male voice wearily. "I've just gotten off the phone with your neighbor. I'm sorry about the mistake. When someone asks for isolation, I always choose that cottage since it's at the end of the road. This is the first time I've had to rent both sides together."

"I understand. Is the man next door going to move?"

"No. We're booked solid and so is everyone else. There may be a few cancellations for a room in one of the high-rise hotels but not for these cottages. We've got a waiting list."

"He seemed angry." She couldn't imagine her neighbor settling down without putting up a fight.

"He is. If he gives you any trouble, feel free to call. You're Minta Cordero, aren't you? I've got your card out."

"Yes. But don't worry about me. I can take care of myself." A smile crept into her voice. The man next door would find he had met his match if he tried to cause her any trouble. Actually she felt relieved. If both of them wanted privacy, it was likely they wouldn't bother each other.

"Okay, but ask for Richard Long if you need anything."

"Thanks, I'll remember."

After hanging up the phone she peeled off her wool blazer and went into the bathroom to splash cool water on her face. A glance in the shell-framed mirror revealed the softly bronzed swells of her full breasts.

She'd forgotten about unbuttoning her blouse in the car earlier. Now she could understand the sensual darkening of her neighbor's eyes as he leaned nearer her outside. As she remembered the scene, a high tide of emotion made her blood pound in her temples. Her quickening response to every thought of this man amazed her.

She rebuttoned the blouse and stripped off her hose before going outside. The warm sand squished pleasantly between her bare toes as she ran toward the car. After gathering up her purchases from the front seat, she reached for her garment bag and then locked the car. The only sign of her neighbor was his car sitting beside hers.

She had finished a quick shower and was debating what to wear when she saw the newspaper, open on a round wicker table in the living room. She reached for it to pitch it in a wastebasket, and her eyes zeroed in on a photo in the lower right-hand corner of the front page. It's caption read: "Robotics Whiz Missing."

Her eyes widened slowly. The identity of this person was known to her. Less than thirty minutes earlier she had been grasping his arms in the sand in front of this cottage. She held the paper closer and began reading the article.

Brad McMillan, robotics genius and owner of the Austin, Texas, Galactia Enterprises, was reported missing today by Ron Williams, manager of the company.

Genius. She took a minute to digest that and then continued reading.

According to Williams, Mr. McMillan did not attend a scheduled meeting of the board on Tuesday. A check with friends revealed no information as to his whereabouts. Williams asserts this behavior is completely out of character for McMillan.

Williams explained, "Brad has always marched to a different beat than most mortals, but he'd never cause his friends any worry if he could help it. I think there's a strong possibility of foul play."

Minta glanced over at their shared wall. *Foul temper is more like it, if the realtor can be believed,* she thought. She read on, "The police declined to say whether or not they were involved in the case."

Typical, Minta thought, grinning. It was a running battle between journalists and law-enforcement agencies. While she agreed the press had a responsibility to keep the public informed, she also understood the need for secrecy while vital evidence was being gathered. The best solution was still the trite but effective, "No comment."

Her smile faded as she scrutinized the photo more carefully. It was an informal shot. Brad McMillan wore a pale shirt that molded itself over his sinewy chest, and she got her first glimpse of the muscular arms she'd felt under her fingertips. Beside Brad stood an engaging robotlike creature.

The photo had a fuzzy quality, but it was clear enough to remind her of this man's tremendous appeal. There was an arrogant tilt to the head she hadn't noticed in person, but the determined chin was as visible as ever. *Genius. The man's conceit must be stifling,* she decided, fanning herself with one hand.

She wondered if this should be a concern of hers. It didn't sound as if Brad was suspected of any criminal activity. She had always believed people had a right to their privacy, and he seemed hell-bent to preserve his. On the other hand, it was obvious he had left friends worrying about him. Of course, they could be well-meaning but too inquisitive. She sometimes felt a need to escape from everyone periodically, so she could empathize with Brad.

But the potential police involvement was another matter altogether. No one knew better than she how thinly stretched law-enforcement agencies usually were. She couldn't allow them to institute a search while he was lying right on the beach under her very nose. The very pretty nose that belonged to one of the youngest and best FBI agents the organized-crime division had ever known.

Stop, she reminded herself sharply as she dumped the paper with its intriguing picture in the basket. *You're off duty. This is nothing but speculation at this stage. Al Slessor has already made a formal complaint saying you have a tendency to stick your nose where it doesn't belong. Just keep your eye on Mr. Genius, and if you see anything sinister, then report it.*

That thought brought a smile to her lips. Keeping an eye on Brad McMillan sounded like a distinct pleasure.

BRAD MCMILLAN DROPPED THE PHONE back into its cradle and ran a hand through his hair. He'd never been more frustrated. There was no way he could stay here past tonight. He'd offered any amount of money to find an isolated cottage, and all he'd gotten was a promise from Richard Long to try.

Richard had asked him if he didn't find the scenery enjoyable. Damn, the scenery was spectacular, he admitted as he dropped into a chair and stared at the wall separating him from the woman on the other side.

Minta Cordero. That's what Richard had called her. An unusual name for an unusual lady. He'd first noticed her in the airport in Miami. The attraction had been instantaneous, but as he continued watching her, it had grown in intensity. There was a sensual vitality about her that made him not care if she caught him staring.

She hadn't. Her mind seemed totally preoccupied as she had tapped her foot impatiently in the line waiting to board the Cayman-bound plane. He hadn't minded the wait. He'd spent his time watching that curtain of black hair swishing against the curve of her slim hips.

It wasn't hard to visualize that hair swirling over slender bared shoulders and flowing down the coppery skin of her full breasts. He was certain she hadn't been aware that the buttons of her blouse had been open when she'd asked him to help her take off her boots. It was all he could do not to lean over and press his lips against the soft inviting skin.

He tried to imagine what she would have done if he'd tried it and he chuckled. Minta had an air about her that told him instinctively she'd defend herself. He liked that in a woman.

He also liked the way her dark eyes glowed with a sharp intellect. Her tongue was sharp, too, he reminded himself ruefully, remembering her irritation when she'd discovered he'd been right to assume this was cottage nine.

He'd thought he'd seen beautiful women before, but there was something so unusual about Minta that it took his breath away. Her almond-shaped eyes with thick jet-black lashes compelled his gaze. And there was something about her fine bronzed skin, smooth as silk, that almost demanded his touch. He tried to recall who she was reminding him of and then remembered. His grandmother. The picture of his mother's mother when she'd been a young woman. Minta must share his American Indian heritage.

Any other time he would have welcomed the way they kept running into each other. He grimaced, thinking of the idiotic way he'd acted when she had retrieved one of the papers he had dropped. His only excuse was that he'd been caught off balance, concerned for the moment that the case hadn't been jostled accidentally.

When he'd seen Minta standing there, amused at his struggle to gather up the papers before they were seen, he'd wanted desperately to ask her to have a drink with him. But he hadn't dared.

He stood and began stripping off his shirt. After a shower he'd make a trip into town. Tonight he'd have to content himself with gourmet pleasures instead of an evening spent with her.

Cheese, ripe tropical fruit, French bread so fresh it was still warm. And wine. He'd treat himself to the best wine he could find on the island, he decided, reminding himself he could have it worse.

CHAPTER TWO

MINTA PULLED ON A PAIR of white cotton slacks and tightened the drawstring around her narrow waist. The green cotton halter she chose fit snugly over her breasts. Free of the constraints of winter clothes, she sauntered out the door onto the wooden veranda.

Tropical flowers grew profusely on bushes on either side of the duplex. Roses climbed on vines over an arching trellis. A curving walk was outlined with rows of conch shells glowing pale peach in the late-evening sun.

The white sand, holding the afternoon's heat, tingled at her toes. Far out on the horizon the sun was sinking into the limitless expanse of turquoise waters, its dusky roses and purples fanning out in a gentle arc.

She wanted to take her first walk before the darkness fell so she hurried down the winding path until she reached the beach. It was totally isolated from either direction, and she rolled up her sheer cotton trouser legs and began wading into the lapping waves.

The seawater was warm and buoyant against her

ankles as she threw back her head, her hair tossing in wild abandon from the delightful sea breezes. Running parallel with the shoreline, she lifted her knees high, humming a spirited tune.

By the time she dragged herself out onto the warm sand it was almost totally dark, the only light reflecting from the glow of the white sands. She dropped to her knees and leaned over, gasping for breath. This was what she had come for. Cleansing of muscles, of mind, of spirit.

She wondered if that might be why Brad McMillan had come. She had noticed fine lines of fatigue and tension around his eyes. He might have slipped away because the demands of his business had suddenly become overwhelming.

She could empathize. As an FBI undercover agent, there were times when she felt incapable of hearing of another embezzlement, another hostage situation, another crime of any sort. The work she had chosen was never ending. The moment one mystery was solved, another erupted. Perhaps Brad's responsibilities had weighed on him in the same way.

When she started back toward their shared cottage, she could make out only a faint outline. Both sides lay in total darkness. Funny, she hadn't seen Brad leave. He hadn't been on the beach, so perhaps he had gone somewhere in his car. When she reached the veranda, she had to feel her way up the wooden railing on the steps. Her eyes became accustomed to the night by the time she reached her back door and she stepped inside the kitchen.

It was pitch-black. She hesitated a foot or two inside the entrance, wishing she'd remembered to leave a light on. Her fingers fumbled along a wall until they encountered a light switch. Light flooded the room, chasing out an eerie sense of unreality.

Briskly she swung open a door and stared into an empty pantry. She distinctly remembered a conversation with the woman at the travel agency in D.C. She had suggested Minta pay an optional fee that provided for basic foodstuffs. The list had specified exactly what she could expect to find in the kitchen on her arrival.

The refrigerator was just as bare when she looked inside it. She debated calling the realtor but decided she wouldn't bother him until morning. There was nothing to do tonight except get dressed again and find a place to eat.

She showered to get the fine sand off her legs and then dressed in an ice-white silk blouse with matching, softly pleated trousers. Around her narrow waist she knotted a turquoise scarf. She brushed her hair back and held it in place with silver filigree combs. Several quick strokes of mascara and she was satisfied with her appearance.

As she was slipping into a pair of silver sandals, she heard a car drive up. Within minutes came the sound of footsteps on the porch outside. Brad must have come back. She risked a quick peek through the window. Yes, the duplicate of her own red compact was parked in front, at a different angle than it had been earlier in the day.

Her neighbor's door opened and then someone was striding down the hall. She frowned. It was obvious every sound was going to carry clearly in this building.

On impulse she went out on her veranda just in time to see the lights in his kitchen come on. Without stopping to think why, she was knocking on his door.

She watched as Brad tensed slightly and his eyes sought the back door. He strode over to it, calling, "Who's there?"

"Your neighbor."

There was a slight pause, then the door was opened. "Hello, neighbor," he said, his gaze flicking quickly over her. "Come in."

She accepted the invitation, moving past him. He was freshly shaven and wearing a tan polo shirt with cotton trousers. His skin had a clean, outdoorsy pine scent that agreed with him. "I was wondering if Surfside left you any food. They seem to have forgotten mine," she said.

"Food?" He was clearly puzzled.

"Yes, basic foodstuffs. It's an optional service I requested. Didn't you ask for it?" His skeptical expression suggested he thought she had manufactured a flimsy excuse to see him again.

"I haven't looked." He turned and swung open his refrigerator door. The shelves held an assortment of food: milk, butter, eggs. "It looks as if I have yours," he said apologetically. His chagrin delighted Minta. "Shall I carry it to your place?" he added.

His eyes were roaming her face inch by inch, which left her oddly breathless. "No, you're probably being charged for it," she said, her skin tingling from his intense scrutiny. She had never met a man who made her so aware of her own body and all without saying one objectionable word. "We'll have to straighten things out with the realtor tomorrow."

"What are you doing for dinner?" he asked.

She knew what he was thinking, that she'd deliberately placed him in a position where he felt obligated to ask her to dinner. For some reason it wasn't bothering her the way it normally would have. "I'm planning on going out," she said.

There was a long silence, and she sensed he was having an inward battle. One side won out at length. "Alone?" His tone lent the word an intimacy she wasn't expecting. Slowly his gaze locked with hers and held her spellbound for a moment.

Minta sensed her answer was important, that it would make all the difference in how much she enjoyed her vacation. "Yes. You're the only person I've met on the island."

He smiled broadly. "Then that makes us equal again. How about sharing my dinner?" She followed his glance over to the cabinet and saw a flimsy box on the counter. Out of it spilled a crusty loaf of bread, mammoth strawberries and a tall bottle of wine beaded with droplets of water. A small bunch of dewy fresh violets graced the collection. Already on the counter lay a can of pâté, a round of Brie and a small jar of caviar. Her taste buds quivered, even as her gaze narrowed on the flowers.

"Where did you find this feast?" she asked.

"A waiter in one of the hotels was most obliging." He took her acceptance for granted as he continued, "See if you can locate the flatware while I wash the lettuce."

As he moved to the sink she watched, thinking that this lean fit body was not what she would have expected of a genius. But then she'd never been in the presence of a genius before. The thought made her smile and as he turned to face her, he said, "Did I say something funny?"

Her shoulders lifted slightly, and she pulled open the nearest drawer. "Sorry, I was thinking of something I'd read recently," she said. "How about taking this food down to the beach? I was there just as it turned dark. It's fantastic."

He didn't glance her way. "I'm expecting a call."

"Of course." Silence. "Did you get any napkins?"

He shook his head, and she walked over to the pantry. Inside the small room the shelves were fully stocked. She heard muffled words and grabbed for a package of napkins. "Sorry, I couldn't hear you," she commented as she emerged.

"I was saying we can take the food to the back porch. I'm sure I can hear the phone ringing from there."

"Lovely idea." She tried ignoring the curiosity building inside her. Even if she could hear what he said on the phone, she didn't intend to eavesdrop. She'd already made a decision to allow him his privacy, and she intended to stick to it. Still, if someone was calling him, it meant his disappearance wasn't a complete secret. Obviously at least one person knew his whereabouts.

Picking up the flowers, she regarded them thoughtfully before setting them aside. On impulse she asked, "Expecting company? These flowers are delightful."

Out of the corner of her eye she saw him stiffen. There was a long silence before he spoke reluctantly. "Toss them out of the way. I bought them from a pushy street vendor. It was the only way I could get rid of the fellow."

Minta knew instinctively there was something he wasn't telling her. It was her nature. She couldn't help being sensitive to any sort of mystery. Silently reproving herself, she turned back to her work.

She rinsed off the strawberries and placed them in a bowl, while he removed the wrapper from the Brie and began opening the can of pâté. As they went about their tasks their bodies brushed in brief, potent contact. Minta stared up at him, her body reacting with an instant flooding of desire that caught her by surprise.

For a moment he stayed against her, his thigh brushing hers, his arm pressing gently into her breasts. There was a feathery dryness in her throat as his eyes made a slow, sensuous study before he turned away abruptly.

"I'll check the table on the porch and see if it needs to be wiped off," he said.

The husky timbre of his voice told her she hadn't been the only one affected by their brief contact. "How about telling me your name first?" she asked, intensely curious to see if he'd lie to protect his identity.

He stopped at the door and turned, laughing. "You're right. We haven't introduced ourselves. I'm Brad McMillan."

"Hi, Brad," she said, pleased he was being honest with her. She was already accustomed to thinking of him as Brad, ever since she'd seen that picture in the newspaper. Lucky she hadn't slipped and called him that before. "I'm Minta Cordero."

"I know, Minta. Richard, the realtor, told me." He repeated her name, lingering on it as though he enjoyed saying it. "Minta suits you. I don't think I've heard it before."

"You won't, unless you know another Zuni Indian," she said, stacking the last of the food back into the box. "Even then, I'm not sure you would have heard it. It's unusual."

"Zuni. Another point of equality between us. I'm Indian, too. At least on my mother's side." He hadn't moved from beside the screen door.

His enthusiasm had wiped the traces of tension from his face. "What's your nation?" she asked, using the Indian designation for tribal distinctions.

They went out on to the porch together. He waited to answer until they were seated at the glass-topped table, the food scattered in front of them. "My mother was a Coastal Indian."

"The ones that carved totem poles?" Minta asked.

"Not really. Most of the totem poles were carved farther north. My ancestors were the ones who wove rain hats out of the bark of redwood trees."

"I remember. Tall dark hats."

"That's right," agreed Brad, laughing. He slipped the cork out of the bottle of champagne.

Minta glanced at the label and then looked back to be certain she'd read it correctly. *Dom Perignon.* Galactia Enterprises appeared to be profitable. At least for its owner.

"Is this a special occasion for you?" she asked, a smile curving the corners of her lips.

"It's special now. Shall we toast our common heritage?" He poured out the delicate, bubbling beverage into the two plain glasses she'd located in a cabinet.

"To us," he murmured, touching his glass to hers.

Their eyes met and Minta's senses were acutely aware of the moment. The luminous stars poking holes in the velvet sky, the tide surging in the distance, the heavy sweet scent of jasmine and roses and the man across from her.

It was almost as if she had stepped outside herself and was viewing this scene from a different perspective, light years away. She could visualize a cameo frame around their sepia-toned images. An image that would still be significant when other memories had faded or disappeared.

She leaned back, dazed, aware he was waiting for her. "To us," she whispered, and then added in a firmer tone. "Two native Americans."

After a small sip she set her glass down. "Do you always eat this lavishly?"

He scooped up caviar on a small cracker and handed it to her. "I frequently get so busy working I forget to eat. But I think it's a shame people don't treat themselves occasionally. Be honest, don't you usually serve the best to guests?"

"Of course. What do you suggest? Send out for hot dogs for my guests and then stuff myself with delicacies when they leave?"

"Why not?" he insisted. "Do you ever taste what you serve company?"

She took a nibble from the cracker he handed her. "Mmm, delicious." When she finished swallowing she added, "I see what you're saying. When I have someone over I go into a tailspin making certain everything is perfect. I'm usually so keyed up I have no idea how anything tastes."

"My point, exactly." He accepted a slice of the creamy Brie. "Think backward is my motto."

She laughed and he looked up. "Do that again."

She glanced down at the slice of bread in her hand to see if she'd done anything particularly clever with it. "Do what?"

He leaned across the table and put his hand on her arm. "Laugh for me again. You have the most beautiful laugh. It's...so uninhibited. So completely natural."

She was acutely aware of his touch. She stared down at his strong, tanned fingers, a close match for her own bronzed skin. An awareness flowed through her that she knew was threatening to get out of hand. She drew her arm back slowly. "I'll have to think about that to see if you've complimented me," she said. "Tell me about your dad, Brad. From what you said, I assume he isn't Indian."

The smile in his eyes told her he was aware of the adept way she'd diverted the focus of their conversation. "No. My father, Alex McMillan, was a red-haired Scotsman. He died when I was five. How about your parents, Minta?"

"Both Zuni. They live near Santa Fe, New Mexico."

"That's your home, too?"

"Washington, D.C.," she corrected. "How about you?" She felt as if they were fencing, each delicately parrying off the other's thrusts to make certain things didn't get too personal.

"I live in Austin, Texas now. I'm originally from Oregon, so I love beaches."

"This is like another world, isn't it?" she said, making a sweeping gesture down to the beach.

"Another planet. If you had been the first person on this island, what would you have named it?"

Minta allowed him to top off her glass again but decided to leave it untouched. It wouldn't take much for her to believe she was on another planet with him. She fingered the rim, watching the bubbles rise to the surface for several minutes. "Something astral. Mars. Venus. No, those are too prosaic. Do you have any suggestions?''

"We must be on the same wavelength, Minta. I named my company in Austin Galactia."

She cringed guiltily, wondering if she'd been probing subconsciously. "What do you make? Space suits?" she asked casually, reaching for a strawberry and popping it in her mouth. He must not be aware his picture was plastered all over the front page of today's news, she decided. She wished she could mention having seen the story about him, but she didn't want to intrude on the intimacy of this moment.

"Me or my company?" he asked.

"It's not the same?"

He shook his head. "My company is involved in manufacturing industrial robots. I'm an inventor."

"Aren't all inventors a little crazy?" she asked.

He was leaning back in his chair, his long legs crossed at the ankles. "I told you I think backward," he said comfortably.

She wasn't used to a man as relaxed as he was. She found most men too intent on impressing women with their abilities. But every action of this man was so open, so unaffected. He attracted and intrigued her at the same time.

"What are you inventing now?" she asked.

"Personal robots that walk and talk. Not just the little arms that take the place of workers on assembly lines."

"Can I put my order in? I'd like one that can

vacuum my floors, take the dishes out of the dishwasher and fold clothes.''

"I have one that can do most of that. Hilda can even greet guests and mix drinks.''

She sat up, indignant. "Hilda? Why not Herbert? It sounds a bit chauvinistic to give your household robot a female name.''

"Hilda is not a servant," he protested. "She's a friend. She also speaks in five languages, sings my favorite operatic arias in a voice uncannily similar to Beverly Sills and has been known to remind me that my socks don't match when I'm leaving the house.''

Minta leaned back, laughing. "You're putting me on, Brad McMillan. There is no such thing as a robot that can do all that.''

"Maybe I'm exaggerating a little," he said sheepishly, "but you'd be amazed how quickly technology is expanding in the robotics field. Hilda is amazing, and she's improving all the time.''

Taking another sip of wine, he swiveled around in his seat to face her fully. "What's your line of work?''

"Guess," Minta countered, her heart thumping uncomfortably. She didn't want to answer questions about her own work right now.

Brad let his gaze drift over her slowly, appraisingly. If eyes could be said to undress, then his had done their work well, thought Minta as she eyed him levelly. A breeze lifted the silky fabric of her trousers, and she felt as if a finger had traced down her spine. "I give," he said at length. "You can't possibly be involved in anything ordinary. Tell me what you do, Minta."

Before coming on this trip she had decided on her cover story. Assuming an undercover identity was second nature to her now. The one she used most often was partially true, and it came out naturally now. "I'm a silversmith. I design and make a line of jewelry." She touched one of the combs in her hair.

He reached over and slipped it out, watching as a curtain of hair drifted over one side of her face. Fingering the delicate filigree design on the comb, he commented, "Yes, this fits with one side of you, but how do you handle your wild nature?"

His perceptiveness caused her to become momentarily uncomfortable and she laughed shakily, "Wild? First you call me uninhibited and now wild. I don't remember doing anything to give you that impression."

He moved his chair around and brushed back her hair with one hand. Minta's muscles went fluid at his touch. She waited for his hands to slide down her shoulders and draw her closer. She was quivering with desire to turn slowly in his arms and meet his lips. When he replaced the comb and moved back, she was filled with an inexplicable feeling of emptiness.

He inhaled deeply. "I'll fix us some coffee."

When the door closed behind him, she leaned back, slowly regaining her natural composure. It had been a long time since she'd felt such desire.

No, that wasn't totally correct. Even with Peter Hammond, she'd never experienced such an intense longing to be held, to be kissed.

She and Peter had been total opposites. Sparks had flown from the time they had first met. Elizabeth Forrester, her favorite friend who happened to be a psychiatrist, had never approved of their relationship. "It's a love-hate relationship," she had explained. "Your differences are what attract you, but that's not enough for marriage. Lovers must also be friends."

She hadn't listened to Elizabeth at first. It was Peter who had suggested she pursue a career in the FBI rather than with the New Mexico police as she'd first planned. She had spent a year in Quantico, Virginia, at the academy there. During that time she and Peter dated frequently and then became engaged.

She'd been twenty-two at the time, over four years ago. They'd be married now if the unthinkable hadn't happened. No one had suspected what Peter was involved in. Not even his closest friends. Still she wondered why she hadn't been more perceptive.

"Cream? Sugar?" Brad's low voice issued from the shadows behind her.

"Black, please." Minta accepted the interruption of her painful thoughts gratefully, reminding herself that she was wrong to assume any blame for what Peter had chosen to do with his life. "I think I'll place my order for a robot exactly like you," she told Brad.

"Oh?" He settled down beside her. She liked the shape of his mouth, the slow thoughtful way he was smiling at her that made her forget everything else.

"One that provides a feast like this and then fixes the coffee. Have you considered using yourself as a model?"

"What makes you think I'm not a robot?" Brad's voice was warm and teasing.

Without warning, Minta's cheeks flushed and he began chuckling softly. "I like that answer, Minta."

She rapped his shin with the toe of her silver sandal. "Enough, McMillan. Remember, I haven't learned to think backward yet."

He laughed aloud. "You're getting there."

"I'll bet you read science fiction."

"I devour it."

"Is that what got you started on robots?"

He took a sip of his coffee. "Not really. After my dad died, my mother opened up an electronics shop. One that sold kits. After school I'd assemble the kits to demonstrate to customers how they worked. It was terrific fun. My favorite kit was a robot."

Memories darkened his eyes, and he looked out toward the sea. In the silence that followed, the steady roar of the surf that had only been background music became the focus of their attention. The sound effect was oddly soothing and she leaned back, wanting to remain here as long as possible.

The phone rang shrilly and Brad jumped. "Excuse me," he said, and strode inside the cottage.

His abruptness startled her and she stood, gazing

after him. For a man on vacation he was certainly edgy. Going over to the porch railing, she leaned against it and stared up at the sky.

Brad McMillan was a compelling man. He was also very puzzling. Take his nervousness over this phone call, for instance. He had been relaxed enough while they were eating, so relaxed, in fact, she'd found it hard to believe he had left so many people to guess his whereabouts. There must be some simple explanation for that picture in the paper. Probably a mix-up of some sort.

The secrecy surrounding him still bothered her, though. It was obvious he had something important on his mind that demanded a great deal of privacy. Idly she sifted through the reasons he might be in the Caymans. Vacation? Possibly, but there was something more. She was sure of it. Money? These islands were famous for their banking practices, guarding secrets as jealously as Switzerland.

Sifting through the images in her mind, she remembered the violets that had been on the kitchen counter. Could love have brought Brad to the Caymans? Was he planning to meet someone there? For a moment her thoughts hovered over this unpleasant possibility, then she rejected them heartily. There was no mistaking the way Brad had been looking at her. Unless he was a practiced ladies' man, he'd been genuinely attracted to her. No, she didn't think Brad was here to meet a woman. Still, questions about his motives niggled at her.

Disgusted by the time she was wasting on speculation, she inhaled deeply, sniffing appreciatively at the fresh salty air. This was her vacation and as of right now, she was going to concentrate on nothing but leisure.

Turning back to the table, she began gathering up the leftovers and dishes. She banged the door behind her as she went into the house so Brad wouldn't think she was eavesdropping, and set the remains of their feast on the counter. The violets lay there, soft and enticing, and she resisted the urge to question him further about them. After all, wasn't a man entitled to buy himself a few flowers? But Brad didn't seem the type to choose violets. She would expect him to choose something with bolder colors and sleeker lines.

In spite of her efforts to ignore the sound of Brad's voice, she heard him saying, "Didn't you get my message? Damn, I can't believe things are backfiring this way. At least I'm glad you've informed the *Chronicle* I haven't skipped the country. I'm not exactly in need of a nursemaid."

As she slipped the perishables into the refrigerator she heard him add, "I'll call you back tomorrow after I've moved." The phone was slammed down with unnecessary force.

She almost slid across the floor in her haste to be gone before Brad reached the kitchen. Safely out of the door, she breathed a sigh of relief. When she saw him through the screen she called, "I'm just leaving. Thanks for the lovely dinner."

He whipped open the door and came outside,

dark red staining his cheeks. "How about a walk along the beach? I need to cool off."

She hesitated. "Bad news?"

He laughed harshly. "You could say that."

Minta wanted to be with him. Her fierce longing was so acute she had to struggle to form her words of refusal. "Things usually seem better after you sleep on them," she said. "I think I'll have to say no to the walk on the beach. I'm exhausted."

"A walk might help you sleep better." He moved beside her, and she could sense that he needed her.

Still puzzled over his reasons for being on this island, she resisted. "I'm about to fall asleep on my feet."

He walked beside her until they reached her back door. As her fingers touched the knob she felt his hands on her waist. She tensed, not certain what she wanted, and he slowly shifted her around until she was facing him.

His hands drew her closer to him, giving her every opportunity to stop him. The warmth of his body, his clean masculine smell mingling with the rose-scented breezes—all heightened her senses. It seemed the most natural thing in the world to move closer into the circle of his arms and settle against the hard, taut length of his body.

His head bent over hers, and she felt his warm, tingling mouth cover her own lips in a firm yet gentle kiss. All the questions fled from her mind as their mouths melded. Her hands moved restlessly, pressing into the smooth muscles of his shoulders, sliding up into his hair. She could feel the firm peaks of her breasts straining through the silky fabric of her blouse as they contacted his firm chest.

His fingers spread across her back, smoothing down her sides, stopping only long enough to caress her narrow waist and then moving to the soft swelling of her hips, shaping her body against his. She floated on a fiery tide, weightless in his arms, her only reality this man and this moment. Nothing, nobody else mattered.

He drew back first, moving slowly away until he held her at arm's length. "Sure you don't want that walk?" he prompted.

She looked into the dark eyes, somewhat confused by the rush of emotion he'd aroused.

Inexplicably the image of the picture in the paper began slowly replacing the reality of the man standing before her. An inner voice was warning her not to get mixed up in the mystery surrounding Brad McMillan. "No," she said, louder than was necessary and then added, "Good night, Brad," in a gentler tone.

He glanced down, letting go of her hands without speaking.

CHAPTER THREE

BRAD STARTED DOWN THE STEPS leading to the beach. He'd given up smoking years earlier, but right now he would have given anything for a cigarette.

Damn, talk about bad timing. All his life he'd dreamed of meeting a woman like Minta. Sensitive but strong. Vulnerable but aggressive. Beautiful but definitely not arrogant. It was such an unlikely combination he'd quit trying, satisfying himself with feminine companionship that demanded nothing more from him than an enjoyable evening.

And now, he might have met her. The woman of his dreams. He was finding himself strongly attracted to her in spite of his best efforts. *Now.* When his time wasn't his own. When he was already committed to something that excluded her. He felt like raging against fate.

Three times before in his life he'd known total frustration. Once, when his mother had told him his father was dead. The laughing, fun-loving father who carried him on his shoulders and told stories with a thick Scottish brogue.

The second time had been when the doctors told

him his mother didn't have long to live. At least, then, he'd been able to do something for her. It wasn't much, but it had helped to provide for the best care, to take her on the trip around the world she'd always wanted, to make her last days full and rich. And she'd outwitted them, living nearly four years. Yes, that had definitely helped.

The last time...that had been in Vietnam. His hands clenched as the memory began to form and he put it away quickly, locked it back into that part of his mind he never explored. But tonight he felt that same outrage, that same overwhelming helplessness. And there wasn't a thing he could do about it.

He couldn't explain his instant reaction to Minta. He'd always scoffed at the idea that a man and woman could meet and know instantly they'd be important to one another. He'd never doubt again.

One look at Minta and his world had turned upside down. He'd been able to handle the tide of emotions at first, thinking they'd never meet again. But now, to be side by side, to have shared a meal, to have felt her response when he'd touched her and to have to walk away....

Cursing inwardly, he remembered the violets. That had been a stupid impulse he'd given into. He wasn't a schoolboy buying a bunch of flowers for a girl he admired.

But he hadn't been able to resist. Coming out of the hotel with his food, he had passed a vendor's laden cart. The violets had reminded him of the shadowy depths in Minta's eyes. He had bought them without stopping to think, knowing even as he counted out the change he'd never give them to her.

He reached the water's edge and pulled off his clothes. As he waded into the water, the cool spray washed over him, clearing the sensual fog from mind and body. He had to believe there would be another time. In a few days, or a few weeks at most, his job here would be over. He'd plan a trip to D.C. then and surprise Minta with a visit to her little silversmithing shop.

The pleasure this brought him ended abruptly as he remembered what lay ahead of him first. There was always the chance he wouldn't get out of here. No, this certainly wasn't the best time for adding any romantic complications to his life. He was already involving Ted Miller and his wife, Lydia, in his troubles. He hadn't meant to but Ted's ship, *Lydia*, had been chartered for his tests several months earlier, and it was too late to try to find another. But at least Ted was an old friend and he'd understand. Plunging into the water, Brad released the anger and tension that gripped him in a sweeping crawl through the water.

IN WASHINGTON, D.C. five men sat around the table in a spacious conference room in the FBI building. The man at the head presided with an air of informality that was deceptive. At thirty-eight, Jerry Richards was the highest-ranking black American in the agency. Those who knew him well never underestimated him.

He had begun his intelligence career in the navy. When he got out he had joined the FBI as an undercover agent. The work was exhausting and filled with sleepless nights, clandestine meetings and covert activities that skirted dangerously near to criminality at times.

Recently his wife, Marla, had commented that his professional life was destroying his marvelous sense of humor. He didn't argue. Some days it was becoming increasingly hard to find anything to laugh about.

This meeting, for instance. They were here to decide the fate of a fellow agent. She was one of Jerry's own protégées and that bothered him. How could he be certain his judgment was clear and unbiased since he and his wife liked her so much?

He studied the men around him. Al Slessor sat on his right. Jerry had known him for years and recognized his ability as a top fighter against the underworld. But he also knew that Al was too ambitious and could be petty.

Al had brought the charges against the agent whose code name was Horizon. They were serious charges alleging that the woman had gone beyond the call of duty in handling some of her cases. While too much zeal didn't sound like a fault, Jerry knew it could have serious consequences if an agent refused to obey a superior's orders to drop an investigation. The other men were experienced field agents themselves, so Jerry was counting on them to see both sides in this issue.

He waited until there was a lull in the conversation before saying, "Let's get down to business, gentlemen. As you can see from the folders on your desk, this is a top-secret classification. Our subject is a twenty-seven-year-old female undercover agent. Code name: Horizon. Assignment: Organized Crime Unit."

He paused as several of the men's eyes scanned the sheets on the table before them. When Jerry had their attention once more, he said, "Al, I'd like you to present your charges now."

Al Slessor squirmed in his chair, his florid face even redder than usual. "Charges are a little harsh, Jerry. I'm concerned about Horizon's fitness for her work. That's all."

Jerry nodded and Al continued, "As the record states, Horizon began to butt heads with me from the time Jerry departed to take over the defense security department. Personally, I think she had hoped for the job I got."

"No personal opinions," interjected Jerry sharply. "Tell us what happened that's pertinent to this investigation."

"She went over my head to get some information I didn't think we needed."

"Why?" asked a white-haired man. Jerry silently applauded. At least someone was willing to listen.

Al sputtered in his anger. "What difference does that make? She disobeyed orders."

"I was a field agent for a long time," said the man. "In certain circumstances it is necessary to think for oneself if the superior officer isn't at hand. What was the result of Horizon's actions?"

"She was lucky," said Al. "She got some vital information but that doesn't excuse her. She's like a hunting dog with its nose to the ground once she scents a mystery. Nothing's going to stop her until she's satisfied."

"That doesn't sound too bad," said another man.

"It is when you've been told to drop an investigation," insisted Al.

"How did you handle the situation at the time?" asked the elderly man.

"I'm not on trial here," said Slessor, glancing around belligerently. "I told her to shape up or ship out, and she stalked out of my office."

"I'm not excusing Horizon's actions, but shouldn't you tell them she'd been on twenty-four-hour duty for three weeks when that happened?" inserted Jerry gently.

"Perhaps all the agent needs is a long rest," suggested the man on Jerry's left.

"She's getting it," snapped Al. "I ordered her to take a vacation. Look, Minta Cordero...."

"No names," said Jerry. It was obvious that Al was fast losing control of his emotions.

"Okay. Okay. Agent Horizon has been spoiled from the day she finished the academy," said Al. "She's a native American, a female and looks like a damn beauty queen. With all that, she thinks she can't be touched with a ten-foot pole.''

"Let's look at her record," interrupted Jerry, trying to give Al a minute to cool off. He hadn't realized before how deep-seated Al's antagonism really was. "Look at page eight. Her efficiency ratings are mostly outstanding.''

"Except for the one I've given her," said Al. "I know what you're thinking, but it's not a personality conflict.''

"It's difficult to know when you're involved . . . .''

"No, don't try telling me that. I think I'm the only one brave enough to admit the truth. I ask you, Jerry. Would you say Horizon is obedient?''

Jerry laughed cynically. "Are any of us? I judge a person under my authority by how interested they are in getting the job done. Horizon rates tops in that.''

"She's too interested. That's my whole point. She gets emotionally involved with her cases and then functions irrationally. So far she's lucked out, but one of these days, who knows? She might even cause another agent's death.''

"No melodrama, Al," said the elderly man. He turned to Jerry with exasperation. "Isn't Horizon the agent who was engaged to Peter Hammond?''

Jerry flinched inwardly. Personally, he didn't consider this information anyone else's business except Minta's. But from the interest brightening the faces around him he saw he'd better allow it to be discussed freely. "Yes. What of it?''

One of the men spoke up. "I wasn't in D.C. at the time. From the rumors I heard Hammond was taking payoffs from the underworld in exchange for information leaks."

"Something like that," said Jerry. "I understand he got himself deeply in debt. One of the crime syndicates found out, and before Peter knew it, he was too deeply involved to back out. It wasn't something he did lightly."

"Was Agent Horizon under any suspicion?"

"No," said Al. "I checked that out with Wolf Larsen. You know he came back from retirement temporarily to handle the Hammond case. I guess he never forgave himself for not catching Hammond when he worked with him."

"Yes, I heard that," the elderly man agreed. "What actually happened to Hammond?"

"Officially, he lost control of his car and spun into a river," said Jerry. "We suspect, though, that he ran to the underworld for protection when his cover was blown. We can't prove it, but I have a gut feeling they were responsible for his death."

"How did Agent Horizon react?" asked the elderly man.

This is getting to me, thought Jerry. "She didn't fall apart, if that's what you mean. In fact, she handled her shock and grief better than anyone expected. She's a strong woman."

"Very interesting. Frankly, I think Agent Horizon will probably return from this vacation rested and ready for her next assignment. Have you considered transferring her out of your department, Al?''

"I don't want that. It might go down on my record as inability to get along with my subordinate."

"Then it looks as if it's going to be up to us to decide her fate," said Jerry. "I'd like all of you to take this report with you and read it thoroughly. Then we'll meet at the end of the month and make a final decision. Thank you for coming today, gentlemen."

As the men left the room, Jerry watched Al Slessor through narrowed eyes. He suspected the man was afraid of Minta. She was good at her work, almost too good, in fact. In a few years she'd be pressing for promotions, and that might threaten Al's own advance.

The door closed behind the last man, and Jerry began gathering up the papers before him. There was only one thing to do. He'd have his wife invite the Blairs over for dinner. Elizabeth Blair, or Dr. Forrester, as she was known professionally, was Minta's closest friend. She'd know where Minta had gone on her vacation.

He'd slip a little word in Elizabeth's ear that she should pass along a warning to Minta. A warning for her to toe the line for the next few months. She'd have to keep strictly to her own assignments, her own projects. Even if the biggest case she'd ever heard of fell in her lap, she'd have to walk away from it unless Al had assigned it to her. It wouldn't be easy, but she'd have to agree.

As he pushed back his chair and stood, he vowed

to himself that he was going to make damn sure Minta retained her status as an undercover agent. For the sake of the agency he refused to sit by and see her railroaded by an insecure superior.

When he reached his office, Jerry paused beside his secretary's desk. Jill Harvey was absentmindedly twisting a strand of her honey-blond hair around her finger as she talked on the phone. He waited until she was finished. "Jill, could you get my wife on line one for me?"

"TWO CROISSANTS AND A CUP OF COFFEE." Minta pointed to the flaky rolls inside a glass case. After an early-morning swim she'd located this bakery in George Town, the capital of the Cayman Islands. As soon as she saw the tables lining the sidewalk in front of the small bakery, she'd known this was where she wanted to have her breakfast. It was too glorious a day to waste one moment inside.

She carried her tray outside and chose a seat that faced away from the street. It was a warm day, made for relaxation. Pots of scarlet and white flowering oleanders shielded the patrons from one another. Minta sipped her coffee slowly, at peace with the world.

When the last buttery crumb was finished, she drew the postcards from her purse and began writing notes to her family. Her parents, her three married sisters and one brother plus an assortment of nieces and nephews would each want one. And each had to have a special message showing how deeply she cared for them. Her pen poised over the post-card she had chosen for Grandfather Tony, and her forehead wrinkled. He was sharp, too sharp. She could just see his face when he got the card. He knew how little time she had free, so he was bound to conclude she was absent from work for more than reasons of pleasure.

Finally she scribbled a few lines of meaningless vacation jargon on the card. "Having a good time. Wish you were here." At least that much was true. She would love to see her grandfather right now, share with him her problems at work.

Next came the cards for her friends in D.C. A big one to be sent to the department. Then one for Jill Harvey, a former roommate that Minta had helped get a job as Jerry Richards's secretary. Last she wrote to Elizabeth and Nathan.

Whenever Minta became discouraged with her job, she always recalled that Christmas in New Mexico when she'd first met the Blairs. She'd been in college at the time and had jumped at an opportunity to work with the FBI.

Minta could still remember the fears and excitement of watching Nathan and Elizabeth fall in love as they all waited to see if the Ferrel gang would be captured before they could kill Nathan. Since then she and Elizabeth had grown to be close friends. Without her, Minta wasn't certain how she could have coped with Peter's tragedy.

Glancing around as she finished the last card, Minta realized the rest of the tables were empty.

Next, she needed to locate a post office and buy some of the beautiful Caymanian stamps.

A tall man brushed by her when she reached the post office. For a moment Minta thought it was Brad. It wasn't, but the tight feeling she experienced in her chest every time she thought of him returned. She was surprised she couldn't seem to get him off her mind. Speculation about what he was doing on the island was so futile and exactly the opposite of how she intended to spend this vacation.

This morning she'd heard his shower. By the time she returned from her swim, his car was gone from its usual parking spot.

Good, she told herself. *Today you're going to stay out of his path. Let him know he doesn't have to contend with a nosy neighbor.* She'd already checked to see if the sand on the side of the cottage was hard enough to hold the weight of her car. That way she could park it out of sight. She'd use the back door, and barring any accidents, they needn't see each other again.

Her next stop was at Surfside Realty. Richard Long called out her name as she came in the door. "How did you recognize me?" Minta asked. Richard was younger than she had expected with a thatch of sun-bleached hair.

"Diane, the woman at the car-rental firm," he explained. "She described you as terrific, but that wasn't right by half." His accent was as delightfully English as Diane's had been.

"Unfair," said Minta, taking the seat he pulled

out on the other side of his desk. The trim white shorts she'd chosen showed off her long slender legs to their best advantage.

"Why unfair?" Richard asked. "I thought women loved to receive a compliment."

"Not when it disarms them. I'm here to complain." Her smile softened the forthright comment. Actually it was true. She was here to complain about the food missing from her cottage. However, she could have done that by phone. She'd really been driven by a curiosity to know whether Brad had complained any further about having her for a neighbor.

Richard groaned loudly, but his blue eyes sparkled with amusement. "Have mercy. I've just dealt with your neighbor."

"He was in?"

"Yes. You should have heard the amount of money he offered me to let him have the duplex alone."

Minta's black eyes glowed briefly. "He offered you money to get rid of me? Any idea why?"

Richard shrugged lightly. "There's no telling. Lots of people come to the Caymans for reasons they don't reveal. Bankers, for instance. We're an international tax haven."

Minta regarded him thoughtfully. She'd thought of that herself. The Cayman Islands were famous for their secretive banking practices. "You're right," she said slowly. "Lots of businessmen hide their money here, don't they?"

Richard nodded. "George Town has over four hundred banks, some of them little more than postal boxes for larger banks. Only London and New York have more. We're right alongside Switzerland, Hong Kong and the Bahamas in providing discreet banking services. In many ways, we're an island of secrets. You could say that almost everyone who comes here has something to hide. We Caymanians never tell anyone's secrets."

Minta was lost in her own thoughts. "What did you tell him? About getting rid of me, I mean?"

"I was tempted," he admitted. "Bonuses don't drop in my lap every day."

"Don't you mean bribes?" The thought of Brad insisting that she be moved at any price left a bitter taste in her mouth. "Where could I go?"

"That's just it. There's nothing except a room in one of the hotels. Interested? We could split the bribe, love."

"Not interested," she said, suddenly determined not to be shoved around by Brad McMillan.

Richard grinned. "Your choice. As a consolation prize how about having dinner with me some evening?"

"Still trying to divert my complaints?"

He held up his hands to show his innocence. "What's the problem?"

"No food."

"Ah, is that all?" He leaned forward. "Mr. McMillan told me what had happened. He wants to keep his, so I'll send someone around to stock your kitchen this afternoon. You didn't choose the daily maid service, did you?''

''No, I don't want anyone knocking on my door if I decide to sleep late.'' She stood. ''Do I need to be at the cottage when the food is delivered?''

He rose and came around the desk to see her to the door. ''No, we've got keys. How about that dinner?''

''Sounds good, but I don't know my plans.'' She softened her refusal with a smile.

Hurt feelings were a new sensation for Minta, or at least one she couldn't remember experiencing for some time. She was fairly thick-skinned and considered herself immune to slights, but it bothered her that Brad wanted her to move that badly.

It was last night, of course. He was afraid she might keep popping up at his back door, and if he had something to hide, that would be damn inconvenient.

Suddenly she decided she would have to avoid Brad. Otherwise her vacation would turn into a working holiday, and she couldn't allow that. The things that went on in the Caymans weren't all illegal. They were only secret, and as far as she was concerned, Brad could keep his secrets. She intended staying out of his way.

Within minutes she found it wasn't all that easy to do on an island that measured only twenty-two by eight miles. At almost the same instant Brad and she pulled into the same service station from opposite directions. He swung out of his car and indicated the man was to fill her tank first. "Hi, Minta," he said, coming over to her window.

It was impossible to remain angry with him when he smiled, she decided. He was wearing a pair of khaki drill shorts and a snug forest-green tank top. In the sunlight she noticed a sprinkling of dark-red hair on his chest and remembered what he'd told her about his father. Her hand, resting on the window, was the same bronze shade as his arm. This reminder of their common heritage made her drop her hand to her lap in an abrupt movement. "Taking it easy?" she asked.

He pushed back a lock of his hair as he leaned down to get a better view of her. "Yes, but I should be working."

"Isn't this a vacation for you?"

"Not on your life. I should be keeping my nose to the grindstone twelve hours a day." His hand stroked back several strands of her hair that had drifted over a bared shoulder as he studied the snug red elastic bandeau that molded over her breasts. She regretted she hadn't worn something less revealing.

She tensed at his touch and he moved back, asking, "What have you been doing this morning?"

"Having fun." Glancing in her rearview mirror, she saw the attendant had finished filling her tank. She reached for her purse and stretched out her arm past Brad to pay for her gas. "See you," she said before pulling out of the drive. In her rearview mirror she saw him standing and watching her.

The encounter left her shaken, and she drove faster than she should. Driving had always been a way of releasing tension for her. In New Mexico she'd taken long solitary drives over the high mountain roads north of her home in Santa Fe whenever she had something bothering her.

In Washington, D.C. she had to limit her pleasure to weekends when she would get her Austin-Healey from the parking garage and drive through the lush Virginia countryside. She remembered one day, in particular. The day she'd made the final break with her fiancé, Peter Hammond. She could never drive through that stretch of the state without remembering the tears that had streamed down her face.

Today she would drive the length of the island, she decided. She'd make a mental note of the restaurants she passed and then look them up in her guidebook when she got back. She was also interested in taking a fishing trip and of course, scuba diving. One of her reasons for coming was to explore the deep Cayman trough with its world-famous coral reefs.

She was glancing at one of the bright billboards when a car shot out of a side road. Her reflexes were quick, and she braked after a quick check in the rearview mirror to make certain no one was tailing her too closely.

Her car swerved slightly, and then she felt the jolting impact of metal crunching into her rear fender.

Blazing fury was her first reaction. After pulling to the side of the road, she jumped from her car and ran toward the culprit, a small black car with several passengers crowded inside it.

"Weren't you watching where you were going?" she demanded. "I was on the main road. I had the right of way."

The driver of the vehicle was a slender man with small eyes and pale-blond hair. He looked at her and then glanced away furtively as if checking with his passengers before deciding how to handle the situation.

Minta's outburst of temper was slowly ebbing, and she regretted her harsh words. The memory of her argument with Al Slessor just before she'd left D.C. had left her with some doubts about her ability to control her emotions.

Anyway, these people were probably tourists, like herself. Perhaps the driver had looked the wrong direction out of habit. After all, it was only a minor accident, and she didn't need to blow up like a volcano.

The man stepped outside, and she saw his dark slacks and dress shirt were loose on his thin frame. "I think you were speeding," he said in a slow correct manner that alerted her English was not his native tongue.

"We need to call the local police to settle this," she said firmly.

"No." He seemed anxious to avoid the police, speaking up quickly and firmly. "*We* will settle this." He walked over and glanced at the bent fender, dismissing it with a shrug. "It's nothing." He reached in his pocket and held out a roll of Caymanian dollars.

"No, I can't accept that. This is a rental car," Minta explained carefully, smiling at him to show she understood he wasn't familiar with the correct procedure. "Let's walk over to that store and see if they'll call the police for us." She pointed to a convenience store a short distance down the road.

"I will see," he said, moving back to his car and sliding inside. A babble of conversation erupted in a language she didn't recognize. She studied the others in the car. On the front passenger's side sat a taller, broader man. His hair was bushy and dark, and when he glanced her way she saw straight, dark eyebrows bridged his nose. The penetrating stare he directed at her was definitely unfriendly and her irritation returned.

She stood her ground, sweeping her gaze to the third passenger, a young woman in the back seat. Her head was bent, but her profile was attractive with classic features and a halo of softly curling red hair. Minta moved closer and tried to listen to the conversation, but she couldn't catch anything.

Disgruntled because they were ignoring her presence, she almost missed the sound of the key turning on the engine of the black car. She stared as the car suddenly shot past her, so closely she had to jump back to avoid being hit. The driver made a roaring arc and sped down the narrow dirt road where he'd first appeared, leaving a cloud of dust behind him.

CHAPTER FOUR

FOR A LONG MOMENT, Minta stood staring down the narrow side road, her mind a complete blank. Pulling herself together, she made a spring for her car, climbing in and starting the engine smoothly and quickly. She glanced out and saw a group of bicyclists meandering past her. It was a group of young men and several waved at her, calling out friendly greetings. It was all she could do not to scream for them to get out of her way.

Once under way she turned on to the dirt road her assailants had taken. *No one,* she fumed, as nothing but empty road loomed ahead. *Absolutely no one is going to get away with hit-and-run tactics without getting a good fight from me.*

She bounced over the rough road, glancing at the ramshackle huts she passed without seeing any sign of the other vehicle. Within minutes she had reached the end of the street and was staring out at the sparkling blue ocean. She jumped out of her car and scanned the beach in both directions. A few children playing with a dog were at the water's edge. A couple lay on a beach towel, looking only at each other. Little chance they'd spotted a car.

She got back in her car and drove to the first house up from the beach. An elderly man answered the door after a long wait. He shook his head when asked if he'd seen a black car. "I was asleep," he explained.

"I'm so sorry," Minta apologized.

She stopped at two more houses where there were signs of life but no one had seen anything. Defeated, at length she drove back to the main road and turned toward the airport. Some vacation this was turning out to be! First a mystery man and now a hit-and-run accident. Either she had a natural knack for getting into trouble or this was just a particularly dangerous island.

When she reached the car-rental agency Diane was once again behind the desk. "I've run into some trouble," said Minta, slightly out of breath.

"Oh?" Diane gave Minta's brief apparel a piercing appraisal. "If you're having mechanical trouble we'll be glad to exchange yours for another vehicle." Smiling slightly, she added, "In that outfit you're bound to run into trouble."

"The trouble ran into me. Literally," Minta added when Diane looked puzzled. "Someone hit my car. The back fender is crunched."

Diane's expression didn't change. "Did you bring in the police report? We'll need it for the insurance claim."

Minta explained briefly what had happened. "They simply vanished into thin air. What should I do now?"

A hint of sympathy appeared in Diane's eyes. "I have a brother on the police force. I'll call him to come down and get your statement. If you'd like some coffee, there's some in the back office."

"Thanks," said Minta. She chose a cola from a machine instead and was sipping on it when Diane reappeared.

"Bobby is on his way. Are you going to want another car? We've got two available."

"No," said Minta. "I'm a little shaken up. How about a bicycle for a few days?" Both women laughed and the tension relaxed.

It was nearly an hour later before the last detail was cleared up and Minta was free to leave. Diane's brother, Bobby Hall, was pleasant and understanding. He agreed to keep a close watch for the black car and told Minta to call him if she spotted it. So far her vacation hadn't been exactly the restful idyll she'd resolved to have.

After a wobbly takeoff Minta cycled smoothly down the road on a sleek ten-speed bicycle. In college she'd owned one similar and wondered why she hadn't thought of renting a bike in the first place.

Grateful that the island was flat, she continued down the road until she came to a restaurant advertising seafood. She parked the bike in one of the racks and locked it with the chain provided by the rental agency. All she'd need to make today an absolute disaster was to have this bike stolen!

The restaurant was crowded with a waiting line in the small lobby. A dark-eyed waitress asked her name and when she heard Minta was alone said, "Would you like to eat at the bar? I think there's still a seat available."

Minta agreed and was led past the line of tourists. Paddle fans whirred softly in the large room and luxuriant tropical plants drooped from the ceiling. In one corner a man was singing a catchy reggae tune. Minta glanced around for an empty stool facing the square bar in the center of the room.

"Hi, again." She heard Brad's husky voice and saw him pointing to a stool beside his.

Minta felt like swearing. She could have kicked herself for not checking the parking lot for his red car before choosing this restaurant. It was logical he would be there; it was only a short distance from the turnoff for their cottage. Humor seemed the only logical defense, she decided, sliding onto the stool. "We've got to quit meeting like this, dahling," she teased in a husky Marlene Dietrich voice.

Brad's appreciative laugh sent a shiver rippling down her spine. "Small world, Ms Cordero," he said, holding up his glass. "May I buy you one of these?"

"I don't dare," she said. "I've already had one wreck this morning."

"What did you hit? A fiddler crab?"

"I got hit."

The smile vanished from his face and he leaned closer, making her all too aware of those probing tawny eyes. "A car came out of a side road and hit my rear fender." She asked the bartender for Perrier and continued, "Worst of all, the creeps took off without letting me get their names."

"Were they locals?"

She hesitated, and decided against telling him all the details. Some of them sounded so melodramatic that she was beginning to wonder herself if they'd happened. "I don't think so. I'm going to keep looking for their car. It can't be hidden on this small island."

"Did you get a license number?"

She shook her head. "They took me off guard. I followed as fast as I could but it was too late. They'd vanished into thin air."

"Don't worry about it. Most ordinary citizens don't think to look at a license number anyway." Brad was frowning. "Were you hurt?"

Minta almost choked on her Perrier. What would Brad say if he knew she was an FBI agent, trained to notice far more than license numbers. If she hadn't been so curious about the passengers in the car, she would have remembered to check the license. Noticing such details was simply routine. In fact, she tended to treat even the ordinary incidents in life as if they were an investigation. She decided on a brief reply to Brad's question. "I'm fine. Just fuming over being a hit-and-run victim."

The waitress appeared at that moment with a heaping plate of fried seafood. Setting it in front of Brad, she asked Minta, "How about you? Would you like the same?"

"I'd like a crab salad with several wedges of lemon on the side," replied Minta.

"No dressing?" The waitress eyed Minta's over-slim figure disapprovingly.

"Just the lemon, please," Minta said firmly.

When the waitress moved away Brad picked up their discussion as if they hadn't been interrupted. "It is upsetting to be hit like that."

"It's not just the fact I was hit that makes me angry," Minta said more emphatically than necessary. "Perhaps they were careless or thinking of something else. I could understand a mistake. But running away like that. That's just a blatant disregard of the law."

"Some people don't have much respect for the law," Brad said finally. She noticed he had trouble meeting her direct gaze.

Minta wanted desperately to say something. She sensed that Brad meant more than he was saying. Perhaps he was trying to tell her something unpleasant about his own nature. But no, she couldn't imagine Brad as a disrespector of the law. The image didn't fit.

Brad forestalled further discussion by holding out a golden-brown shrimp by its tail. "Have a bite."

Minta shook her head, but he put it closer to her lips. "Go on. You're a little pale from your accident," he coaxed.

Minta opened her mouth as her eyes glowed with amusement. Grasping his wrist, she took several bites of the delicacy. "Thanks," she said when she finished swallowing.

"Want some more?" he teased.

"Eat, McMillan," she ordered, reaching for her glass of sparkling water. She felt strangely weak and wondered if she was having a delayed reaction to the accident. She rejected the idea. Brad's kindness was more likely the cause. She was used to being independent, handling her own concerns with no quarter asked or given for human frailties. His unexpected gentleness presented her with something to think about.

"How badly was the car hurt?"

"Well. . ." she said mischievously. "I traded it in on a bicycle."

"You would," he returned, laughing. He lightly placed one hand on her shoulder. "Why did you come to the Caymans, Minta?"

She glanced down briefly, wondering what he'd think if she told him her boss had insisted she choose a place where she'd be alone to recover her equilibrium. Eyeing Brad levelly, she said, "The beaches. The ocean. I love scuba diving. Aren't those the reasons why most people come here?"

"Many people come to stash away money. It's famous for its secret bank accounts."

"With all those custom agents searching us in Miami?" She laughed easily but she had tensed. "Was that your reason for coming, Brad?" she asked.

"No, I'm here to work," he said, and resumed eating.

"How come you were on that flight from Miami?" Minta asked casually. "If you're from Austin, you could have come through Houston."

"They don't have daily flights, and I wanted to come yesterday. So I caught a connecting flight to Miami." Brad was equally casual as he added, "I'm glad I did. One passenger on that plane was very enchanting."

Minta's smile was meant to chide him gently, but she couldn't help feeling warmer inside. She literally itched to probe further, but restrained herself with an effort.

She left before Brad, taking only a few bites of her salad and then pretending she remembered an appointment. She hated deception, but she hated Brad to think she was following him around the island even more.

After locating the waitress and paying for her lunch, she went outside. The sun was high overhead, casting a sheen on the road as she started out. The noonday heat combined with the high humidity made the pedaling more difficult than it had been earlier.

She slogged on with determination, mentally planning a leisurely afternoon. She'd take one of the novels she'd bought and stretch out on the hammock on the back veranda. And she wouldn't allow her thoughts to drift. Not even for a moment.

A horn sounded behind her and she jumped, almost losing her balance. She swiveled her head slightly, uncertain what the driver of the car wanted. She was already as far over on the side of the pavement as she dared be without going into the soft sand.

Her eyes widened as the horn sounded again, and she caught a brief glimpse of black metal looming behind her. Her eyes sought out the driver and she screamed, certain that she was staring at the same man who'd hit her car earlier that day.

He stared back, and she realized he had recognized her as well. For an instant she felt the automatic instinct that she was being hunted down. Not certain if the car's wheels were swerving, she veered toward the side of the road, heading for a grassy ditch. Her front tire hit something hard, and she felt herself catapulting over the handle bars.

She lay in the soft grasses, trying to sort out her chaotic thoughts, unsure if she'd been injured or not. She heard a car stop and then another, but her head seemed too heavy to lift. Then she heard voices.

"Is she badly hurt? What happened? Why didn't the driver of that black car stop? He must have done something to make her drive off the road like a crazy fool." The voices continued, chattering excitedly somewhere above her head.

With a supreme effort she pushed up on one elbow in time to see brown muscular legs running toward her.

A familiar voice called, "Minta. Are you okay? What happened?"

A moment later she was cradled in Brad's strong arms.

Minta's eyes focused slowly on Brad's face. It felt so good to look up and see the concern in his amber eyes and to feel the strength and gentleness of his arms. For a moment she succumbed to the warmth seeping through her. She told herself it was acceptable to let him handle the crowd gathering around her, to check on what the witnesses had to say about the driver of the black car, to see if the rented bike had been destroyed in the accident.

Then she realized that she was acting like a docile child, and she'd never been one of those. With an unexpectedly supple twist she tried to pull free of his arms. "Help me stand, please. I need to talk to those people."

He ignored the urgency in her voice, bending his head, his lips brushing across her forehead. She closed her eyes, accepting momentarily his genuine interest in her welfare. "Lie still and let me get an ambulance." His words were soft, spoken against the shining mass of her hair, his breath caressing the side of her neck.

Ambulance, doctor, her mind associated freely, and she pulled back, forcing her feet to the ground. "Please, help me up, Brad," she said. It was ridiculous to be lying here like this. She knew she wasn't hurt that badly. At least nothing felt broken, and she had never been one to make a big deal over a few cuts and scrapes. It would be humiliating to be the center of a big fuss with an ambulance rushing to her side.

Brad obeyed reluctantly, his movements sure as he kept his arm around her and helped her to her feet. There was a deep frown on his face as she faced the onlookers. She glanced around sharply to see if the driver of the black car was standing there. It was no surprise when she didn't find him.

Suddenly her professional instincts took over. So thorough was her training in handling emergencies that she automatically began noting and filing away details, asking questions, conducting an investigation.

"Did anyone see what happened?" she asked, her voice once more in control.

"There was a black car in front of me," said a slender woman holding the hand of a boy about eight or nine years old. "The driver honked at you and you turned back. The next thing I knew you lost control of that bike."

"Was the driver deliberately trying to drive me off the road?" demanded Minta.

"Minta..." Brad began, his arm tightening around her.

She pulled free and stepped shakily to one side of him, turning her back on him firmly. The skepticism in his voice reminded her of the inquisition she'd undergone at work on her last day.

"I don't know," said the woman. "Are you hurt? I'd be glad to drive you to my doctor's office?"

"No, thanks," said Minta with a slight smile. "I'm fine. Did you get the license number of the black car by any chance? I see they didn't bother to stop." She glanced around the crowd of bystanders with an inquiring look.

"Sorry," said an older man. "I was the next car in line. You were definitely on your side of the road, so I don't see why that crazy driver honked at you."

"He honked twice," said the small boy.

"Hush, Eric," said his mother. "Don't interrupt grown people."

"But I saw the number," he protested.

Minta knelt down stiffly in front of the boy. In her work she frequently found children to be better observers than adults. "What was it, Eric?" she asked.

"It started with a Y and a 3 but that's all I remember."

"That's wonderful," said Minta. "What else happened?"

"Eric's got a big imagination," said his mother with a worried frown. "I wouldn't want him to get involved."

Minta watched Eric as he continued, "Two people were in the car. A woman and a man. The man was driving crazy. He acted scared to meet another car. He kept way over on his side. Maybe he doesn't know how to drive too good."

"Anything else you remember? The car's make and model? Any dents on the car? The color of the man's hair?"

"No, that's all," he said. "You sure looked funny when you saw that man. I think you scared him."

Minta smiled. "He needed scaring. Thanks,

Eric." She stood. "Would someone get a list of everyone's names and addresses for me? The bike's rented, so the agency might want to talk to witnesses in case the bike's damaged." She caught a quick glimpse of a curious expression on Brad's face.

"I'll do that," said the elderly gentleman, taking a card out of his pocket.

"Your bike doesn't appear to be damaged," said Brad as he turned and lifted it from the grass. "Even the frame doesn't seem to be bent." He pushed it a short distance as Minta watched, distracted momentarily by the way the strong sunlight turned his hair into a rich auburn shade.

She thanked each of the people who had stopped as they started back toward their cars. "Would you like the name of my doctor?" asked Eric's mother. "I take it you're a tourist here."

"No," said Minta quickly.

"Yes," said Brad in almost the same breath.

"I'm not hurt. I'm not going to a doctor," returned Minta stubbornly.

"There's an emergency clinic about three miles down the road," said the elderly gentleman. "It might be a good idea, miss, to get a quick check. They're very efficient, and if you started feeling pain in the middle of the night, it would be nice to have a doctor on call."

Minta shook her head with a smile as she accepted the card with a list of witnesses printed neatly on the back. "Thanks so much, everyone. If the bike's not damaged, I doubt you'll be hearing from anyone concerning this.''

As the cars drove off she turned back and saw Brad carrying the bike down the road. "Hey, where do you think you're going?" she yelled, hobbling painfully after him. "I need to ride back to the cottage on that.''

"I'm putting this in my trunk and then driving you to that emergency clinic."

"You and who else?" demanded Minta, stopping and placing her hands on her hips.

His laughter was as warming as she remembered it. "I'll have to rely on my charm, I guess."

"Sorry, I hadn't noticed any," she lied, trying to make her voice sound cold.

He laughed again as he opened the hatchback on the small red car and attempted to place the bike inside. "You could have left me with my illusions," he said easily. When he finished he started toward her. "Say, that was quite a performance. I saw you flying through the air and wondered if I had lost my marbles."

"Is that what geniuses have for brains? Marbles?"

He stopped, only inches from her. "Genius? What gave you that idea?"

She could have bit her tongue for such a stupid slip. Maybe she was suffering from a mild concussion. "As far as I'm concerned, people who understand electronics must be geniuses," she said quickly.

He accepted her explanation with a smile. "It's

because we've invented our own language to keep the public fooled. Anything hurting yet, Minta? Sometimes there can be a delayed reaction after an accident."

"Speaking from experience?"

"I spent four years in the navy," he said softly.

She watched him steadily as she filed away this new piece of information. There was an aura of quiet strength about him she hadn't noticed the evening before. Like a granite boulder at the sea's edge that could withstand the thundering tides and raging storms. She sensed it would feel so right to lean on that hard masculine strength until she could regain her own, but she wouldn't allow herself to succumb to the urge. Male strength could be such a deceptive, harmful illusion if you depended on it instead of taking care of yourself.

"May I drive you to the clinic now?" he asked.

His deference turned the tide. If he'd given the slightest hint of running roughshod over her own wishes, she could have resisted and even walked every step of the way back, if need be. But there was nothing terribly threatening about his concern. He would have extended the same to anyone stranded along a roadside.

"Thanks. Maybe it would be wise," she said, and started toward the car.

He walked beside her, not attempting to help her and then stopped suddenly. "Your hair," he said.

"I'll bet it's a mess." Her strength seemed to be returning gradually with each step she took.

"No, one side's loose. Did you lose one of your silver combs?"

She felt and confirmed what he was saying as her hand slid over the silky mass. "It wasn't silver. Only tortoiseshell."

"I'll look," said Brad after opening the car door.

She slid into the car and watched as he strode back down the road. Her curiosity grew as she noted the graceful rhythm of muscles in masculine shoulders, hips and legs. There was much more to this man than appeared on the surface, and she was certain that it would take an infinite amount of time to learn all there was about him. It was a shame she'd never have that opportunity.

She became aware of a scratch of paper against one of her legs, and she reached down and retrieved a newspaper she'd seen Brad shove to the floor of the car before she got in. It was from the States, the same as she'd bought in the airport, except it was a later edition.

Brad had left the paper opened to a back section, and as her eyes scanned the sheet they settled on the article he must have been reading. With a hurried glance out the window to make sure Brad wasn't returning she read:

Police today reported that Ron Williams, general manager of Galactia Enterprises of Austin, Texas apologized for involving them needlessly in his search for Galactia's owner, Brad McMillan.

When contacted, Williams stated that a note McMillan had left on his desk saying he was going out of the country on vacation had been covered up by the company's cleaning crew.

Speculation about Galactia has been rampant in the past few weeks. Conflicting theories have been proposed. Some insiders are certain that the company is planning on revealing a new robot that will revolutionize underwater exploration. In that case, most financiers agree the company will go public.

Others in the business community are equally certain that Galactia is in serious financial trouble. A source who requested he not be identified stated, "If you ask me, McMillan's disappearance is a ruse to. . . ."

Minta glanced up and saw Brad striding back toward the car. Hastily she shoved the paper onto the floor beside her feet, her curiosity burning over what the unidentified source had been about to disclose. Probably not much. This was a national newspaper, not a gossip sheet.

Brad held out the square comb when he was seated in the car, but when she reached for it he murmured, "Let me have this pleasure." He made it sound as if he was a humble supplicant requesting a favor from a ruling monarch.

She turned her face toward him and his fingers eased through her hair, brushing the strands off her warm cheeks with a touch so gentle she could hardly be sure she'd felt it. When the comb was securely in place his head came down and his firm, tender lips moved over hers. She wondered how she could have ever thought anything about this man was like granite as his mouth became miraculously soft and warm, making a gentle assault on all her senses.

He gave freely, demanding nothing, filling her with the taste and warmth of himself until she sighed with pleasure and returned his kisses. When he finally lifted his mouth, she was barely able to think straight. "I think I better take you to that doctor," he said rather reluctantly as he started the car.

She leaned back against the seat, closing her eyes, not trusting herself to speak. She only wanted to savor the memory of those intimate moments when she had been drowning in the sensual depths of this man beside her. She didn't look around until she felt the car turning off the road onto a gravelly path.

Brad parked in front of a pink stucco bungalow. Several other cars dotted the small parking lot. "Why don't you remove my bike and I'll ride it home when I'm finished?" she asked, her hand on the door handle.

"I'll wait for you."

"It may be a long time."

"I haven't any plans."

"I thought you told me earlier you had a lot of work to do," she reminded him.

"I do. Thinking. Inventors carry their work around in their heads all the time."

"Very handy," she said, smiling at him. It wasn't fair for any man to be this attractive, she decided, her fingers tingling with a desire to trace the bulging curves of muscles beneath his dark-green shirt. "At least, stay here in the car to do your thinking. The waiting room's probably filled with all kinds of aggressive germs."

"That doesn't worry me, but I don't want your bike to be stolen," he said, settling down in the seat. "Stick your head out the door and give me a signal if you need me."

"Will do." She slid out of the car and forced herself not to reveal any sign of injury as she crossed the parking lot.

Her name was called in a surprisingly short time, and the bald-headed doctor exuded a competent manner as he tested her reflexes. "Everything seems to be in good working order," he told her. "You may have some soreness tomorrow, but I have a feeling you landed the correct way to minimize injury."

"I've had training," she answered without thinking, then quickly added, "gymnastics." God, why was she being so careful about protecting her identity. Habit, she guessed. An FBI agent never got to live a really normal life in that respect. There was always the tendency to protect one's identity in case it became necessary to pretend to be someone else.

When she was ready to leave, the doctor handed her a small cellophane packet containing two capsules. "These are for the pain you may have tonight. Your muscles will probably ache a little. Follow the directions on the front."

Doubting she'd need them, Minta took them rather than argue. She didn't like to cloud her mind with drugs if she could help it. After paying for the visit at the front desk, she hurried outside to Brad. "Going to live?" he asked, his eyes bright with welcome as he leaned over to open the car door for her.

"Until I die. The doctor agreed I wasn't injured."

"Then what's that?" asked Brad, his gaze fixed on the packet of capsules.

"Insurance. For the doctor. So I won't call him in the middle of the night saying I have a pain. Thanks so much for being right behind me, Brad. You've been a great help."

"Our paths seem to be crossing with amazing regularity," he answered. "Now any other errands you need to run?"

Minta tried to decide if his remark had a sarcastic edge, but Brad impressed her as the type of man who wouldn't resort to innuendos if he had something to say.

"No errands," she said.

When they reached their cottage, he invited her inside for a drink. "A little something stronger than mineral water seems called for at this point."

She agreed. "But don't tell me you can invent while you entertain guests. As soon as I've finished my drink, I'll get out of your hair."

"I hope you're very thirsty," he returned with a grin. Opening the cottage door, he ushered her inside, not giving her any time to digest or analyze his remark.

CHAPTER FIVE

THERE WAS A CASUAL DISORDER about the room. Several opened books lay facedown, a newspaper was scattered over the polished wood floor and a half-filled glass sat on the low coffee table. "This is Hilda's job at home," he apologized, gathering up the items with a shrug.

"Poor Hilda. What does she get in return?" asked Minta, sinking down on the sofa with a sigh of pleasure.

"My undying devotion."

"Hmm, doesn't sound like enough to me. She deserves sick leave, regular raises and a paid vacation."

"Not Hilda. She only lives to please me."

"Every man's fantasy," answered Minta.

"It's mutual. I spend a lot of my time thinking of her."

"Thinking of ways to get more mileage from her, you mean?"

Brad stopped in the doorway leading down the hall, his face serious. "What did he do to you, Minta?"

"Who?" she asked coolly, her stomach clenching with tension.

"The man who gave you such a suspicious mind."

She tried to grin, but it came out crooked. "Which one?"

Brad measured her with narrowed eyes. "The one you loved."

"Thought I loved," she corrected. "I found out I didn't know the first thing about him, so I was only in love with a figment of my imagination."

"Or one side of him. He might have wanted to be the man you imagined him to be. None of us is perfect, Minta."

She sucked in her breath. It had been so long since she'd allowed herself to remember anything nice about Peter she wasn't certain she could handle it. His betrayal had been so unexpected that her only protection had been to focus on its depths. But there was truth to what Brad was saying. Peter had hated himself in the end. "I know," she said softly, lowering her eyes to shield her thoughts from Brad's intense gaze. "I'm really not a bitter woman. I like men immensely. It would be a dull world without them."

Brad laughed softly. "That's a relief. I'd like to get to know you much better, Minta."

"It shouldn't be difficult. I'm basically your standard uncomplicated model."

"No secrets?" he probed.

She flinched. "What would I be without a few secrets, Brad?"

"Still mysterious. I've never met two women who

were alike. Each comes with an amazing individuality.''

"Then why did you name your robot Hilda? You must have seen some resemblance to basic femininity.''

"That name really bothers you, doesn't it?''

"You're evading my question. Does Hilda remind you of a special woman friend?''

He laughed briefly. "Wrong. But that doesn't mean I've got some lurking, primal male urge to subjugate females.''

She widened her eyes as a mocking smile curved her lips. "Now did I say that?''

He was watching her with a peculiar intensity. "Not out loud.''

"Don't tell me you read minds? I may be in more trouble than I thought.''

Brad smiled. "I do my best. Now, how about that drink? What would you like?''

She relaxed. "Whatever you're having.'' Brad had a way about him that made it impossible for her to stay mad. He seemed so willing for others to have a differing opinion that she was constantly disarmed.

When he returned from the kitchen carrying two squat glasses, he settled down on the sofa beside her. "Your hospitality is becoming too generous for me,'' murmured Minta. "My Zuni ancestors will be dishonored if I can't repay your generosity.''

"You have repaid it. Many times,'' he answered softly.

She swirled the amber liquid in her glass, avoiding his gaze. "How have I repaid it?"

"Being here with me. Letting me touch you, run my fingers through that fantastic hair...."

She held up the glass as a sign of protest. Her voice was cold. "Those are things you can't buy, Brad. I had something like meals or drinks in mind."

She knew her words had wounded him when she saw his amber eyes darken. His reply was brusque. "Sorry. I thought you were referring to any kindness I might have shown you by picking up your bike and taking you to the clinic. If you don't like being in my debt, send over some canned goods."

"Brad...." Shame flooded her. She had misconstrued his words terribly. Setting down her glass, she leaned over, framing his face with both her palms. His skin felt warm against her cool hands. Sincerely she whispered, "I'm sorry."

He remained rigid for a moment and she leaned over further, stopping when her lips lightly grazed his. She felt him tremble, and waited as he set down his glass to wrap his arms around her.

"Minta," he whispered over and over, his lips covering hers, gently at first and then with increasing passion. His hands slid against the bared skin of her back with a silky, sensuous touch that set her on fire.

When his tongue touched hers, he made a deep hungry sound in his throat and Minta molded her body closer to his lean, hard frame. His hands explored the shape of her shoulders, the curve of her spine and the smooth skin of her midriff. Her mouth wasn't submissive, but active on his, seeking the slow, sure movements of his tongue.

When his fingers began exploring the elastic band covering her breasts, her skin began burning, aching for him to smooth away the thin fabric, for his hands to cradle her breasts, for his mouth and body to consume her as a wild surging wave crumbles the lonely sand castle on the shore.

Instead his kisses slowly subsided and his hands slid down her rib cage as he moved away from her. "I can't handle this, Minta," he said in little more than a groan. His eyes held a wild fire that hinted of passion mingled with torment.

She lowered her head, moving away, attempting a smile. "See, the Zunis never remain long in debt to anyone."

He ignored her attempt at humor as he picked up his drink. Moving away from her, he stared morosely at the wall. "Do you ever wonder why things work the way they do, Minta?" he said at length.

She lifted her shoulders slightly and took a swallow from her own glass. "Doesn't everyone? What were you thinking of?"

"Timing."

She waited silently until he continued. "Timing is just a little thing but so important. For instance, if you're in the right place at the wrong time, it's no good. Or if you're with the right person at the wrong time, it's sheer hell."

She braced herself for whatever he was trying to tell her and then decided to stop him. "Hilda must be smarter than I am if she understands everything you say, Brad," she said.

He turned toward her, chuckling softly. "Hilda has an advantage over you. She doesn't try to spare my feelings. When I start philosophizing she cuts me off by saying, 'Bad message. Bad message. Press escape to delete.' "

"I love her already," said Minta, joining in his laughter. She glanced at her watch. "I've got to run. I know you have work to do."

The phone rang. Brad reached for it, saying, "Please wait until I've answered this before you leave."

After a short, friendly greeting he began smiling broadly. "That's great, Ron. I'll be at the airport to pick her up. Be sure she's under wraps. I wouldn't want anyone to see her."

Minta felt as if she'd been punched in the stomach. With an artificial smile pasted on her face she rose and patted Brad on the shoulder, whispering, "I have to go."

He frowned, covering the mouthpiece of the phone with one hand. "What? You're not going anywhere in your condition!"

"Don't worry about me. I've just got a phone call to make. See you, Brad."

She ignored his protest and left. When she reached her side of the cottage, she went straight to the bathroom and began running the tub full of hot water.

One hint of apology out of Brad and she knew she would have crumpled. Her mind had a will of its own, though. She wondered who the woman was that Ron was supposed to be keeping under wraps.

As she was drying after a long relaxing soak, Richard Long called. Draped in a towel, she listened as he teased her. "What's this I hear about you being a menace on our roads?"

"I've only had two wrecks so far today," she countered.

"Two? I was only told about one."

"That's because I'm afraid to tell Diane I came close to totaling the bike she rented me."

"Diane can be formidable," agreed Richard, and while his voice was solemn, Minta had no trouble imagining the way his blue eyes were twinkling. "What are you trying to do? Give our fair island bad publicity?"

"Is that all you think about? For all you know I may be severely injured."

"May I come over and check?"

"No need," she said quickly. Richard was an irrepressible flirt, but he did it so charmingly, she couldn't really be angry. "I don't even have a scratch to show for all my adventures."

"I'll be glad to search and see if there's one you might have overlooked."

"No doubt," she replied dryly. "But you'd better check with Officer Bobby Hall. He's my protector."

"That guy! Always trying to take over the women I meet. How about that dinner with me tonight? I think you deserve to be shown a better side of the Cayman Islands after your day.''

She started to refuse and then remembered Brad might be bringing a woman to the cottage after he'd picked her up at the airport tonight. With such a thin wall separating them she knew she'd be able to hear nearly every sound they made. The thought appalled her. "I accept," she said. "What time?''

"Eight okay?''

"Great.''

After dressing she went back to the phone to call Bobby Hall to tell him about her latest accident. The police dispatcher told her Bobby was on another line but promised to have him call her. As Minta waited, she forced herself to go over the moment on the road when she'd first heard the car's horn sound behind her.

If she was honest with herself, she'd simply admit that the car was the same car she had encountered earlier. She closed her eyes and got a clear picture of the man's thin face, the pale-blond hair and that moment when his eyes had widened in recognition. There had been an angry intention in the deep-set eyes that made her skin crawl.

On the other hand, she might have been mistaken. She'd dealt with too many witnesses at accidents not to know that people tended to see what they wanted to or what they feared. The human mind was capable of playing strange tricks. But when that happened, it was a signal that the person involved needed help.

Al Slessor had implied her imagination was out of order, running amuck. Due to overwork he had said, his only attempt to be conciliatory. At the time she had scoffed at his allegation, but now she was beginning to wonder. Perhaps the person in question was the last to realize they were having problems.

Suddenly angry, she stood and started pacing the room. Damn, she was normal. It was entirely possible she had encountered the same driver twice. And she shouldn't rule out a slight possibility that she was being pursued. She'd dealt with the underworld too long not to have a healthy respect for their methods.

If she'd stumbled on something unknowingly in her last case, they might have followed her here. It would be stupid not to question whether she might be a target of revenge.

The phone rang and she grabbed it up, still debating whether or not she should tell Bobby about her own involvement in the FBI. Since this was another country, she was not bound by professional courtesy to reveal her identity. Still, was she being unfair? No, she was under absolute orders to stay out of trouble and that meant keeping herself uninvolved. She wasn't here on FBI business, so her status as an agent was not an issue.

Bobby's voice broke into her reverie. "Minta, I was about to call when I got your message. I may have found where that black car disappeared."

Minta was instantly alert. "Where is the car?" Now maybe she'd get some answers to what was bothering her. "Can I come down and identify it?"

"Hold on," he said, laughing at her enthusiasm. "I haven't seen it yet. Remember that house where you told me an old man came to the door?"

"Yes. He said he'd been sleeping."

"Well, behind that house and the others on that street are a lot of tall bushes."

"I noticed." Officer Hall's slow delivery of information was setting her teeth on edge.

"Those bushes hide a huge estate. There's a narrow entrance somewhere, between some of those houses."

"Can we go out there and see if the car's parked at the estate?"

"Not without a search warrant. We have laws here, too, you know."

"I'll come down to the station and swear out a complaint."

"It won't help. Without more proof than we have, we'd never get a warrant."

"So where does that leave us?"

He sounded slightly aggrieved. "At least we have an idea of where the car might have gone."

"For someone supposed to uphold the law you sound a little too disinterested," she said accusingly.

"Minta, I do my best," he said in a weary voice, and she felt instantly contrite. How many times had she known that same feeling of helplessness when victims of crimes had become impatient at the slowness of the justice system. "You may as well forget it now. The insurance is supposed to take care of everything," he concluded.

"It wasn't money...."

"I know. You have to understand something about the Caymans. We're a little blob in a big ocean. We don't have many natural resources to help us survive. We've become a haven for the rich. Whoever owns that huge estate wouldn't like it if we started probing too deeply. Of course, if you'd been injured, we'd give them hell."

"Could you at least find out who owns the estate for me?"

He sounded relieved. "No problem. I'll check the records office and get back to you. By the way, what was it you wanted when you called me?"

In the light of what he'd told her, Minta was reluctant to mention her latest escapade but she plunged on anyway. "I had another little accident today, Bobby," she said.

"Tell me all," he said with resignation.

Minta described her fall on the road briefly, hesitating when she had to tell him she suspected that the black car had been the same one. There was a long silence on the other end of the phone when she finished.

"Are you sure it was the black car?" Bobby asked her at length.

Minta paused and debated. "No," she admitted. "I'm not positive but I'm pretty sure."

"Well," Bobby said heavily. "Keep an eye out for the car, and if you see it again, try to get a license number. I'll alert my men to watch for it as well. How about staying on the beach tomorrow. It might keep you out of trouble."

"Sorry, Bobby. I'll try to keep from bothering you with more accidents." They hung up without saying anything further.

MINTA FOUND IT IMPOSSIBLE to concentrate on Richard's rambling conversation over dinner that evening. Her head throbbed, and she felt the first twinges of aching muscles. Her mind kept returning to Brad, dreading the thought of overhearing him with his lady friend.

Her bed was against the wall that joined his cottage, and if his was against the other side, she knew she'd be able to hear the slightest movement. At that thought she suddenly lost her appetite for the sweet dessert in front of her.

"Anything wrong?" Richard asked, his tone solicitous.

"A headache," she admitted. "Too much excitement in one day, I guess."

"Then I'll take you home immediately." He signaled the waiter for their bill.

When they arrived at the cottage, Minta spotted Brad's car sitting discreetly at the side. A light was burning in his living room, but she tried not to think about it as she assured Richard there was no need for him to see her to the door.

Once she was on the porch, Brad's light went out. Her heart sank like a lead weight as images of him flickered through her mind. She should have bought herself a radio to camouflage the noise, she decided, clicking on her living-room light with a decisive gesture.

In spite of her best efforts she found herself listening intently. Encouraged when she couldn't hear anything, she started for her bedroom. Once there she undressed quickly and slipped on a shorty gown. Without warning she heard the sound of someone whistling. Brad! Damn, he sounded so happy, she almost hated him.

Not willing to wait for more unwelcome sounds, she pulled on a matching robe and grabbed up a pillow and coverlet from the bed. She'd read. On the sofa in the living room. Surely one of those novels would do the trick.

Her head was throbbing painfully when she huddled on the couch. After a few minutes of forcing her eyes to scan the pages of the paperback book, she gave up. It wasn't going to work. She needed to talk to someone. Glancing at her watch, she decided to risk calling Elizabeth in D.C.

It was late but Elizabeth and Nathan were both night owls. They stayed up late at night and then slept late. As a freelance photographer, Nathan set his own working hours. Elizabeth didn't see her first patient in her psychiatric practice until ten each morning.

After telling herself she'd hang up if they didn't

answer by the fourth ring, she dialed direct. Elizabeth answered almost immediately. "Dr. Forrester."

"Elizabeth. Minta."

"How wonderful. Nathan and I were just discussing you. How's your island paradise?"

"Beautiful. Why was I the subject of your conversation? Should my ears be burning?"

Elizabeth laughed, and Minta had no trouble visualizing the smoky gray eyes and softly curling auburn hair of her friend. "Not at all. But I do have something I need to discuss with you. Nathan and I just returned from dinner at the Richardses'."

"Nothing wrong I hope?"

"Not with Jerry and Marla."

There was a hesitancy in her voice that alerted Minta. "Elizabeth! What's bothering you?"

"Jerry took me off for a little talk. He wants me to pass along a warning to you."

"Al?"

"Yes. Jerry thinks he's out to get you."

"I know that. I don't think he can. I do my job well."

"Don't be naive, Minta. If Jerry's worried, then I think you better take him seriously."

Minta took a deep breath. Elizabeth wouldn't be this disturbed unless it was worse than she had thought. "What's the warning?"

"To walk the straight and narrow. You're not to do anything except what Al assigns you."

"I'm not planning on it."

"Good. I don't quite understand why Jerry was worried. He said to warn you that even if a spy walked up and bit you, you're to pretend you didn't feel it."

Minta gave a shout of laughter. "That Jerry! I guess he does know me, all right. Do you think I'm acting a little strange, lately."

"No stranger than usual. Why do you ask?"

"Al said I'm close to a nervous breakdown."

"Oh, the big NBD scare," scoffed Elizabeth. "First of all that term is just a catchall for anyone who's under stress. I'm surprised you'd even remember such a petty accusation."

"Me, too. But I find it keeps popping into my mind."

"That's why it's so terrible to label people," said Elizabeth. Minta smiled, remembering how passionately her friend defended the right of people to differ from the norm without being accused of mental problems.

"It's just that you've never run into anyone before who doesn't recognize how special you are," added Elizabeth. "Admit it, all your life you've met with approval, so Al's disapproval is coming as quite a shock to you."

"You could be right. But do you think I'm too nosy?"

"If you weren't you'd never be good at your work. You're very observant. When you come to see me, you always notice if anything's different about the room we're in. And you were the first to see if Nathan, Jr., had a new tooth or more hair. Don't try to change yourself.''

Minta laughed. "Okay, enough about me. How are the members of your family? Tell Nathan there's beautiful scenery begging to be photographed down here. Maybe you can fly down for a visit while I'm here."

"I wish, but we're both swamped." Before hanging up, Elizabeth added one last message. "I almost forgot. Jill Harvey, Jerry's secretary, called my office today for your number. Shall I give it to her?"

"Yes, but I'll call her myself tomorrow. She's picking up my mail while I'm gone."

Silence descended on the cottage after Minta replaced the receiver. As she reviewed the warning from Jerry that Elizabeth had passed on, her head began pounding once more. For the first time she realized that her job, her whole career, might be in danger.

She wouldn't leave without giving Al a fight, she vowed. But it seemed so senseless. All she wanted was to do her work to the best of her ability. As her head began aching intolerably she remembered the capsules the doctor had given her. When she passed the bedroom, she heard a door closing in Brad's adjoining room, and she knew she would have given anything in the world to be held in his arms at that moment.

With a muttered oath she cursed herself for being such a fool and hurried into the kitchen. The packet lay on the windowsill. Her hands shook slightly as she filled a glass of water and then swallowed one of the capsules. Tonight she desperately needed a long restful sleep.

She awoke sometime during the night, her muscles cramped from the position she'd assumed on the sofa. Lifting her head, she glimpsed the moonlight filtering through the sheer curtains covering the open window.

She didn't have the slightest notion where she was. She forced herself to look around the room but it wasn't familiar. The wicker rocking chair, the satiny quilt covering her. None of this belonged to her. Where was she? Damn, she shouldn't have taken that pill.

Then she heard the sounds. Voices. Near. On the other side of the wall. A man's voice. And then another. She strained to hear and realized what the problem was. They weren't speaking English. Without warning, her head began drooping and she sank back down on the sofa, pulling the coverlet over her, too weak to care. Tomorrow was soon enough to think.

CHAPTER SIX

THE BEACH WAS TOTALLY ISOLATED the next morning. Dressed in a brief red bikini, Minta waded into the warm salty water. When she reached a depth for swimming she turned over on her back, floating under the brilliant blue sky. Waves washed over her sensuously, the currents exploring her inner thighs and caressing her full breasts. The sea reminded her of a gentle lover, teasing, tantalizing, arousing. A lover such as Brad must be.

Feeling a shiver from head to toe, she turned and struck out for shore with swift, sure strokes. Suddenly her dream from the night before surfaced. She struggled with the memory and then gave up, convincing herself it was only a result of the medication she'd taken. Once out of the water she flopped onto a large beach towel she'd spread on the warm sand.

Her gaze drifted toward the cottage behind her but she glanced away. His side of the duplex had been quiet when she'd awakened. Several children came running out of a cottage and spilled onto the beach, their laughter filling the air.

She stretched out on her stomach and within

minutes had fallen asleep. When she awoke she leaned up on one elbow and saw Brad in the distance, lounging on a similar towel. Her stomach muscles tightened, and she began filtering warm sand through the fingers of one hand.

He was leaning on one side, also, engrossed in the book he was reading. Probably something to do with his work. Her hand tingled to push back the lock of silky hair that had tumbled down over his forehead. He turned a page of his book and she watched, feeling oddly aroused by this simplest of movements.

She could imagine herself, squeezed onto his towel beside him, her hand running gently over his muscular torso, sliding around his waist. She forced her thoughts away as they skirted dangerously lower. What had happened to her? She'd never been one to rhapsodize over a man's physical attributes this way.

Disgusted with the way she couldn't get him off her mind, she gathered up her towel and walked back to her cottage. Evidently his friend was still sleeping, she decided, as she prepared herself a cup of coffee. If there was a friend. She was so confused by what had happened during the night. That pill had knocked her out completely.

And then there were those voices she remembered. Or thought she remembered, anyway. Something had been going on at Brad's place last night but she had no idea what. She didn't remember hearing any female voices.

She was studying the phone book to decide which scuba-diving offer intrigued her most when she heard a rumbling sound on the back veranda. She waited, uncertain what was making the noise, and then heard a loud knock.

An adorable cone-shaped metal machine confronted her when she opened the back door. Multicolored lights were flashing around its gleaming circumference, and the portion of its face where a mouth should be was shaped in a wide smile.

"Minta. Would you like breakfast?" it intoned.

"I don't believe it!" Minta began laughing and opened the door. "Please come in."

The creature obligingly rolled through the open doorway and then stopped. A door opened and a tray slid out. On the tray sat a platter of sweet rolls and two glasses of orange juice. "Mind if I come in?" said a deep voice from the doorway.

Minta glanced up and saw Brad. He was brushing off the powdery sand from his calves. No man had ever attracted her more than he did at that moment. She wanted to freeze the image of him in her mind, just as he stood, his hair gleaming, his chest and taut stomach sprinkled with a vee of silky red hairs. If it was possible, she'd keep that image of sensuality nearby her forever.

"Did I smell coffee?" he asked.

"Brad!" Minta struggled to slow down her racing pulse. "Is this Hilda? When did she arrive?"

He came inside. "Last night. I had Ron send her down so I could make a few refinements."

"Negative. Negative," said Hilda, and Minta began laughing again.

"Sorry, sweet one," said Brad, patting the robot affectionately. "You're right. I sent for you because I was missing you."

"Does she understand you?"

"Ask her."

"What do you think of Brad?" asked Minta, facing the robot.

Lights began flashing brightly and a series of chimes beat out a marching tune. Minta shook her head at Brad. "You've programmed her to do that," she teased him. "How does she understand what we're saying?"

Brad reached for the plate of rolls and two glasses. "Run along outside, Hilda," he said. When the robot disappeared through the door, he continued, "I wouldn't want her to hear me talk about her."

"Brad, you're impossible," sputtered Minta. "I think you really believe she's human."

"Not me. She's the one who thinks that. Am I invited to stay for breakfast?"

Minta nodded and poured out another cup of coffee before joining him at the table. She tried to decide if it was possible that Hilda was the woman he'd been expecting or if the real one was asleep next door. She decided she had to find a way to ask him. "Is Hilda jealous of the women in your life?"

He laughed. "I haven't tested her lately. I'm not involved with anyone, Minta. How about you? Anyone special in your life?"

"No." She felt better than she had since she'd met him. "Level with me, Brad. Can Hilda make independent decisions?"

"A few," he said. "Her brain is a computer. Voice activated. She sees through a camera lens. Basically she's only capable of doing what I program her to do."

"Can she do any household tasks?"

"She can at my home in Austin because I've designed the house around her. But at the moment, personal robots aren't really equipped for the general public. They have to be individually designed to suit each person's habits."

"How long have you had her?"

"Since I was twelve. She's gone through a lot of refinements, of course. When I learn something new she has to be reprogrammed."

Minta bit into one of the sweet rolls. Brad must have gone to a bakery before she got up. "Then robots are basically only a hobby?"

"Personal robots are. Industrial robots are the wave of the future. Unlike humans, they do exactly what they're told to do, and they do it the same way every time. They're revolutionizing industry. One of these days they'll free mankind from all the humdrum tasks in life."

"What kind does your company build?"

He glanced away as if undecided whether to tell her, and she felt that same buzz of curiosity she had when she'd first met him. "Underwater exploration is my specialty," he said.

"Jacques Cousteau of the robot world?" she said innocently.

His smile revealed even white teeth. "I see you've got the directory open to scuba-diving companies. Planning on engaging in some exploration of your own today?"

"I might have better luck dodging fish than cars."

He frowned. "Any pain today?"

"No, I took one of those pills last night...." She stopped, suddenly remembering her dream. "Does Hilda speak any foreign languages?"

He tensed. The hand that had been turning the directory pages stilled. "Why?"

She shrugged lightly. "I had the dumbest dream last night. I thought I heard some men talking."

He was too interested. She knew that, but she wouldn't let herself wonder why. "What language?" he asked.

"I'm not sure." She took another nibble of the roll. "It wasn't Spanish or French. Wait! I've got it. It was one of the Slavic languages. I'm sure of it. Polish, Czech, maybe."

He watched her carefully. "Are you familiar with those languages?"

Although she wasn't able to carry on a conversation in many languages, she had taken a basic linguistic course to help in identification. "Not really. In college I belonged to a foreign-film club. We even watched films with subtitles, so I can usually recognize most languages. That medication must have made my dreams a little wild."

When he smiled slightly, she sensed he seemed relieved. "Where did you go to college, Minta?"

"University of New Mexico. It's in Albuquerque. Ever been there?"

"At a robotics convention last year. It's quite a state. I don't see how you could have traded it for D.C."

"It wasn't easy."

"Couldn't you sell your silver jewelry just as easily from Albuquerque?" he persisted.

"A leading Washington jeweler was the first to handle my line," she offered by way of explanation.

He seemed content, glancing back down at the directory. "Have you called any of these diving companies?"

"No, I can't decide on one."

"Mind if I come with you?"

She could have hugged him but she resisted the urge. Her spontaneousness bothered most men. They seemed to feel threatened when a woman took the lead in touching first. "If you like," she said with considerable restraint.

He stood and started toward the phone in the living room. She watched him until he was out of sight and then sipped the orange juice he'd brought. Now that Brad had said he wasn't involved with anyone she sensed their relationship was likely to take a new twist. While one side of her welcomed it, another was reluctant to simply be swept along on the tide of his irresistible male attractiveness.

Soon she'd be leaving, returning to her hectic life-style. She doubted if Brad or any other man would ever be content with a woman who had to disappear periodically without being able to say where she was going or when she would be back.

If she was less drawn to Brad, then she could have enjoyed a brief interlude with him. She knew instinctively that he would be a perfect lover. His every action indicated consideration and tender-ness. Getting involved with him would be a total ex-perience, and she wasn't certain how she'd handle it when they had to part.

She stood and went over to the sink to rinse out the glass, thinking that she was foolish to deny her-self the pleasures she was certain Brad was capable of bringing her. Footsteps sounded behind her and she half turned as Brad entered the kitchen.

"Minta, why did you sleep on the couch last night?" he asked quietly.

For the life of her not a single excuse would come to her mind. "Damn, Brad. I thought you had a woman in bed with you," Minta said, refusing to lie to him. "How did I know you were picking up Hilda at the airport?"

His soft laughter was not what she expected. "Funny, is it?" she continued, her anger growing. "Well, just stuff this into your little microchips. I'm not even the jealous type, and here I am having a fit over a simple robot."

He rested his hands on her shoulders and turned her to face him fully. "And I thought I was the one having a jealous fit last night."

Minta couldn't hide her pleasure as she tilted back her head to gaze into his eyes. "You, too?" she whispered. She felt his fingers tighten on her skin, and when his lips moved to her throat she arched her neck back farther to grant him total access. He let his lips wander to the crest of a high cheekbone, then on to her temple, moving slowly, as if savoring each square inch of her exquisitely smooth skin.

She could feel the world slip out of focus as if she was underwater, weightless, moving effortlessly with the rippling currents in a world containing only the two of them. Her skin burned where his lips touched, her body aching for more. She murmured something that wasn't intelligible. If this was madness, then she would gladly go mad.

His fingers slid over her shoulders and, with an easy motion, removed the small scrap of fabric to expose her breasts. He ran a fingertip over the curve of first one and then the other, creating an almost unbearable torture as he traced the deep hollow between. He lowered his head and his tongue followed the path of his wandering finger, and she went up like kindling, the flames roaring in her ears.

Pleasure cascaded through her, making her skin glow and her blood pound in her temples. She sifted her questing fingers through his hair, pressing the slender tips against his head when she feared she might not have the strength to stand on her trembling legs.

He raised his head, wrapping his arms around her, lifting her off the floor. Their eyes locked, their lips joined in a searing kiss, as if all the hunger and thirst they'd ever known was to be satisfied in that one moment.

A sensual sigh of pleasure escaped her as their kiss deepened, his tongue seeking the inviting recesses of her mouth, probing, searching, exploring all the innermost secrets with flickering thrusts that only created increasingly insatiable demands.

She didn't question why she was so sure his kiss was different from any other she'd ever known before or why she was so certain they belonged together. She wanted only to be with him, to experience the moment fully, to suspend time forever.

His grip on her tightened, pressing her against his firmness, and she tore her lips from his and began kissing his cheekbones, his eyelids, his dark lashes and his square, clefted chin. She kissed him over and over, and with each kiss her hunger grew. She could feel his heart pounding, and she knew the tide was running as strong in him as it was in her.

Suddenly her mind latched on to thoughts that refused to go away. No matter how attracted she was to Brad, she knew it was more than a physical attraction. She wanted more from him than a casual sexual encounter. She needed to know more about him as a person, more about his own life and personality, before she committed herself to him.

"Brad," she whispered against his lips, and he drew back reluctantly. "What about that diving trip?" she asked rather breathlessly.

For a moment he seemed about to protest. Then a

small smile curved his lips. "Okay, Minta. I guess I was pushing things too far. But damn, you're so gorgeous!"

"I'm not saying no," she said softly. "Just 'not yet.'"

He chuckled softly and said, "Fair enough." Touching her cheek with a finger, he added, "Don't disappear on me while I'm getting ready."

"When will we leave?" Minta forced her mind to return to the everyday details of the day.

"Say half an hour. Why not pack an overnight bag? We might stay over on Cayman Brac tonight. That way we won't have to rush our diving trip."

Minta debated for a moment and then gave in gracefully. "Sure. See you in half an hour."

BRAD'S THOUGHTS KEPT RETURNING to her over and over as he changed out of his swim briefs. Minta. Her body had been so warm, so willing when he'd held her. He hadn't wanted to let go of her. His hands had itched to explore, excite, unlock the secrets of her soft curving body.

It was better this way, he told himself. He had to remember to go easy. To play it by ear. To retreat the moment there was even a remote possibility that he might be involving her in his own private nightmare.

When he'd first met Minta the answer had been simple. Ignore her attractions. Then had come their dinner together. He smiled to himself, remembering the discussion they had over their Indian heritage.

He hadn't thought about his mother's people for a long time. But then he had never been around a woman so at ease and so proud of her native American heritage, either. In many ways he envied her.

He knew now that it had been an impossible solution to think he could turn his back on Minta. She'd invaded his mind like water into a dry sponge, crumbling his defenses, imbuing him with daydreams he'd given up long ago.

She was different from any woman he'd known before, but he hadn't tried to analyze how. He only knew that he was obsessed with wanting to know her better.

To know means to be known, he reminded himself, moving to the closet to throw a change of clothes into a bag. He was a fool to risk intimacy with her. If he held her in his arms, if he made love to her, he'd be vulnerable; unable to carry on pretenses no matter what the cost.

He zipped up the bag with impatient fingers, suddenly angry with the trend of his thoughts. A romantic fool. That's what he was. Caught up in a tidal wave of longing by the sudden impact of meeting a woman he'd never dared dream existed. Enjoy her today. That's all she's offering, he told himself in a burst of temper.

But how about tomorrow? Or the next day or the day after that? He knew that every second he spent with her was going to make it harder to walk away when the time came that he had no other choice.

He tried to decide how long he had. Last night

The Trio had found him, as he'd known they would from the beginning. They grated on his nerves as much here as they had in Austin. Money, they'd offered, watching with their expressionless eyes to gauge his reaction. As if dollars were as vital as air to a human's existence.

The vicious rumors spread by a competitor about Galactia's financial problems had targeted him. And like wolves circling caribou herds until they located the sickest animal, they'd sought him out.

"Deal with us and your troubles will be over," they'd said, reminding him in the next breath that if he didn't someone else would. Someone high up, in the Pentagon even, they'd hinted. He believed them. Once burned, twice shy wasn't just a folk-saying in his mind. But he'd refused to lose faith. Until now.

If only he'd had more options. But the final tests on Hugo were already planned for now and he couldn't change them, not without losing any chance for having his bid accepted. It still bothered him how The Trio had known all the details.

No matter how long he racked his brain, he couldn't pinpoint the source of the leaks. No one had known his plans. He'd made his own plane reservation. He had arranged personally for this cottage. He'd even slipped away without telling anyone, thinking a note to Ron would be sufficient. He should have known there'd be a slip.

Or a catastrophe would be more like it. His picture splashed on the front page of the paper. He regretted now the way he'd lost his temper with Ron. Especially since the police hadn't shown the slightest interest in him.

Anyway, he hadn't given The Trio the slip. They'd arrived on the island before him and left a message with the realtor. A strange sense of hopelessness had swept over him as he'd opened that envelope at the car-rental agency and seen their note.

The Trio had arrived at the cottage late the evening before, just as his old navy buddy, Ted Miller, was leaving. Ted had stared curiously at them, or so it had seemed. Puzzling though, how he had hurried out so quickly, almost as if he'd been aware of the tension in the air.

Brad had given them one diagram, just enough to send them scurrying for confirmation from one of their own experts. If he'd made it cryptic enough, it would give him the time he so desperately needed. Based on Ted's analysis of the tides, it would be a day or two before they could begin the tests. Any delay now was wearing on his nerves.

Brad frowned suddenly, remembering what Minta had told him about her dream. Damn, he hated the way he'd lied to her.

If she mentioned it again, he'd tell her a little of the truth. Not much. Just enough so she'd relax. That's what he needed right now. Minta, relaxed and happy. And with him.

That thought cheered him, and he checked to make certain the front door was locked before going out on the back veranda. Hilda was waiting for him, and he surveyed her speculatively. "What do you say we ask Minta if she has room in her cottage for you this afternoon, Hilda?" he asked.

"Affirmative," she answered solemnly.

MINTA WAS CHANGING into a striped cotton minidress when she remembered her promise to Elizabeth to call Jill Harvey. When she finished twisting her hair into a sleek roll on the back of her head, she hurried to the phone.

Jill lowered her voice confidentially when Minta identified herself. "I can't say much now," Jill said.

Minta was amused. Jill was a petite blonde with enormous china-blue eyes that gave her a childlike expression. Since she had gone to work for the FBI, she had developed a habit of making everything seem like a major crisis. "About what? Did I get some strange mail?"

"No, it's Jerry. He talked to Elizabeth last night and...."

"I know," Minta interrupted, somewhat irritated that she was the subject of office gossip. "She passed along his warning."

"Warning?" Jill's voice vibrated with interest. "I didn't hear about that."

Minta could have kicked herself for jumping to the wrong conclusion. "Forget it. I was just joking. What did Jerry say to you?"

"He wanted to know why you chose the Caymans for your vacation."

"Damn! What's going on?" demanded Minta, suddenly tired of all the ferment about her in her absence.

"I don't know. He seemed upset. I told him I had no idea why you went to the Caymans."

"There's nothing mysterious about it. I wanted to scuba dive and remembered that the Caymans are supposed to have some of the most fantastic diving spots in the Caribbean. Didn't Jerry give you some idea why he was so interested?"

"None. Shall I tell him you're diving?"

"Only if you two run out of anything more interesting to discuss. Jill, tell Jerry if he wants to talk to me, he can get my phone number from you or Elizabeth. I'm not doing anything illegal." After a pause she added, "Did any bills come in my mail?"

"No. A travel brochure from a cruise company is all. I glanced through it, and it has the most marvelous trip that covers all the Med. It even stops in Yugoslavia...."

Yugoslavia. Minta's attention was diverted as she remembered her dream. The language she'd heard might have been Yugoslavian. "Do me a favor, Jill," she said impulsively.

"Glad to. What is it?"

"The next time you have to check the computer files for Jerry, call up a name for me."

"Have they got you working?" Jill asked indignantly. "I'd refuse if I were you."

"It's not exactly work."

Jill gave a short, cynical laugh. "I'll bet. What's the name?"

Minta hesitated, wondering why she was doing this.

"I've got a pencil," Jill persisted.

"Brad. Brad McMillan, short for Bradley, maybe. He's from Oregon originally. He's got a company named Galactia Enterprises in Austin, Texas. It manufactures robots."

"Mr. Star Wars?" Jill suggested.

Minta laughed, feeling slightly embarrassed and guilty. It couldn't hurt to check Brad out. After what had happened to her with Peter, she couldn't be too careful. But he only asked you to go scuba diving, she reminded herself. "I've got to run now. I'm leaving for my first dive in a few minutes."

"Lucky. Shall I try to catch you this evening?"

"Don't make a special trip to the computer files for me. We'll talk later in the week, Jill."

Minta heard Brad whistling on the porch as she replaced the receiver. "Come in," she called out when he knocked.

The robot rolled in beside him. "Do you have room in your closet for Hilda? Mine's filled with her packing crate. The cleaning woman is due today, and she might die of fright if she caught her by surprise."

Minta avoided his gaze, remembering her directions to Jill. "Hilda or the cleaning woman?" She led the way to her bedroom.

"Hilda? Afraid? She'll never forgive you if she

hears you say that.'' He casually opened the front panel on the robot and said, ''I'll be out in a minute. I just want to program her so she won't miss us.''

Minta thought she saw Brad slip something from his pocket. . . some kind of disc or miniature tape. Deciding there was no time to ask for a detailed explanation, Minta shook her head and smiled. ''Show me how she works when we get back, okay Brad?''

''Love to,'' he called after her as she left the room.

A few moments later he joined her in the living room. His eyes swept over her, admiring the expanse of slender legs showing beneath the short, flared skirt she wore. ''Ready?''

She nodded. ''I'll need to rent diving equipment, though.''

''As long as you have your C-Card, Ted will have everything you need.''

Minta patted a small leather envelope that was looped over her belt. The C-Card was simply a diving licence. ''Right here.'' She reached for her canvas gym bag containing her swimsuit, some underclothes and cosmetics. ''Who's Ted?''

''A friend of mine. He's captain of the boat we're going out on.''

Minta stopped. ''Didn't you call one of the diving outfits in the yellow pages?''

''Why would I? Ted's ship is docked here. I've chartered it for some tests on an underwater robot I'm developing.''

Minta thought about this new piece of information. Brad hadn't mentioned anything about this project when she'd asked him why he was in the Caymans. "Then this isn't your first trip to these islands?"

He grinned. "Are you always this curious, beautiful?" With his fingers on her elbow he guided her toward the door. "This is my first time staying on Grand Cayman. Ted is a resident of Cayman Brac, so I usually stay there when I'm running tests. Any more questions?"

His answer opened up a dozen more but she decided to say nothing. As he swung open the passenger door on his red car a phone started ringing, and they both turned. "Let's forget it," Brad said.

"Is it yours?"

He shrugged, and she began laughing and slid in. "I'm all for ducking out, myself."

He backed out into the road. "Let's declare this an official holiday. Freedom Day. Everyone is free to do what they want today."

Minta leaned back against the seat, letting the breeze waft over her. "If you ran for president on that platform, you'd probably win every vote."

"Not interested. Government work would stifle me. Four years as a navy SEAL taught me a lesson I'll never forget."

"A navy SEAL. That's the special underwater division, isn't it?"

"Yes." Brad was tight-lipped, and Minta refrained from probing. He obviously didn't like discussing his military experiences. She wondered for a moment what he would think if she flipped out her FBI ID card the way she'd seen it done on the old TV shows. It was tempting, and he'd given her a perfect opening by bringing up working for the government. For some reason, a reason she herself did not completely understand, she couldn't make herself reveal that information yet.

He glanced over at her. "You're smiling that little secret smile again. Are you laughing at me, Minta?"

"Definitely with you, McMillan. I'm so excited about finally getting a chance to dive in the Caymans I can hardly sit still."

He smiled at her exuberance. "How much diving have you done?"

"I belong to a club that dives once a month around D.C. Mostly in the Chesapeake. Last year we went down to the Keys. Compared to a navy SEAL, my skills are in the amateur class."

His eyes had darkened when he glanced back over at her. "Depends what skills you're talking about."

"You are incorrigible," she said unable to suppress a grin. The toe of her shoe rustled against a piece of paper, and she leaned over to push it aside. It was a copy of the paper she'd seen the day before, the one explaining Brad's disappearance. "Brad, I have a confession to make," she said as she brought the paper to her lap.

His hands gripped the wheel tighter. "What?"

"I knew who you were when I knocked on your door the other evening."

He glanced toward her in surprise. "We haven't met before. I'd remember you."

She shook her head. "I saw your picture in the paper. Are you really a genius?"

He laughed. "God, no. That was just sensationalism."

"Now you tell me," she said, feigning disappointment. "And I was all ready to write my friends back home I'd gone diving with a genius."

He lifted his eyebrows. "Don't forget to add I'm a disappearing genius or didn't you read the story?"

She patted the paper on her lap. "I read the follow up in here. Did the cleaning crew really hide your note?"

"Misplaced it. Don't you know what happened to Pandora when she got too curious?"

"I don't believe in myths that put down women. Why didn't your manager know where you were going? Were you trying to keep it a deep, dark secret?"

Brad kept his eyes on the road ahead. "I don't check in on a day-to-day basis with my company. Anyway, Ron is a worrier. Our friendship goes back to when we were in school together in Oregon." He paused as if carefully weighing his words before adding, "In case you're wondering, neither of the rumors about my company are true. We're not going broke and we're not going public."

"I'll be sure to tell my stockbroker," she said

lightly. "Now it's your turn. What would you like to ask me?"

He remained serious. "Why didn't you ask me about my disappearance when you first met me?"

Her voice took on its husky quality. "I didn't know I'd be interested."

CHAPTER SEVEN

THEY REACHED THE WATERFRONT and drove along it, passing rows of modern hotels. Minta rolled down the window on her side, sniffing the salt-scented breezes floating in from the sea. Along the quay, fishing vessels, yachts, speedboats bobbed in the water, while out on the sea, sails fluttered against the naked blue sky. Here and there an occasional bird soared skyward holding aloft a prize fish in its beak.

Brad stopped at the far end of the road, in front of a large vessel that lay low in the water, its white paint chipped and scored. The water in the harbor sloped comfortably against the solid timbers as Minta stepped outside, her bag slung over her shoulders. *"Lydia,"* she read on the side of the boat.

"Ted's wife," Brad explained. "I'll introduce you to her if we get a chance. She and Ted moved here right after he returned from Vietnam. She's always full of questions about the States. I suspect she misses her old hometown in Florida sometimes."

"Beside taking you out for tests on your robots, what does Ted do with his boat?"

"He and Lydia run a fishing service. It's both a commercial and tourist operation. And of course, they're always happy to accommodate divers. Ted was a SEAL in the navy, too." For a moment Brad's eyes seemed to cloud over. Minta eyed him curiously but didn't ask him any questions about Vietnam. She'd found that many people who had served in Vietnam didn't like to talk about their experiences. It dredged up memories they didn't want to recall.

Minta walked past several sailors who were lolling back against a railing. Their eyes followed her lithe movements with more than a passing interest. Brad moved beside her as they started down a wharf. "This is a much larger boat than I was expecting."

"She's a good vessel." Brad waved at a man emerging from the small wheelhouse as they scrambled on board.

The man was sturdy with a fringe of curly brown hair curving around a generous bald spot. In many ways he appeared to be older than Brad, but the bright-blue eyes welcoming Minta had a youthful look. He fingered a thick beard as he came toward them.

"Minta, Ted Miller. Captain of *Lydia*," Brad announced proudly.

Ted hesitated a moment, eyeing her carefully, and then extended a calloused hand. "You're the best-looking robot Brad's brought on board yet."

Minta laughed. "But not nearly as docile as most

of them.'' She glanced around the ship. ''Nice boat. Mind if I look around?''

Ted nodded briefly in Brad's direction. ''It's up to the boss what he lets you see.'' Minta thought she detected an unfriendly look in his eyes. No, it wasn't exactly unfriendly. Just cautious.

Minta turned toward Brad, her eyebrows raised in speculation. ''Am I treading too near someone's secrets?''

Ted tensed suddenly, even as Brad frowned. ''You're welcome to wander anywhere you like,'' Brad said shortly. ''Ted, let's run Minta out to The Bay so she can explore the reefs.''

''Aye, aye, sir,'' Ted said, his eyes darting toward Minta. ''By the way, who were your friends last night?'' Although the question was asked casually, Minta could tell that the answer was important to Ted.

This time it was Brad's turn to tense. Minta felt the muscles in his arm contract as he brushed against her. ''They weren't friends, just business contacts,'' he said.

''Down here to meet you?'' Ted persisted.

Brad's laugh sounded forced. ''Among other things. Why?''

''That was a strange time of night to be doing business. It must have been after midnight when I left.''

Brad's voice was deliberately cool. ''Europeans live by a different time schedule.'' After a pause he added with a hint of anger, ''Everyone doesn't have the luxury of choosing the people they do business with, Ted.'' He turned to Minta. "Ted's an independent cuss. If he doesn't like one of his passengers, he takes them back to shore and returns their money.''

Minta glanced from one man to the other, uncomfortably aware of the tension between them. She herself was reminded once again of how uneasy she felt about her dream of the night before. But now she knew it had not been a dream. Realizing both men were watching her, waiting for her response, she tried to be light and breezy. ''I'll try to behave, Ted.''

Ted clamped a hand on her shoulder, glaring at Brad. ''Now see what you've started, man. You'll have Minta thinking I'm terrible.'' It was the first really friendly gesture Ted had made toward her and she was surprised.

One of the crew shouted for him, and he moved away after giving her a reassuring wink. Brad stared out over the water, his features grim. Minta stood beside him as the roar of the engine throbbed assertively in the background. *Lydia* made her way slowly out to sea.

Brad turned toward her abruptly. ''What? No questions from Ms Cordero?''

She shifted awkwardly. ''About what?''

''I think you know what I'm talking about.''

His attitude angered her. ''If you insist, I am puzzled over why you didn't tell me you had European visitors late last night. It explains what I thought was a dream.''

He shrugged coldly. "My visitors chose that time because they didn't want to be seen."

She brushed back several strands of hair that had drifted free of the coil on the back of her neck. "I didn't mention having seen anyone."

Brad turned toward her, motioning to a bench. They moved toward it and seated themselves. When he didn't speak after a long silence, Minta said stiffly, "None of this is my business, Brad."

His short laugh was harsh. "Of course it is. I lied to you. You have a right to ask why. That is, if you intend to spend any time with me."

Minta opened her mouth, then shut it again without making a sound. A slow smile animated her heart-shaped face, transforming the planes and angles into breathtaking beauty. "I do, so why?"

His hands reached out and grasped hers tightly. "Thing are hectic right now, Minta. I'm caught up in something of a nightmare. If I don't get these tests finished on time...."

She tried to disengage her fingers. "I don't want to keep you from your work. Perhaps we should cancel the diving trip."

Brad laughed as he kissed the crown of her head. "I'm hopelessly distracted."

Minta lifted her head. "Ted can always turn back."

"It wouldn't help. I've got a reel of Minta Cordero running constantly in my head."

"Maybe you need to punch the off button on your movie projector."

"I'm minus willpower." He placed one hand on her cheek. "You have me bewitched, Minta."

A little gasp escaped her lips as she felt a sharp twist of desire. The same desire she saw in his eyes. She wanted to touch him, to reach out to him, but her hands remained powerless to move.

He dropped his hand from her face and shifted away, shattering the moment. "I'm sorry I changed the subject. I believe you wanted to know why I lied to you."

She watched him carefully. "You're the one insisting. I've accepted you had business reasons."

"I wish it were that simple. What I do..." he started only to begin again. "Robotics are the hottest thing around right now. Everyone is trying to get in on the act. Some of my competitors, foreign and domestic, would stop at nothing to get their hands on my inventions."

"And your visitors last night?"

"I don't like them. But I'm involved with them. That's why I think it would be wise if you moved out of the cottage and stayed away from me."

She laughed shakily. "How did we get back to that? I thought you'd admitted I'd bewitched you with my Zuni charms."

He smiled, and in his eyes was a recklessness she'd never seen before. He buried his head in her neck. "Hell, why am I doing this to myself? Minta, forget what I've been saying. Everything will be fine, I know it will."

His mouth caressed her throat, and Minta felt

herself go up in flames. It occurred to her briefly that she might be passing up her last chance to stay out of this man's life. She brushed her hand along the back of his neck and let the warning slide by, unheeded.

His lips moved to her mouth and he kissed her slowly, deeply, with a gentleness that melted her. She was the first to move back, smiling into his eyes. "No more lies, Minta," he whispered. "I promise."

She touched his cheek with one finger. "If there's anything I can do to help, let me know."

The amber flecks danced in the depths of his eyes. "You have no idea how much that means to me, Minta."

As they neared Cayman Brac, one of the three islands that make up the Caymans, Ted pointed out the diving equipment he carried on board.

"It's more professional than I'm accustomed to," Minta said.

"And heavier, I'll bet. Go below and change into your swimsuit while I try to locate the smallest vest we've got." He nodded his head toward a ladder leading below deck.

There were three small bunk rooms, connected by a hallway lined with storage cabinets. At the far end was a small galley and a charting table, which probably doubled for mealtimes.

Minta changed into a navy maillot that skimmed over her full breasts. When she came back to the deck, Ted was waiting for her, holding a buoyancy vest in one hand. He helped her slip it on. "Brad says you have your C-Card."

"I left it downstairs. Let me get it."

"I trust you, Minta. And Brad. He vouched for you."

"You've known him a long time?"

His fingers fumbled with the fasteners on the vest as he nodded, suddenly serious. "Brad's a great guy. But he's a crazy fool when it comes to taking risks. He's not afraid of tackling anything." He glanced up, smiling at her. "Have you known him long?"

She shook her head as she adjusted the straps. "Only a few days but I agree with you. He's a great guy."

When Brad came on deck, she assisted him with his vest. "Ever been kissed underwater?" he asked when Ted moved away to locate the best spot to anchor.

"Hmm, I'll never tell."

"Then I'll have to make certain you can say yes." He opened up a metal cabinet and removed an underwater watch from a shelf.

She refused it. "It's too large. I'll have to depend on you. What buddy system do you use?"

"Standard." He slipped a whistle attached to a nylon cord around her neck. "What depth are you accustomed to?"

"I've gone over a hundred feet several times. I'd like to extend as far as possible."

"We'll see how you're doing." As the vessel

shuddered to a halt, they went over to the side, watching as a diving platform was lowered by two crew members.

When everything was in position, they climbed onto the platform. Ted handed over their tanks and they strapped them on. Minta tingled with anticipation as she swayed on the platform, slipping on her flippers and then the hood. Brad leaned over and slipped the regulator mouthpiece between her lips, whispering, ''I've been meaning to tell you how great you look in a bathing suit.''

She glanced up, but he had turned away and was giving last-minute instructions to Ted. Somehow the comment hadn't been flirtatious or crude. Brad was genuine about his feelings, and he said what he felt. He liked her body, but she could tell he liked her as a person first. For a second her thoughts shifted to the evening ahead. By agreeing to stay on Cayman Brac tonight she had been tacitly agreeing to sharing time alone with Brad. Would it lead to lovemaking?

She had to admit she was bored by casual love-making. The past few years had taught her a lot about life. One thing she had learned was that sex was no antidote to loneliness. For sex to be meaningful, you had to care about the person, you had to have some sort of committed relationship. Most of the men she knew these days weren't willing to be committed to anyone. And that had made her wary.

Yet instinctively she knew Brad was different. He wanted a relationship, not just a one-night stand.

Dismissing her premature worries, she decided firmly to accept whatever happened, to make the most of their time together and to stop being so analytical.

Brad started down the ladder first. She followed and slipped into the warm waters. For a moment she was disoriented by the unaccustomed weight of the equipment. Within seconds she adjusted to it and began the slow, passive free-fall down. Down. Down.

It was an incredible sensation. Free motion. Weightlessness. The sensual slide of the water over her skin. All doubts, all insecurities slipped away and she was mesmerized, enchanted and the master of infinite space.

Below her she saw Brad poised beside a coral reef, grasping one edge of it, waiting for her. Everything that had happened in the past few days suddenly made sense. All her life she'd been waiting for Brad, suspended in space and slowly drifting toward this linkup with him. What marvelous luck they'd found each other.

As she neared Brad, she began to feel reality return. He gave her a thumbs-up signal and she responded, her heart pounding with pleasure. Two large groupers floated near them and then veered away as if resentful of this invasion of their privacy. She wanted to call after them and reassure them that she would not hurt them, that she had her mate, too, and they could share this world together.

Grinning over her romantic thoughts, she kept

swiveling her head, watching the colorful reef fishes floating among the brightly colored coral heads. The Cayman reefs were even more fantastic than she'd imagined. None of her other diving experiences had prepared her for the spectacular, clear, turquoise waters and the swirling surrealistic landscape stretching before her.

Sheer heaven, she decided, reaching out to let a school of small fish filter through her fingers. Brad was pointing down and she followed the direction of his finger, gasping at the awesome scene below them as the paler gradations of color gave way to deep, darkening blues. As if in a dream, she glided downward to what seemed like immeasurable depths.

The emotions cascading through her seemed almost too intense to absorb. All her past diving memories were lost, swallowed up by the awe-inspiring panorama below.

She responded to the pull of gravity as if to an irresistible force. The parallel between this and how she felt about Brad was evident. Fighting her strong response to him would be as futile as resisting the laws of nature.

Dreamily she thought about his invitation to stay with him at Cayman Brac. She conjured up images of the time they would spend loving and learning all about one another. Minta knew she wouldn't, she couldn't, refuse.

A large fin brushed against Minta's bare leg, startling her out of her flight of fancy. She glanced over at Brad to see if he could guess at her thoughts, but he was turned away from her, inspecting a strange coral formation at closer range. She maneuvered her way slowly to his side and he took her hand in his, brushing it against the long skeletonlike fingers of the coral. The softness surprised her, and she caught the pleasure in Brad's eyes.

He pointed to her depth gauge. They were at fifty feet now, and they started down the side of the sheer cliffs. The cliff was a living wall of trees, shrubs, mushroom forms that were actually animals, living corals and sponges. Around and through the graceful shapes, fish, shrimps and mollusks soared and jumped, walked and glided, expressing a joy of the life flowing through them.

She located Brad and pointed to several shapes, indicating her wonder over the vast range of breathtaking colors—bright yellows, reds, oranges and blues in every shade imaginable. An artist's paradise. A new design for her jewelry began to form in her mind, and her fingers itched for the feel of the malleable silver under the blows of her hammer.

Brad rolled over and Minta followed suit, gaining a spectacular view of the receding surface. She pointed to the boat above and Brad nodded, as long wispy columns of bubbles rose endlessly from them toward the light.

When they began descending again, Minta kept checking her gauge. One hundred feet. One hundred twenty. One hundred thirty slid past almost too easily. A slight fuzziness in her brain alerted her to nitrogen problems, and she took a deeper breath from her tank. Brad signaled to her several times, and when her answers came back slower and slower, he motioned for them to start back.

Relieved, she nodded. Just then, from out of one of the canyon walls, there came an undulating streak of silver. Minta watched with total detachment as her mind identified the object as a barracuda. The animal postured himself so she and Brad could get a full side view of its impressive six-foot length, and Minta glanced over for Brad's response.

Brad moved cautiously to position himself between the barracuda and Minta. Minta pushed forward, her hand on the sheath strapped around her waist, which held a long knife. The barracuda turned for a front view, displaying prominent, wickedly sharp teeth, and Minta felt her heart flop.

She angled her body away from the fish. As it turned and glided away, she breathed a sigh of relief that she, a mere spectator, had not been forced to war against a creature in its own home. With one last look down, she turned and began the long, slow climb toward the sunlight.

Following their dive line, they surfaced at length near their ship. One of the crew members was waiting on the platform, and he grasped Minta's shoulders, dragging her onto it. Ted came down the ladder and assisted her in removing her bulky equipment. "How was it?"

Minta could only shake her head. "Go on down and get into something warm while I fix us a pot of coffee," said Ted, the gleam in his eye indicating that he understood she was too overwhelmed to put her feelings into words.

Minta waved at Brad as he climbed out of the water and went onto the deck. Once in the small cabin where she'd left her clothes, she leaned against the wall, regaining her breath. Still caught up in the indescribable beauty she closed her eyes, reliving the glorious sensations.

She heard the door open and glanced up to see Brad in the opening. "Mind if I come in?" he asked softly.

"If you hadn't I would have gone looking for you," she answered. "It was all so wonderful, Brad. Thank you for bringing me here."

"My pleasure." He moved closer, his eyes burning brightly. He reached for a dry towel. "Need some help?"

"Please."

He slipped off the straps of her bathing suit, exposing her breasts to his scrutiny. With gentle strokes he dabbed the sparkling drops of water off her soft skin, sending her into paroxysms of pleasure. When he finished he fitted his hard palms against her taut nipples, and she took a sharp breath as her knees trembled beneath her.

Raising her head, she parted her lips, flicking the tip of her tongue over them in an unconscious invitation. He reacted instantly, moving his lips down to cover hers. His tongue, soft and sweet, moved between her teeth to play with hers. "I almost went crazy wanting to make love to you down there," he murmured.

When he drew back, he moved her away, gazing at her full breasts with their dusky-rose nipples. After a long sigh of pleasure he touched her arms, gathering her against his hard chest. "Let me feel you," he said huskily. "You're so soft, so perfect. I need you."

She was acutely aware of his clean, masculine scent. With tiny flicks of her tongue on his neck and shoulders she tasted his salty skin, and felt the tremors coursing through his body. His trembling hands stroked down the silkiness of her arms as her lips sought out the hollow at the base of his throat.

"Minta," he said huskily. "Did you decide if you'd stay with me at one of the inns on Cayman Brac tonight?"

"Do you really need to ask?" She leaned back, gazing at him through half-lowered lids, glorying in the sensations engulfing her body, a woman's body that seemed destined to blend with the man holding her. "I thought we'd settled that."

"Not the part about your staying *with* me," he murmured. "Am I asking too much too soon?"

Minta couldn't have denied him anything at that moment. He was so gentle, so caring, and so over-whelmingly attractive.

He pushed back slowly. "While I still can, I better get out of here. I'll have Ted radio to see if any rooms are available."

Her legs were unsteady as she moved away. "I need to rinse the salt out of my hair," she said, pulling the pins away to let the strands fall down her back.

He watched intently. "May I stay for that?"

She pushed him away gently, smilingly. "You better get back on deck before Ted starts to think we're suffering from the bends."

"That's not what he's thinking," returned Brad before closing the door behind him.

When she came up to the deck, Ted came forward. "Ready for that coffee, Minta?"

"Am I ever." She accepted the mug he held out as she glanced around, looking for Brad.

"He's in the engine room." Ted's perceptive blue eyes brought a slight flush to Minta's cheeks. "Checking out his beloved robot. That guy's got a one-track mind, you know. He talks to those machines as if they're human."

"Shh, it would break his heart if he found out they aren't. What's the name of this one?"

"Hugo. Want to see it?"

"Love to." Minta placed her nearly empty mug back on a shelf holding several others.

Ted pointed toward the engine room again. "I'm sure Brad will want to give you the guided tour."

Brad was down on one knee, peering into a metal box that contained a computer screen. He glanced up with a warm smile as Minta entered. "Ted told me you'd introduce me to Hugo," she said.

He stood immediately. "I thought you'd never

ask. These are the controls," he said, his face lighting up with enthusiasm. "Hugo is stuffed in the room beside this one." He pointed to a door.

"I suppose because you call him Hugo, he has a far more exciting life than Hilda." She crossed the room with Brad close behind her.

"What do you want to bet she wouldn't trade places?"

"You are crazy, you know," she said affectionately.

"Of course. It's required in my line of work." He put a palm on her waist. His voice lowered, "Ted checked at the inn. There are plenty of rooms."

Minta leaned back, resting momentarily against Brad. His meaning was unmistakable. By mentioning rooms, he made it clear she was free to choose whether she shared with him or not. Such thoughtfulness and lack of pressure delighted her, making her feel truly liked and appreciated.

Brad drew away finally and turned his attention to a combination lock on the small door. Bending over he entered the small room first to click on a light before motioning to Minta.

"You're serious someone might try to steal Hugo," she said.

He nodded grimly. "I damn well better be." He pointed to the squatty machine. "Minta, meet Hugo. He's a combination two-man sub and working robot." As his hand patted several metal parts he explained, "His eyes are a small stereo camera capable of taking 15mm slides and simultaneously sending pictures back to a television on the ship.

"He's equipped with two arms with adjustable hands that can collect delicate marine samples. The scientists inside can spend much more time working at close range than they could while they were only able to dive."

Brad's tremendous skills became a reality to Minta as she listened to him. A gulf yawned between them, reminding her of how divergent their lives were. "What are Hugo's uses?"

"Many. Biologists will explore the depths of the ocean for new food sources. Oil companies can locate new oil fields and with adaptations, Hugo can pioneer a whole new field of missile and submarine guidance." He paused and frowned before adding, "It's in this last area that Hugo is exceptionally unique."

"And the plans are all in your head?"

"Basically," he said matter-of-factly. "Some of them are inside the computer in a code only I can decipher." For a moment Brad looked as if he was having some unpleasant thought, but the next minute he was restored to his usual good humor. "Hey, why are we talking like this when we could be kissing?"

She avoided his mouth, and he settled for scattering kisses over the top of her head. "Aren't you worried someone will kidnap you, Brad?"

He nibbled along the column of her throat, his breath tickling her skin. "They'd have to have my cooperation. Like I need from you right now."

Minta collapsed against him, laughing. "Stop, Brad. Hugo is getting embarrassed."

"Now who's crazy?" he said, eyeing her quizzically. Minta surrendered, melting against him, meeting his lips with an intense passion. They were soon oblivious to everything, engrossed only in each other.

CHAPTER EIGHT

CAYMAN BRAC WAS A DELIGHTFUL SURPRISE. Minta stood by the railing as they neared the small ribbon of land that met with sea in an arc of snowy-white sand.

Brad hurried her off the boat, leading the way up the beach to a path hidden by a ring of trees. "We can walk to the inn," he told her, taking her hand and pulling her against his side.

The inn was set on a shiny crescent of sandy beach. All around the small building rose the glossy domes of mango trees, while a wall covered with a blanket of magenta bougainvillea marked the front entrance. The inn was ice-cream pink and white, two stories high, with wide verandas on all sides.

"It's wonderful," Minta said delightedly.

Brad's eyes showed he was pleased. "I hoped you'd like it. It's a special place."

Minta laid out her American Express card when they reached the desk inside the lobby. Brad glanced at her with a quizzical expression before smiling to show that he understood. He waited as Minta requested a room and was handed her key and then asked for his own. They were given adjoining rooms.

"If you hurry you should be able to make it before the dining room closes for lunch," the woman behind the desk said. She started to direct them down the hall, stopping when Brad explained he'd been a guest there before.

"Hungry?" Brad asked as they walked down the hall, their bags slung over their shoulders.

"Diving always leaves me starving," Minta replied.

The dining room was moderately large, with round tables scattered in random groupings. The pastel linen tablecloths contrasted pleasantly with the unglazed terracotta floor tiles. Graceful urns filled with tropical flowers lined one wall of the room, and on another a wide expanse of the sea could be viewed through floor-to-ceiling glass.

Only a few of the inn's guests remained in the dining room, and most of those were lingering over cups of coffee. Minta and Brad chose a table with an excellent view, and almost before they were seated a waiter appeared. After explaining that the service was buffet style for lunch, he took their drink orders.

When he left, Minta and Brad went up to the buffet, enticed by the tantalizing smells of rich foods. Minta piled her plate high with rice, spicy curry and condiments, while Brad chose a fish soup and an assortment of fresh, crisply cooked vegetables.

For the first few minutes they ate in silence. Minta savored the contrast between the smooth cream sauce and the crunchy peanuts, plump raisins and shredded coconut. When she tasted the mango chutney she sighed with pleasure. "Fantastic. Next time I come to the Caymans this place will be my first choice." She held out a fork full of the savory condiment. "Want some?"

"Definitely, if you're the one offering," Brad responded suggestively. His tongue licked the chutney off the fork in a sensuous movement.

Minta smiled gently as his hand grasped hers before she could withdraw it. "Thank you for sharing this place with me, Brad."

"It's my pleasure," he insisted.

The intensity of his gaze made her slightly nervous, and she knew he was aware of her response by the way his hand tightened reassuringly over hers. Slowly he removed the fork from her hand and leaned over to rub her palm against his cheek. A warm glow spread through her as she silently conceded the absolute rightness of being there, alone with Brad, isolated from everything familiar and completely vulnerable to his unique sensuality. Some instinct told her that she had found what was missing in her life. She made no effort to hide her excitement.

As the waiter moved toward their table, Brad released her hand. Minta tried to concentrate on finishing her lunch. When Brad suggested dessert she refused and asked for coffee instead.

Her shoulders burned under her thin cotton dress as his eyes narrowed on her. "I want to know everything about you, Minta," he said, studying her closely.

Her voice held a firm promise. "You will." She sensed that he wanted her to know him, too, in a way that few were ever allowed to. It startled her to realize how clearly they were beginning to understand one another.

Resolving to tell all, to withhold nothing about herself even if it changed everything between them, she cleared her throat lightly. "What shall I tell you first, Brad?"

"I told you I think backward. Right now, I'd like to hear you say that you want us to make love."

His directness took her by surprise. "I thought I already had," she said after a pause. "In a million ways."

The muscles in his shoulders relaxed as he smiled. "I didn't want to misunderstand."

"Misunderstand what?" she asked.

His voice was vibrant. "The way your breath quickens when we touch. The scent of crushed, wild violets I smell when we're kissing. The pressure of your arms around me when I'm holding you. If I'm reading more into these than you want me to, let me down gently, Minta."

Minta's voice was little more than a husky whisper. "I want you, Brad. That's all I'm sure of right now. Is it enough?"

His smile was slow and slightly crooked. "I've always been known as a risk taker, Minta. As long as you promise to keep leveling with me, I'm in this to the finish."

She glanced up through thick, dark lashes. "Me, too."

THEY MADE THEIR WAY silently along an outside balcony to where their rooms were located on the second floor. Brad stood behind Minta as she fumbled with the lock on her door. He hesitated when the door swung open.

"Brad?" she asked, and he followed her into the room.

The room was almost dark. Minta dropped her canvas bag and flipped on a lamp on a low round table. She turned toward Brad, and he drew her into his arms with a rush, almost as if he could wait no longer. "God, I want to love you," he said. "Since I saw you at the airport in Miami I've been thinking about having you in my arms. Warm, soft and so wonderfully beautiful, Minta."

Minta leaned back, her hair covering his hands. "Miami? I didn't think you saw me until you dropped those papers in Grand Cayman."

"I'd seen you all right." His fingers gathered her hair loosely and lifted it off her neck. He buried his face in the shiny mass and sighed. Slowly he located the zipper on the back of her dress. "One look and I was lost."

"Do you make up your mind about everything that quickly?" She was savoring the unhurried manner in which his fingers were caressing her spine.

"Never." He buried his face against her neck as

one hand found the smoothness of her back, unfastening her bra. Both of his hands united in encircling her waist before moving around to her breasts. From the sound of his breathing, she sensed that he was holding himself in check, waiting for her to decide on the pace she wanted.

For a moment she found herself hesitating. Loving Brad would not be simple. There would be nothing purely physical about it. She sensed she was committing herself irrevocably, and knowing so little about him, it was almost frightening. Caring about another human being deeply meant you shared their triumphs and their troubles, and today she'd sensed that Brad was in some sort of trouble.

She hadn't sought him out, she reminded herself. And yet they were together. She couldn't refuse the warmth and caring he was offering her. She had been alone and empty for too long.

As his mouth settled against hers with a seductive gentleness her misgivings were swept aside in a relentless tide. If she was making a mistake, she would have to deal with it later.

With slow deliberation she began unbuttoning his shirt, slipping her fingers inside to tangle in the hairs on his chest. She felt the sharp intake of his breath when her fingers moved down to stroke his taut stomach. He leaned back, slipping off her dress as she unfastened the button on the band of his trousers.

His fingers teased her nipples with a lightness that made her cry out with pleasure. He bent down, swallowing the soft sound with his mouth, kissing the corners of her lips and then moving invitingly into the recesses with delicate probes.

His movements were timed perfectly, allowing her to savor each new sensation with a lingering appreciation. Slowly she continued to help him undress until they were touching, clinging, caressing in a lover's tight embrace. The heat from his body spread through her, his hard masculinity straining against her, and wordlessly she led the way to the bed. They lay down together, facing each other.

He leaned on one elbow and smiled down at her, the amber flecks in his tawny eyes glittering in the soft light. She sensed the sensual enjoyment she was affording him as his eyes drifted across her face, down to her breasts and then gazed at the triangle of darkness at the apex of her slender thighs. "Perfection," he murmured. "Am I dreaming?"

She traced the hardness of his muscles, running her fingertips across his chest. "If you are, so am I."

His head bent over hers, and she pressed her fingers into the strong muscles of his back, drawing him closer with a swift motion. His lips searched hers in a more demanding way, and she met the pressure with an urgency of her own, guiding his hands back to her straining breasts.

His palms moved across the firm mounds, stopping at length to cup them with a breathtaking gentleness. When she felt she might burst he moved down and drew each breast in turn into the soft darkness of his mouth, catapulting her into a whirl-wind of passion.

She wanted to protest when his mouth ceased caressing her breasts and began roaming over her shoulders, sliding down to her rib cage and against her flat stomach, but the heat rose too swiftly inside her and she felt herself dissolving into a dreamy mist.

She tensed slightly as he sought out her warm moistness, but she relaxed as he stroked inside her. "Brad," she murmured, granting him fuller access and arching to meet the perfectly timed caresses that threatened to drive her into a frenzy.

Strong pulsations ran the length of her arms and legs, and she raised her head, meeting his mouth with a desperate hunger. As she laced her fingers through his hair their tongues met and he moved over her, her muscles closing tightly around him as their bodies merged.

Automatic responses took over as he found her burning center, and their thrusting moves drove them closer and closer to ecstasy. As her passion pushed her ever onward, she gave herself over to Brad, opening her mouth to moan her pleasure. Waves of pleasure she'd never known existed welled inside her, threatening to spill over in a rampaging flood.

Desperate for surcease, she heard him joining in her incoherent cries and she soared into mindless bliss, her breasts crushed against his chest, his passion rampant inside her. "Minta," he whispered hoarsely, and they roared to the crest of the wave together, teetering precariously on the edge and then sliding down, down, down in an undulating drift that left her weak and breathless. It was long moments before she felt herself drift safely back to the bottom of their own private world.

A strange mist covered Minta's eyes, but she didn't care. No man had ever understood her needs as Brad had, and she knew she'd never been this deeply affected before. Secure in the warmth of the protective arm Brad had cradled around her, she nestled her cheek against the curly hairs on his chest and heard his murmur of satisfaction. "Minta, that was...." He stopped and leaned on an elbow. "I can't describe it."

"I know." He brushed the hair back from her face. "It was for me, too."

"Utter bliss. Like free-floating when you're on a dive." He brushed a kiss across her cheek.

She wrapped an arm around him, drifting contentedly. His mouth nuzzled her ear. "What if I confessed I'm addicted to you? We've just made love and I'm already dreaming of the next time."

"Is that bad?" she said suggestively, moving her leg comfortably nearer his body.

"If that's not an invitation, please say so quickly," he warned her.

She slid her hands down his spine to caress his warm length. "Who's talking?"

Brad reached to snap out the light and then gathered her into his arms, murmuring private words of caring and desire until she forgot everything but the man, the time, the place.

The room had darkened even more when Minta pushed back the stray lock of hair flopping over his forehead. "Why is the hair on your head so dark and...." She ran her palms lightly over the silky curls on his chest, finishing, "Red everywhere else."

He chuckled. "I was a redheaded lad."

She attempted to imitate a Scottish brogue. "You're a strange combination, Brad McMillan."

"Neither fish nor fowl, my love. From your lofty pinnacle as a pure native American, you are sneering at my lowly half-breed status?"

"You're perfect. Just the way you are," she murmured. "There's nothing about you I would change."

Minta was the first to get up. She leaned over to pick up her dress. "Do you realize all I have to wear to dinner tonight is this wrinkled mess?"

"You look wonderful to me the way you are now."

"You're a big help," she grumbled. "I hadn't quite pictured this lovely inn when you suggested we spend the night. Somehow, I'd pictured roughing it on the beach. Why don't I rinse this out and hang it up to dry? We can put on our swimsuits and walk on the beach while it's drying."

He folded his arms behind his head, watching her intently. "Great idea."

She stepped into the legs of her maillot, aware of the way his eyes sparkled with amusement as she struggled to pull the damp fabric over her hips. "Aren't you going to get dressed?"

"When the show's over."

She picked up his trousers and flung them toward him. They landed over his face, blocking his vision. "It's over."

"Not for lack of interest," he said with a chuckle as he swung his feet off the bed.

A short time later they were strolling along the beach, barefoot, holding hands. Far out on the horizon, slender figures could be glimpsed, casting fishing nets off small vessels.

"How do the natives of Cayman Brac make a living?" Minta asked.

"Mostly from tourism, I think. It was once a great turtling island."

"I've heard about that. Are there any turtles left?"

"It's a shame how few. The natives did no harm by the few they consumed in their world-famous bowls of soup. But the tourists grew to love the delicacy. Soon they were demanding turtles be exported. It's one of the many disgraceful wastes of natural wildlife."

"I'd like to visit the turtle farms on Grand Cayman."

Brad's hand tightened. "Together," he said, making it sound like a promise.

They passed several tanned, indolent sunbathers sprinkled along the sand and continued walking until they located a secluded inlet, sheltered by several large rocks. Brad gestured toward a flat ledge. "Let's talk, Minta."

She sank onto a rock, leaning back and stretching out her long legs in front of her. "If I'd known about this island, I'm sure I would have made my reservations to stay here."

Brad shook his head. "Impossible. Then we might never have met."

He glanced out to the sea, much more serious than she. "I thought we'd agreed to quit fighting it. Why aren't you involved with anyone, Minta? You have so much loving to share. I find it hard to believe you aren't married or committed elsewhere."

She kept her eyes down, fingering a small cone-shaped shell, wishing Brad would save this discussion for later. For now, she was too happy, too carefree, too eager to revel in the aftermath of their newfound intimacy. "I haven't found anyone I wanted," she said at length.

Brad gave a loud laugh. "God, you're honest. What are you looking for? The perfect man?"

She blew the sand off the shell carefully. "Maybe. How about you?"

"I've never found anyone who would put up with my craziness."

"Isn't that something you've chosen to be?"

"Maybe. Maybe not."

"People can change."

He lifted his shoulders slightly. "I honestly don't think I can. I might pretend to be a young, upwardly mobile man, making all the right moves. But eventually I'd revert to form and where would that leave a relationship?''

She smiled disbelievingly. "Are you really that impossible?''

"I've been known to be terribly forgetful. I get shut away in my own world. I told you I'm a concentrator. The extension of that is I shut out the rest of the world when I'm caught up in one of my projects. I doubt I'm ever going to change into any woman's ideal.''

The serious tone of their conversation bothered Minta. It filled her with a jumble of questions that she knew had no easy answers. Wasn't she pretending to be something she wasn't? Sensing Brad wanted to discuss what was happening between them, she knew she should join in. But she wasn't ready. Not now. Some instinct told her not to say anything she might regret later.

She jumped up. "Race you out to where it's deep enough to swim, Brad!''

"You're on," he shouted, jumping up and running across the beach before she realized his intentions.

She followed, sputtering with outrage. "That's no fair.''

He reached the edge of the water and turned to wait for her, white teeth gleaming against his brown skin. "What did you expect? A handicap for being a woman?''

"You...." Minta leaned over and splashed water on him. He grabbed her, and they began tusseling in the shallow water until both landed on the soft sand, laughing together.

Brad sought her lips and kissed her with a thoroughness that made her legs and arms cease their movements. "I've always wanted to ravish a mermaid," he told her when he leaned his head back.

She brushed back the wet strands of her hair. "Mermaids are usually blondes, McMillan."

"Not Indian mermaids. They have long black hair and eyes with violet centers."

His words triggered something. "Tell me, Brad," she said. "Who did you buy those violets for the other night?"

He groaned. "Don't ask."

She gave him a kiss on his cheek. "I already have."

"You."

"Ha, that's a bunch of nonsense. Remember, I'm the one you were trying so desperately to get away from. Even offering bribes to realtors to see if they would move me."

"I swear it's true. The velvety texture of those violets reminded me of your eyes, so before I could stop myself I was paying for them."

It was her turn to laugh delightedly. "Did you intend to leave them on my doorstep and run like a bashful lad?"

"I don't know. I was acting like a love-struck fool. All part of the fantasy I started building up at the airport about you, I guess."

She sat up, splashing water against her skin to remove the damp sand. "That sounds fascinating. Describe this fantasy for me, Brad."

"In public?" He stood, pulling her up beside him. "You've got to be kidding, Ms Cordero. What kind of a guy do you take me for?"

"Silly. This beach is absolutely deserted."

He swiveled her head around with a light touch, pointing out a flock of blue herons fishing in the shallow water nearby. "Those are really journalists in an elaborate disguise. They work for an international gossip sheet," he said in a whisper.

"What makes you think you're famous enough to interest them?"

"Didn't you see my picture in the paper?" he pointed out with indisputable logic.

With an exasperated laugh, Minta tugged on his hand and they started wading into the sea. As the water became deeper, they paused several times to catch their breath. Within moments they were both swimming around in lazy circles, gliding close to each other and then retreating like the fish they'd seen below the surface during their dive.

Minta's thoughts were circling just as aimlessly, skirting on the edges of what was bothering her and then veering away. Each moment she spent with Brad she knew she was sinking deeper and deeper into turbulent waters.

There was no way she was going to be able to walk away from him with only a fond farewell. Somehow, she was certain she would always remember these rapturous moments. Moments when they'd reached out and made a mystical connection that went far beyond even the excitement of their bodies touching.

With an impatient shrug she quickened her pace, striking out away from Brad, reminding herself that it would be foolish to deny herself pleasure now because of the possibility of pain in the future. Today was all she and Brad had. She intended to enjoy it fully. Tomorrow would have to take care of itself.

As THE LAST OF THE SUNSET'S brilliant purples washed away in the sea's billows, Minta and Brad sat in the resort's open-air bar sipping on glasses of the inn's specialty, rum punch. It was a delicious concoction of lime juice and rum, flavored with sugar and nutmeg. Brad leaned over. "Having fun?"

Minta felt the same surge of excitement she had when she'd first met Brad. She wondered what it was about him that made him so totally different from the men she dated in D.C. "Surely you don't need to ask," she answered, letting her husky voice convey the depths of emotion she felt.

As his fingers began twining through her hair, she heard someone calling his name. "McMillan."

They both turned as Ted strode toward them. "Mind if I join you for a drink?" He directed his question to both of them.

"Please do," Minta replied, patting the chair beside her. Remembering that Ted had mentioned fishing that afternoon she asked, "How was your catch?"

He sat down, making a circle with his thumb and finger. "A big fat zero but Lydia had a great afternoon." His eyes softened at the mention of his wife, removing some of the tension from his face. "She caught a blue marlin you wouldn't believe."

"Did you position Hugo?" Brad asked.

"Set him down right where you said. I told him he better work right or I'd dent his metal cage." Ted's voice was smooth and friendly but Minta's skin prickled. She'd heard something else she couldn't put her finger on. Fear? Anxiety?

"Did you leave him all alone?" Minta asked. "I thought someone was supposed to be in him."

"Not this time," Brad explained, taking a sip of his drink. "Actually, Ted does have some of his crew keeping watch over Hugo. Just to be on the safe side."

"Don't worry, Brad. Everything's fine," Ted assured him quickly, and this time Minta was sure of her instinct. Something was bothering Ted. Something he was trying hard to hide, even from Brad.

Ted was continuing, "Lydia wants to be sure to see you two before you leave the Caymans."

"I'd love that," Minta accepted at once. "Do you have any children?"

She had asked the question out of pure routine friendliness. But there was a long pause that made her wish she'd kept her mouth shut. "No, but we'd like to," Ted said finally.

"I've offered them a baby robot," Brad put in.

Minta and Ted laughed together. "Brad's strange, Ted," Minta said.

"You're telling me? Has he mentioned the time he...."

Brad leaned forward. "Whoa, Ted. Leave Minta a few illusions about me."

As the desultory conversation floated back and forth, twilight came. Several men leaned on the teakwood bar connecting the outside lounge with the inside, and Minta was aware of their eyes drifting in her direction. An old waiter puttered around several tables, refilling the ice surrounding bowls of fruit and boiled shrimp. In the air a warm scent of rum and fresh fruit and tropical flowers mingled with the faint aroma of freshly brewed coffee. Strains of calypso music made the whole scene strangely unreal to Minta.

When Brad and Ted started reminiscing about a trip they'd gone on, Minta's thoughts returned to her talk with Brad on Ted's boat that morning. His deep concern bothered her, making her want to help him. Maybe if he told her more about those Europeans who were interested in Hugo, she'd tell him about the FBI agents who fanned the country, trying to find both foreign and domestic thieves who raided the technology of American companies. She reached over absentmindedly and stroked Brad's arm, receiving a long, lingering look in return.

Ted rose as if on cue, saying, "I'm running by the ship on the way home to check Hugo's signals."

"Keep me posted," Brad said.

Ted hesitated as if he wanted to say more and then shrugged his shoulders. "Don't worry, Brad. I'll take care of things."

After he'd left, Brad was silent for a while. Minta broke into his reverie. "Your friend seems a little worried about something," she commented.

"Ted?" Brad's face didn't quite convince her he was surprised. His eyes were thoughtful as he took a long swallow of his drink.

"You were in Vietnam together, you said?" Minta was probing and she knew it.

"Yes," Brad's voice was clipped, but she persisted.

"In the same unit?"

"Yes."

"It's nice that you've kept up your friendship. Do you keep in touch with the other members of your unit?"

She wasn't prepared for Brad's reaction. His hand clenched on the glass he held, almost breaking it as his face contorted with pain. "There are only a few of us left," he said shortly.

"Oh, I'm sorry." Minta wanted to erase the pain on his face, but whatever she could think of to say seemed inadequate. "Want to talk about it?" she asked lightly.

"No. No, I don't think so." Brad had effectively shut her out, and Minta looked at him thoughtfully. At least he was being honest. She could respect that.

CHAPTER NINE

DINNER WAS SURPRISINGLY LIGHTHEARTED. Brad seemed to have recovered from whatever had been bothering him. The owners of the inn circulated among the tables, talking to their guests between musical acts performed on a small stage in the center of the room. Minta and Brad drank a bottle of dry white wine to complement the whole fish that had been sautéed in butter and covered with slivers of toasted almond. Dessert was a delicate kiwi lime pie covered with mounds of whipped cream.

When they finished, they ordered cups of espresso. "Tell me about yourself as a child, Minta," Brad said. "Was your hair always this long?"

"If you weren't a native American, I'd give you my stock answer to that question."

"Which is?"

"What would you expect out of Pocahontas?"

He shook his head with a grin. "And I suppose you wore beaded deerskin clothes and carried bows and arrows to protect you from the pale skins?"

"Don't steal my line," she protested with a laugh. "Did your mother grow up on a reservation, Brad?"

"No. I think our grandmother did. My mother's parents didn't care much for my dad or at least, they didn't want my mother to marry him because of her age. After he died, my mother couldn't seem to get over being angry with them. We seldom went to see them, so I didn't spend much time with any of my Indian relatives."

"And yet you're proud of your heritage, I think. Tell me a little about those Coastal Indians, as you call them. Don't you know your tribe?"

"The Coastal Indians weren't tribal oriented. We're mainly distinguishable by our language. My mother's relatives spoke Bella Coola. It's derived from the Kwakiutl language, but all the Coastal Indians are closely related."

Minta took a sip of her coffee. "I saw a Bella Coola mask once in the museum in D.C. Why didn't your people carve those massive totem poles like the ones farther up the Pacific coast?"

"The masks and totems are related, both memorials to the dead. Maybe my ancestors were like me. They didn't want to be caught up in a lifetime artistic endeavor. They were too busy living. But enough about me. Tell me about the tribe you come from, the Zunis. I don't know much about them."

"They're a peaceful people. Everything centers around the home and family. A Zuni child is always loved. In my case, I was the youngest child, so I was definitely spoiled."

"If you're typical, I can understand why. Do you miss your family?"

"Terribly. I usually spend most of my vacation with them." Her fingers tightened around the handle of the cup as she remembered that she had intended to do just that this year. But that was before Al Slessor's tirade. He had stressed she needed time alone to think. Her mouth curved in a gentle smile. She doubted if being with Brad was exactly what Al had in mind.

Brad traced her lips with a fingertip. "I love that secret smile of yours but I feel left out."

"Sorry, I was just thinking about my family. They're quite special."

"They'd have to be to have you for a daughter."

"Please, no more flattery. I'll get such an inflated opinion of myself you won't be able to stay in the same room with me."

His eyes shone. "Am I being invited?"

As the waiter brought fresh cups of espresso, Minta shivered involuntarily. "Cold?" Brad asked. "There's a breeze coming from the open door. If you'd like to move. . . ."

"No, I'm fine." She didn't feel cold. She felt apprehensive. She was having a strange sensation that she had experienced several times in the past; the certainty that someone was watching her. She took a sip of espresso and tried to forget her uneasiness.

She shifted her attention back to Brad as he was asking, "Did you leave New Mexico because there weren't any opportunities for the young people of your tribe?"

She shook her head. "Unemployment is high but

all of my sisters stayed. They and their husbands are doing great in traditional jobs. One's a nurse, another works in a hotel. It's possible to stay in New Mexico if you want.''

''But it wasn't for you?''

The cold shiver ran through her again, and this time the hair on the back of her neck quivered. She was being watched! She knew it! Her intuition never failed her. She forced a smile. ''I am feeling that draft you mentioned. I think I'll slide over to your other side.''

Brad moved quickly, pulling out her chair and shifting her coffee over to the place on his right. ''Better?''

She nodded, scanning the guests she'd been unable to see before as covertly as she could. She spotted him almost immediately: a slender silver-haired man with a youthful face, dressed in a dark, impeccably tailored suit. He was staring at her openly, his grayish eyes making a careful study as if he was memorizing each detail for later reference.

Minta shifted so she was partially hidden by Brad, gradually becoming aware that he was speaking again. ''Does your mother work?'' Brad asked.

''Since I was in high school. She owns a gift shop in Santa Fe. Handmade crafts are her speciality.'' On one hand, Minta was answering his questions, while on another she tried to determine why the man was staring at her. His boldness made her rule out anything sinister. But it seemed highly unlikely that he thought she would be interested in him when she was seated beside the most attractive man in the room.

"Minta, is there something about your family that is bothering you?" Brad asked softly.

She tilted her head back in surprise. "No. Why do you ask?"

"You're taking longer and longer to answer my questions," he said, his expression thoughtful.

She smiled apologetically. "Maybe I am a little homesick. As I said, we Zunis tend to be clannish. I think I'll call my mom when I get back to Grand Cay."

"I envy you. You never know how much you love someone until they're gone."

Minta forgot her worries momentarily and laid the palm of one hand on Brad's cheek. "I can't imagine how it must feel to lose both parents, Brad."

He grasped her hand. "We won't be lonely tonight, Minta. We have each other." His promise whispered against the soft skin of her palm.

She relaxed against him, leaning her head on his shoulder so she was completely out of sight of the silver-haired stranger. She sensed a meshing of Brad's needs with her needs, fusing them into one. Tonight was theirs. No one, especially not a total stranger, was going to intrude.

"Mr. McMillan. Telephone. In the lobby." Their waiter spoke softly, but Minta jumped as if he'd shouted.

Brad stroked her hair, gentling her with the tenderness one would use on a spooked horse. "It must be Ted. I'll be right back. Don't disappear on me, okay?" He was gone before she had a chance to ask him why he seemed to think it was necessary to say that to her.

She straightened up and took another drink of her coffee before lifting her head to view the curious man head on. He was still staring, but this time there was a difference. He was nodding to her, with a smirk on his face that infuriated her.

Minta jumped to her feet and strode over to the table where he sat alone. "Do you think you know me?" she demanded.

His eyes blinked rapidly several times, but aside from that he handled his shock well. Standing, he pulled out a chair. "Please sit down. I knew you'd come over the first opportunity you had."

His slickness unnerved her, but she refused to let him see it. "Cut out the nonsense. I don't appreciate the way you've been making a fool out of yourself," she said, her words cool and with a sharp edge.

"On the contrary. It is you that is making a fool out of yourself, *mademoiselle*. Please sit down before the others think you are trying to pick me up."

His French accent was faked, she decided instantly, but there were no clues to his nationality. About forty-five, she guessed. Well educated, expensively dressed with a diamond ring on the small finger of his right hand that glistened under the candlelight. She sat down smoothly. "Perhaps we do know one another, *monsieur*. Don't tell me. I want to guess. Was it Bermuda? At the festival last year? Perhaps you were one of the houseguests of Viscountess Ratteray? You remind me of the one whose yacht came in second.''

He was amused. ''No....''

Minta leaned forward, tapping him on the shoulder. ''Of course, I remember now. Scottsdale, Arizona. The Arabian horse show. What class will you be entering this year?''

He took out a package of cigarettes and without asking put two into his mouth. After lighting them, he leaned over and pushed one into her mouth with a seductive smile. ''Try Kitzbühel. Easter. Last year. We spent a memorable night together. I've never known a woman with your appetites before. But your name? It's slipped my mind. Perhaps you would be so kind as to refresh me.''

She allowed him a moment of triumph, hating the dissipated smile on his face so much she wanted to hit him. But she tried to refrain, deciding instead to attack more subtly. She timed it perfectly. The beginning of an erotic smile on her lips. The crossing of her slender legs as a large expanse of thigh was exposed to his avaricious eyes.

Leaning over so the curved neckline of her dress gaped, revealing the curve of her full breasts, she slid the cigarette out of her mouth and thrust it back between his lips.

''Thank you, but I don't smoke,'' she said softly, her eyes challenging him to a duel that promised to be bitter and cold. "I don't like phonies, mister. The closest you've ever been to any of those places is on a postcard. Take this as a warning to stay away from me. If I have any more trouble from you, you're going to think you've tangled with a wildcat."

She started to leave but he was up before her, blocking her way, speaking softly but urgently. "I would suggest you leave this island and Grand Cay as well. The dented fender on the red car? The twisted bicycle?" He paused dramatically and glanced at the table where she had been sitting with Brad. "They are nothing compared to what happens next if you don't leave."

Minta started after the man as he crossed the dining room. A waiter stopped him at the door and she paused, dropping behind a tall tropical plant. "What is your room number so I can put your dinner on your bill?" the waiter asked.

"I'm not a guest at the inn." The silver-haired man thrust several bills in his hand. "I'm in a hurry."

"But this is too much," protested the young waiter. "Let me total your bill for you."

"Keep it." The stranger pushed past him.

Minta followed but was stopped by the waiter who was smiling faintly. "Do you know him?" he asked her.

"No, but I'd like to. . . ." She paused, aware the young man was grinning at her knowingly. "I need to know his name," she added firmly.

The waiter held up the bills. "Even if I knew, this would seal my lips. He gave me the biggest tip I ever got."

"Just be sure it's not counterfeit," snapped Minta, stalking through the door. Just as she suspected the lobby was empty when she reached it.

With several doors to choose from she hesitated and then started forward, almost bumping into Brad before she saw him. He steadied her with his hands. "What's wrong, Minta?"

She debated telling him what had happened but decided it would only complicate matters. Not only that, she knew she would have to tell him about her work with the FBI and she wanted to do that at the right time. Until she figured out what that little scene had been all about, she was going to keep her mouth shut and her eyes open.

During the years she had been working as an agent, she had learned one thing. Threats were meaningless nine times out of ten. When someone intended to have an enemy harmed, they didn't go out of their way to announce it. No, this man was only trying to frighten her. The question was, why?

Who was the man? And what connection did he have with the black car that had hit her? Those were questions that could not be solved tonight, would perhaps never be fully solved. She would keep alert until she came to some conclusion. There was no sense bringing Brad in on it if the meaning was still unclear in her own trained mind.

"I wondered what was keeping you so long, Brad."

"Ted. He insisted I explain some of the messages Hugo is sending back, so I couldn't get him off the phone. Finished your coffee?"

She nodded. "Let's go to the upstairs terrace for a few minutes, Brad."

Later, as they sat holding crystal glasses of Cointreau, Minta watched the play of moonlight on the cresting waves of the Caribbean. All around the inn rose the glossy dark domes of mango trees, and a lighted flower garden in a courtyard below blazed with color. They were in a secluded alcove, but the tinkle of glasses and the soft conversation of other guests emphasized the comfortable silence that enveloped them.

The last traces of uneasiness over her encounter with the man faded away, dulled no doubt by the drinks she'd had throughout the evening. She felt herself becoming drowsy from the combination of diving, fine food and wine, and she leaned back into the soft cushions of her chair. Brad smiled over at her. "Still enjoying yourself?"

"Loving it. You?" Her supple body flowed into the contours of the chair.

"Mmm," he agreed softly. "Go to sleep. I promise to carry you to my room, if you like."

"Sounds delightful." Her eyes closed as she felt him lift the glass from her limp fingers.

When she awoke he was holding her in his arms, attempting to retrieve the key in his pocket as he stood before his door. "I'm sorry," she murmured against his neck. "I didn't mean for you to really carry me."

Ignoring his protests, she slipped to the floor, pushing down her skirt. "How many other guests did you meet on your way?"

"Several. They congratulated me for having such a lovely bride."

"Sorry." Fully awake now, she preceded him into the dimly lit room, her eyes automatically searching every nook and crevice before she advanced to the center. "I don't usually sleep so soundly."

Brad was behind her, his body warm against her back. "You're light as a feather and shaped like you were meant to rest in my arms."

Her hip brushed against his thighs as she turned toward him, and he pulled her against him, his lips finding hers and his tongue exploring the soft interior of her mouth. One hand lifted Minta's hair from beneath, twisting it around and around.

Brad knew he was helpless where she was concerned. He hungered for her so that he ached. He couldn't believe the way she was affecting him. Only when he was holding her, caressing her, making love to her could he gain temporary respite from the overpowering desire the mere thought of her generated in him.

Anger and jealousy were fueling his desperation now, and he despised himself for it. He was still shaken over the way she had crossed to the gray-haired man's table the moment she thought he was gone. He had returned to the doorway of the dining room to ask what line his call was on and he had seen her, smiling at the man, leaning forward. His mouth sought hers desperately as he struggled to forget.

He wished now he hadn't been so noble, turning and leaving instead of watching to see what happened. He wondered what he would have learned if he'd stayed and watched the two of them together. Did Minta know the man? For the first time a faint seed of doubt planted itself in his mind. Perhaps Minta was not the innocent tourist she appeared to be. God forbid, perhaps she was connected with The Trio.

He rejected the idea immediately. It didn't make sense. Nothing about Minta suggested she could have any possible association with the people who were making his life miserable. The man might have been someone from the plane, even. A casual acquaintance. Still, why hadn't she mentioned him?

As Minta pressed herself against him, he expelled his breath sharply. Tonight she was his! Tonight he would savor the softness of her lips, the swiftness of her response when he stroked the silky skin between her thighs. The memories of the love they'd shared that afternoon made his desire rage out of control.

With impatient fingers he unzipped her dress and slipped it down, nuzzling his lips against her nipples as he hooked his fingers inside the elastic on her bikini briefs. She moaned softly and began unbuttoning his shirt.

His hands worked across her flat stomach, eliciting sighs of pleasure as they moved to the roundness of her hips, kneading the smoothly textured skin with soft, measured strokes. When he slipped down to his knees and began kissing the soft skin of her abdomen, she trembled and stroked his hair.

"Oh, Brad," she protested as his intentions became plain. But he continued his gently relentless assault, feeling the ripple of pleasure that shook her as she moved to give him fuller access.

He slid her dainty briefs down her hips, burying his face against her, kissing the downy softness over and over. His tongue sought out the core of her pleasure until she relaxed against him, her body shaking with tremors of passion and ecstasy.

They moved to the bed together, arms intertwined, sharing a deep kiss that exchanged a hundred different emotions, asked a thousand questions and gave away their undeniable attraction.

When he'd left both of her breasts pleasured and swollen with passion, his lips moved to her mouth. His tongue played a game with hers as her hands stroked the length of his body. Slowly Minta became the giver, rising slightly, melting over him, drawing him inside her soft inner moistness with an exquisitely smooth movement that threatened to drive him out of his mind.

She made love to him slowly, her head thrown back, her hair fluttering in the ocean breezes wafting through the open window. He hung on as long as he could, his hands clenched into tight fists, determined to prolong the sweet pleasure her undulating hips were providing.

As his last restraint snapped, she leaned over, gazing deeply into his eyes. He felt as if she were a pagan goddess, offering herself to him in an ancient ceremony that would fuse their souls forever. Without reservation he accepted her sacrifice, giving his all in return as the urgency inside him exploded. He grasped her hips as he felt her smooth contractions beginning. With arms wrapped tightly around each other, they rode out the storm together.

THE SOFT TROPICAL AIR caressed Minta as she crossed to the hotel dining room the next morning. She had left Brad sleeping, surprised that the sounds of her shower had not made him move a muscle.

Awakening out of a troubling dream with a heightened sense of danger, she remembered sitting bolt upright in bed, gazing around as if she expected to see danger lurking in every corner.

When she saw Brad's sprawling body beside her, a rush of tenderness had filled her and she had leaned over, kissing him lightly on the cheek. Her anxiety had vanished as swiftly as it had come.

Dressed once again in the short cotton dress with her hair braided and coiled at the nape of her neck, her manner was once more brisk. First on her agenda for the day was a good breakfast. Then she wanted to slip away for some time alone. A time to review what was happening to her on this vacation.

Vacation? She smiled ruefully. A fender bumper? Losing control of a bike? A man threatening her if she didn't leave the island? She'd been on many cases that didn't involve as many puzzles as had this vacation.

She chose the buffet service on the terrace and heaped her plate with sliced melon, oranges and fresh mangoes circled with sugared strawberries. Two sweet rolls and several curls of butter fit on the edge of the plate and she settled down at one of the tables to enjoy the feast.

When she finished and had folded the snowy linen napkin, she was ready to tackle anything that lay ahead. First she went down to the desk and located a woman that Brad had pointed out as one of the owners of the inn the day before.

The woman was in her fifties, with reddish short hair. "Do you have many diners who aren't guests at the inn in the evenings?" Minta asked her.

"Very few. The locals come occasionally, but I don't remember seeing any last night. Why?"

"There was a man dining here. Very distinguished looking. Wearing a dark suit."

"Thick gray hair?"

Minta nodded. "Sort of silvery. Do you know him or where I can reach him?"

"No. He paid cash."

"I know. I met him. . . ." Minta bit her lip, hoping this woman didn't know Ted or Brad well. From the way she was staring at Minta, it was certain she'd mention it if she did.

"I'm sorry, but it was the only time he'd been here. He made quite a splash by giving his waiter a huge tip. Would you care to leave your name with me? If he returns I'll mention you to him."

"Thanks, but no." Minta changed the trend of the conversation, complimenting the woman on the lavish amenities of the inn. They parted finally and Minta went outside, staring up at Brad's room. The door was still closed.

The walk to the beach was deserted, but once she reached there she saw several others enjoying the early-morning sunshine. She settled down on a rock and stared out at the tranquil blue waters, trying to bring order to her chaotic thoughts. She tried to make a mental list. Brad. First priority was thinking about Brad. But she decided to leave the pleasant part until last. The man who'd warned her last night was the most bothersome. She couldn't dismiss him as lightly as she'd first thought.

Two possibilities for his behavior came to mind. One was that she had been followed to Grand Cayman. The last two cases she'd worked on had been particularly violent. There was no doubt in her mind that the underworld had a stake in frightening her to the point of making her transfer to another department.

On the other hand, what had happened to her might be completely unrelated to her work. It was possible the driver of the car that had hit her was involved in smuggling or any of a myriad of illegal activities that were so difficult to control on a small island where every square inch of the coast offered constant opportunities. If he was involved in something illegal, he may have been afraid she could identify him. So he had sent someone to deliver her a warning.

Criminals were seldom the brave, fearless individuals portrayed in movies. Rather, they panicked easily, constantly paranoid over everyone who looked at them. If this were the case and the man indeed was a criminal, she needed only to ignore the warning. When she returned to Grand Cayman she'd contact Bobby Hall and see if he had learned anything.

This second scenario seemed more likely than the first, she decided, leaning her back against a smooth rock. At least, it was more in agreement with her own wishes. She didn't want to leave the island now. Not as long as Brad could spend time with her.

Reluctantly she turned her attention to her dilemma concerning Brad. Admittedly, it was a delightful dilemma. The memories of their lovemaking could still make her cheeks burn and her skin tingle with excitement. But that was part of the problem and definitely not the answer. Each moment she spent with him she was digging herself into a hole where there was no sane or safe exit.

Enjoying him on a vacation was one thing, but when it ended? Then what? This was exactly the sort of situation she had determined to avoid in her life from now on. She was tired of the singles life, tired of meaningless associations that led nowhere, leaving a person empty and cold afterward.

It had been hard to stay quiet the afternoon before when Brad had tried to tell her that his lifestyle was a difficult one for anyone else to accept.

At least it was in the realm of most people's imagination. But her job? How many young, female field agents were there? A precious few and since their identities were concealed, the public never gave them a thought.

She had known two women agents who had married. Both had now given up their fieldwork. One had left the FBI altogether at her husband's insistence. The other worked in a branch office near the place where her husband's job had taken them.

Minta knew she wasn't ready to give up her career. She had dated men who gave lip service to a woman's right to have a firm commitment to such an unusual career, but she felt that's all it ever amounted to. She suspected that if she married, any man would quietly sabotage her right to come and go as she needed to. Even male agents complained over their wives' lack of understanding and failure to adjust.

Somehow she had seen herself going on in fieldwork for a long time, eventually moving into administration when she was no longer so young or eager to taste the action herself. Before she was eligible for administration she would need more schooling and that was a big step for her at this time.

With a distressed sigh she leaned over and dug out a shell embedded in the sand. It was early in her career to be thinking of marriage and commitment, but that was how her mind worked when it came to Brad. But the real heart of the matter was that she wasn't ready to tell him about her work yet. She wanted to be with him, to let their relationship develop, without that barrier in their way.

Twenty-four more hours? Was that asking too much? She laughed aloud. Happy-go-lucky Minta, as her mother always called her. Sitting there worrying when she ought to be enjoying every minute. Maybe Al was right. She really did need a vacation if she'd started taking herself this seriously.

As she stood she made a firm decision. She would wait until Jill called and she had the all clear on Brad. That would be as good a time as any to be completely honest with him.

The other conclusion she came to as she hurried back toward the inn was that she needed to mention the silver-haired man to Brad. If she'd been thinking clearer the evening before, she would have told him then. Maybe he would have some clues to the man's identity.

CHAPTER TEN

BRAD OPENED THE DOOR to his room as soon as she knocked on it. Nude except for the towel wrapped around his waist, he smiled broadly when she walked in. "I wondered if I'd imagined you, Minta."

There was a certain shyness in his voice this morning that charmed Minta, and she put her arms around him. "I'm real, Brad. How about you?"

"I don't remember ever being more alive," he answered emotionally, his arms tightening around her. His warmth surrounded her, filling her world, making her concerns vanish as surely as the graceful sailboats she'd seen disappearing over the edge of the world.

She caught a whiff of after-shave as she buried her lips against the beating pulse point in the hollow of his neck. She wondered how she'd ever imagined for one moment that she had the strength to turn her back on this man.

Tilting her head to get a better look at him, she smiled. He began kissing her, a warm rain upon her cheeks, her brows, her slender curving throat. One hand played with the braided coil at the back of her neck, and she felt it falling free, cascading down her back, as his fingers gently sifted through the thick strands.

She was on fire, savoring this ever-new, intense pleasure of the way her body instantly surrendered to the overwhelming pull between them. He was becoming more important to her than she had anticipated.

She needed him, needed his love as she never had needed anything before, and she refused to listen to any of the voices inside her head crying out to beware of becoming too dependent on his kisses, his ministering hands, his lean strength.

"Brad," she murmured, and the sound of her soft voice seemed to excite him even more as he slipped off her dress. She tried to tell him how she was going up in flames, but the velvet explosions his hands were triggering made the words flutter in her throat and softly die there.

She pulled him down on her as they slid to the bed. Knowing that she had only twenty-four hours with Brad made her respond to him with the urgency of a life-or-death situation.

He joined her on the fiery wheel of pleasure, his hands stroking, his mouth pleasuring, his body molding with hers in a cataclysm of roaring sound and brilliant light.

They lay wrapped in the sheets afterward, their bodies trembling for long minutes. Leaning up on one elbow, Brad smiled down at her, brushing back her hair. "I didn't ask if I could unbraid it," he apologized softly.

She was still dazed by the intensity of their need for each other. "I don't mind."

He turned her face, so she was looking at him fully. His voice was serious. "I know there's something bothering you, Minta. I wish you'd tell me."

She traced the sensual curve of his full lips with her fingertips. "I would like to talk to you about something, but after you've had some breakfast."

He insisted he wasn't hungry but she was just as adamant. She won out, and after they showered and dressed they walked toward the terrace. "I hope you're not too late for the buffet," Minta said.

"If it's gone, I'll get a cup of coffee. That should hold me until lunch. What time did you get up, early bird?"

"Before seven."

"All that energy puts me to shame."

She stopped, sniffing the heavy fragrance of gardenias mingled with other scents she couldn't identify. "It's heavenly here, Brad."

"Our private paradise. I've thought about building a home here." He glanced at her as if he wanted to say more and then started walking again.

She bridged the awkward moment. "Can foreigners own land without restrictions?"

"No problem. The Cays are friendly folks."

They reached the stairs leading to the terrace and walked up them side by side. The buffet table was still laden with a fresh assortment of delicacies. After Brad had selected what he wanted, they both poured cups of coffee and settled at a table where they could view miles of snowy-white beach sliding away into the cerulean-blue waters. A gentle breeze cooled their cheeks.

"It's always the right temperature here," Brad said.

"Trade winds. What exactly are they?"

"A wind that almost constantly blows in one direction. These islands always have a steady sea breeze from the east. The windward side of the island is where you feel it most. If I build here, that's the side I'm interested in."

Minta tried to gauge his mood as she thought of a way to tell him about the warning she'd received. She knew he was going to be shocked no matter how she handled it.

Keeping her voice low, she said, "Did you happen to see a man with silvery gray hair in the dining room last night?"

His head shot up and he stared at her, his lips pressed together. For a moment she wondered if the man was an acquaintance of his. "The one who couldn't keep his eyes off you while we were eating?" he snapped.

She smiled. "I didn't know you noticed."

"How could I help it? I had an urge to go punch him."

He was looking at her as if he expected her to tell him something. Was it possible he'd seen what happened between the two of them? "I went over to his table while you answered the phone," she said evenly.

Brad didn't answer. She continued, "I wanted to confront him. He bothered me."

"I saw you."

Brad spoke so softly it took Minta a moment to understand. "When?"

"I had to talk to the waiter to find out what line Ted was on. Minta, do you know that man? Is he the one we were talking about the other day?"

She stared at him in astonishment before she understood Brad's distress. Reaching out, she placed her hand over his. "I never saw him before in my life."

"Then why in hell would you speak to him?"

"I resented his invasion of my privacy."

Brad stared at her. "You never cease to surprise me, Minta."

"That's because you insist on treating me as if I'm fragile."

"Don't you ever get yourself in trouble?"

"Certainly, but it's better than being a shrinking violet."

"What did he say?" Brad returned to the discussion so quickly it took Minta a moment to follow.

"I pretended I recognized him, hoping to find out who he was."

"And?" he prodded, his gaze intent.

She recounted quickly what had transpired between the man and herself, stopping just after the moment she had jabbed the cigarette between his lips. The expression on Brad's face changed from worry to amazement. "Where is he now?" he asked when she paused. "I'd like to get my hands on him."

"He wasn't a guest at this inn. I tried to find out his name from the owner this morning but she didn't know it."

"We'll describe him to Ted and see if he knows him. His looks are distinctive enough that it would be hard to forget him once you've seen him."

"I think he's gone now. I have more to tell you."

Brad leaned forward, a frown creasing his face. "What?"

"I started to walk away, but he blocked my path for a moment and gave me a warning." Quickly she repeated word for word what the man had told her, watching Brad closely to see his reaction.

His coppery skin reddened with anger, and when she finished he swore under his breath. "So you were right. The two accidents were connected." He consulted his thin gold watch. "If we hurry you can be on that plane to Grand Cay. I'll call the airport there and get you a reservation and then see if Richard Long can go by the cottage and pack your suitcase."

"Hold on," Minta interrupted. "Who said I was leaving? I hope this doesn't come as shock to you but women have brains. I'm capable of doing my own thinking. I'm not leaving the Caymans today or any other day until I'm good and ready."

Brad settled back against his chair and regarded her broodingly. "Aren't you afraid you're in danger?" For the first time since they had met, he seemed to be suspicious. Even his eyes were narrowed in speculation.

"Danger?" Minta decided to play it cool and innocent. "Just because some man decides to play cloak and dagger?"

"Those two accidents were hardly child's play, Minta." Brad's voice was cool and almost accusing.

"Actually I was wondering whether you could tell me anything more about the man," Minta said slowly, eyeing him steadily.

"Me?" Brad's eyebrows rose, and he remained perfectly still. If he was faking the surprise he was certainly cool about it, she decided. "I've told you I don't know the man."

"Well, you see, that's what's so strange about this. Neither do I. Now why would he be warning me to leave the islands?" In the moments after she finished speaking Minta could have cut the tension with a knife. Brad was quiet, too quiet. His expression had grown alarmingly distant, almost worried.

"What's your theory?" Brad said at length.

Minta nodded in approval. "Now we're talking. I think I've stumbled into a nest of smugglers. Why else would they take off from the scene of the accident, unless they're involved in something illegal? They're probably afraid I'll describe them to the police. The officer who is investigating, Bobby, has had a bulletin out on the car, but no one on the island has seen it."

"That's hard to understand on an island that small."

"They must have hidden it somewhere."

Brad nodded. "Or taken it off on a ship. Ted and I have watched a lot of strange actions around the private harbors. Not necessarily on the Caymans but in the whole Caribbean. These seas are impossible to patrol. Then you're not worried about the warning?"

"No. If you were going to get even with someone, would you make a point of telling them in advance?"

He grinned. "I see what you mean." The smile didn't quite reach his eyes. "Are you going to go on as if nothing has happened?"

"I'll be extra alert, and I'll report this to Bobby. Aside from that I refuse to let some wise guys playing cloak and dagger ruin my vacation."

He leaned back. "You amaze me, Minta. You're taking this in stride, as if it were nothing unusual. Most people would be fit to be tied. Why are you so calm?"

The tension between them mounted as Minta floundered for an answer. God, she supposed she must look awfully blasé about the whole thing. To her, this was kid stuff. She was so used to dealing with threats and conflicts that nothing surprised her, at least nothing this trivial. Still, was she being too calm? That could be a mistake. She might be overlooking something very important.

Something was very definitely wrong in this island paradise. The vibes were unpleasant, threatening. Or was her mind playing tricks on her? Perhaps she had imagined most of this or blown it out of proportion. Suddenly her mind was whirling with a thousand questions. With a sudden movement she stood. "Come on, McMillan, the day is going to waste."

When they left the terrace, Minta stopped by the gift shop in the main lobby. Brad watched her go in before he turned and crossed to the phones.

His thoughts were far away as he paused in front of the booth. Something was bothering him but he wasn't sure exactly what. Yes, he was sure. For a woman who'd been in an accident, been run down on a bicycle and threatened, she'd scarcely turned a hair.

Perhaps he'd been acting like a fool, living in a pretend paradise, acting as if he had the right to fall in love. Maybe he'd walked right into a trap. A trap baited by the most beautiful, fantastic woman he'd ever met.

Was she lying to him about the threat? Why in hell would anyone have threatened Minta? Was it because of him? Were they trying to get to him through Minta? Of course, that was it! They were counting on her repeating the threat to him. They were watching him. They were using every dirt trick in the book to get him to do what they wanted.

He would have to be very careful. For the rest of the time they were together there on Cayman Brac, he'd never let her out of his sight. And he'd talk her into leaving the Caymans entirely. That was his only hope.

INSIDE THE GIFT SHOP, Minta asked the clerk, "Do you carry any clothes?"

"A few." The young girl led her over to several racks. "The sizes are scattered, so you'll have to look through them. If you want to try anything on, there's a fitting room through that door."

Minta slid the garments down the racks, scanning each one carefully. They were her type of clothes. Bright. Sporty. Some with ethnic origin. Unlike women who worked in large companies, she was free to indulge herself in a rainbow of colors as long as she dressed in muted shades when she was actually involved on a case.

Her hand stilled when she reached a sheath with vivid purple, turquoise and blue diagonal stripes against a silky white background. Giant tropical flowers in the same colors were splashed randomly between the stripes. With its straight-cut neckline and wide trapunto-stitched shoulder straps, she knew it would look stunning against her coppery skin.

On the next hanger was a matching bikini. There was even a giant scarf to drape over the dress or cover the swimsuit.

"Perfect," a low voice commented behind her.

Minta whirled and almost collided with Brad. "Oh, I didn't recognize your voice."

"And you're as jumpy as a cat," he pointed out.

"I'm on red alert," she admitted.

He frowned. "That takes me back to my navy days. Were you ever in the military, Minta?"

"With my two left feet?" Turning back to the clothes rack, she added, "You really like these?"

"They're made for you. I'd ask if I could buy them for you, but I'm not in the mood for a lecture on women's rights."

"Smart thinking." She looked over at the clerk. "I think I'll try these on."

Brad was scanning the magazine rack when she returned from the small dressing room to pay for her purchases. He joined her at the counter. "Good fit?"

She nodded. "Any plans for today?"

"Lydia invited us over for dinner this evening. I told her I'd check with you and let her know later."

They walked toward their rooms. "Don't you need to go back to work, Brad?"

"One more day, Minta. That's all I'm asking of your time. One more day." He made no attempt to hide the depth of his longing.

"I have the time, Brad. I'd love to spend it with you, but don't let me keep you from your work, promise?"

"Tomorrow I'll have to go out with Hugo. Today is ours."

They separated at the doors of their respective rooms and Minta went inside. She checked inside the closet, under the bed and even in the shower stall before undressing. Although she'd been confident with Brad, she was definitely on guard. And jumpy, too, she admitted to herself.

She admitted also that she thrived under these

conditions. She'd always had a need for action, for adventure, and even for danger. Her family had recognized this at an early age. Her mother constantly complained about all the risks Minta took as a young child.

Only her Grandfather Tony had understood her. He was a deputy sheriff and had encouraged her to go into law enforcement. As a youngster she remembered listening to him tell of capturing "outlaws" in the days when New Mexico was considered a wild place to live. Her three sisters preferred to gather around their grandmother for more traditionally feminine pursuits.

This need to live on the edge, to seek excitement, had not diminished as she'd grown older. Now that she accepted it as an integral part of herself, she capitalized on it in her work. She also accepted that her career would always win out when it came down to a choice. No matter how much she tried to mold herself into a more conventional standard, she would fail and make herself and anyone close to her miserable.

Surveying herself in the mirror as she slipped on the bikini trunks, she smiled suddenly. *Leave it alone, Cordero,* she told herself. *All McMillan has asked for is one more day of your time. Why are you trying to make it into such a big deal?*

ON A YACHT anchored off the far side of the island, Andre Mirabeau slammed a file down on his desk and called out loudly, "Lex, get in here."

The cabin was paneled in rich dark wood, Andre's desk a smooth gleaming expanse of oak. When the slender blond-haired man entered the cabin quietly, Andre looked up. "I've read your report," he said flatly. He eyed the other man speculatively. Lex was one of his right-hand men, a man who'd grown up in Eastern Europe but had escaped to make his living in the desperate but lucrative world of mercenary spy activity.

"The information he gave us was correct," Lex said as his eyes roamed restlessly. He was nervous; Andre could sense his anxiety and it irritated him.

"Correct," he bit out the word. "But totally worthless. I don't like it. McMillan is moving too slow. What's he playing at?"

A half smile broke across Lex's face. "Right now, he's playing with a very beautiful young woman."

"Damn," Andre muttered under his breath. "I don't like this at all. We've got to get that information and we need it now."

"Until he's finished the tests, the robot is worthless to us," Lex reminded him.

"Surely he has plans. Why do we have to wait for him to finish?"

"Without McMillan...what have we got?" Lex said, shrugging his shoulders. "He's known for keeping the key information in his head until he's good and ready."

"McMillan's no fool," said Andre. "He's made a tape, and unless he cooperates with us we'll have to get our hands on it."

"What do you suggest?" said Lex cynically.

"Put pressure on him," Andre ordered.

"We've already threatened the girl," Lex snapped.

"Who is this girl? Do we know anything about her?"

Lex waved his hands dismissively. "Just a tourist. She's his woman, that's all."

"Why would he bring a woman with him when he had a pretty good idea we would contact him?"

"He didn't bring her," Lex explained. "They just happen to be sharing the same cottage on the main island. Obviously they've gotten to know each other quite well."

"Pressure him. Get his mind off that woman and back on that robot. I'm tired of waiting for the information. My buyers are tired of waiting. You know what to do."

Lex stepped forward and twisted his hands together. "What about Miller?"

"You know what to do," Andre eyed him sharply, and Lex moved away, nodding his head before slipping out of the cabin.

TED MILLER SAT behind the desk Lydia had arranged for him in their cottage. It was a nice desk, but then everything Lydia did for him was nice. She was a nice person. A wonderful person. He hadn't realized that when he'd been in Vietnam. He'd been too young, too rash, to recognize the gift he'd been given in his wife. It had been his lack of appreciation that had triggered the chain of events that embroiled them all now.

Pulling open the bottom drawer of his desk, he glanced up to make sure Lydia was not in the room before pulling out a small packet of envelopes at the back of the drawer. A picture fell out of the package, and he stared at it. The boy was growing up now, his features young and eager. The pain twisted like a knife inside him, and for the hundredth time he wondered if he'd made the right choice. It had all happened so fast, and he'd been so young and so shocked by the horrors of Vietnam.

Footsteps sounded in the hall outside his door, and he hastily shoved the photograph and papers back in the drawer just as Lydia entered the room. "Good morning," he said, smiling at her quickly.

"Good morning," she replied, but her voice was lacking in enthusiasm. She'd been like this lately, depressed, apathetic. He knew how much she wanted a child, a baby to replace the one she'd lost while he was in Vietnam. She'd lost that baby all by herself, alone and frightened, and he hadn't even been thinking of her at all.

His voice was infinitely gentle as he rose and put his arm around her. She was so precious to him, and he was scared to death of losing her. His arm tightened around her, and he bent his head to kiss her. Even as their lips met he was vowing silently that, no matter what the cost, he would protect her, keep her from suffering any more pain. It was a promise he had no idea how he was going to keep.

MINTA AND BRAD enjoyed a perfect day. They rented a small sailboat and went out during the morning. After lunch at the inn, they went beachcombing and collected shells. In the early evening, they dressed and waited in front of the inn for Ted to come by.

"I'm glad you didn't let that man scare you off," Brad said, his arm wound tightly around her waist.

She leaned back into the crook of his arm. "I wanted another day with you."

"You could go out on the boat with Ted and me."

"And distract you some more? I'll fly back to Grand Cay in the morning. I've got some work to do myself."

"You're right," he said. "You'd be bored out on the boat anyway." Inwardly he was cursing himself for inviting her. What kind of fool was he? He was probably endangering her life. These guys were playing for keeps. He needed to keep his senses alert, to keep his eyes peeled for every possible sign of danger.

"Can I ask what you'll be working on?" he asked after a pause.

"While we were diving I thought of a design for my jewelry. First I'll sketch it, and then I'll make one up to see if I like it."

"Did you bring your equipment?"?

"I always bring a few of my favorite tools with me. And enough silver so I can actually work something up. I have a special permit to carry silver. It gets me past the customs agents."

Brad slid his fingertips along her arm. "What made you choose silversmithing?"

"Only another native American would ask that!"

"Why so?"

Minta sighed and smiled back at him. "Most people connect all Indians with silver and turquoise."

"Isn't that a traditionally Navaho craft?"

"That's what I mean. You view Indians as distinct from one another, but most people I meet lump us all together. Haven't you ever run into that kind of thinking, Brad?"

"I'm seldom confronted with my Indian heritage. Unless someone knew my mother, they don't get past the red hair and the McMillan name."

"In D.C. I'm constantly being taken for a native of India. If I slipped into a sari and dropped a jewel over my forehead, I'd only confirm their beliefs. You'd be amazed how people phrase their questions. What nationality are you, dear? Were you born in this country? It gets on my nerves, especially since my ancestors were the first real Americans."

He was laughing as an old beat-up Jeep pulled to a stop in front of the inn. "Jump in, you two," Ted ordered in his deep voice.

As they roared down the road, he turned to Brad. "I asked around about that guy you mentioned on the phone this morning. No one remembers seeing him. How'd you meet up with him, anyway?"

"He gave Minta a rough time," Brad explained.

Ted kept his eyes on the road. "Why do you say that? Did he make a pass at her?"

"No," Brad said, suddenly tight-lipped. "It was probably nothing. I just wondered if you knew him."

Ted glanced at Brad curiously and then shifted his gaze to Minta. For a long moment they stared at each other, and Minta sensed that Ted was eager to find out more. However, he said nothing more and Brad avoided the subject as well.

"I hope you aren't too hungry," Ted said, changing the subject. "Lydia says you've got to sing for your supper."

Minta patted her flat stomach. "Sounds like a good time to diet."

"By sing, Ted means we have to catch our meal. Whenever his freezer gets low, he always pulls this on me."

"Don't believe a word of what Brad is telling you," protested Ted. "We're going lobster progging."

"Lobsters? I thought they flourished only in cold water," Minta said.

"These are the European variety. *Langouste*," conceded Ted. "I've got a secret spot where they're as easy to get as picking up candy."

Minta felt a surge of happiness as her wind-whipped hair flew across her face. Today had been a perfect vacation day, just the sort the doctor would have ordered. Suddenly her worries seemed groundless, and she determined to enjoy the evening to the fullest.

CHAPTER ELEVEN

TED'S WIFE, LYDIA, was waiting on the front porch of their lilac stucco bungalow when they arrived. She was stunningly beautiful with dark wavy hair that fell around her shoulders. Her skin was creamy white, and her eyes were a translucent shade of gray. She looked like a *Vogue* model. Even the lightweight jump suit she wore had the look of a designer's label. She walked out to the Jeep and put her arms around Minta. "I'm so happy to meet a friend of Brad's," she said sincerely.

Minta found it hard to connect the fragile Lydia with Ted as she returned the friendly hug. They went inside. The interior of their home was furnished with sturdy oak furniture that looked as if it had come with the squat stucco dwelling. On one wall was a huge bookcase lined with antique, leather-bound volumes. The room seemed totally at odds with Lydia, too.

Lydia fingered Minta's silky dress. "This is so lovely. But we'll have to find you something sturdier to wear. I think I've got something that should fit." She led the way down a hall, past a rather nice-looking masculine study.

When she opened a door at the far end of the hall, Minta was unable to stifle an exclamation of pleasure. It was the most exquisite child's room she'd ever seen. The pale-yellow walls, the hand-carved cradle, the dotted-swiss curtains. Even the shelves were filled with stuffed animals and children's picture books.

"Do you like it?" Lydia asked.

Minta schooled her voice carefully, remembering what Ted had said the evening before about their desire for children.

"It's lovely."

Lydia sighed. "It's been ready for several years now. Actually some of these pieces came from the States with me. I've been pregnant twice but miscarried both times." She smiled suddenly. "But you're not here to listen to me talk about that." She opened a closet door and began rummaging through until she pulled out a strapless jump suit. "How about this?"

"Great, if I can fit into it," Minta said, leaning over to slip her new dress off her head. She stepped into the suit and pulled it up over her hips.

"It looks like it was made for you."

As Minta started to leave, she saw a picture on the dresser and picked it up. It was a younger Ted, in a navy uniform, his face smiling and carefree. "Ted and Brad were in Vietnam, together, right?"

When she turned she saw that Lydia's face had clouded. "Yes." She bit her lip and stared down at the floor for several moments. "That's when I lost the first baby. Ted was gone, so I put that picture in the nursery in case the baby arrived before Ted came home. It's part of the room now.''

''Why did you lose the baby?'' Minta asked sympathetically, sensing the woman needed to talk.

Lydia shrugged her shoulders. ''The doctors aren't certain. I'm going to have some more tests run next month. Then, there may be a possibility of help. My doctor has been studying all the new literature on treating problem pregnancies.''

Minta hugged her impulsively. ''I'll be cheering for you. You and Ted have so much to offer a child on this lovely island. Have you considered adopting?''

''If the treatments aren't successful, I'm going to look into it.''

Brad's eyes swept over Minta appreciatively when the women returned outside. The four of them climbed into the Jeep and sped along a curving road that skirted the coast until Ted braked to an abrupt halt. ''Here's the boat,'' he announced.

Minta looked up, expecting to see *Lydia* but saw an old flat-bottomed skiff. She climbed in, hoping it was sturdy. The engine purred to life on the first try, and soon they were chugging out toward a shelf of reefs where Ted promised *langoustes* were lurking by the hundreds.

After Ted dropped anchor, Brad and he lowered a glass-bottomed box over the side of the boat. Minta sat still, spotting the crustaceans lying motionless in the still, shallow clear waters. ''I thought these would be small. Some of them must weigh two pounds."

Ted handed her a pronged stick. "That's small compared to the cold-water lobsters off Maine. When you sight one that you think you can catch, go after it. Hook it between the prongs and drop it in the box."

"Just like that, huh?" Minta asked, grinning.

She leaned over the side and made several wild tries before she caught her first one. "Go for it," shouted Ted and soon the four were engaged in a fast-paced contest. Minta stole several glances at Lydia and was pleased to see that she seemed stronger than she had at first glance.

When they clambered ashore, Brad and Minta gathered up driftwood for a fire. When it started to blaze, Lydia put a pot of seawater on to boil. She poured in a good measure of vinegar, explaining to Minta that the vinegar kept the meat tender.

"This time, Brad," Lydia said. "Twenty minutes ought to be about right for this size." In another pot of boiling fresh water she dropped shucked ears of corn. As the steam rose around her face her cheeks flushed, and she looked brighter, more cheerful somehow. Glancing at her, Minta chanced to see that Ted was staring approvingly but anxiously at his wife. His eyes were filled with such pride and love that Minta was deeply moved.

She turned, seeking out Brad's gaze. He was already looking at her. Smiling, he grasped her hand and squeezed it warmly, communicating his own response to the emotions she was feeling.

When the time was up, they removed the *langoustes* and broke off their tails. Minta decided the succulent pink meat, dripping with butter and lightly salted, was possibly the most delicious food she'd ever eaten.

After they stuffed themselves, they lounged around the fire, finishing off the last of the smooth dry white wine Brad had brought from the inn. "Remember that time you brought your mother here, Brad?" Lydia asked.

"And she caught more than any of us?" Ted added.

Brad smiled but his eyes were sad. "I can never thank you two enough for the good time she had here."

"We loved having her," Lydia said, turning to Brad. "If I ever have a son, I'd want to have the same relationship you and your mother had. You two were friends. And you were so good to her, especially near the end."

Brad glanced down, and Ted broke the silence with a short laugh. "Sounds like Lydia's trying to impress Minta with all your good qualities, Brad."

"Don't accuse me of that," Lydia said, stirring the fire with a stick.

The conversation turned to Brad's work on his robots. Minta listened, noting Ted's interest. He seemed knowledgeable about electronics as Brad explained some of the technicalities. A yawn overtook Minta before she could stop it and Brad stood, "I think we better get back to the inn, Ted."

They gathered up the remains of the picnic and drove back to their cottage. Minta went inside to change back into her own dress and stared sadly around the room prepared for an infant that never arrived. When she went outside she hugged Lydia goodbye.

"You and Brad seem right for each other," Lydia whispered. "I hope everything works out for you two. I know I'll be seeing you again."

It was late by the time they returned to the inn. Ted and Brad made last-minute plans to meet the next morning. When Ted drove off, Minta and Brad started for their rooms. "I had a great time," Minta said. "But I feel so sad for Lydia. Have you seen the baby's room?"

Brad nodded tersely. "Yes, it is sad."

"Why don't they adopt?"

Brad hesitated before answering. "Ted needs to change his attitude about adoption."

"Oh, what's that?"

"He refuses to consider it." Brad said shortly.

Minta digested this piece of information, trying to put it together with what Lydia had said. "Want to stop on the terrace and have some coffee?"

"Mmm, better not," Minta said. "It would probably keep me awake. But I would like something cool, like a soda."

They lingered on the shadowed terrace, sipping the icy drinks, basking in the warm breezes. Finally they headed for their rooms. Minta had just turned from making a comment to Brad when she caught a glimpse of someone taking the steps that led down from the balcony fronting their rooms two at a time. Something about the slope of the man's shoulders was familiar to her. He disappeared before she got a good enough look to identify him. Somewhat distracted, she turned back to Brad. "I'm sorry, did you say something?"

"I said I'd check to see if there are any messages at the desk. Would you like a paper?"

Trying to suppress her uneasiness, she said, "No, thanks, I'll see you in a few minutes."

She walked across the courtyard and started up the darkened staircase, noticing for the first time how the tall bushes surrounding this wing tended to isolate it from the rest of the building. It was silent all around her, no sounds of conversation, no music drifting out from the bar, not even the sound of the surf reaching her ears.

When she made it to the top of the staircase, she paused and glanced around cautiously but the balcony appeared deserted. She knew it was foolish, but she couldn't help thinking that anyone heading for one of the rooms would make a perfect target for a mugger. But why should that come to her mind here? Cayman Brac probably had so few violent crimes that no one gave it a second thought.

In spite of her logic, Minta hurried across the balcony and stopped in front of her door, reaching automatically for her shoulder purse before remembering she had decided against carrying it. Brad had her key. She'd handed it to him and asked him to keep it in his pocket.

Impatiently she positioned herself against the wall to wait. A cool breeze brushed her shoulders, and she wrapped her arms over her breasts for extra warmth. What could be taking Brad so long?

She checked the luminous dial of her watch. Three minutes. She'd give him three more minutes before she went in search of her key. Her vague anxiety bothered her. Unlike the instant alertness the evening before when she'd known someone was watching her, this feeling was too nebulous, too emotional to be of any help.

The longer an agent was involved in dangerous assignments, the more acute the senses became. People close to undercover personnel frequently accused them of having a sixth sense.

When she'd first become involved with older more experienced agents, she'd been awed by this ability they had. But now she understood it. They had developed an awareness of everything around them to the extent that they knew if the slightest thing was out of sync. A leaf fallen on the ground from a tree that wasn't there. The faintest hint of fresh cigarette smoke in a room that should have been unoccupied for hours. The slightest sound that was undetectable to most human ears.

Ordinarily she assumed this state of constant vigilance only when she was actively working a case and that was what was wrong now. She had no reason to be overly concerned. Her encounter with the silver-haired stranger was not all that ominous. She'd been given much more malicious warnings in the past.

There was only one difference that she could see. The way the man had glanced over at the table where she and Brad had been sitting. This was the first time she had ever involved someone important to her, someone she cared for, someone she suspected she was beginning to love, in anything even remotely connected to danger.

Always before she had sympathized with agents who worried about their wives being attacked or their children kidnapped by vicious underworld criminals. Yet she had never really understood their feelings. With her own family thousands of miles away, she had never been personally affected. But now there was Brad. Dear God, she knew she'd never forgive herself if she was the cause of anything happening to him.

Footsteps sounded on the staircase, and she stiffened momentarily until she recognized the distinctive step. She started forward, her voice radiant with relief. "Brad."

He rounded the corner and came into sight, his presence the only reassurance she needed that all was well in her world. His slow smile caressed her as they reached one another and he hugged her to him. "I thought I'd never get off the phone to Ron. What are you doing outside?"

Very carefully she eased out of his arms, surprised by the rush of emotions the mere sight of him had generated. "I left my key in your pocket."

"Damn, I forgot. Why didn't you come looking for me?"

"Too lazy, I guess."

"I'd wager you've never been lazy in your life." He located the key as they reached her door. Grinning down at her, he inserted the key in the lock.

At that instant she froze. Her sixth sense hadn't gone haywire after all. Something was wrong. Very wrong indeed.

Habits. Something they drummed into your head before they let you out of the academy. Always be aware of your own habits. She knew hers like the back of her hand and that was what had alerted her.

Minta grasped Brad's hand, wrenching it off the doorknob.

His eyes narrowed as he turned to face her.

"Shh." Minta laid a finger across his mouth before motioning with her head for them to move into a shadowy corner that housed a cleaning closet.

He followed, frown lines etching his forehead.

"My lamp's on," she mouthed when they were against the closet door.

"So are most of the others . . ." he said, and then paused. "Oh, I see. You didn't leave yours on."

"No." Her lips formed the denial firmly.

"Maybe the maid?" The inflection in his voice indicated he was clearly skeptical of the need for speaking in whispers.

"Maybe. Let me have my key. You stand aside, and when I push open the door with my foot, stay out of sight." She had his full attention, she realized, but her mind was working too hard to do more than make a mental note of the way his eyes widened in amazement.

"You're too old to play cops and robbers. This is ridiculous."

Minta ignored him, moving across the balcony and inserting the key soundlessly in the lock. She waited a few seconds before turning it and then kicked the door open in a sudden rush.

A soft, fluttery sound greeted them, and she noted that the window was open. The sheer panels that served to diffuse the sunlight in daytime were fluttering in the night breezes. That meant the heavier drapes had been opened since she'd left. A maid wouldn't have done that.

She motioned to Brad and then went quickly into the room. It was empty but someone had been there. Someone had very definitely been in her room. All the drawers on the dresser were opened, the closet door gaped widely and her few clothes and cosmetics had been strewed across the floor.

Minta paused, speechless, her mind working overtime. What on earth was going on here? Brad gave a low whistle of surprise behind her but said nothing. She turned to look at him finally, noticing that his face was very grim.

"Someone searched my room," she said needlessly.

"Any idea why?" Brad studied the chaos silently and then added, "Looks like burglary to me. Is anything missing?"

Minta got down on her knees and pulled her

purse out from under the bed. Brad watched as she rifled through it quickly. "No, everything is here. My passport, my credit cards and traveler's checks."

"Did you have any jewelry with you?"

Minta shook her head. "No, I left most of my things back on Grand Cayman. All I brought was my gym bag and a few essentials."

Brad was suddenly furious. "What's going on here, Minta? Are you in some sort of trouble you're not telling me about?"

Minta regarded him carefully. Was this the time to tell him about her FBI connections? *No,* her inner voice warned. *No, not until you hear from Jill. Until then, you don't know quite enough about Brad to give him that information.* The air of mystery that surrounded him had thrown her off balance these past few days, and for some reason, she was beginning to feel that all was not as it should be with him.

To be quite honest, she had to admit that none of this had begun happening to her until she had met Brad. Was he telling her everything she should know about his own life? As the silence lengthened between them his eyes narrowed. "Well, are you going to answer me or not?"

"I don't like your tone, Brad," Minta said coldly.

"Hell, who cares about my tone? Are you always this prone to getting into trouble, Minta?" His voice softened as he said her name, and she realized he was more concerned than angry. Some people showed their concern this way. When they were terribly worried about you, they yelled. Mothers did that with little children when their safety was threatened.

"Look, Brad—" Minta rose to her feet "—I don't know what's going on here, myself. You're right, most likely. Someone was probably robbing my room but didn't find my purse. When they saw how little I had in the drawers and closet, they gave up."

"I don't like it," Brad said under his breath. "Look, let's call Ted and get him to run you back to Grand Cay in one of his smaller boats tonight. You can talk to Bobby about this, maybe move to one of the big hotels where you'll be safe."

"Safe?" The surprise in Minta's voice was genuine. "That's an odd word to use, Brad. A burglary in my room while I'm out hardly threatens my physical well-being."

"I was thinking about what happened last night," Brad said.

"I have a better suggestion. Let's go down and report this to the desk clerk. Maybe they've had this problem before, and they'll be able to tell us what's going on."

"Okay," Brad agreed slowly.

"Why don't you go check your room to make sure nothing is wrong. I'll pick up these clothes while you're gone," Minta suggested.

Brad started to protest and then thought better of it. "Right. Be sure to lock the door behind me."

Minta looked at him reprovingly as he made for the door. "I'm not totally without common sense, Brad," she said, and he left the room.

IN HIS OWN ROOM, Brad noted that nothing was out of place. It didn't make sense. Why would someone search Minta's room but not his? Was he wrong about that warning to her being a veiled threat to him? But no, this incident tonight fit in. They were harassing Minta and by doing so, hoped to get at him. This was their way of telling him to forget about her and get on with his business in the Caymans.

Well, he didn't feel like being threatened. He'd learned a few things these past few days. He'd found out that there were more than just The Trio involved in this thing. That man last night. He wasn't anyone Brad had seen before.

He had also found out that they were dangerous. They would stop at nothing to get what they wanted, even if it meant hurting Minta. Had the first car accident been deliberate or had it been a coincidence?

Suddenly he knew he had to get this thing over with. Tomorrow morning he would begin testing Hugo, and with any luck he would have the information he wanted and be gone before anything worse could happen. Meanwhile, he was going to get Minta out of there. That much he was sure of. Tonight she would stay with him, and tomorrow he'd see that she went back to Grand Cayman and talked to Bobby.

That worried him, though. By talking to Bobby, she was involving the police. Would that hinder his project? He had tried to get help before he left Austin, but the doors had been closed to him. No one had listened, and he had decided to risk it alone. One thing was certain; testing Hugo was top priority right now. He wanted that contract, and he had to have the results of those tests to get it.

First things first. First he had to get Minta out of there. Then he could concentrate on his own problems. The rest of the world be damned.

MINTA LOCKED HER DOOR behind her and hurried down the staircase with Brad. The lobby was deserted except for a woman behind the desk. Minta recognized her as the one she had spoken to that morning.

Brad greeted the woman by name, asking, "Have you been here all evening, Paula?"

"Why, yes, I have, Brad. Why?"

"Did you see anyone unusual hanging around here?"

"No," Paula said with surprise. "No, I didn't. Why?"

Minta spoke up for the first time. "My room seems to have been broken into."

Paula looked horrified. "A burglary? What did they take?" She looked so agitated that Minta felt the need to reassure her.

"Nothing, actually. But my things had been scattered around the room."

Paula came around to the front of the desk, wringing her hands. "Oh my dear, I'm sorry. But how did they get in? Did you leave the door unlocked?"

"No," Minta said, frowning. "At least I don't think so. I'm pretty sure I locked it."

"I'll come up right away," Paula promised. "Do you think I need to call the police? Oh, dear, I hate to have something like this happen in my inn. We've never had any trouble here before. My guests will be terribly upset."

Minta experienced a wave of sympathy as she watched the woman. The woman's agitation was genuine. "Why don't we forget about it since nothing was taken," she urged.

"Oh, no," Paula protested. "I couldn't do that. It might happen again."

Minta saw her point. "Why don't you call the police privately tomorrow. They can send someone over to help you tighten your security, maybe keep an eye on the place for a while."

Paula looked grateful. "That's a good idea. But if you discover anything missing, let me know at once. My insurance will cover it. Meanwhile, I'll send a maid up to clean the room."

"Thank you," Minta said. "I'm sorry to have to tell you this. I've had a lovely time here."

After a few more moments Brad and Minta made their departure. As Brad headed back toward the stairs, Minta said, "I'll be up in a minute, Brad."

"Where are you going?"

"I just got an idea," she said thoughtfully. "I want to talk to someone."

"I'm going with you," Brad said firmly. "You're not getting out of my sight tonight."

"Now wait a minute," Minta said, not sure if she liked his attitude. "I don't need a keeper." She wasn't used to being taken care of, and she wasn't sure if she felt comfortable or not.

"You have no choice," Brad said, and she decided not to argue after a look at his face.

Leading the way to the semidarkened dining room, Minta stopped and glanced around. The room was nearly deserted. In one corner several waiters were huddled together. "There. I see him," Minta said with satisfaction.

"Who?" Brad asked, but she ignored him.

The young man looked up as they neared and he visibly paled. Minta quickened her pace until she reached him. "I'd like to talk to you, alone."

His eyes darted around the room. He looked different than he had when the gray-haired man had handed him the large tip the evening before. Shaken, somehow. A little upset. "I've still got some cleaning up to do," he hedged.

"I'll handle it for you, Sean," said another waiter. "Go see what the foxy lady wants."

Minta ignored the remark as Sean followed Brad and herself out of the room. When they reached the lobby she glanced around for a private place to talk. There was no reason to create a scene. After all, she could be wrong. "Is there anywhere we can be alone?" she asked.

Sean was belligerent. "Why should I go anywhere with you?"

"Maybe you want Paula to hear this," Minta said softly, and his face reddened.

"We can go down the hall. There's a uniform room."

When they were inside the small room with the door closed, Minta spoke first. "Did you let anyone into my room tonight?"

Brad started when she asked the question. She felt his gaze on the back of her neck and paused for a moment.

Sean looked horrified. "Oh, no ma'am. I wouldn't do a thing like that!"

Minta regarded him sharply. "Well you're acting funny about something. What happened tonight?"

"All I did was talk about you a little," Sean protested quickly. "That's all. There's nothing wrong with that."

"Who did you talk about me to?"

Sean's eyes darted between her and Brad. "It wasn't the man from last night," he mumbled.

"But you know it was his friend." Minta was not asking a question.

"Yeah, he mentioned what happened last night with the tip and all."

"Who was it?" Brad demanded, advancing toward Sean menacingly.

Minta stopped him with a hand on his arm. "How much did he pay you, Sean?"

Sean's chin trembled. "Just a tip. For a little information, he said."

"What sort of information?"

"He said he wanted to know more about you. You're so pretty and all. He said his friend was interested in you."

"What happened next?" Minta said, determined to be relentless.

"I finally told him that I'd watch to see when Paula took her break from the desk. She usually gets one of the girls from the kitchen to help out for a few minutes. Tonight she picked Josie, a friend of mine. While she was working, I went over and looked through the register until I found your name...."

"How did you find her name?" Brad interrupted.

"You were the only single girl to check in yesterday," Sean answered, directing his gaze at Minta.

"So you told this man Minta's name and her room number. Then you gave him her key...."

"I never. I wouldn't do that," Sean protested. "Well, I did tell him her name and room number, but I didn't give him any key. He didn't even ask for it. He left about five minutes after I gave him the information."

"Did he threaten you?" Minta asked.

"Yeah. He told me not to mention this to anyone or I'd be sorry."

"Big threat," muttered Brad, his voice strained with anger.

"Who are these men, Sean?" Minta asked.

"Honestly, I don't know. I'd never seen them before in my life. I'm telling the truth."

"When you bragged about your big tip to the other waiters. Did anyone say they knew who the men were? Think hard."

He cleared his throat nervously. "Honest to God, the only other thing I know is that Charlie said the man who was here last night lives on a big yacht. It was anchored down at The Point."

"What's her name?" Minta demanded.

Sean gulped. "Charlie said it's called the *Omen*. Can I go now?" He shifted restlessly. "I won't tell anything about you to anyone else, ever again. I promise."

"Where's Charlie?" Minta asked.

"He's over on Grand Cay now. He's off work for a few days."

Minta started to let him go and then added, "You better keep your mouth shut from now on, Sean. I want you to tell Paula all about this."

"Oh no." Sean cringed.

"That man broke into my room tonight. Paula is worried about it. She's calling the police tomorrow. You better tell her anything you know, or I'll see to it you're fired."

"Yes, ma'am," Sean said reluctantly.

"I'll be checking up to see if you told her," Minta promised, and Sean left after a quick respectful glance back at them both.

Brad was quiet for a while after Sean left. "You've got quite a technique there, Cordero. Sure you haven't been in the military?"

"I'm sure," Minta said lightly. "I just grew up

reading Nancy Drew stories. I learned my technique from them.''

"It's effective,'' he said quietly, and she sensed that he wasn't saying everything he was thinking.

"Well, at least we know who broke into my room.''

"Do we?'' Brad straightened up and stared at her. "All you know is that some man is attracted to you. Funny way he has of showing his passion. Searching your room.''

"I'm sure there's a logical explanation for all of this, McMillan.''

"Depends on what you call logical, I guess.'' He paced back and forth a few times and then stopped in front of her. "I want you to leave here first thing in the morning, Minta.''

"Hey, wait a second,'' Minta said, putting her hand up to push him back slightly. "I'm not under your command. Don't try using your navy tactics on me.''

"I'm asking you,'' Brad said softly. "Please.''

"Please, what?'' Minta answered stubbornly.

"Please go back to Grand Cayman. Get yourself a room in one of the big hotels. Enjoy your vacation and stay out of trouble.''

"I like my cottage,'' she said flatly. "I don't intend to leave it.''

"Well at least talk to Bobby,'' Brad said. "When are you leaving Grand Cay?''

"I don't know yet,'' Minta said, intentionally vague.

"In case I don't make it back before you leave, how about giving me your address in D.C.?"

"I'll probably be on Grand Cay for a while," Minta replied. "You're only going to be testing for a few days, aren't you?"

"Just in case I run into a delay. I don't want to lose you, Minta." His voice was so low she had to strain to hear.

"Okay," she said after a pause. "Got a pencil?"

Brad pulled a pen from his pocket and took a card out of his wallet. "Here, write it on this."

Minta scribbled her address on the card, squinting in the dim light. "There. Feel better?"

"Not yet. But I will if you promise to spend the night with me tonight."

Minta pretended to debate the question for a long time. She relented at length. "Sounds great." His eyes darkened, and he gathered her into his arms for a long, intense kiss.

CHAPTER TWELVE

MINTA WAS IN THE SMALL PLANE that ferried passengers back and forth between the islands several times a week before she had time to think again. She hated to leave the resort. It would always hold special memories of the time Brad and she had spent there together. In spite of the unpleasantness of her encounter with that man and the invasion of her room, her mind was filled only with memories of Brad.

She leaned her head on the plane's soft seat, trying to picture what he was doing at the moment. Probably inside Hugo, she decided. Far below the surface of the water. Much farther than most men dared to go. Taking risks. That's what Ted had said about him. For the first time she understood what it was like to worry about someone else's safety. It was much more difficult to fear for someone you loved than to handle danger yourself.

She had shed her last doubts about loving Brad. Some time in the midst of their passionate lovemaking the night before she had surrendered to the knowledge that he was vital to her happiness.

The love she felt for him went much deeper than

the romantic infatuation that had swept over her when she'd met Peter. Then she had ignored the fact that they had nothing in common, argued constantly and had little or no respect for each other. That was why she felt so guilty when she learned the truth about him.

She had known that if they had truly loved each other, he would have felt free to confide in her at some point. He had needed a stronger relationship, someone to notice how troubled he was.

But the way she felt about Brad was totally different. She not only felt the strongest of physical attractions to him but she liked him as well. This morning she felt totally optimistic. Sure, there were problems to overcome in their relationship.

First, she had to tell him about her work. It would be a shock to him, of course. But she was beginning to realize that Brad was a very flexible person. They would work something out.

Then came the task of learning to make allowances for each other's unique life-styles. They'd handle it! She knew they could. The times they had to be apart would make their moments together even more tremendous and passionate. In the rosy aftermath of their lovemaking, Minta was certain that nothing could come between Brad and herself.

When she arrived at the airport, Minta stopped by to say hello to Diane Hall at the car-rental agency. Diane seemed pleased to see her. "Bobby's been looking for you. I think he has some news about the car that hit you. Where have you been?"

Minta's heartbeat sped up over the thought of learning more about her assailants. "Scuba diving. I spent a couple of nights at Cayman Brac."

"Beautiful place! What do you think of our coral reefs?"

"The best I've ever seen. Do you dive much?"

Diane flushed. "Not very often. I'm ashamed to say that I get nervous underwater."

Minta grinned sympathetically. "Is Bobby at the station today? I'll give him a call to see what he knows."

"He goes on duty later. If he comes by I'll tell him you're back."

When the taxi stopped in front of the cottage, Minta felt almost as if she was returning to a familiar house. She paid the driver and walked through the thick sand, remembering that first afternoon when Brad had helped her to remove her boots. She'd made a fool of herself that day. Going hot and cold at his touch. But he had as much as admitted he'd been just as smitten. Thinking about the violets he'd bought and then been too embarrassed to give her made her lips curve into a generous smile. Only a few more days and she'd be back in his arms.

Propelled by that thought she ran up the steps and fished out her keys. As she unlocked the door she scanned the porch absentmindedly. It looked as if it had been recently swept. The cleaning crew Brad had paid for, she guessed. Then she caught a glimpse of the door leading to Brad's side. It was ajar.

Stepping back to get a better view, she saw that it had definitely not been shut. Had Brad been careless? No, she remembered that he had turned the knob to make certain it was locked before they'd gone to his car.

She swore softly under her breath. Damn. The cleaning crew must have failed to pull the door shut. She hoped that didn't mean they'd been as careless with Brad's possessions. She started toward the door when she heard a phone ringing inside the cottage. Her side. The investigation into Brad's partially opened door would have to wait until she took care of that call.

It was Elizabeth on the phone, her voice bubbling with the kind of excitement that Minta recognized immediately. After the usual greetings, Minta broke in, "Tell me your news!"

"How did you guess?"

"Just say I've been a friend long enough to read you like a book. Okay, give."

"I'm pregnant again."

Tears clouded Minta's eyes. Since the birth of Nathan, Jr., over four years earlier, Elizabeth had been longing to have another child. "That's wonderful! When's your due date?"

"Seven more months. You're the first person I've told. Now I've got to figure out a way to tell mother and Sarah at the same time so neither of them will feel left out."

Minta laughed, her concern over Brad's open door forgotten for the moment. "I'm voting for a girl this time."

"Me, too. So is Nathan, for that matter. But Nathan, Jr., has demanded a brother. I think he imagines the baby will be ready to play soccer when it's born."

"Wait until he sees the little red, wrinkled creature. He'll think E.T.'s come back. How are you feeling?"

"A little tired, but I don't think it will last long. I'm in excellent health, so I'll bounce back quickly. I tried calling you last night but you weren't home."

"I'm glad you're not my mother or I'd be blushing."

Elizabeth laughed. "Who is he?"

"It would take me hours to even begin to tell you. He's fantastic!"

"I'm impressed, but since I'm paying for this, I'd rather be impressed in person," Elizabeth teased. "This doesn't sound like the carefree Minta who can take them or leave them."

"It's not. I think I've got a terminal case, doctor."

"Best news I've heard from you in a long time. What does he think of your work?"

There was a long pause, then Minta cleared her throat. "I haven't exactly told him about it, but I think he can handle it. He's a little unique himself."

Elizabeth laughed. "Then it should be a perfect match. I've got to run now. My next patient is here. Oh, by the way, I can report to Jerry that you're following his advice, can't I?"

Minta hesitated, remembering the past few days. No one could blame her, though. She wasn't trying to get involved in any trouble. "Absolutely," she said firmly.

"I knew it. Keep me posted on the man in your life. I'm dying to meet him."

"Will do. And tell Nathan I'm so happy for you two. Your baby's mighty smart to have picked you for parents."

As she hung up the phone she thought of Lydia. Sometimes life didn't seem totally fair. But she was happy for Elizabeth! Humming softly to herself, she started for the bedroom when she heard a loud shout from next door. Minta began running, letting the door slam behind her as she rushed onto the front porch.

A middle-aged woman dressed in a spotless pair of white overalls was holding her hands in the air. "It's awful. Absolutely awful. I can't believe it," she screamed.

Minta reached out and shook her by the shoulders. "Calm down. Tell me what's wrong."

The authority in Minta's voice restored the woman to a measure of calm. She pointed toward Brad's side of the cottage. "Go in there and see for yourself."

With a feeling of dread, Minta pulled open the door, bracing herself for the sight of some catastrophe. She stopped in the doorway and her mouth dropped open in shock.

The sofa was overturned. Pillows were ripped

open, stuffing scattered over the wooden floor. The braided rug, identical to her own, had been rolled up and lay sprawled against a wall. The glass base on the lamp had been shattered, and the shells it had once held lay in a heap. When she glanced up and saw that the glass cover on the overhead light fixture had been removed, she knew nothing had been left untouched.

Minta assessed the damage with detachment, her professionalism taking over and blocking out all thoughts of personal involvement. There was nothing random or amateurish about this. Nor was it even particularly violent although a casual observer would have thought so.

Instead, a methodical search had been made of every square inch of the room. A quick look verified what she had already guessed. Even the light switch and electrical-outlet coverings had been removed to locate any hidden recesses in the room.

She walked through to the bedroom and saw the same havoc had been wrought. Mattress and box springs slit open. Drawers overturned and left on the floor. The closet door was open, and its contents scattered around the room, including the discarded remains of a packing crate.

Hilda! Minta's mind reeled and then she remembered. The robot was in her own closet. Or at least she was supposed to be.

Running outside, she encountered the woman standing in shock on the porch. Minta grabbed her hand. "Why don't you come in and fix a cup of tea? When you feel like it, call Mr. Long so he can report this to the police."

The woman followed her in, eager to talk. "It wasn't my fault. I was here yesterday morning. Left about ten o'clock. Everything was in good order, but I'm sure I pulled the door shut behind me. It must have been teenagers. Probably tourists. We don't see much vandalism on the island but sometimes these rich kids have nothing better to do. Bored, if you ask me."

"While you're at it, I'll take a cup of tea, too," Minta told her, aware the woman's ramblings bordered on hysteria. "There's a bottle of wine in the fridge if you'd like a glass for your nerves," she added. "It's the strongest thing I've got in the house."

Minta opened the closet door and was rewarded by the sight of the sturdy robot. She felt a rush of gratitude and patted her the same as she'd seen Brad do. "I'm glad Brad brought you over here, thought about your safety...."

She stopped, not only because she didn't want the woman in the kitchen to think she'd cracked up, but because a thought had just occurred to her. Why had Brad insisted on leaving Hilda in her closet? She couldn't help wondering if he'd suspected that his cottage might be searched. Was he worried about something more than having his robotic ideas stolen? These criminals had been looking for something specific. Something small. Drugs? Diamonds? A wave of guilt swept over her, and she slammed the door shut. Was she really thinking these thoughts about Brad?

She returned to his cottage and finished a quick survey. The mess in the kitchen was the worst yet. Every carton had been opened and its contents shaken out. Every jar emptied wherever the searcher had been when he grabbed it. It staggered her imagination to think what they had been looking for.

A short time later she heard a car drive up. She met Richard as he ran up the stairs. "What's wrong?" he said, though he was clearly out of breath. "I got a hysterical call a few minutes ago."

"I hope you're fully insured. It's bad," Minta answered.

Richard walked inside and swore loudly. "Where's McMillan?"

"Offshore."

"When did you get back?" Richard's eyes glazed over as he surveyed the damage.

"Less than an hour ago." Minta idly dusted off a countertop with her fingertips and then stopped.

"And your side wasn't touched?"

"No."

"Must have been some party! A year ago some college students on spring break broke into a house and messed up the place. But it wasn't half as bad as this." He grimaced. "Why did it have to be McMillan? He'll probably sue me for not putting better locks on the place."

"Not Brad," Minta said. "Surely he'll know it's

not your fault." She walked over to the door and looked at the lock. "An easy entry all right."

"Don't touch it. I'm sure the police will check for prints," Richard cautioned her.

Minta knew there wouldn't be any. No amateurs had been involved in this operation. This hadn't been caused by any college students on spring break. It had been a professional search pure and simple. The mess they'd left behind had been incidental. It was only evidence of their methodical haste to find something and then get away before they were caught. Had they found what they were looking for?

"Have the police been called?"

"Yes. They're on their way," said Minta.

"Good," said Richard, looking a little more relaxed. He surveyed the mess. "I think my insurance will cover this, but it may take a few days to get cleaned up. I hope McMillan's going to be gone for that long."

"Shouldn't he see it before you clean it up?"

"What for?" He walked into the bedroom with Minta behind him. "Nothing's worth saving except for the stuff that belongs to him. Where did you say we could reach him?"

"We can't. He's out on a boat. I could try calling some friends of his."

"Whatever the police decide." As if he suddenly remembered, Richard added, "Where have you been? I called a couple of times to see if you wanted to go out to dinner again."

"I've been diving. With Brad." She waited for his reaction.

Richard smiled knowingly. "So you two made up your differences? That's cozy. I forgot to mention that I do charge an additional fee for matchmaking."

"Try and collect," Minta retorted, glad that Richard was taking the damage to his property as calmly as he was. She wondered if the police would be as calm. They might suspect as she did, that Brad was the target rather than the victim.

Bobby Hall was the policeman on duty. "More trouble?" he asked when he joined them inside the cottage.

"Afraid so, but it's not my place," Minta answered.

"Wowie! This is one helluva mess," he said. "In all my years of experience I've never seen worse."

"How many years is that? One?" Richard asked dryly. "You know I'm expecting you to apprehend the persons responsible for this by nightfall?"

"Yes, boss. If you insist, I'll wait that long."

"While you two clowns are performing, I think I'll check on the cleaning lady. She may have passed out by now," Minta said.

"Don't go anywhere before I get a chance to talk to you," Bobby said.

"Good Lord, Bob," Richard growled. "You surely don't suspect Minta had anything to do with this? I can verify she was off the island."

Bobby and Minta glanced at each other and

began laughing. "Bobby wants to see me about something else," Minta told Richard when she had recovered her composure. The laughter had released some of her tension and put things in perspective. "When you're finished photographing or whatever you need to do, I'd like to gather up Brad's things. The cleaning lady won't know where to start."

IT WAS SEVERAL HOURS later before Bobby and Minta sat down at her table over sandwiches. "I've got a theory about this," Bobby said.

Minta continued eating, her nerves taut. "I think someone who stayed in this cottage in the past hid something here," Bobby said.

"Oh?" Why hadn't she considered that herself? Because she'd been too busy jumping to nasty conclusions about Brad, an inner voice nagged.

"It's possible. Say they were hiding drugs. They might have left them here and then returned to their own country, planning to get them on their next trip."

"Why would they have to tear the whole place apart? Wouldn't they know where to look?"

Bobby appeared nonplussed by her arguments. "Not if they weren't the same people. Maybe the original guy bragged...."

"I saw a TV show like that once," Minta said dryly, but she was intrigued by his theory, in spite of herself.

"Laugh all you want to but you'd be amazed how

frequently crimes are committed like ones seen on television.''

"Critics say the programs plant ideas in criminals' minds," Minta said. "Do you think Richard will give you the names of the people who've stayed here before Brad?''

Bobby shrugged. ''He may balk if it's someone who came incognito. As I've told you, people come to the Caymans because they're safe. No one asks too many questions as long as you're not caught causing any trouble.''

''That reminds me,'' Minta said. ''Diane said you had some news about the black car for me.''

''Not much. Remember the old man you told me had been sleeping when you knocked on his door?''

''Don't remind me. I still feel badly over waking him. He looked so frail.''

''Between his hut and the one next door, I located some ruts. I think there's a road leading to the estate behind the houses along there. As far as I can see, it's the only space wide enough to accommodate the width of a car.''

''Is there a gate?''

''I think so, although I couldn't see it well because of the undergrowth. It's possible a car could go under the branches.''

''Why would the owners of the estate go to such elaborate lengths to hide their entrance?''

''It probably started out as a pirate's dwelling. Remember you asked me to find out who the property belongs to? Well, I found out it belongs to an

Arab sheik. He may have bought it as a retreat where he and his family could vacation safely. Rich people have to guard themselves against kidnappers."

"The men I saw were definitely not Arabic."

"I know. I also found out the estate's up for sale. Until it sells, it's available for lease. I tried to find out the name of the current tenants but no luck. Like I told you, secrets are safe on the Caymans."

"Then we're right back where we started," Minta said, clearly disappointed. "That's not much news."

"I have more, but I hate to ruin your vacation."

"Tell me. I won't fall apart."

"Okay, if you're sure you want to hear this. When I questioned that old man the day I saw the gate, he was plainly terrified about something. He begged me not to come back any more. One side of his face was bruised...."

"When was this?" Minta inquired sharply. The one thing she hated most was the feeling she had caused an innocent person to suffer because of something she'd done.

"The day after the accident. Just long enough for any marks to turn the purplish shade his were. I suspect the people we're looking for are responsible. When they found out he'd talked to you, they worked him over. But he denied it. It makes me mad as hell to see an old man like that mistreated."

Minta burned with rage. "Think how I feel. Surely this puts things in a different light. Can't you get a search warrant and find out what's happening behind those walls?''

"I don't want to go that far, not yet anyway," Bobby said frowning. "I guess it's best to let it all die down and hope they don't have any more accidents."

"I have news for you," Minta said. She lay her sandwich down. "I've received some threats connected to that accident." Calmly she went over what happened on Cayman Brac, beginning with her encounter with the silver-haired man and then the forced entry into her hotel room.

Bobby's youthful face hardened. "Damn, that's awful. What a thing to have happen on your vacation. I guess you want to leave here right away."

"Not yet. Don't you agree these must be idle threats or something worse would have already happened to me?''

"But why? What does anyone have to fear from you?''

"I wish I knew. The only one from the black car I could identify positively would be the driver. And, of course, I remember everything about the silver-haired man. None of it is making much sense to me, Bobby. If only we could get inside that estate. Could I talk to the chief of police?''

"I'll mention it to him again, Minta." He stood. "My home phone's on that card I gave you. If anything else happens, call me immediately. If you're afraid to stay here after what happened next door, Diane would be glad to have you share her room.''

"No, thanks. I'm not afraid. You're not making a connection between my threats and what happened to Brad's side are you?"

"It could be someone thought it was yours but I doubt it. I'm still sticking to my theory that the intruders were looking for something they'd hidden earlier in the cottage."

MINTA SPENT SEVERAL HOURS that afternoon going through the chaos in the other side of the duplex in an effort to locate Brad's possessions. The expensive safari shirts and walking shorts, the linen sports coats and hand-stitched shirts were all salvageable. The cleaning lady offered to drop them off at the cleaner's when she left if Minta would inventory them.

Even Brad's colognes, hair gel and toothpaste had been slit open and the contents squished out into the bathroom sink. Whatever the intruders were looking for must be small, she concluded. That seemed to reinforce the possibility of diamonds or drugs. This plundering of his personal possessions made her long to talk to Brad, to prepare him for what awaited him when he returned. But he'd emphasized how pressed for time he was, and this would only be a distraction. Hilda was safe. The rest of these items could be replaced easily, she concluded.

She was in bed that night before she remembered that she hadn't called Jill. Tomorrow was soon enough, she decided sleepily. It had been a foolish impulse to ask her friend to run a computer check on Brad, anyway. Or maybe it was only an occupational hazard. Like the dental hygienist she'd roomed with in college who'd insisted her boyfriend have his teeth X-rayed before she'd marry him. Or her banking friend who warned never to date a man who didn't reconcile his bank statement each month.

Smiling at the trend of her thoughts, Minta turned over and gave herself up to memories of the time she'd spent in Brad's arms.

MINTA FELT IN CHARGE of her vacation when she awoke the next morning. Next door was a beehive of activity. First Richard and an insurance adjuster arrived and then later a team of workmen who removed all the damaged furniture and began scrubbing out the place.

After breakfast she put a call through to the FBI, but Jill's phone was answered by a woman she knew only vaguely who worked in Jerry's office as a typist. When Minta asked for Jill she learned she was out for several days. "To get a little rest," the woman confided. "Jerry's been working us to death around here before he leaves." Minta was proud of the way she squelched her curiosity and didn't ask his destination.

Jill wasn't at home either, so Minta tried Jill's sister, Lana. She told Minta Jill was out of town for a few days. "She's been working too hard, so she and a friend went in search of the sun. Anything important you needed to talk to her about?"

"She's been taking care of my mail."

"I'm doing that for you. Would you like me to run over what you have? I'm waiting for Jill to get back to pay these bills with the money you left her."

As Minta declined, she marveled how the events of the last week had eclipsed her normal world. "I'll talk to Jill when she gets back, Lana. Thanks for helping with my mail."

THE REST OF HER TIME apart from Brad fell into a pattern. Mornings swimming and snorkeling. Afternoons exploring the island on her bike and the local buses. Evenings she spent sketching designs for a silver tie clasp for Brad.

She wanted it to be special. A unique reminder of the time they'd shared together. She finally settled on an abstract design with flowing lines that reminded her of their diving trip. The first of many she hoped they'd take together.

By Thursday afternoon she finally perfected the design. With the surge of adrenaline she always felt when she reached this stage, she opened her silversmithing kit and drew out a thin sheet of rolled silver.

Cold and gleaming dully in its unworked state, the silver showed little of its allure to the uninitiated. But she knew that beneath the blows of her hammer it would become alive and almost infinitely responsive. If she failed to mold it into the shape she wanted, she knew she would have no one to blame but herself.

Minta had first become interested in silver when she joined an Indian Arts Council in high school. One of her teachers, a Navaho, had painstakingly passed on his love of the metal men had been known to die for. "Being a silversmith has brought me years of joy," he had told her. "Through it I can make a personal statement about the beauty of life."

Minta had fallen in love with the intricate art almost immediately. She accepted that it was tense, demanding work. Few people realized how emotional it was, also.

When she was involved in a project, she knew she became difficult to be around until she achieved the design she was seeking. Perfection was always the goal and this quest created a high level of anxiety. But the serenity that flowed through her when she held up a finished piece was worth every effort she expended.

Reaching inside her case, she located her favorite hammer. It was priceless and could never be replaced. The hammer to a silversmith is what a paintbrush is to an artist, almost an extension of the craftsman's own arm. This particular one, which she'd found in an antique shop by mere chance, was alleged to be more than a hundred years old. She liked to imagine what its original owner had made with it.

The soft taps of the hammer rang out clearly now as Minta worked with a small strip of silver. She divided it into two slender bands, twisting one over the other with deft movements. She held it up, pleased with the dramatic way the curved line of the design played off the linear one.

She pictured the moment when she would hand it to Brad. The way his face would light up in that slow smile, the pleasure something she'd crafted herself would bring him. She knew he was like her in that way. She sensed that Brad would feel much as she did that a gift that costs its giver nothing but money was meaningless.

Holding the delicate object against an anvil-like device, she struck the curved band repeatedly with light blows. Each blow coaxed the metal into more fluid lines. When her arm tired, she leaned back, surprised to see that it was almost evening.

As she stood to stretch she heard a car stopping in front. Bobby? Or one of the workmen who'd forgotten something? Sliding her tools back in the case, she stood and went outside, smoothing down her full skirt over her slim hips. She recognized Brad's red car turning in front of the cottage.

CHAPTER THIRTEEN

"BRAD," SHE CALLED, running down the steps.

He jumped out of the car and came toward her. When they reached each other, both stopped, their eyes filled with welcome. He held out his arms saying, "I've been dreaming about this moment for so long I can't believe it's real." His voice was as deep and soothing as the sound of waves on the beach behind them.

She melted against him, enjoying the feel of his cheek, rough against hers, and the way his heart pounded against her soft breasts. He seemed to understand her need to savor his warmth, his powerful body, the scent of his skin and the hard strength of his muscular form, and he remained still for a long time.

"I'd forgotten how incredibly soft your skin is," he murmured against her cheek. "Like silk. God, I've missed holding you, Minta."

She made soft indistinguishable sounds. He bent down to kiss her neck, deafening her with a roar of excitement. When he pulled away momentarily, he bent over and lifted her into his arms, carrying her toward the cottage.

"Did you finish your tests?" she asked, her arms around his neck.

"Later." He pushed open her door with the toe of his shoe. Without a word, without giving Minta a chance to even close the door behind her, he crossed to the bedroom. "Here?" he asked.

His urgency thrilled her, and she nodded against his chest. Gently he placed her on the bed and sat down beside her. The sunlight slanting through the open window played across his features, bouncing off the high planes of his cheekbones, proudly proclaiming his ancient heritage. Minta watched silently, trying to absorb each detail through the pores of her skin.

"What do you want?" he asked in a low voice, that sent shivers of sensual promise radiating through her.

"You," she answered softly. "All of you."

"Show me."

The corners of her mouth curved slowly into a smile, and she slid into a more comfortable position, aware of the way a tiny muscle flickered in his jaw revealing his state of arousal. Aside from that his self-control was absolute as he remained immobile beside her.

She reached out and slowly undid the first two buttons on his shirt and spread it open, revealing a mat of hair. With tantalizingly slow movements she stroked through it, her eyes fixed on his, watching sparks dancing in the amber depths.

His banked fires lit flames inside her, beginning

deep within and pulsing throughout her body. She leaned up and rubbed her lips against his, tormenting him with the tip of her tongue as her hands slid into the thick, cool strands of hair at the back of his head.

"Kiss me," she commanded huskily before parting her lips against his, silently enticing him to enter.

He settled his mouth firmly over hers, his tongue flicking sensually inside, teasing the inner softness. She felt him trembling above her and she pulled him down, gripping his head in her hands. Hunger tightened his muscles as he stretched out against her, pressing the length of his body along her soft curves. He said her name softly, his lips moist on hers. He was determined to capture her sweet essence with long heady kisses from the depths of his velvety mouth.

She drew back to keep from drowning, and then resumed kissing the corners of his mouth, tracing the contours of the sensual lips as her hands kneaded his shoulders. She sensed how much he wanted to hold her closer, to run his hands over her. Despite his intense hunger he restrained himself, waiting for her to set the pace. She loved him all the more for this evidence of his sensitive, caring ways.

When she felt the hard proof of his masculinity straining against her, she leaned back. "Undress me, Brad."

He took a deep breath and leaned over her, his eyes glowing. His hands slipped under her skirt and caressed the tender flesh of her thighs. Alive in every cell, Minta watched as his mouth found the contour of a nipple through the thin fabric of her blouse and began to gently caress it with his mouth.

One hand slipped inside her lacy briefs as the other circled her breast. His gentle, seeking, supple fingers stroked her too quickly to a fever pitch of desire until she pushed back, guiding his hands to help her strip off her clothes.

When the last garment fell on the floor, he settled back against her, this time circling the soft bare skin of a breast with his tongue as his fingers returned to the downy triangle between her thighs. He knelt over her for a long time, stroking her, seemingly as much for his own pleasure as hers, refusing to stop even when her first gasps subsided. She gazed in wonder as he brought her over and over again to inarticulate heights of desire.

She reached for him, removing his shirt, unfastening the button on his shorts with fumbling fingers. "Now, Brad."

He leaned back, smiling down at her. "Don't hurry my pleasure, little Zuni maiden. Time is standing still for us."

Leaning down, he lifted her hips and slowly circled her stomach with kisses, his tongue seeking out all her pleasure points until she cried out in ecstasy once more, too dazed to notice when he had removed his last garment until he leaned over her in all his masculine splendor.

She reached out, touching him with loving motions. "Teach me how to love you, Brad."

"You know how," he whispered hoarsely. "My God, you know how, Minta."

His lips found hers and he kissed her hungrily as she lovingly traced the swelling ridges of muscles on his back. As he settled against her, his mouth moved down, roaming over her breasts, gently kissing and caressing as his hands ran lightly down her body, molding her closer and closer into his contours until he entered her, sliding into her welcoming moistness and expanding with each gliding stroke.

She joined in, matching his rhythms, watching his fierce concentration until the last of his restraint broke and he cried out. Release shuddered through him in a series of gasping waves that inflamed her into a matching ecstasy. For a long moment her soul glided outside her body, and then she settled down into his arms, whole once more, slowly regaining her senses as he sighed in contentment.

He lay still beside her as little by little Minta began to feel the results of his lovemaking. Completely reborn, burst free from her old self, she was aware of everywhere Brad had been. He had made her more alive, happier to be a woman than she'd ever dreamed possible. This love was so much more than she'd ever known.

He moved beside her and leaned on an elbow. "Did I say hello to you yet?"

She stretched lazily. "Your body language communicates well."

He bent over and gave her a kiss. "Stay here. I've got a surprise for you."

"I love surprises." Minta sank back onto the pillow and watched as Brad went into the bathroom. Still basking in the afterglow of their lovemaking, she watched when he emerged dressed a short time later.

"Wait there. I'll be right back," he said.

She swung her feet off the bed when he left and went into the bathroom. As she was dressing, she was reminded of the break-in in his side of the cottage. Damn, why hadn't she mentioned it the moment she saw him? Smiling silently, she remembered he had literally swept her off her feet without giving her a chance to say much of anything.

Still pulling the brush through her hair she ran out on the porch just as Brad's head emerged from the rear of his car. He was holding a large box. "Courtesy of McMillan's," he announced, grinning. "You're invited to my potlatch."

"Your what?"

"Don't tell me I know something about Indians you don't," he said triumphantly. "A potlatch is the name for the famous feasts given by my branch of American Indians."

"Oh, I remember about them." Her mind was busily trying to find a way to mention what had happened while he was gone. "Brad..." she added hesitantly.

He seemed unaware of her attempt as he walked toward the porch. "I bet you've hardly been eating since I left you." With one hand he dug into the box and held out a bunch of violets. "Flowers for a lovely lady."

Her voice softened as she murmured his name again. She accepted the flowers and leaned up to kiss him. Afterward she buried her nose into the delicate black centers of the flowers and followed after him into the cottage.

"By the way, how's Hilda?" Brad asked.

"She's in the closet...." Her voice died down to little more than a whisper.

Brad whirled around as they reached the kitchen. "What's wrong, Minta?"

"Someone broke into your side of the duplex while we were both on Cayman Brac, Brad."

He was watching her intently. "Who did it?"

"No one knows. Richard thinks it was college kids on spring break. Bobby Hall thinks some prior guest may have hidden something and come back for it."

Brad shoved the box onto the counter, forgotten. "Let's go see what they did."

"Everything's been cleaned up now. Richard even had the walls painted and most of the furniture replaced. When the cleaning woman found the place in such a mess, she almost went into shock."

His expression was serious. "That bad?"

"Unbelievable. They ripped out the light covers, emptied out the food cartons in the kitchen. Bobby brought by a set of the pictures he took. Let me get them for you."

Brad followed her back to the living room. She took the pictures from an end table drawer and handed them to him silently, watching his eyes as they narrowed. During her college training she had worked an apprenticeship with the robbery division in the Albuquerque police. Many times, she'd witnessed victims of crimes as they viewed the destruction of their homes or businesses for the first time.

The reactions were usually predictable. First disbelief, then outrage that something evil could invade their life so suddenly, without any warning. Last would come fear, the victims worrying that if this had happened once, how could they ever feel secure again? It took weeks, even months before they settled into a more comfortable routine but the scars were permanent, making the criminal guilty of far more damage than the cost of the items stolen.

Brad's expression reflected none of those emotions. Instead his usually coppery skin turned deep red and his fingers curled tightly around the photos. Revenge, Minta realized, surprised at how clearly she was able to identify his emotions. Brad was planning his revenge. A thought flashed through her mind: *He knows who is responsible for this.*

She waited quietly beside him until he finished studying each picture. Then he turned to her, ''Were you the first one in the cottage after it happened?''

''No, the cleaning woman I mentioned was. I noticed your door wasn't closed all the way when I arrived home. Just as I started to investigate my phone started ringing. While I was answering it she arrived and the next thing I knew she was shouting for me to come and see it.''

''I'm sorry you had to be involved, Minta.'' He laid the pictures down. ''I suppose I'm going to need to get some new clothes.'' His voice was unemotional.

''I salvaged yours. Richard paid to have them

cleaned, and they're back in your closet. How about your papers, Brad?''

He glanced at her sharply. ''What papers?''

She gave him an irritated glance. ''The ones you didn't want me to see in the airport. I couldn't find any papers at all in your cottage.''

He hesitated, measuring her up for a minute. ''The specs for Hugo, you mean. They're safe aboard Ted's ship.'' He ran his hand through his hair, still studying her. ''What's bothering you about this break-in, Minta?''

She eyed him levelly. ''Bobby says this wasn't a routine robbery. The criminals were searching for something specific. They were professionals.''

''And...'' he probed, his eyes searching hers.

''Do you have something to hide, Brad?''

He laughed without humor. ''Doesn't everyone?''

She flushed slightly. ''We're talking about you.''

''I've told you a lot of people would like to learn what I'm doing.''

''And they thought they could find what they needed inside your toothpaste tube?''

He flung out an arm angrily. ''Hell, Minta, why don't you come out and say what's on your mind?''

She remained facing him. ''I haven't accused you of anything, but I'll admit this bothers me. Are you involved in something you shouldn't be, Brad?''

He flinched as though she'd struck him. ''If you have to ask, then I think I'm in the wrong house. Right now I'd like to believe you felt you could trust me.''

Minta was caught off guard by the intensity of his anger. She tried to speak but she couldn't. He strode from the cottage and closed the door behind him with unnecessary force. Still paralyzed, she listened as his front door opened and slammed shut.

When Brad reached his living room, he leaned his head against the wall, clenching his hands at his side. The fierce pounding inside his head blocked out every other sound. He was sickened with rage over this latest assault from The Trio.

They hadn't kept to their part of the deal. Now they were after the tape, and he knew they'd stop at nothing to get it.

He couldn't believe the way he'd blown up at Minta when she'd questioned his involvement. It was just that he had needed her trust, needed desperately to think someone believed in him.

He had to tell her the truth. Had to let her know that he was involved in a deadly game with people she could never understand. For reasons no one but he, himself, could ever fathom. If she couldn't handle that, he'd have to accept it.

He sank down on the sofa, dropping his head into his hands. *Why not be honest with yourself, McMillan,* he told himself. *She's not going to believe you. You're in this mess alone. She can't be expected to see your side. You've been down this road before. Even the best of friends don't stand behind you when all the evidence seems to be against you.*

He was certain now that what he felt for Minta was love. But that didn't mean she felt the same for him.

If she was still wrestling with her feelings for him, it wasn't fair to expect her to trust him without reservation.

He frowned, trying to remember exactly what she'd said. How much had she guessed?

She was puzzled. Wondering why the persons searching his cottage had been looking for something so small. But that was a normal thought for anyone to have. What was a problem was that he had already lied to her once. He had denied he'd had late-night visitors and then been forced to tell her the truth. Damn! No wonder she was suspicious. Blowing up at her hadn't helped either. *She was only asking questions and you fell apart, you fool,* he told himself angrily.

But there was still a chance. *Why not go back and apologize? She cares for you, McMillan. She'll forgive you. And one more evening together. What can it matter now? If you're being watched, they've seen you carrying her into her cottage, so they know that she's important to you.*

He sat up, remembering that The Trio had failed to get what they were after. They'd be more cautious now. Watching his next move to see if he connected what had happened to his cottage with them.

As he continued to think, he began convincing himself that he owed it to Minta to be with her. She wasn't about to leave until her vacation was over. It was his responsibility now to make certain that The Trio didn't use her any more to get to him.

He stood, his mind clear and ready for action

again. Now that he'd thought it through the solution seemed so simple. And so perfect. His job was to protect Minta until she left this island or his mission was completed, whichever came first.

As he stood he ignored the voice that reminded him that the man who fools himself is the biggest fool of all.

MINTA REMAINED STANDING in the middle of the living room for several minutes after Brad left. How could things have gone so wrong? Only minutes earlier they'd been in each other's arms. Brad's anger had stunned her, and she frantically searched her mind for a plausible explanation.

Perhaps she had sounded too clinical, too detached, she decided. What would the person who had no experience in law enforcement do if someone they cared for had been a victim?

Suddenly she knew the answer. Normally people would commiserate, offer their sympathy, show anger at the criminals. Instead, she'd done the opposite. Instead of offering her sympathy, she had practically accused Brad of being responsible for the crime. Oh God, no wonder he'd been angry. She'd have to apologize.

She started toward the door and then stopped. There was only silence from the other side of the duplex. A silence that was more worrisome than his outburst of anger only minutes earlier.

Not certain she could handle it if he was still angry with her, she decided to give him more time to cool off. She remembered the box he'd left in her kitchen. A perfect reason to see him again, she decided, and started down the hall to see what it contained.

The box was sealed and the violets lay on top, their dark centers seeming to stare at her accusingly. After all, Brad had cared enough to buy them for her on his way home. She laid them aside carefully, and examined the box more closely. Air freight. From Austin, Texas. Brad must have called and had a delivery made.

Before she could have second thoughts she grabbed a knife and slit the box open. She began to smile as she saw the top layer: Fresh flour tortillas and underneath were cans of refried beans and jalapeño peppers. On the bottom there were crispy nacho chips, carefully wrapped to keep from being crushed.

She set the items on the cabinet and as the stack grew higher, her taste buds began to quiver. There was even Mexican chocolate almond coffee. Now how could Brad have guessed that was exactly the way she loved to finish a New Mexico Indian feast?

Refusing to think about how she'd spoiled his surprise, she started to set the cans back inside the box. She'd have to return it when she apologized. Trying to decide what words to use, she felt a pair of hands slip around her waist. Instinctively she whirled, striking out with a bent elbow as she prepared for her next move.

"Damn," Brad screamed, staggering back and hugging his rib cage. "What are you trying to do? Kill me?"

Minta couldn't stop laughing. "Brad," she sputtered, as much in relief as humor. "I...didn't know it was you."

He steadied himself and gingerly rubbed his ribs. "That's the last time I'll ever try to show you Bella Coolas can sneak up on Zunis. Have you considered having your arms registered as lethal weapons?"

She managed to stop laughing. "I was about to go to your place to apologize."

He took a deep breath. "I'm the one who owes you the apology. I had no right to blow up at you."

"No, it was my fault," Minta insisted. "I was acting as if the victim is the one on trial. Forgive me, Brad."

"You're welcome to ask me any questions you want."

"But there's nothing to ask. Like Bobby said, one of the other guests must have hidden something in the cottage. I could have been the unlucky one as well as you."

The corners of his mouth softened into a smile. "Are you sure this change of heart isn't just because you've been snooping in my potlatch?"

"It might have influenced it," she admitted, grinning. "Where did you find all these luscious things?"

"I had Ron send them on today's flight."

Relieved to have the tension between them cleared up, Minta forced a pretend sigh. "But I can't eat them."

"Don't tell me you think you're getting too fat?"

he said, running his hands down the sides of her body. He stopped at her hips and spread his fingers over them. "Just right. In fact, there's still lots of room for expansion."

She pulled away, laughing. "I'm not dieting, silly. It's just that I remembered what happens when you're invited to share a potlatch and I don't think I can afford it! I already owe you one dinner for all the other times you've bought my meals."

"You mean you're afraid to share my potlatch because that means you're supposed to repay me double for every kind deed I do for you? Let me see how that works. If I give you one kiss," he said, pulling her toward him, kissing her, "then you'll have to give me two kisses in return." He leaned over, kissing her nose, her cheeks, her chin until she dissolved into laughter. "Now, you're my slave. You can never repay me, little Zuni maiden." When he started kissing her again, she twisted away.

"You know you're absolutely. . . ." Minta said.

"Hopeless?"

She nodded, her eyes bright. His voice was unsteady as he said, "Are you accepting my apology for walking out on you that way?"

"Please, Brad. Let's forget it. I think both of us are bewildered by what's been happening since we got to Grand Cayman."

His amber eyes darkened. "Have you had any more threats?"

"Not a peep out of anyone. I think I was right. They just wanted to frighten me. Or maybe they don't know where I'm staying here on Grand Cay.''

"Then how would they have followed you to Cayman Brac?" he pointed out. "No, Minta. I've spent hours thinking about everything that's happened to you, and I don't like it. I'd feel a whole lot better if you'd just leave the island," he said sincerely.

"Oh, Brad. You're making too much of this," tried Minta.

"I am? Who's to say that the accident and the threat aren't somehow connected with the break-in on my side? What does Bobby Hall think?"

"I told you. All Bobby knows for sure is the break-in was a professional job. He's still trying to locate that black car that hit me just in case there is some connection." She stopped, smiling. "But why are we wasting our time talking about this? Let's see about getting this feast on the table."

"I'm for that," agreed Brad replacing his frown with a smile.

They worked on the meal together, each arguing good-naturedly about the best way to prepare the New Mexico delicacies. Minta dipped the rims of two glasses first in stiffened egg white and then in salt for the margaritas. Brad distributed the refried beans, peppers and cheese on the chips before sliding the nachos into the oven to crisp.

Both of them worked on the sopaipillas, with Minta mixing the dough and cutting it out in a thin sheet. Brad cut the squares and fried them until they were a puffy, golden brown, ready and waiting to be drenched with streams of thick yellow honey.

When they sat down to eat, Minta sighed in appreciation. "I get so tired of all my friends dreaming of mama's home cooking. All they know about is macaroni and cheese, rice pudding and frozen waffles. When I get nostalgic, this is what I dream of. How about you, Brad?"

"I grew up on fried salmon, blackberry cobbler and wheels of Tillamook cheese, Minta. I didn't learn how to cook Tex-Mex...."

She interrupted, outraged. "Tex-Mex! Don't insult my native state's cooking! This is pure New Mexico Spanish-Indian cuisine. Just because Texas is so big doesn't give it the right to steal our delicacies and call them theirs."

He bit into an enchilada, smiling indulgently over her outburst. "Mmm, you're right. This is much better than anything I've had in Austin."

Minta was mollified slightly. "I guess I better admit I've never heard of Tillamook cheese, Brad."

CHAPTER FOURTEEN

As Minta dried the last plate and replaced it in the cabinet, she said, "Aren't you ignoring your favorite woman, Brad?"

"She's right beside me."

"I'm glad Hilda can't hear you."

He leaned against the counter, smiling. "You're right. She might go berserk. Let's get her out."

Minta reached for the violets. "As soon as I spread these out in a bowl. I want every little face to be visible."

Brad left and Minta followed a few minutes later. When she reached the bedroom, she saw Brad kneeling down, removing a cassette from inside the robot and slipping it into his pocket.

"Are you stealing her brains?" Minta asked.

The muscles in his shoulders tensed. "Not really."

His nerves are on edge, Minta noted. *He must be the type that holds everything inside.* Feeling a surge of tenderness she flopped down on the floor, sitting cross-legged beside him. "Teach me to work Hilda, Brad."

He appeared pleased by her request. "First, you

have to know the code for activating her." He punched several buttons in sequence, explaining their significance as lights flashed on. "Hello, Hilda," Brad said.

"Welcome, Brad. Elapsed time since last contact: Six days, five hours, thirty minutes, fifteen seconds," the robot answered in her strange monotone.

Minta's eyes widened in surprise. "It's hard to believe what I'm hearing. How did you program her to do all this, Brad?"

"This is the showmanship part, Minta. When I was in college Hilda and I hired out at trade shows to earn money. In the early days, it was mostly bluff. She was remote-controlled with a mike hidden inside her. But gradually, I began programming her and refining her as I learned more about computers. I'm more interested in practical applications than in the razzle-dazzle stuff now. Personal robots still have a long way to go before most people can own one who does all Hilda can."

He turned to the robot. "Minta wants to be your friend, Hilda."

"Friend," Hilda repeated. "Companion. Sidekick. Chum. Crony. Confidant. Soul mate. Acknowledge if all available words for friend in French, Spanish, German, Japanese or Swahili are requested."

"Negative," Brad answered.

"I think she's avoiding having to relate to me," Minta said with a smile. "Let's see if I can break through that barrier. Hilda, what does Brad do each morning?''

The computer chips whirred faintly. ''Morning schedule. Bradley McMillan. Wake-up call. Seven o'clock. No movement. Second wake-up call. Seven thirty. Bring coffee to bed. Shake sleeping figure. Place cup firmly in hand. Further details available upon request.''

''She's incredible, Brad,'' Minta said, choking with laughter.

''Incredible,'' Hilda repeated. ''Extraordinary. Superhuman. Fantastic. Fabulous. Awe inspiring.''

Brad raised his voice in exasperation. ''Quit showing off for Minta.''

''Voice level not acceptable,'' Hilda answered. Minta could have sworn she detected a trace of humor in the robot's voice. She could imagine how popular the team of Brad and Hilda must have been entertaining visitors at trade shows.

''Smart mouth,'' Brad remarked to Hilda. ''Want to see her go through some paces, Minta?''

''I'd love to.''

''Walk three feet. Turn around two times. Return to place of origin, Hilda.''

The robot obeyed instantly. Minta clapped.

''Thank you,'' Hilda said.

Brad grinned. ''She's beginning to like you.''

''What else can she do?''

''In her home environment she's capable of a number of actions. You'll have to wait until you come to Austin to see most of them.'' He pushed several buttons and a small green screen appeared at the same time as a keyboard slid out from her tummy. "Watch while I show you how to bring up a menu." He demonstrated the correct keys to strike. "Feel free to learn how to operate her. She's programmed for some voice-controlled games you might get a kick out of playing."

He pointed to the words on the screen. "Type in the number of the operation you want and all the instructions will appear on the screen."

Minta peered around his shoulder, reading, "'Language Subroutines, Relational Expressions, Memory Maps, Sequential Files....'" She paused, then added, "Is this the Swahili she mentioned earlier?"

Brad chuckled. "No, it's self-explanatory when you bring up the menu."

"If you're familiar with the restaurant," Minta said dryly. "Hey, here's one I can read. Alarm Systems."

"That's Hilda's favorite job. She loves playing female supercop." He brought up the alarm system sequence on the screen and ran through the procedure, explaining, "In this mode her heat and light sensors are active. If anyone comes inside her range she'll challenge them for their ID. If she doesn't recognize the intruder, she starts running around shouting, 'Exit immediately. Deadly rays. Deadly rays.' A friend of mine almost had a heart attack one day when I forgot to inform Hilda I'd given him the use of my home."

"What's the identification signal?"

"Everyone has a different one. I'll program her to recognize your name, so you'll never get the scare treatment out of her."

"Could anyone else use my name?"

"No, she recognizes voice patterns of individuals."

Minta leaned back. "I'm impressed, McMillan."

He tugged on several strands of her hair, "What do you think I've been trying to do, Cordero?"

Later that evening as they sat on one of the porch swings with their arms around each other, Brad's voice grew serious. "Let's leave Hilda in your side of the cottage with her alarm system on."

"Are you worried about Hilda's safety or mine?" said Minta.

"You'll never know," said Brad with a grin.

"Well, I doubt if your intruder will come back and they've had all the opportunity they need to frighten me while you were gone. Anyway, Bobby's half convinced they got what they were after."

Brad did not look directly at her as he asked, "What does Bobby think they were looking for?"

"Drugs. Diamonds. Small gold ingots. Anything small and valuable. I guess the Caribbean islands are teeming with contraband." Aware of his strength and the warmth of his body beside hers, she moved closer inside the circle of his arm. She didn't want a rehash of the mysterious happenings they'd both encountered. Not tonight. Not when she had something much more intriguing on her mind.

Brad's voice interrupted her thoughts. "Let's put Hilda to bed shall we? And then I'll see about putting you to bed."

"Your place or mine?" teased Minta.

"Mine," said Brad. "Very definitely mine."

IN THE EARLY-MORNING HOURS, just before dawn, the rustling of sheets as their bodies moved against them mingled with their soft murmurs of pleasure. Minta had lain in Brad's arms all night, her head in the hollow of his shoulder, her arm thrown across his coppery chest. Unwilling to fall asleep at first, she had lain awake, storing up memories of their lovemaking for the days that lay ahead when they would be parted.

A persistent thought had kept nagging at the back of her mind. The thought was that they needed to speak of commitment. Only a tentative commitment, one in its earliest stages, she told herself.

What they had was so fragile, so precious. When they parted she feared they would be blown apart like fragments, each hurled into his or her own world, as if they'd never met. This thought made her feel strangely insecure, and she had finally moved closer to him until she'd fallen into a restless sleep at last.

She had awakened gradually to the stroke of Brad's hands. "Brad," she whispered.

"Shh, darling. I didn't mean to wake you," he answered.

She traced the outline of his mouth with her

fingers and then kissed him, feeling the tremor that went through him when her lips touched his.

She kissed him slowly, thoroughly, until he reached for her, covering her, entering her willing body and bringing her to joyful spasms that matched his own. Then he lay back, his hands gently soothing her, bringing her back down from the heights they'd ascended together.

She loved this time of intimacy, these moments after making love when the differences between them melted away. He whispered his love for her, and she knew the time was right to tell him she felt the same. Brushing back his hair, she moved her mouth against his ear, wanting to be sure he heard every word when she spoke her love. Her lips nuzzled against his skin as she prepared to bare her soul to him. . . .

A shrill sound pierced the air, followed by clanging and clattering noises. Minta bolted upright as something metallic crashed against a wall next door. "Identify. Identify. Last warning to identify," she heard.

Brad slid off the bed in one fluid motion, fumbling for his clothes. "Hilda," he muttered hoarsely.

Minta rose to her feet, trying to decide whether to flip on a light and deciding against it. Best not alert the intruder. She groped around, making contact with the back of a chair. Locating a pair of briefs, she struggled into them in the dark.

Hilda's shrill cries changed. "Exit. Last chance to leave immediately. Deadly rays. Deadly rays."

"You take the front. I'll take the rear," Minta said as she pulled her dress over her head, her mind busy working out the best plan of action.

"Like hell," Brad snapped. "You're staying here this time."

In the dark Minta could see Brad leaving and she ran behind him, watching to make certain he was going toward the front before she moved to the rear entrance. She unlocked the back door and opened it soundlessly as Hilda's cries sputtered to a halt. Wondering if that meant the intruder had discovered a way to render her harmless, Minta slipped on to the veranda, her back sliding against the wall.

The back door of the cottage was open and she knew, without even checking, that the intruder had fled. Running to the side of the veranda, she glanced toward the beach but couldn't see anyone. Whoever it was had known enough not to risk being seen in the moonlight.

The screen door swung open and Brad stepped outside. "Gone," Minta said. She noticed Brad had turned lights on inside her cottage.

"Did you see anyone?"

"No, but the back door was still swinging when I got here. Is Hilda okay?"

"A little shook up. Her sensors had difficulty determining the boundaries so she bumped into the walls. She needs to be programmed for the rooms she's patrolling."

Minta tried to suppress her nervous laughter. "Hilda must have scared our burglar half to death."

Brad crossed over to her and put his arm around her. "Let's go inside and see if anything was taken."

After making a thorough search, Minta informed Brad nothing was missing. Brad had the front of the robot open. Once again, she noticed that he was retrieving the cassette and slipping it into his pocket. "What's that?" she asked.

"A tape. Hopefully, Hilda recorded some clues. I'll have to listen to it."

His explanation left Minta as much in the dark as before but she decided against probing. Now hardly seemed the time for Brad to stop and give her a lesson about how Hilda's computer brain worked. "What do you think is happening, Brad?"

His face was grim, his jaw covered with a fine, reddish stubble. "I'm stumped, Minta."

"Another warning for me to get off the island," Minta said faintly.

"And another connection between my so-called friends and yours?"

"But what connection? It all seems so senseless. You come here to the Caymans to run some tests on a robot that your competitors would like to steal. We happen to rent adjoining sides of the same duplex."

"Then you're the victim of a hit-and-run accident," he added slowly. "*If* it was an accident."

"No, that doesn't make sense. When my accident happened, we barely knew each other." She assessed him for a long moment. "I have an idea.

Why don't you introduce me to those late-night visitors of yours and see if I recognize any of them?''

Brad's breathing became shallow. ''They didn't leave me anywhere to contact them. If I hear from them, I'll tell you.'' He put his hand out toward her. ''We're not going to be able to decipher all of this on our own. Why don't we call your police friend and have him check for clues in your cottage?''

His suggestion didn't satisfy her, but she had nothing better to offer. ''How about fixing some coffee while I call?'' she said, with a sigh.

Minta called Bobby and told him about this latest break-in at the cottage. He arrived in a few minutes and fell in love with Hilda the moment Brad demonstrated the way she'd alerted them. Minta was grateful for the way Bobby's expression did not change when he realized she had been spending the night with Brad. If it had been Richard he would have felt compelled to make some off-color remark.

The three of them inspected the sand for footprints and saw that the trail circled around the house and to the road. Bobby decided to make a cast of the print. ''I've got the necessary equipment in my car.''

When Bobby finished they sat on the veranda, enjoying the cool morning breezes as they drank their coffee. Bobby filled them in on the clues he'd uncovered relating to the break-in in Brad's side of the duplex. ''Richard gave me a list of the guests for the last couple of years. We've already learned that several were using assumed names but that's not too unusual on this island. So far, none have anything in their background that makes me suspect they'd have hidden something in the cottage during an earlier visit.''

"And now this entry into my side," said Minta. She glanced at Brad, wishing he'd say something. She thought it was odd that Brad didn't say anything to Bobby about his late-night visitors. After all, they had wanted information about his robot. But Brad sat silently staring out at the beach.

Bobby sat down his cup as he stood. "Time for me to be running along now. I'll keep working on this case, Minta. If you ever get tired of Hilda, I'll adopt her, Brad."

"I'll remember," Brad answered. "And thanks for coming so quickly. We must be the most bothersome guests you've ever dealt with."

"No, the record goes to a woman who reported her dog was kidnapped," answered Bobby. "We looked everywhere until her husband told us she didn't own a dog."

Minta laughed appreciatively, remembering some of the crank calls her agency received. After Bobby drove off, Brad said, "He's a nice guy. I hate to be putting him to so much trouble."

She slipped her arm around his waist. "What are we doing today?"

"How about me fixing our breakfast?"

"Sounds great. Then I've got a surprise to finish

for you. I was working on it when you came back yesterday.''

"Can I watch?"

"You may not! Why don't you go snorkeling? I rented some equipment, and it's hanging in the broom closet. The reefs around here are fabulous.''

"After all that's been happening, I'd rather we stayed together." Brad's tone was somber.

"Silly. I'm not going anywhere. Anyway, Hilda will be here to protect me.''

He stood, laughing softly. "I guess I am over-reacting. If you're sure you don't mind, I would enjoy a little time in the water after breakfast.''

When he had left, Minta called the FBI office. Jill would be in later that day, she was told. She left a message to have her call returned and then brought out her silversmithing tools and settled down once more at the kitchen table.

Within a half hour she finished putting her initials on the back of the tie clasp and had given the graceful shape a last burnishing until it glowed under the light. After slipping it into her purse until she decided the right moment to give it to Brad, she walked down to the beach. Brad was nowhere to be seen.

Feeling restless for some unknown reason, she walked back to the cottage and decided to see if she remembered anything Brad had taught her about Hilda. Within minutes she had the robot activated and obeying some simple voice command. "Come out on the front porch with me," she told the robot.

Hilda rolled through the door as Minta held it open. She stopped obediently in front of the chair when Minta sat down.

"Now, let's see," said Minta, frowning in fierce concentration. She punched several buttons but nothing happened. "Come on, sweetie," she coaxed. "How do I get this menu to come up?"

"Try punching Shift and C10 simultaneously," said the robot.

"Thanks." Minta scanned the menu that appeared on the screen, selecting one labeled Interviewing. As the instructions slowly filled the screen she began laughing. "This is great, Hilda. I can see you and I are going to have fun together."

The words: *Ask Question. Punch M4,* popped onto the screen. Minta debated briefly, but her curiosity overruled her usual respect for another's privacy when she asked, "What does Brad say about Minta?"

"Inappropriate question," Hilda answered in what Minta could have sworn was a censuring tone.

"Why you're just jealous, Hilda."

"Repeat. Inappropriate question. Please reword."

Minta gave up, laughing softly. "Okay, you win. Where does Brad work?"

"Galactia Enterprises, Austin, Texas. The company is privately owned, operating under a state license. It's..."

"Cancel," said Minta. "I want gossip, not facts,

silly. Won't you share any little tidbits of gossip about him with me?''

"Request not comprehended.''

"You, my dear, have been brainwashed,'' said Minta with a grin. She erased the section from the screen and called back the menu, trying to decide if she was in the mood to play a computer game or not.

From the end of the street she heard the sound of a car's engine as it turned the corner. She glanced up, but the glare of sunshine off the hood of Brad's car made her look away, shielding her eyes. Her decision made, she punched in the Games number only to be greeted by more choices. "Chess or Blackjack, Hilda?'' she asked. "Which do you recommend?''

"Check bank balance before proceeding,'' advised the robot.

Minta had leaned back to laugh over the computer's bossy ways, when she saw a car swerving across the sand toward her. She leaped to her feet, screaming at the driver to stop, certain he had lost control of his vehicle. Doors on both sides swung open as the car's brakes screamed. Men began running up the steps.

Too late she realized what was happening and instinctively she crouched over the robot, as if she was protecting a child. A pair of hands pulled Minta back, knocking her to the floor. Two other men wrestled the robot away from her and then the first man dumped the chair she'd been sitting in over her, effectively pinning her to the porch.

Hilda added to the confusion, screaming, "Help.

Help.'' Anyone listening would have sworn it was a child's crying.

The vehicle, filled with the men and robot, veered away almost as quickly as it arrived. Minta pushed the chair off of her, struggled to her feet and ran down the steps toward the road. She caught only a glimpse as the car sped out of sight but it was enough. The black car had struck once again!

Minta ran for the phone and dialed the police station's number as quickly as she could. One ring. Two rings. The feminine dispatcher's voice came on the line.

''Quick! I need Policeman Hall,'' said Minta.

''He's in the patrol car. What's the nature of your emergency, please?''

''A kidnapping.'' Oh God, not another lady with a dog story, she realized as soon as she'd said the words. Would Bobby think she was playing a practical joke?

''Hold on,'' came the excited voice of the dispatcher. ''I'll radio Officer Hall immediately.''

Minta was desperately wishing Brad would return as the dispatcher contacted Bobby. The woman came back on the line. ''Describe the victim and location of the kidnapping.''

''Location: Surfside Beach Cottage #10. Witnessed by Minta Cordero.''

''And the victim?''

Minta searched her mind wildly. ''Hilda. Hilda McMillan. Officer Hall was introduced to the victim this morning.''

Bobby's voice came through the receiver when the message was radioed to him. "That robot! Ask Minta if she has any idea of the kidnappers' identities."

Minta came on the line quickly. "Yes, it's the black car we've discussed previously. Tell Officer Hall to check the estate's entrance without delay."

The dispatcher sounded confused when she came back on the line. "Officer Hall reports he is on his way to the estate. Stay where you are, and he'll contact you shortly."

"Thanks. I'll be here."

As soon as she replaced the receiver she ran outside and started toward the beach. Brad was emerging from the water, holding his mask in one hand as he removed the flippers from his feet. She shouted his name and he looked up. The moment he saw her face he started running. "What's wrong, darling?"

"Hilda. She's been kidnapped." Minta buried her face against Brad's chest when she reached him.

He stared down at her. "Maybe I didn't hear you right, Minta."

She explained what had happened quickly. "Damn, I can't believe it," he answered.

"I'm so sorry, Brad. I know what she means to you."

"I'm not worrying about Hilda," he said. "I'm furious I left you alone this morning. Do you realize you could have been the one kidnapped?"

"But it's all my fault. If I'd used my head I wouldn't have taken her out on the front porch. Can you ever forgive me?"

"Hilda's not gone, Minta. Only her outer shell is. I can reproduce her brain. They didn't get what they were after."

She leaned back to get a better look at him. "Then you think you know who kidnapped her?"

"I can make a good guess. It's those late-night visitors I told you about. Now they've definitely made the connection between you and me."

"I can't even think about that now. Hilda was crying for help, Brad. She expected me to rescue her and I was helpless. Can you imagine how I felt when she screamed?"

He was smiling indulgently at her and she felt a wave of embarrassment sweep over her. With an attempt to calm down, she added, "I called Bobby and he's checking on it."

Bobby arrived shortly afterward and reported no activity around the estate. "I may have been too late but I don't think so. The sand leading toward the location where I think there's a gate wasn't disturbed. My guess is that the kidnappers are heading to the docks. I've issued a bulletin...."

"Please drop it," said Brad tersely. "I've already caused the Caymans enough trouble."

"But it's my job," returned Bobby.

Brad was adamant. "No, I mean it. This case is closed."

Bobby shrugged uncomfortably. "It's your robot."

Minta couldn't believe her ears. There was a long awkward silence while each of them considered the implications of Brad's directive. Finally Minta broke the silence. "Thanks for coming," she said looking at Bobby but not at Brad. She had never expected Brad to react so strangely to his beloved Hilda's disappearance. Maybe she only thought she was beginning to know him.

When Bobby left, Minta turned toward Brad. "I don't understand."

"I'm tired of causing the Cayman police force problems. I think I'll cruise the island and see if I can spot any sign of the kidnappers. Want to come along?"

"You know I do, but I still don't understand," she said. When she received no answer she added, "let me get my purse."

They circled the island several times and gradually Minta began to see why Brad had been reluctant to ask for more help. It was true that between the two of them they had caused a constant stream of police reports. Like the little boy who called wolf too many times until a real wolf appeared and no one believed him, perhaps Brad was afraid that Bobby might get the wrong impression.

"No sign of Hilda," Brad said at last. "Maybe we should stop for lunch before we return to the cottage."

"I'm not too hungry," Minta said.

"But you need to eat." He turned in at the seafood restaurant where they'd eaten once before.

When Minta only stared at the menu morosely, Brad ordered the Caesar salad for two. As the chef prepared it on a cart in front of them, Brad tipped up her chin with one finger. "Cheer up, Minta. It's not the end of the world."

"But I feel so guilty for taking her out on the porch."

"I told you I'll make another Hilda."

"Do you discard all your women so easily?" she asked.

A slow smile crept all the way up from his mouth to his eyes. "Only ones with a spare brain."

She returned his smile. "Then I'm safe."

When they returned to the cottage, they saw Bobby's car sitting in front. He was walking down the front steps. "There you two are. I've got great news. Some boys called the station to report they found a strange contraption down on the beach."

Brad's eyes lit up and Minta realized how much it must have cost him to pretend it hadn't mattered when it really had. "Where?" he asked.

"Hop in and I'll run you down there," Bobby said.

"If you're sure we're not keeping you from anything more important," Brad began.

"And miss the conclusion of our first legitimate kidnapping?" Bobby said, grinning.

He drove quickly down the main road, heading north into a secluded area until he turned on to a side road.

"What's around here?" Brad asked.

"One of the natural harbors. My guess is that someone was waiting for the kidnappers in a boat.

Then it would be only a short run out to a yacht,'' Bobby answered.

"The *Omen*,'' Minta said, reminding Bobby of the vessel the waiter on Cayman Brac had named. "Could you question Charlie? He's the waiter who is supposed to have seen the yacht?''

"Good idea,'' Bobby said. "I'll call over this afternoon and see if he's still on Grand Cay or back at work.'' He glanced over at Brad, adding, "That is, if you don't object.''

Brad shrugged lightly. "What can I say at this point?''

Several dark-skinned children were standing at the edge of the road and they pointed excitedly when they saw the police car. Bobby swung off the road and stopped. "Are you the boys who called the police?'' he asked.

The children nodded and led the way to the shore's edge where they pulled back a tangle of bushes. Hilda lay sprawled in the dirt, wires hanging out of her, her lights missing, her surface filthy. "We found this. Tim was the one who called the police,'' said one boy of about ten.

"Good for you, boys,'' Brad said, reaching in his pocket. "How many found her?''

"Four. We're all here,'' the one designated as Tim answered. "Can we keep this robot? It's all messed up.''

Brad shook his head, placing several crisp bills in each child's hand. "You'll have to build your own robot. This ought to be enough to get you started with a mail-order kit, if you're interested."

"Thanks, mister," they chorused.

Brad picked up Hilda and brushed her off. "Just as I thought. They've stripped out her insides but it won't do them any good. Unless you know the exact way she's put together, the individual parts are useless."

"Why do you think they wanted her?" Minta asked.

Brad waited a moment before saying, "Beats me. Maybe someone else is interested in building a personal robot. Stealing Hilda would give them a good start."

"Could it have been one of those men you told me about?" Minta asked quickly.

"Who?" Brad replied, obviously preoccupied. Before she could explain, he added, "I don't think this calls for an investigation. Let's drop it, shall we?"

Bobby was staring intently at Brad as he talked but he said nothing. Minta could tell he was as puzzled by the whole thing as she was. She hesitated, wanting to probe further, but the grim look on Brad's face stopped her. It wasn't her job to find out what was going on. She couldn't interfere.

CHAPTER FIFTEEN

MINTA WAS ALMOST ASLEEP that night when she remembered she hadn't been home for Jill's call. By the time she and Brad had gone to the police station and filled out a report on the theft, it had been after five in Washington, D.C.

She tried to stay awake to decide when she was going to tell Brad about her job with the FBI. Her decision to wait until she'd heard from Jill was becoming ridiculous. Each day she put it off, Brad would have more reason to wonder why she had felt it necessary to conceal from him.

Tomorrow, she told herself before snuggling against Brad's sleeping form. Tomorrow she'd make one last try to reach Jill.

Even if she didn't, she would tell Brad every little detail about her work. She knew, deep inside where it counted, that he'd accept it the way no other man ever had.

The next morning they woke late and then took a leisurely shower together that led to lovemaking. Afterward Brad helped scrub her back. She was rinsing off the suds under the shower's spray when the phone rang.

"I'll get it," Brad volunteered.

"No, I will," Minta insisted.

"Afraid your grandfather will wonder who's sharing your beach cottage?" Brad teased.

"You bet." She wrapped a towel around herself tightly and ran for the phone, afraid the caller would hang up if she didn't hurry. "Hello," she answered, breathless.

"Minta. This is Jill. Sorry I've been gone. I've had this information for days, but we couldn't seem to connect."

Minta glanced nervously toward the bathroom. She wished she'd never asked Jill to check on Brad now. "I shouldn't have bothered you, anyway," she said quickly.

"Bother? It sounds like you'll soon be part of our department, so I'll be doing work like this for you all the time."

Minta stared at the phone as if she hadn't heard her friend correctly. "What are you talking about, Jill?"

"You. On the Cayman case. You could have given me a hint."

"Jill! Start at the beginning and tell me what's going on."

"The Bradley McMillan file you asked about. I called it up, and I couldn't believe all the red flags on it. I guess this is one of the biggest cases we've had going since I came to work here."

Minta froze. "I need a complete update, Jill."

"Jerry will have to give you the supersensitive material when he arrives tomorrow."

Minta's pulses were thundering in her ears. Trying to sound casual, she said, "Let me get a pen and write down the hotel he's staying in."

"Don't bother with a pen. The Holiday Inn was the only one with any vacancies. I've reserved room 301 for him."

Minta made an enormous effort to sound calm. She glanced toward the bathroom and was reassured by the sound of the water still running in the shower. "Tell me all you can about that file."

"Bradley McMillan's company, Galactia Enterprises of Austin, Texas, is involved in bidding on the navy's latest superweapon. It's some kind of underwater robot that can destroy enemy subs with laser beams." Jill stopped. "Now here's where we come in. Bradley McMillan is suspected of leaking the top secret specs to counteragents. Can you believe an American would be a traitor to his own country?"

Minta sucked in her breath. "Jill!"

"I know. I shouldn't get personal but it does disgust me. Anyway, the files indicated that evidently Mr. McMillan was brought before a naval board of inquiry when he was on active duty as a SEAL in Vietnam. Almost everyone in his unit was destroyed under strange circumstances."

The implications became unbearable and Minta felt herself growing cold. "I'm sorry, Jill. I don't see what that has to do with what's happening now."

"Well, the bottom line is he was suspected of doing the same thing back then. The only difference is that this time he's leaking specs and last time it was top-secret maneuvers information. He maintained he was innocent, but he resigned his commission a short time later. The board never could find enough evidence to press charges against McMillan, but he's been under active surveillance ever since."

"For a bunch of innuendos that couldn't be proven?" Minta defended instinctively.

"His work is extremely important to enemies of this country, Minta," Jill explained patiently.

"Nothing else suspicious has ever occurred in the intervening years?" Minta was trying desperately to find some reason to refute what she was hearing.

"Nothing in the record until lately. He was spotted in the company of known counteragents in Austin several weeks ago. Jerry is furious because our Austin bureau lost track of him. Then his company manager reported him missing. Later this same manager claimed he found a note from McMillan, but he insists McMillan can't be reached by anyone."

The missing pieces of the puzzle were thudding into place, destroying Minta's last hopes as Jill continued. "A CIA operative reported McMillan was seen in the Caymans the other day, so Jerry left here. He's scheduled to arrive in Grand Cayman this afternoon. But I'm sure you know most of this, Minta."

"Some." But she hadn't allowed herself to believe it.

"I can't believe Al actually agreed to a transfer or did Jerry pull rank on him?"

"I'm still with Al," Minta said quietly.

"Oh, is this Cayman case just a temporary assignment?" Jill persisted.

"What's going on here is definitely temporary. Look, I need to get off this line. When I see you, I'll tell you everything."

"I hope so. Tell Jerry everything's under control around here when you see him."

Minta answered weakly. "Will do." She glanced up and saw Brad standing in the doorway studying her. Her heartbeat became erratic as a chill swept over her.

"Brad," she mumbled unnecessarily as her gaze locked onto his.

"You'll have to speak up," Jill said. "This line must be having trouble."

"I have to run now," Minta answered quickly. "We'll talk later."

She replaced the receiver carefully her thoughts chaotic. For a moment all she could think of was catching the first plane out of the Caymans. She'd stumbled into a nightmare, and she knew only that she needed to escape before it was too late.

Would Brad allow her to leave? The idea that she'd even think of such a thing stunned her. But if he had heard enough to guess the truth about her career, he might try to forcibly prevent her from leaving the island.

Brad didn't move. They kept on staring at each

other, the lengthening silence becoming tenser by the moment. Not certain what to do next, she waited, watching the expression on his face. She was utterly confused by what she saw.

He spoke first, his voice rough. "I didn't intentionally eavesdrop, Minta."

She groped for words, deciding at length to say as little as possible. "It doesn't matter, Brad."

His body tensed and his eyes glowed with a sudden anger. "Doesn't matter? God, you're cold."

When she didn't speak, he continued, "I knew this was all too good to be true. I knew I must be dreaming to think a woman like you appeared in my life with no attachments. I recognize I have no right to pry into your past. But temporary, Minta? Is that all I am to you? A temporary affair you'll explain away when you get home?"

Her velvety dark eyes widened in astonishment. She tried frantically to recall what she'd said to Jill that might have made him think she'd been talking about her relationship with him. Then she remembered having said something about still being with Al, about all this being only temporary....

"Brad, I'm not sure what you're thinking. Did you think I was talking about us to my friend, Jill?"

He gave his shoulders an angry shrug. "Don't try fooling me any longer. It's better for me to find out the whole truth at once instead of being let down in easy stages."

Her mind was working frantically. What to tell

him? What cover story could give her the time she needed to escape? "You're all wrong, Brad." Her voice broke with emotion.

Clasping the towel around her tighter with one hand, she added, "I just got some bad news about... my business."

He was clearly skeptical. "What news?"

She improvised rapidly. "It was about Al. He's one of my salesmen for the jewelry line. It seems he's flubbed a deal. Jill, my assistant, thinks I ought to fire him, but I like to stick with my employees."

There was a long thoughtful pause before Brad offered her a tentative smile. "I feel a little foolish for jumping to the conclusion you were talking about me. I'm sorry about this, Minta. Is there anything I can do to help? I have a friend in Austin who owns several jewelry stores. Maybe I can give him a call about your line."

Minta was confused for a moment. Brad seemed so utterly sincere. Then she forced herself to remember what Jill had told her. "No, thanks, Brad. I'll work this out. Right now I need some time alone. I've got to think about Jill's news, and when I'm with you I can't think straight."

She brushed past him to go to the bedroom and felt his eyes staring at her back. After a few seconds' delay he followed. "Maybe talking about it would help. I've been involved in the business world a long time."

Her voice came out angrily, "I don't want your help."

He took a step back as if bewildered. As she pulled out a pair of lemon slacks and a white blouse, she tried frantically to think of a way to ease the tension between them. Letting him see she was angry was the worst route she could take. When she finished dressing she turned toward him. "Brad, I'm sorry I'm such poor company right now. I think I'll bike into George Town and have breakfast at the bakery on the main street."

Brad continued to watch her, silently, as she braided her hair. Picking up her mascara, she began to brush it on her eyelashes with careful strokes. In the mirror she caught a reflection of Brad's eyes. They were not happy. She turned and smiled at him, hating herself for having to pretend. "Are you mad at me?"

"I'm baffled, Minta. I think something is bothering you more than you're letting on."

She lowered her eyes. "You're right, Brad. Losing that contract is a catastrophe. But I'll handle it. Once I figure out a solution, I'll be fit company again."

"At least let me drive you to the bakery," Brad said.

But she was busy trying to think of some logical explanation that would absolve Brad of treason. He could never be involved in such a thing. Not the Brad she had come to love. "I need the exercise," she said without much conviction.

"After all that's been happening around here, I'd rather stay close to you, Minta. Things may not be too safe."

She brushed past him, forcing herself to lean up and give him a quick kiss on the cheek. She swayed momentarily, his nearness reminding her of moments best forgotten. "I'm a big girl, Brad. I can take care of myself."

He smiled. "How long will you be gone?"

"Until I think of some answers to my business problems."

He followed her out onto the back veranda and watched as she unlocked her bicycle and carried it down the steps. "Take care, Minta. I wouldn't want anything to happen to you."

She faltered for a moment, a huge lump forming in her throat. "Dammit," she said to herself when she was out of his range. It was taking all her resolve not to turn around and run back to Brad.

The sand was soft and she had to push the bike around the side of the cottage until she reached the marl road in front. She climbed on and began pedaling, not allowing herself to look back even though she knew Brad had followed her around and was watching her.

Waves of depression alternated with anger as she went over the events of the last ten days. First had come her confrontation with Al during which her career had been threatened. She had arrived here on Grand Cayman confused and perhaps vulnerable, she admitted. But ripe for a love affair with the first man she met? The very thought appalled her.

Brad had seemed so different. As if he were the man she'd always been waiting for. He was the complete opposite of Peter Hammond.

Her foot slipped from the pedal and she felt herself veering toward the side of the road as the resemblance between Brad and Peter struck her for the first time. Regaining her balance, she analyzed the resemblance carefully and the conclusions she was forced to reach were painful. Both Brad and Peter were double-crossers. And both had done one hell of a con job on her.

Peter had sold information to the underworld and Brad to enemies of his country. Was there something wrong with her that she was attracted to these kind of men?

She must have radar in her brain. If she were in a room full of men, she would be attracted like a magnet to iron to the one that was a total cheat, the one devoid of conscience, the one who had no regard for the truth. There must be some reason that she should care for men like that.

It hurt much more to learn the truth about Brad, she realized. Even though she had known him such a short time, she loved him much more deeply. With Peter there had been constant friction. They had always settled for a superficial solution of their differences rather than any real coalescence. But with Brad there was total harmony, total loving from the beginning. She'd held nothing back, and now she felt as if he'd robbed her of everything worth living for.

She yearned to talk to someone. To someone she trusted, respected. Someone who cared for her.

Jerry! Jerry would be here on Grand Cay this afternoon. She need only hang on for a few more hours. Then she'd go to the hotel, surprise Jerry and tell him all that she knew.

But why was she feeling like such a traitor to Brad? She knew she couldn't give in to her longing to tell him he was under surveillance and that he needed to escape. No, she'd have to stay away from him to resist the temptation. No matter how much it cost her personally, she had a duty to perform.

Then she remembered the warning she'd received through Elizabeth and her suppressed anger switched to Al Slessor. Damn the man for eroding her confidence. If she'd arrived on this island in her normal state of mind, she would have reported Brad the moment she'd seen that picture of him in the paper. Before she got so deeply involved. Before she had fallen in love.

Lost in her thoughts she was surprised how quickly she arrived in George Town. She glanced around for a pay phone and located one in front of the bakery. After parking her bike she hurried to the phone, before she lost her nerve, and dialed an emergency number known only to field agents.

While the phone was ringing at the FBI head-quarters, she reviewed what she intended saying to her boss. It was time she confronted him, time she let him know she didn't agree with his assessment of her or her performance.

"Al Slessor," she told the switchboard operator. "Tell him it's an emergency."

Al was slightly irritable as he acknowledged Minta. "Get a lot of rest?" he asked.

"Too much. I want you to know that you were wrong, Al," she said without any of her usual pleasantries.

"Oh? In what way?"

"I wasn't having a nervous breakdown as you said. Because I listened to you, I walked right past an important case. There's not much I can do now, but I just wanted you to know that a good agent can never ignore important evidence without regretting it."

"You're not on duty, Minta."

"Maybe not for you, but I am still an undercover agent for the FBI, Al. And I intend to stay on no matter what it takes to prove you're wrong."

"That almost sounds like a threat, Minta." His voice was cold.

"Take it as a friendly warning."

"Is that all you have to say?"

"That and the fact that I'm going to hand over all the evidence I've managed to collect to Jerry when he arrives here."

"I think you're making a mistake, Minta."

"And I think I've already made one." She felt a weight lifting from her shoulders now that she'd made her feelings known. "I won't keep you from your work any longer, Al."

There was a long pause before he added, "We'll talk more about this when you return to work."

"Yes, lots more. I'll make an appointment as soon as I return."

AFTER AL REPLACED THE PHONE he wandered over to the window and stared down at the busy streets of the nation's capital below. The call from Minta couldn't have come at a worse time, as far as he was concerned. Several of his key personnel had just left his office, threatening to resign unless he changed his methods.

Their arguments had made sense to him, and he had lost some of his conviction. He had been so sure that he always knew what was best for those under his command. And now Minta. She had sounded so sure of herself, not at all like the exhausted woman who had sat in his office a short time ago. Although she had been ready for combat, he had still managed to get to her with his arguments that she was mishandling her work.

Since his meeting with the board of inquiry, headed by Jerry Richards, he had been having second thoughts about Minta. Her record was impeccable. Her efficiency ratings all excellent except for the one he had given her. And he knew that Jerry, his predecessor, thought he was wrong about Minta.

It was true that he didn't really think women belonged in the field. But he had kept that view well hidden from his superiors during his years with the agency. And the last two cases he'd handled hadn't gone well, and he knew that he was being closely watched now.

There was only one thing to do, he decided suddenly. Striding over to the phone, he punched Jerry

Richards's extension. When his secretary answered he told her, "Jill, this is Al Slessor. Please contact Richards and tell him Agent Horizon has been authorized to hand over all pertinent evidence on his current case."

MINTA WALKED INTO THE BAKERY when she ended her call to Al. She wondered why she hadn't done this the day after Elizabeth had given her Jerry's warning. Even though she had always believed in following orders to the best of one's ability she realized that her position as an agent demanded that she exercise her own judgment to a much higher degree than most positions. From now on she would do just that. If she made mistakes, she'd have to live with them, but at least they'd be her own mistakes.

She was willing to recognize her weaknesses. Perhaps she was too dependent upon the excitement of life as an undercover agent. The time might come when she would need to consider moving more toward the administrative side of her work. But she'd do so according to her own schedule and not because someone had told her she was doing her job too thoroughly.

She ordered a roll and a cup of coffee and located a small table in one corner of the crowded room. With her mind clear of self-doubts, she began mentally listing all the evidence that she'd been ignoring about Brad. As it began to pile up, her last hope that she'd been judging him too harshly vanished.

She was trying to decide whether to get in touch with Bobby Hall or wait at the hotel until Jerry arrived, when she spotted a man at a table across from hers. He was half-hidden from view by one of the tubs of flowering pots, so she wasn't sure whether she recognized him or not.

Her heart skipped several beats as she tried to study him without being obvious. Tall, thin, blond-haired. Yes, it was possible he was the man who had been driving the black car that had hit hers.

At length she walked to the counter to refill her cup, keeping the man in her peripheral vision. She got only a moment to observe his full face but she knew instantly who he was. The small deep-set eyes were exactly as she remembered, and his clothes were as ill-fitting as ever. Her glance dropped to his shoes for a final verification. Yes, they were poorly constructed. Eastern European, she surmised as the parts of the puzzle continued to fall into place at a steady pace.

Now what? She wondered briefly if she were being followed but then decided that the man was totally unaware of her presence. She paid for her second cup of coffee and moved back to her table, stationing herself well out of the blond man's sight as she waited for him to make the first move.

She didn't have long to wait. He stood and started through the crowd and she followed behind, leaving enough bodies between them to avoid suspicion. The crowds were dense on the sidewalk outside. Each time she thought she'd lost sight of the blond man, he bobbed back into view and she continued her apparently casual surveillance.

When he stopped in front of a shop window, she came to an abrupt stop, causing an outcry from the woman behind her. Minta turned, irritated over having attention drawn to her. She murmured an apology when she realized the woman had dropped a package. Bending over, Minta scooped it up and handed it to her before moving away.

Just in time she caught sight of the blond man entering a shop. Edging her way close to the stores, she stopped as she reached the shop's display window. Grateful for this moment to catch her breath, she leaned against the wall beside it, careful to keep out of sight. Her heart was pounding, her color was high and her mind was working at top speed. Active surveillance, the cat-and-mouse game, was undercover work at its best. She was known as one of the top operatives in this field.

She edged closer to the glass and peered inside. The shop was large and crowded with tourists. She scanned each counter until she located the blond head. Moving quickly, she entered the store and began fingering some merchandise on one of the counters.

It was a duty-free shop. Forcing herself to look at each item carefully, she located Scottish woolens as soft as a cloud on a counter next to bottles of French perfume, blue-and-white delftware bowls and boxes of Swiss chocolates.

A clerk broke her concentration. "We're having

a sale on our hand knits today. Do you see anything you like?''

Minta shook her head, relieved when the clerk moved on quickly to another customer. She noted that the man was at the cash register, taking money out of his pocket to purchase one of the boxes of candy.

Minta waited until he'd completed his purchase and was out of the doorway before she lay down the shawl she was admiring and followed after him. When she reached the open door she paused and glanced quickly down the street. Almost too late she realized the man was staring in the display window on the other side of the door. Had he recognized her?

Retreating into the safety of the shop, she maneuvered past two men and turned her back on the window, seemingly absorbed in a group of colorful round tins filled with imported cookies. Inwardly she was reminding herself that it never paid to take chances. It was always possible that she was the hunted rather than the hunter. Never underestimate your enemy was a lesson she'd had to learn the hard way.

The next time she glanced up, the man had disappeared from sight. She went outside and started down the sidewalk, mingling with the crowd. Just as she decided she had lost her target, she caught sight of him a half block away.

Too easy, she decided instantly. He was acting as she would if she was trying to be followed. She slowed her steps, moving diagonally under a colorful awning in front of another shop. If he slowed, she'd know that he was well aware of her presence.

He did the opposite, sprinting forward suddenly. She leaned forward, surprised by his sudden action and then saw him turn the corner and hurry across the street. She expelled her breath, elated once more that she was still the one in control.

She waited until she saw him enter another shop and then crossed at the corner herself a few minutes later. When she arrived, she checked the shop quickly. He was inside. Acting like a typical tourist buying presents for those back home. Did this mean he was preparing to leave the island soon?

Minta made a quick reconnaissance of the store and decided it was safe to enter the noisy, crowded souvenir shopper's paradise. Its garishness was appalling. Coconut shells carved to resemble grotesque shrunken heads were strung along a pole from the ceiling. Delicate shells transformed into a nightmare collection of gaudy colors and weird shapes lined the shelves.

The man was fingering a lamp. A conglomeration of shells glued together to resemble a pelican. In the beak of the crudely rendered bird was a shade with a bulb dangling below it. Minta watched in amusement as the man motioned to a clerk and asked the price.

She heard his voice clearly, identifying the heavily accented English as the same one she'd heard before. A male clerk stopped beside her. "Shall I ring that up for you?"

The man glanced up as if he'd heard the clerk and Minta turned around, fumbling for money from the purse at her waist. "Yes. How much?" she said absently.

The clerk reached for an object off the counter and Minta realized she was purchasing a sloppily executed clay ashtray in the shape of a shark. *In the future, watch where you put your hands when you're making fun of someone else's taste,* she reminded herself with a silent groan.

A half hour later Minta was exasperated. The blond man was a tireless shopper and had already made several more purchases. She clutched the ashtray in her hand, watching for a litter barrel in vain. At least she had made some discoveries about him that might be helpful. A thin scar along his jaw. A nervous twitching under his left eye. And his purchases gave her some idea about his personal life. Beside the lamp, he'd bought a purple-and-pink wraparound skirt, two dolls and a small plastic helicopter. A wife and three children were the most likely guesses.

Totally relaxed by now, Minta stayed close behind him as he left at a shop at the far end of the shopping section of George Town. He turned at the next corner and started down a street leading toward the sea.

Minta dropped farther behind him, gradually lengthening the distance to over a block as they left the crowds behind.

The streets sloped slightly, and she kept out of sight as well as possible, satisfied when he kept to a steady pace that he wasn't aware of her presence. Her heartbeat quickened as they neared the harbor. If he boarded one of the yachts, she'd have more valuable information for Jerry.

Minta hesitated as he reached the quay. A long line of luxurious yachts lined the harbor. On the walk in front were groups of people: tourists clicking cameras, sidewalk vendors pushing gaily colored carts filled with peanuts, popcorn and ice-cream bars, and several huddles of roughly dressed sailors watching the scantily clad women sauntering by.

She lost sight of the man momentarily and then saw the blond hair bobbing along as he hurried away from the throngs. Minta crossed the street and followed after him, dodging through the crowds and ignoring several women hawking knickknacks out of baskets.

Breathing rapidly, Minta realized her quarry was picking up his pace and she pushed forward, bumping into a tall bearded man dressed in a pair of frayed jeans and a denim shirt. He grabbed her by the arms. "Let go of me," she demanded angrily.

He grinned insolently at her, his eyes running down the length of her body. "What's your hurry?" he said.

She wrenched free, ignoring the laughs of his friends as she started forward. Damn, she'd lost him. She walked on slowly, scanning the area and then stopped. Almost at the end of the marina she decided he had vanished into thin air.

Consoling herself that she had still learned something important about the driver of the black car, she started to retrace her steps. Below her a voice called, "Looking for someone?"

She glanced down sharply into the appreciative gaze of a young man. He was dressed in brief shorts and an expensive polo knit shirt. His styled brown hair, thin gold watch and gold ingot dangling over his chest suggested he belonged to the wealthy class who frequented this island. Smiling at him, she said, "Yes, I am. You didn't see a blond man boarding one of the ships around here?"

"Why don't you come on board and take a look from this angle?" he offered. "My name's Rick."

"Minta," she said, reaching for his outstretched hand and climbing aboard.

"At the end of the deck you can get a better view of the vessels over there," Rick said in a friendly voice.

Minta started across the deck just as she felt a prickling at the back of her neck. Too late, she decided that she had made a mistake. She didn't know this man from Adam. She breathed deeply, determined to keep a level head while she decided what kind of mess she'd gotten herself into. She moved closer to the rail to keep in sight of the tourists, calculating her chances of escaping by jumping over the railing into the water.

Using her razor-sharp mind, she concluded

Rick's accent was not American as she'd first thought. British? No! That same accent the blond man had but Rick concealed it better. She edged closer to the rail, keeping him in her peripheral vision. "Have you been on the Caymans long?" she asked casually.

"A long, long time." Rick said moving closer. "Have you found the man you're looking for?"

"Not yet." She touched the railing with one hand.

Rick laughed and she felt a hand on her shoulder. She whirled but it was too late. The heavy hand of an unseen assailant yanked her around and clapped a pad over her nose. The smell was familiar and she struggled to fight off her attacker to no avail. A violent blow struck the back of her head. A flash of lights. Searing pain. Then utter darkness. Her body betrayed her, sagging to the deck as a moan escaped her throat.

CHAPTER SIXTEEN

BRAD COULD NOT REMEMBER ever feeling quite so helpless as he watched Minta pedaling down the road in front of the cottage. Something was terribly wrong and he knew it. Even though he'd wanted desperately to believe her story about a business problem, he knew he wasn't convinced.

He kicked a pebble out of his path and started back for the cottage. It was his fault. He should have let Minta know he was in the hall, overhearing her phone conversation. But it hadn't been deliberate eavesdropping. He hadn't even realized she was still on the phone until he had reached the doorway.

He could still remember how shocked he'd been by the emotion in her voice. But what had upset her so? Was she that worried about her business problems? He couldn't buy that explanation, no matter how much he longed to. No, she'd definitely learned something that had both stunned and infuriated her. Something she was so upset about she was willing to lie to him.

As he let himself into the cottage, he decided that was what was bothering him the most. Minta's lies. She'd always seemed so open before. But that kiss on his cheek and her smile as she'd left the cottage. Neither one had been the least bit sincere. She'd been determined to make him think nothing was wrong, nothing was bothering her, but inside she'd been seething. And her rage was directed at him, he realized suddenly.

His heart was pounding as he gathered up his shaving equipment from her bathroom. If he even had the slightest inkling why she was so angry. He knew the trouble had nothing to do with another man. No, her brown eyes had been glittering with anger. A barely suppressed anger instigated by something she'd heard during that phone call.

The tension in her body as she'd braided her hair, the crisp tone of her voice as she'd said her farewells. All had been attempts by her to keep from blowing up at him over some wrong he'd committed. But what? That was the unanswerable question.

He could follow her to the bakery. Demand to know what he'd done wrong. Try to straighten things out between them. But what right did he have to demand anything of her?

Their love was so right, so perfect. Not just for him but for Minta, as well. One of them had to break down the wall she was trying to build between them.

Hell, he didn't have any pride where she was concerned. If getting down and crawling was what it took to put things right, he would do it. He'd go to the bakery and beg her to level with him.

He glanced at his watch and decided to give her a

few minutes to arrive at the bakery. He didn't want to pass her on the road. If she saw him now, she might change her mind and go somewhere else. The more he thought about Minta's phone call and her subsequent anger, the more confused he got. As he crossed the porch to his side of the cottage he discovered his phone was ringing.

He answered it, hoping it wasn't anything that would delay him. It was a woman's voice. "This is the police station. Officer Hall is on his way to see Mr. McMillan. Will he be there?"

"This is Brad McMillan. I'll wait for him."

Brad waited on the porch, impatient for the young officer to arrive. When the official car stopped in front, he walked out to meet him. "What's happening?" Brad asked.

Bobby stepped outside the car. "In a few minutes I'm interviewing Charlie. He's that waiter from Cayman Brac that is supposed to know about the yacht. I thought maybe you and Minta would like to be there."

Brad hesitated and then decided this was too important to miss. "Minta's gone bike riding but I'll go. Give me time to leave her a note and I'll follow you in my car."

The police station was set back from the road. Brad stopped in front and walked inside, his mind mulling over his problems with Minta. He regretted his decision to take the time to come here. He was more concerned about patching up the differences between Minta and himself than hearing what a waiter had to say.

Charlie was older than Brad had expected, sitting slumped down in a chair in the reception room. Bobby introduced Brad and the three of them went inside a small room. "Have a seat," he told the man. "Tell us what you know about the *Omen* and her owners."

"I haven't done anything wrong," the man said. The small shiny bald spot on the top of his head glistened with perspiration under the bright overhead lights.

Bobby leaned forward. "You haven't been accused of anything."

"All I did was deliver some fish to the yacht. My family runs a delivery service to the yachts out in The Point."

From the nervous movements of the man's hands as they twisted in his lap, Brad suspected his family ferried more than fish back and forth, but he kept quiet as Bobby continued, "Did you go on board the yacht?"

"Yes, several times. I went below to the galley. It's a high-class yacht. Got a dining room big enough to have a party."

"Who owns it?"

He shrugged, his eyes darting around furtively. "They pay me cash."

"What country are the people on board from?"

"I don't know. Most of them speak something that sounds like German. I can't be sure."

Not German, Brad decided. It was beginning to sound more and more as if the men on the yacht were the same ones he'd been dealing with. As Minta had so accurately guessed, they were from one of the Eastern-bloc nations but to Charlie's untrained ear the slavic language had sounded like German. Maybe Charlie didn't have a good ear for languages, but at the moment he could be helpful in other ways. Brad needed to learn what was going on on board the yacht. "Is the silver-haired man who gave Sean such a big tip the boss?"

Charlie glared at Brad, as if he'd just noticed his presence in the room. "Are you the man who gave Sean such a hard time?"

"I should have done more than that," Brad said, in a menacing voice. "I don't take it lightly when someone gives out my woman's name and room number to a strange man."

Charlie subsided in his seat, plainly bewildered. It was evident Sean had not told him all that had happened that evening at the inn. "The silver-haired man, as you call him, paid me for the fish once. But there's another man on board. Taller. Dresses like a king. He calls the shots, I think."

"What's his name?"

Charlie frowned, deep in thought. "I've heard him called Andre. That's all. Just Andre. He's a Frenchman, I think. But he speaks lots of other languages, too. He's not like the other men on board. I think they're all afraid of him."

Brad's eyes narrowed in speculation. This was an entirely new twist. What in hell was a Frenchman doing mixed up in this deal? After he'd straightened out the mess with Minta, he'd have to give this new information some thought.

When Bobby was satisfied Charlie had told everything he knew, he dismissed him, handing him the fare for his return to Cayman Brac and thanking him for his cooperation. "I hated to scare the old fellow that way, but after all that's been happening to you and Minta I didn't want to pass up the opportunity. Did you hear anything helpful?"

Brad smiled wryly. "We won't know until later," he said cryptically. "Thanks for your efforts."

He drove straight to the bakery when he left the station. All the parking spaces in front were filled and he had to drive around the block until he found one. Hurrying inside, he glanced around. Minta was nowhere to be seen. Carefully he circled the room, checking to make certain he wasn't missing anyone hidden behind the tall pots of flowers. Dejected, he acknowledged he'd missed her.

It wasn't until he reached the cottage and saw she wasn't there either that he remembered he hadn't checked the bicycle rack in front of the bakery. It was possible she left her bike there if she had wanted to visit the local shops.

MINTA LAY SPRAWLED ON HER BACK, aware only of pain and confusion, as she drifted in and out of consciousness. Unwilling to consider where she was or why she was there, she let her mind drift for an indeterminable length of time.

Her first clear thought was of Brad. If only he would put his arms around her and hold her tight, then maybe the pain in her head and the back of her neck would go away.

Brad. As she concentrated on him, it all came back to her. You idiot, she told herself. Don't trust Brad McMillan. He's a liar. And worse. Much worse. Pretending to discuss his business dealings with you so openly. Telling you he checked with the State Department....

The sudden rush of memories was too painful. Now wasn't the time to think about it. Anyway, where was she? Slowly she forced her eyes open, blinking at the sudden onslaught of light. A wave of nausea swept over her as she watched the polished hardwood floor curve upward and then slowly recede.

A stateroom. She was in a stateroom. Out at sea. The yacht she'd boarded. She groaned, remembering her stupidity. Damn, she'd never done anything as foolish in all her years as an agent.

But who did it belong to? And why would they want to drug her? And kidnap her? She forced herself to sit up, noting absently the expensive quilted satin spread she had been lying on.

She studied the rest of the room. A teakwood built-in dressing table. A bamboo armchair with caned seat and antique parchment finish. A wicker trunk at the foot of the queen-sized bed and a table desk framed with brass. This was no ordinary yacht, to say the least.

Sunlight spilled through a small round porthole, reassuring her that she hadn't been unconscious as long as she feared. Or was it another day? She peered at her watch and checked the date. No, still the same day. She couldn't be too far away from Grand Cayman yet.

Gingerly she placed her feet on the floor, fighting off another wave of nausea. With her hand on the back of the bamboo chair she stood, chilled as beads of perspiration popped out on her forehead. Luckily she spotted a narrow door across from the larger one that must have led to the hallway. She lurched toward it, pulled it open and made it into the bathroom just in time to lose the contents of her stomach.

She sank down on the lavender bathroom floor, waiting for the next round of nausea she knew would strike her. Once it passed she was convinced she'd start regaining her strength. She had to find a way to escape. Before it was too late.

According to her watch, over an hour passed before Minta was fully recovered. It seemed more like a day. She slipped one of the deep lavender velour cloths off a rack and dampened it in the marble sink. It felt deliciously cool as she washed her face. Rinsing it out, she wrung out the excess water and folded it into a thin oblong. Once back on her bed she lay the cool compress on her head and willed her headache to vanish.

The drug they'd pressed against her nose—one of the newer forms of the old standby, chloroform, she guessed from its characteristic sweet odor—was safe when used in low concentration. She'd even employed it herself once when rescuing a young hostage she'd feared might scream and alert the captors. But she had been ultracareful about how much she'd poured on the pad. Her kidnappers must have used all they had, she concluded, gingerly running her hand behind her neck. At the moment she felt exactly like a telephone pole had flattened her.

The ache in the back of her head slowly became tolerable and she sat up again. Outside the sun's rays were slanting toward the horizon. Her stomach growled, and she realized she needed to try to find food if she wanted to regain her strength.

She tried the lock on her door and it slid open smoothly. Cautiously she turned the knob and pulled open the door. Peering outside, she saw a long narrow passageway. Thick grasscloth carpeted the floors and teakwood walls gleamed dully. Overhead a series of recessed lights shone down with a startling brilliance.

After checking to see that all the other doors were shut and no one was approaching, she started into the hall. The sound of deep masculine laughter brought her to a halt, and she slid back inside her room. Footsteps pounded down the hall, and she fell back on her bed, pretending to be unconscious as she heard her door being pushed open.

It was all she could do to lie still and listen as footsteps approached her bed. Two men spoke rapidly to each other. "Still out like a light," said one, his voice low and sensual with a decided French accent.

"Faking," said the other. She recognized this man's voice immediately, but she opened her eyes to make certain. She found herself staring into the harsh gaze of the silver-haired man.

"So you are awake," he said, glaring down at her with anger in his eyes.

She pushed up on her elbows. "Why am I here?"

There was an imperceptible pause as the silver-haired man turned to the one beside him. Minta followed his gaze. With almost inhuman willpower, she kept her eyes from widening as she recognized him as Andre Mirabeau, a known terrorist.

"I hope you're comfortable, Minta," he said, his sensual lips creasing into a welcoming smile. He was handsome, she acknowledged wryly, remembering how the society columnists had all had such a hey-day reporting on his latest female conquests when he had been free to roam through Washington, D.C. at will. But there was an evil cast to his features, as if all his infamous deeds had left their mark.

"Of course, I'm not comfortable," she snapped, swinging her feet off the bed. "I've been drugged, hit on the head and left without food for hours. Is this your idea of hospitality?" Inwardly she was desperately trying to remember if there was any reason why Mirabeau might recognize her.

Andre's dark eyes flashed with amusement. "Guests on *Omen* are usually pleased with my hospitality. Please take it easy until you are fully recovered."

WHEN ANDRE MIRABEAU LEFT HER ROOM, he turned
to the man beside him. "I totally disapprove of this,
you fool. Kidnapping this young lady to try to get
McMillan's cooperation will never work. How do we
even know the woman means anything to him?"

The man's hands trembled slightly. "They stay together."

"And that means he'd give us valuable information to rescue her?" Andre sneered. "I thought you
and your countrymen were a little more sophisti-
cated than that."

"Then we'll have a little fun with her and set her
free on Cayman Brac. I know our man should have
consulted you before leading her to the boat but
there was no opportunity."

"Fool. Fool. Fool," muttered Andre. "I am
forced to deal with nothing but fools. There's no way
we can release her now. But from now on, stay out of
this. You're paying me to handle this transaction for
you!"

AS NOON APPROACHED, Brad became more and more
edgy. Unable to stand it any longer, he went back to
his car and drove once more to the bakery. This time
he spotted a bike similar to Minta's as he pulled into
a parking space. He got out and studied it and then
went into the bakery.

A quick survey of the room revealed only a few
people at the tables. Minta was not one of them. He
approached the woman standing behind the counter.

"Did you see a young woman with long, waist-length dark hair...?" He stopped, suddenly remembering watching her braid her hair. "No, hair braided and on the back of her neck," he amended. "I think her bike is parked in front but I can't locate her."

The woman shrugged. "I only came to work a few minutes ago."

"The problem is, it's a rented bike," Brad went on hurriedly, aware the woman was staring at him as if he was acting strangely. "I'm not sure it's hers. Maybe if you could ask the other customers...."

"Ask them yourself," she said, turning back to pick up a cloth.

Brad turned toward the room and saw that the four customers were watching him. He cleared his throat. "Anyone in here riding a red bike?"

Two shakes of the head. One shrug. And one "No." "Thanks," Brad said, and strode outside. The sight of the bike made his chest contract in alarm. He was sure something had happened to Minta.

He forced his breathing to be slow and steady. He couldn't rush back to Bobby and alarm him with no more evidence than this. He decided to walk the length of the shopping district and check in all the shops. And how about the restaurants? She might have decided to grab an early lunch.

Nothing. The more he searched, the more discouraged he became. He went into a coffee shop and peered into each booth. Then he went into a crowded restaurant and asked a waitress if he could check for a friend. She agreed, but Minta wasn't there either.

By the time Brad left the last shop, he felt older, weighed down with a sinking sensation that was making it difficult to even think. The fact he hadn't felt like eating all day didn't help, he knew. But food had been the last thing on his mind.

His mind reeled with thoughts of all that could have happened. But one thought kept returning. Minta might have left the island. To get away from him. She could have parked her bike there and then taken a taxi to the airport. Without returning rented property? It didn't make sense, but then she might have told Diane Hall where the bike was left and paid extra to have it picked up.

He got back in his car, not satisfied with this explanation. Why would she have rushed off without her clothes? He drove slowly toward the airport without coming up with any answers to all the questions rushing through his mind.

When he arrived at the small airport, he went straight to the ticket counter and checked on the passenger list of the plane which had just departed. Minta's name was not on it.

Next he tried Diane but she shook her head. "No, Mr. McMillan. Minta hasn't been here or contacted me in any way today. Is something wrong?"

"Dead wrong. If you see Minta, tell her I'm frantic with worry." Brad strode outside without saying more.

By the time he reached the beach cottage, he was drained. He walked up the steps and went inside

Minta's side first. Still empty. Inside her bedroom closet, her clothes still hung on the racks. A wave of longing for her almost overcame him as he saw the striped cotton dress she'd worn to Cayman Brac. He forced himself to stop thinking about that and continued his search.

A quick check of the drawers in the wicker dresser and the pockets of her canvas hanging bag revealed nothing. Where was her purse? He could swear she hadn't had it with her when she'd pedaled away but it was nowhere in sight.

After a comprehensive search he sank down on the sofa in his side of the cottage, not certain how much more he could stand. If only Minta hadn't left when she was so angry with him. *Calm down, McMillan,* he told himself. *She said she was upset about a business reversal. Why not believe her? Why are you so certain that she was running away from you?*

The possibility that something sinister had happened to her occurred to him but he dismissed it. She'd been here for days now, and although she'd had a nasty threat, no one had tried to harm her. No, he had to deal with her anger toward him. That was what had triggered this disappearance. Perhaps she'd return in a few hours with a perfectly logical explanation.

The sound of the phone ringing shattered his nerves. He leaned across the sofa and picked it up, reluctant to talk about anything but Minta at the moment.

A low masculine voice said, "Mr. McMillan? We have Minta."

Brad felt like he'd been punched in the stomach. "Where is she and who is this?" he demanded hoarsely.

"We've met. In your cottage last week."

"You bastard," Brad swore. "What do you want with Minta?"

"An exchange. An even exchange. The information we need and the diagrams of the weapon in exchange for the young woman."

Brad's mind was working furiously assessing the information. "Where is she? How do I know you have her? As far as I know she's fine."

"You know she's missing."

"Damn if I do." He thought about pretending Minta meant nothing to him, only a beautiful young woman who'd shared his bed for several nights but decided against it. They might get rid of her if they thought she was useless in their scheme.

Brad forced himself to laugh. "This is coming as a shock. I expected a little money. My company's in a financial bind right now." He paused. "That woman means a hell of a lot to me but I need time." He didn't care what they thought as long as he had some time. One night. One lousy night was all he needed. He had to convince them he was serious.

The man on the phone spoke more slowly. "How long do you need to think? Minta is weak. She's been hurt."

Brad's throat tightened convulsively, but he

clung to the desperate hope that the man was bluffing. He'd have to do the same. "I don't believe you. Let me talk to her."

"That's not possible."

"Then you'll have to talk to me again in the morning."

"*We* set the terms," he said angrily. For the first time Brad thought he recognized the voice. It sounded like one of the counteragents who'd come to his cottage that night.

"Not as long as I'm the only one who knows how to build what you want," he reminded him, equally as forceful. "And let me warn you. If Minta is not in excellent shape, you'll never see the information you want. Tell your boss that I said so. Call me at ten in the morning at this number if you're interested in dealing on my terms." He forced himself to slam down the receiver, breaking the fragile connection that was his only link with the woman he loved.

Not allowing himself to give in to the overwhelming emotion filling him, he dialed Ted's house. Lydia answered. "Lydia. Brad. This is an emergency. Tell Ted to meet me at the dock in George Town as quickly as possible. I'll explain when he gets here."

With that call completed, he made one last one. To the inn on Cayman Brac. He asked for Paula, the woman at the desk. "Paula, Brad McMillan. I was a guest at your inn several days ago. Do you remember the young woman whose room was broken into?"

"Why yes, Mr. McMillan. Why?"

"I need to speak to one of your waiters concerning

that break in. His name is Charlie. I'd like his home address.''

Her voice was formal. ''I think he's given all the information to the police.''

''This is private. It's a matter of life and death. The young woman is missing.''

''Oh, I'm sorry. I'll call him and tell him to come here if you'd like,'' she said quickly.

''Good. Have him stay until I can get there.''

WHEN ANDRE AND THE SILVER-HAIRED MAN left Minta alone in her stateroom, she leaned back against the pillows on the bed.

Andre Mirabeau. A leader of one of the most deadly terrorist groups in the world according to the State Department report she had once read. Andre's deportation had made headlines in D.C. for several days. Since then she remembered that he had been accused of masterminding a terrorist attack on a group of Israeli ballet dancers when they'd been performing in Paris.

Now that she knew her kidnapper's identity, she realized the deadly position she was in. *But what did they want with her?*

That was the unanswerable question. She was almost certain that they didn't connect her with the FBI. No, it was that freak hit-and-run accident that had targeted her. Andre hadn't been one of the passengers in the car, but it must have been some of his gang. She had stumbled into a much bigger operation than she'd even dreamed possible.

Where did Brad fit into all this? Although she fought the conclusion as long as possible she finally admitted there must be a connection between Brad McMillan and this gang of terrorists.

With mounting horror she even faced the possibility that he might have arranged this kidnapping. If he'd picked up enough clues from her conversation with Jill to suspect she knew his reason for being on the island, then he might have called his friends and arranged for them to lead her to the yacht. Like an utter idiot she'd fallen in with his malevolent scheme.

Minta heard a knock, and she pushed the hair back from her forehead with a nervous gesture. Positioning herself against the wall beside the door, she called out, "Come in."

A white-jacketed steward entered with a tray. His eyes betrayed surprise when she stepped away from the wall, but he overcame it quickly and located a folding stool. After placing the tray on it, he spoke to her in rapid French. She understood most of the message that expressed Monsieur Mirabeau's wishes that she would enjoy her meal.

A single red rose in a crystal vase graced the tray.

CHAPTER SEVENTEEN

BESIDE THE VASE WAS A NOTE. Minta picked it up and read: "Please honor me with your presence at dinner at eight. Andre."

Please? That seemed a novel approach for a kidnapper. Lifting the metal cover off a china bowl, she smelled the delicate aroma of hot consommé garnished with thin slivers of avocado. Beside it was a delicate china cup and saucer with a matching teapot. She ate everything eagerly and felt her strength returning.

When she finished she tried to analyze Andre's game plan. His courteous manner. His kind treatment. At least she could be grateful the evil-eyed man with the silver hair was not in charge of her.

A few minutes before eight the steward returned to take her to Andre. She had showered and re-braided her hair, ignoring the array of expensive cosmetics and perfumes in the dressing room table in favor of a more subdued appearance.

Except for a mild headache, Minta felt fine by the time she reached Andre's suite of rooms. He greeted her in a sitting area, dressed in a European-styled evening jacket with matching striped pants. She studied him as he poured a glass of champagne for her, noting the finely chiseled features and long slender fingers. She found herself wondering what could have made a man turn to a life of terrorism. Extreme poverty? A life filled with political turmoil that had made him one of the world's homeless? Whatever it was, she was certain he had no loyalty to anyone or any cause beside that of himself.

"Do you like my yacht?" he asked her, gesturing to the luxurious suite furnished in an eclectic mixture of oriental and mahogany furniture.

"It's lovely," she answered, taking a small sip of her champagne. "Do you live here all the time?"

He smiled at her. "I come and I go, Minta. How about you? What are you doing on the Caymans?"

"Vacationing."

"And where do you live?"

She answered without hesitation. "I'm from Santa Fe, New Mexico. I'm a native American Indian." She was relieved when his eyes revealed that he didn't doubt this.

"How fascinating. Over dinner you must tell me about New Mexico. I've never traveled in the western part of your country."

He led the way into a dining room and indicated that Minta was to sit on his right. As a waiter served an icy-cold thick gazpacho, Minta told him a little about the history of the Zuni tribe. He listened closely, asking intelligent questions as if he had nothing more pressing on his mind.

A wine steward circled their table, filling their

glasses with appropriate wines and removing their dishes. The next course was broiled fish and that was followed by rare roast beef, artichoke hearts and Belgian endive salad.

Minta was careful not to drink too much, but she kept up appearances by lifting her glass frequently and exclaiming over the smoothness of the expensive wines. Although she itched to confront him with a myriad of questions, she decided to wait until they had finished eating.

When they neared the end of the meal, Andre requested a platter of cheese and fruit. When the steward disappeared, he leaned back and asked, "Do you have any questions, Minta?"

"A million, but I'll settle for one answer. What plans do you have for me?"

He smiled. "I wish I could decide that on the strength of my own personal feelings, but Brad McMillan holds your fate in his hands."

She was sickened with disappointment. Since she'd regained consciousness she'd been trying to tell herself that Brad was not responsible for her being here. Now it was out in the open, and for a moment it hurt so badly she wondered if this was what it felt like to die. Hoping Andre had not sensed how distressed she was, she answered, "So he's the cause of all this!"

Andre seemed amused by what she'd said. "I'm afraid so, Minta. Mr. McMillan has something we want. We're hoping you're worth enough to him that he'll cooperate with us for your release."

Minta experienced a flicker of hope that Brad was not one of them, after all. "What kind of cooperation?"

"We want to know more about his robots."

"Those?" She laughed lightly and reached for her glass of wine. "I thought those were playthings."

"To me they are, but there are some who will go to almost any length to get them."

"Then who are you? And who is the man with the silver hair?"

"I prefer to be called a soldier of fortune, Minta." He reached for a grape and offered it to her. "But you should never have gotten involved in this. It doesn't concern you. Why did you ignore the warnings you were given?"

"I guess I couldn't figure out what they meant. Did that man I followed to this yacht wreck my car deliberately?"

"You mean Lex? No, he's just a poor driver."

"And the bike accident?" she persisted. "Why did Lex try to drive me off the road? Is he a soldier of fortune, too?"

"Another blunder, I'm afraid."

"And the man who came to my room with you earlier today? Did you send him to warn me?"

Andre leaned back in his chair. "He had you under surveillance for several days. When he spotted you with McMillan on Cayman Brac, we decided you were an unnecessary complication. If only you'd listened."

She gave him her most charming smile. "I'll listen now if you'll give me one more chance."

"Sorry," he said, smiling in return. "You're our bait now. In case McMillan has only been leading us on, we have you for a little added insurance."

"I haven't known him long," she said, sighing softly.

"But he is completely enamored with you."

"I'm not sure."

"Why did you follow Lex this morning?"

She came up with the first answer she could think of. "He owes me money for hitting my rented car. I had to pay what the insurance didn't cover."

"So that's why you were following him?" He eyed her for several moments and then began chuckling. "How much money?"

"One hundred dollars. Lex offered me money at the scene of the accident, but I wanted to wait until I found out what it would cost. Little did I dream he'd take off without reporting the accident to the police."

Andre shook his head as if he couldn't believe such stupidity. "You risked your life for a mere hundred dollars?"

She tossed back her hair in a defiant gesture. "You may think that's not a lot of money but it is to me. Please tell me about those other men in the car. Who are they and where are they from?"

He answered her sharply. "This is not your business, Minta."

When the meal was finished Andre suggested a

stroll on the deck. Hoping to gain a clearer idea of where the yacht was anchored, Minta rose quickly. When they emerged on the top deck, the moon was nearly full, illuminating the darkness with a whispered brilliance.

Minta gazed out across the shimmering waters, wondering what Brad was doing. Andre's remarks puzzled her. If he was telling the truth—and that was a big *if* in her mind—then Brad had nothing to do with her kidnapping. For that, at least, she was grateful.

But it still left him guilty of dealing with the enemy. Why? She had never been involved with the type of individual who spied, but she had always thought that they were people without any loyalties. People devoid of a conscience, really. Brad didn't fit that classification at all.

"The weather forecast is for a tropical storm," murmured Andre. "But right now it seems impossible."

"Life's like that," said Minta. "This morning I thought everything was going my way and now here I am, a prisoner on a yacht, miles from land." She touched Andre's sleeve. "How far from Grand Cayman are we?"

He placed his palm over her hand. "Miles and miles, my dear. Do not think of escaping."

She laughed shakily. "I can hardly swim. Have you told Brad what he has to do to set me free?"

A shiver ran through her and she removed her hand from his and hugged herself. Andre glanced down at her. "It's time you went to your room. You're not to worry. Mr. McMillan knows what our demands are. We expect him to act on them tomorrow."

"I hope so," she said fervently.

As they went across the deck and down the stairs Minta made a quick survey of the layout of the yacht. When they reached the door, she said, "Please don't lock my door. I get claustrophobia."

He leaned over and brushed his lips across her cheek. "I'll leave it unlocked since there is no possible way you can escape. Until tomorrow, then."

She extended her thanks and slipped inside, relieved to stop pretending such naiveté. As Andre had pointed out so cruelly, escape was highly unlikely. But she knew she had to give it a try. No terrorist should ever be trusted. She had little doubt that even if Brad cooperated fully, Andre's plans for her did not include setting her free.

Disgusted she hadn't been able to learn the identities of the other men on board the ship, she checked her watch and decided to rest until several hours after midnight. That was when most people found it increasingly difficult to stay awake. In an effort to find out who was occupying the rooms on either side, she stood and stripped down to her briefs and bra and began a vigorous exercise routine. Humming a march tune loudly, she began running in place.

Within seconds pounding erupted on the wall behind her. "Quiet. It is late." It was a man's voice. Perhaps the blond man. She wasn't sure, but she could rule out the silver-haired man. The accent was too pronounced.

"Sorry," she called out contritely. "Who are you?"

"Quiet please."

She took another shower and dried on one of the thick towels. Searching through a narrow closet, she located several swimsuits. Bikinis with European brand names. She wondered if Andre entertained female friends often enough to keep these in stock or if they belonged to a special friend of his.

She slipped into a bright-red suit that seemed nearest her size and then pulled her yellow slacks and white blouse over it. After rebraiding her hair and coiling it on her head, she lay down. Her watch alarm set, she closed her eyes and tried to fall asleep without letting her mind stray to painful thoughts of Brad.

She wasn't sure how long she lay awake but the beep of her watch alarm woke her out of a sound sleep. It took her several seconds to remember where she was. When she did, she sat up, swinging her gaze to the porthole. A full moon, she noticed. Just her luck when she needed as much darkness as possible.

Going over to the window she peered out. In the distance she caught what she hoped was a gleam of light. Another ship? Or land? Either would be a welcome sight. She glanced around the room one last time and then lifted her head, suddenly alerted by the sound of tapping on the porthole.

With a muffled gasp, she jumped up and ran over to the small round glass. A black apparition gazed in at her. Brad! Even disguised in a wet suit and a diving hood, she recognized the familiar face immediately.

Flipping on her bedside lamp so Brad could see her better, she indicated with an upward motion of her thumb that she would make her way to the deck. He shook his head vigorously. "Stay put," he ordered, mouthing the words. Disappointed, she placed her hands on her hips and repeated her first motion. He once again shook his head, but this time she detected a smile and she knew he was there to help her.

He disappeared from the window, and she flipped off her lamp and crept over to the door. Cautiously she opened it and looked outside. All was quiet. Tempted to disobey Brad, she put one foot outside, but withdrew in a hurry when she heard footsteps above her head. The guard. Brad would be caught.

That thought made her more determined than ever. She listened carefully to the footsteps as they became less distinct. The guard was walking away from the staircase she needed to use. Now was her opportunity.

Her feet bare, she kept to one side of the hall, stopping in front of each door long enough to detect any signs of movement inside the rooms. When she reached the staircase, she started up carefully, her body flattened against the railing.

As she neared the top she heard the footsteps moving toward her once more and she ducked down, waiting for them to pass. As she crouched on the landing she heard a muffled groan and then a distinct thud. Her breath caught in her throat as she pictured Brad falling to the deck, but when she heard no further noises she decided to investigate.

She reached the deck and looked around. It appeared to be deserted. She sprinted across a section flooded with moonlight and stopped in the shadows. "Not bad." Brad's whisper came from behind her.

The shock of hearing his voice made her knees buckle under her. As she started to fall, Brad caught her, pulling her against the unyielding dark wet suit. His hood had been removed, and she noticed he no longer had his oxygen tank strapped to his back. Before she could ask any questions, he spoke against her ear. "Shh. Slip off your clothes and come with me. I've got diving equipment for you over the side."

Minta regained her equilibrium and obeyed without a moment's hesitation. Brad's eyes widened momentarily as he saw the bikini she wore, but he motioned her forward without speaking again.

He indicated she was to wait while he climbed over the railing. She leaned over watching as he clung to a metal ring. Pointing to a tangle of diving equipment attached by a rope to the ring, he whispered, "I'll put this on first. Then you climb over."

She nodded to show she understood and crouched down in the shadows against the railing. Her heart pounded against her rib cage as she strained to hear if anyone was moving around on the yacht. In a few moments, Brad's head appeared at the railing again. "Now," he said.

She climbed over and grasped for the ring where Brad pointed. He let go of his ring and maneuvered his way along the side of the yacht toward her. She could see a spare portable tank, inflatable vest, hood and flippers dangling on him. For the first time she tried to imagine how he had managed to arrive here loaded down with all that equipment.

A navy SEAL, she remembered. Brad must have gone on many missions like this. Through unfamiliar enemy waters. But she refused to dwell on it as she struggled into the equipment with his help. To remember Brad and Vietnam was to be reminded of why she couldn't allow herself to fully trust him.

When he had checked to see that her oxygen tank was working, he handed her a small light. He lifted her hood and placed his mouth against her ear. "Don't turn this on unless we need it. I'll use mine to guide us. You follow close behind me."

"Where are we going?" she asked.

He shook his head, the expression in his eyes clearly forbidding as he motioned impatiently and began to slowly submerge. For the space of one heartbeat she hesitated, wondering if she were trading one set of troubles for another, and then steadied her mask before lowering herself into the depths behind him.

The water was warm and clear, and she had no

trouble following Brad's lighted figure. A school of tiny minnowlike fish swam past her, flicking against her legs. Several large orange fish with enormous fins kept a steady distance ahead of Brad's light as if they had volunteered to guide these strange human intruders to a place of safety.

Minta relaxed as she increased the distance between *Omen* and herself. She would take her chances with Brad over Andre any day, she decided. An eel slithered toward her and Minta maneuvered her legs to let it pass through them, reminding herself not to let down her guard for even one instant.

Brad turned once and gave an okay sign to Minta. She waved, and he turned back and picked up his pace. Minta's legs began to tire first. A creeping numbness that made her efforts more and more difficult. Next her arms began to feel like heavy weights, and then she became aware of an ache between her shoulder blades. She pushed on, knowing that she would have to rely on sheer willpower to carry her through to their destination. Wherever that might be.

As her body tired she found herself forgetting to watch for Brad. She was totally absorbed in her thoughts. Repeating over and over again that she could go on, that she wouldn't give up. After what seemed like an eternity she glanced up and panicked. Brad was not in sight.

She reached for the light he had strapped on her leg and flipped it on, illuminating an underwater cliff. She swam around a corner of it and came upon

Brad clinging to the coral reefs. By the relief in his eyes, she knew he had been looking for her. She joined him and rested beside him. He grasped her arm and squeezed it reassuringly, and tears flooded her eyes. Nothing she had learned about Brad had vanquished the love she felt for him.

He motioned for them to go on and she nodded, keeping her mind on following him so she wouldn't waste her strength on frightening moments again. A sense of euphoria crept over her at one point, and she began to swim effortlessly as if she'd gotten her second wind. When she saw Brad's body starting toward the surface, she knew they'd made it.

The sight of Ted on the diving platform of *Lydia* brought a fresh rush of tears to her eyes. He helped her from the water, and she hugged him awkwardly.

"Oh, Ted, I thought I'd never make it," she managed to say as her legs crumpled beneath her. One of the crew members grasped her arm and steadied her.

"We've been worried sick about you," Ted said, unstrapping her oxygen tank. "How were you treated?"

"Not bad," she whispered hoarsely. "How did Brad find me?" She glanced around and saw Brad removing his equipment.

"We'll talk tomorrow," Brad answered. "How about getting her a shot of Scotch, Ted? Then off to bed for her. It was longer than I thought back to the ship."

Ted and the sailors finished removing her equipment and then helped her on to the deck of the fishing vessel. "Will they come after us?" Minta said between chattering teeth.

"Not a chance," Ted said, his arm still around her. He helped her down the narrow ladder leading to the galley. She pulled open the door of the room she remembered from her previous trip and went inside. "You'll find towels on the shelf. Get those wet clothes off and wrap up in one. When I get back with that drink I want to see you in bed."

"Thanks," Minta managed, her whole body racked with uncontrollable shudders. She slipped out of the bikini top and briefs and located one of the towels. Sitting cross-legged on the bed, she waited for Ted's return, refusing to wonder why Brad seemed intent on avoiding her.

Ted returned quickly and sat down beside her, wrapping his arm around her as he held the glass against her trembling lips. "Drink up, my girl."

She tilted back her head, choking as the fiery liquid burned the length of her throat. Her hand shook as she attempted to brush several droplets off her chin. When the glass was drained, Ted stood. "Crawl between the sheets and try to get some sleep, Minta."

"Where are we, Ted?"

"A long, long way from danger. You're safe now and among friends, Minta."

The liquor was having an effect on her, numbing her brain and she smiled crookedly. "That's nice...."

Ted was grinning at her. "Need any help getting under those covers?"

Minta's words slurred and her eyelids grew heavy. "I can do it my...self." Ted was chuckling loudly as he closed the door behind him. She shrugged off the towels and managed after several frustrating attempts to crawl between the sheets on the narrow bunk.

"WHY DON'T YOU GO BELOW?" Ted asked Brad when he came on deck. "Minta could stand a little warming up."

Brad stared out to sea without turning around. "Is she okay?"

"A little tipsy but she's in bed. She'll sleep it off. Did she say anything about what's happening on *Omen*?"

Brad shook his head. "We haven't had a chance to talk. Head for Grand Cay, Ted."

Ted stiffened. "What in the hell are you talking about, Brad? You know you've got to check the results of that last test on Hugo. My engine's acting up, so I don't want to run it any extra miles."

Brad whirled around, his fists clenched. "Dammit, Ted. Do what I say. Until Minta's safely on a plane and out of danger, I'm not giving another thought to those tests."

Ted held up his hands in defeat. "Okay. You're the boss but I tell you Minta's fine. She'd want you to finish."

"You have no idea what Minta wants," Brad

said evenly. "I know that because I have no idea either."

Ted moved to give orders to the crew to turn the vessel back toward the island, and Brad slipped out of his heavy wet suit. The last few hours were crowding in on him, making him break out in a cold sweat.

God, it had been a close call. If Minta hadn't been so resourceful and found her way to the deck, he wasn't sure if they could have made their escape. Charlie's detailed drawing of the yacht's layout had been helpful, but the waiter had never been in the hall where the staterooms were.

He was still amazed at Minta's determination during their voyage back to Ted's ship. More than once, Brad remembered looking over his shoulder to check on her. Her legs had grown weaker and weaker, and he could tell her arms were aching almost unbearably. But something inside her—spunk was the only way he could think to describe it—had kept her from giving up. His admiration and love had grown even deeper than before, if possible.

He held his breath as the engine on the vessel sputtered and then finally took hold. It had been giving Ted some trouble earlier that evening, but now it was purring like a big cat. He glanced over at the ladder longingly. Maybe Ted was right. He ought to go below and see if Minta needed him.

She was sleeping soundly when he came into the room and stood looking down at her. One shoulder was uncovered and he touched it softly, stroking his hand over the smooth, silky skin that had the power to drive him wild.

A residue of adrenaline still pulsed through his veins, and he felt a stirring of desire as he gazed down at her soft, flushed cheeks. She moved slightly, parting her lips, as if she could feel his gaze upon her.

His body began to respond to her unconscious invitation and he retreated a step, telling himself that he couldn't take advantage of her in her condition. She moved again, her eyelids fluttering open. "Brad," she whispered, holding out one arm.

The blanket slid away and he saw the generous swell of her breasts, the narrow rib cage, the curve of her hips and slender thighs. With a muffled groan, he pulled off his swim trunks and slid in beside her, gathering her into his arms.

To hell with generous gestures, he thought. He'd spent too many hours wondering if he'd ever see her again to pass up this chance to hold her in his arms. Not only that. Unless a miracle occurred, this could well be their last time to spend together.

She moved against him, spreading her thighs and he didn't pause for a second, entering her lavish moistness as his mouth plundered hers. She pressed herself closer and closer, urging him on with murmurs of pleasure as he moved faster and faster, no thought of stopping. He couldn't have stopped, he loved her, he loved being submerged in her depths, in the pulsating rhythms of her welcoming body. He knew he'd make love to her all night if she was this warm and this willing.

As MINTA WAS SHOWERING the next morning, she was filled with thoughts of their lovemaking throughout the night. No amount of willpower could have kept her from responding to him, she admitted. She had wanted nothing more than to be cradled in his arms, safe and secure and loved.

Loved? She scrubbed the rough washcloth over her body vigorously, reminding herself that Brad was involved in selling his invention of a super-weapon to some sort of enemy agents. She had no regrets about the night before. It had seemed like a dream come true. Today she had to deal with reality.

CHAPTER EIGHTEEN

BENEATH HER FEET Minta could feel the vibrations of *Lydia*, and she wondered where they were going. Was Brad holding her a prisoner now? She was almost certain Ted wasn't a part of the mystery surrounding Brad.

After drying she looked around for something to wear but found only the red bikini she'd taken from *Omen*. She slipped into it and hurried outside the small bunk room.

When she climbed the ladder, she glanced up at the sky. It was overcast, and she remembered Andre's mention of a tropical storm. Ted and Brad were standing by the entrance to the wheelhouse. "Anyone have a shirt I can borrow?" she called.

Brad swiveled his head and gave her one of his warm smiles. "How are you, Minta?"

She pointed to her brief attire. "A little chilly."

"I've got some spare clothes down in my storage closet," Ted answered. He pulled out a ring of keys and pitched it to her. "Feel free to wear anything you find."

Minta took the key and retreated. She glanced down the hall and selected what she hoped was the closet door. After trying several keys she found the right one and the door swung open.

The closet was dark, but she could make out a string dangling in the center of it. A quick pull and the roomy storeroom was illuminated with a pale light.

The only garments she could find were huge but she grabbed a shirt and a pair of trousers gratefully. When she tried on the shirt, it drooped down to her knees. The trousers were even a worse fit but she located a ball of twine and twisted together several strands to fashion a belt. By the time she finished rolling up the shirt-sleeves and pant legs, she knew she resembled someone's worn-out scarecrow.

She saw the gun as she was turning to leave.

It was small. A useless weapon in the opinion of law-enforcement officials. But better than nothing, she decided.

She picked it up, fingering it carefully, severely tempted.

Breaking it open, she inspected its empty chamber and saw that it hadn't been fired in a long time. Her gaze roved over the shelves until she located a box of matching cartridges. Forcing herself not to think of having to use it against Brad, she loaded the weapon and slipped it in one of her generously sized trouser pockets. Since her discussion with Al on the phone the day before, she realized she had now made herself an official part of this case. Squeamishness had no part in that role.

She was back in the hallway when she saw Brad

descending the ladder. He dropped down to the floor and came toward her, smiling. "The latest style?" he asked in a lighthearted voice. He stopped in front of her and dropped a kiss on the end of the nose.

The gun in her pocket made her heart pound rapidly. "I need to talk to you Brad."

He tensed. "We have lots to discuss, but there's not much time now, Minta. We're nearing Grand Cay, and you need to catch the first available flight out."

"I need to know what's going on here."

He studied her serious expression for several moments before saying, "I'm needed on deck. The engine's giving us trouble, and it's all we can do to limp back to shore."

When she stared back at him, silent, he sighed. "Okay, I know you're entitled to some information. Come along to the galley, and I'll fix you some toast and a cup of coffee."

When she was seated at the small table, she asked, "Brad, how did you know where I was last night?"

He kept his back to her as he placed a piece of bread in a small toaster. "I got a call from your kidnappers."

"They're friends of yours?"

He turned. "Is that what they told you?"

For the first time she noticed the fatigue lines creasing his face. She suppressed her sympathy. "They said you were involved with them." *Tell me the truth, Brad,* she pleaded silently.

He poured her a mug of coffee and set it in front of

her. "They're liars, Minta," he answered when he was seated opposite her.

She stared at him with troubled eyes. "How about you, Brad? You didn't tell me that you were on speaking terms with the same group that was threatening me."

He reached for her hands but she gestured him away. His face grew grim. "I had no idea the people wanting information from me were the same ones bothering you, Minta. I believe I did mention that I wondered about it, though," he pointed out.

She took a swallow of the hot coffee in an attempt to steady her shaking hands. "I remember. Why have you talked to these terrorists?" she asked.

"Terrorists?"

She tried to smooth over this slip. "Call them what you will. They're not friends, Brad. They will go to any lengths to get what they want, and I don't think they'll use your inventions for a good purpose."

He laughed cynically. "That's putting it mildly. Minta, I don't have time to tell you everything now, but I want you to know that I called the State Department and reported these criminals to them before I left Austin."

She began to feel a flicker of hope. Jerry Richards must be coordinating his efforts with the State Department. "What did they say?"

Brad leaned back, closing his eyes. "They didn't believe me. Minta, remember when I mentioned I'd been in Vietnam?"

She tensed, remembering Jill's information. "Yes."

"I found out then that you can't always depend on those in authority. I don't want to go into details, but I was accused of what amounted to treason over there. Nothing I'd done in the past, nothing I could say was good enough to prove my innocence. The case was finally dropped for lack of evidence, but it left me with no more illusions about the fairness of officials. Since then I've been a loner. I'm handling this problem now about Hugo on my own."

"You can't. You're one against everyone on *Omen*."

He smiled over the sincere anguish in her voice. "Don't forget Ted and the crew. What did your kidnappers tell you they intended to do?"

"Andre said he intended to ransom me for the information he wanted from you."

"Who's Andre?"

She wavered, momentarily distracted by Brad's question. Didn't he even know what a dangerous group he had been dealing with? "The owner of *Omen*. He speaks French. Haven't you met him?"

Brad shook his head. "I'm glad Charlie gave me enough information to locate you. That was one hell of an effort you exerted to keep up with me on our way back here last night."

He was avoiding telling her more about his involvement, she realized sadly. "So that's how you found me. Thanks for coming to my rescue, Brad."

He leaned over and kissed her on the mouth. "It's the least I could do, darling. I'll never forgive myself for putting you in danger."

Minta felt a terrible exhaustion creeping over her: physical, from the drugs and the long swim she'd taken the night before; mental, because she wasn't sure what she should do next; and emotional, because she knew she loved Brad in spite of all the reasons why she shouldn't.

A shout from Ted brought her out of her thoughts. Brad stood. "I better go up on deck. Come up when you've finished your toast."

BRAD KISSED MINTA FAREWELL when they arrived at the quay in George Town. "I have to stay on the ship," he told her. "I want you to leave the Caymans and I'll contact you as soon as I can in D.C." He turned to Ted without waiting for her answer. "Go straight to the cottage and get Minta's things, Ted. Then drive her to the airport and wait until you see her get on that plane."

"No one's going to try anything in broad daylight," Ted said with a bewildered shake of his head.

"They did yesterday," Brad answered, releasing Minta. "I'll call you as soon as I can darling."

She nodded, sensing his mind was far away and wrestling with a million problems. When she and Ted stepped onto the main street, Minta turned and caught one last glimpse of Brad. He was watching her, and her heart skipped a beat when he blew her a kiss.

Ted seemed as distracted as she as they hurried to the lot where Brad had left his car the day before. When they arrived at the cottage, Ted turned to her. "While you're packing I need to use your phone, Minta. I've got to locate a part for the ship's engine."

"Why not leave me here? I can get a taxi. . . ."

"You heard Brad."

"He's a worrywart," she said lightly. "What's he doing, Ted?"

The bearded man glanced at her sharply. "About what, Minta?"

"Hugo and those men on *Omen*. Is he in some kind of trouble?"

"What did Mirabeau tell you?"

"How do you know his name?"

Ted's eyes narrowed. "I think Charlie mentioned it."

Minta felt uneasy over his answer, but she tried not to show it. "Mr. Mirabeau wouldn't tell me much, but I'd like to help Brad, Ted."

He patted her on the shoulder awkwardly. "Brad can take care of himself. I was with him in Vietnam."

"What really happened there?" she asked.

Ted moved away abruptly, as if she'd struck him. "I didn't mean for you to tell me anything that Brad wouldn't," she said, attempting to reassure him.

"What do you know about Vietnam?"

"I don't know much," she admitted.

"Take my word for it. Brad's a great guy, Minta."

Ted's words were warm, but there was an undercurrent of anger that troubled her. "Don't let anything happen to him, Ted," she pleaded.

He swung his gaze away from hers. "I'll do my best."

Once inside the cottage Minta convinced Ted that he didn't need to wait for her. "I'll call and get a reservation and then call a taxi to take me to the airport. It's several hours before the plane leaves, and it would be foolish for you to stay with me."

"Well . . . a storm is brewing in the Caribbean, and my engine's got to be repaired before we can go back out," he said slowly.

"You're going back out to sea?"

Ted nodded. "We have to. Hugo's out there. He's not sending back the right signals, and we've got to locate him before the storm strikes."

"He's lost?" That would upset Andre, she thought grimly.

"We're not certain. Brad's working on the controls now."

"Then leave right now and get that part for the engine," she said quickly. What Ted didn't realize was that she was coming to a firm decision. "How long will it take you to repair it?"

He glanced at his watch. "If everything goes just right, it'll be at least three hours." He gave her a quick kiss on her cheek. "Take care, Minta."

"You, too, Ted. And tell Lydia goodbye for me."

He glanced down. "I will."

When Ted left, Minta stopped for one last look at the cottage. She remembered when she'd first seen it and what high hopes she'd had for a restful vacation. Her whole world had turned upside down since then, and she doubted she'd ever be able to set it right. Determined not to wallow in disturbing memories, she walked briskly into her bedroom.

When she glimpsed her reflection in the mirror, she gasped in surprise over the baggy clothes she was wearing. She'd forgotten to give them back to Ted. Or to mention the gun she'd taken from him, she realized, fingering it in her pocket. Well, she'd just have to phone him later and ask how she could mail back the clothes. But not the gun. If she was able to follow through on the plan of action developing in her mind, the gun might be a handy deterrent.

Before changing out of the loose clothes, she called the hotel where Jerry was supposed to be staying but was told there was no answer in his room. "Would you like to leave a message?" the clerk asked.

"No, but I'd like to make a reservation for a room for myself." As soon as that was completed she called for a taxi and then changed into a fresh pair of duck slacks and a nautical knit shirt. When her bags were packed, she went out on the front porch to wait.

Jerry had not returned to his room when she reached the luxury high-rise hotel located on Seven Mile Beach. She left a message at the desk for him to call her after checking into her own room.

Once she arrived there, she paced the floor restlessly. She wanted desperately to share all she knew about the case with Jerry.

Every instinct was telling her to return to Brad. But he had ordered her to leave the island. Of course, she could slip on board *Lydia*....

She stopped pacing and ran over to the phone. Checking through the services offered, she located one designated as secretarial. She dialed the number quickly. "I'd like to rent a cassette recorder for twenty-four hours," she told the woman who answered the phone.

When the recorder was delivered to her room, Minta settled down in a chair and punched the record button. She spoke clearly. "This is Agent Horizon. On April twentieth I arrived on the Cayman Islands. At the airport I was directly behind a man who dropped his briefcase. When I attempted to help him retrieve his papers, he acted suspiciously...."

When she finished detailing what had occurred on her vacation, she checked her watch. Forty-five minutes had elapsed. The phone rang and she answered it eagerly. Jerry was speaking, "I got yours and Al's messages. Where can we meet?"

They met in Jerry's room. He hugged her when she came inside. "What's this about Al's message?" she asked as she kissed him on the cheek.

He showed it to her and she began smiling as she read it. So Al had decided to act as if he had ordered her to help Jerry. It didn't bother her. As long as he was backing down, she didn't care who got the credit.

"What do you know?" Jerry asked her. "I've got to leave for an appointment right away. On our way, you can fill me in."

"Where are you going?" she asked.

"For a date with a sub, sweetheart."

"Then I'll have to give you this," she told him, reaching for the cassette she'd slipped in her purse. "If you need a player, I've got one in my room."

"I have one. Why are you leaving in such a hurry?" he asked.

"To keep an eye on a creature named Hugo." She slipped the cassette in his pocket. "Everything I know is on that tape, Jerry. It tells you where Brad McMillan and his beloved underwater robot are. It details everything about the men after that robot, including a complete layout of the yacht that belongs to Andre Mirabeau."

Jerry whistled in admiration. "How did you find out about all this?"

"It came up and bit me, and I couldn't help feeling it," she teased.

"You're amazing, Minta. Have you met McMillan?"

Her breezy manner vanished. She swallowed, nodding. "Yes, I know him. Tell me your plans, Jerry so I can help."

"I'm going on board a navy sub and we're going to try to intercept *Omen* before it can rendezvous with *Lydia*."

"Then what?"

He shrugged, clearly puzzled. "We'll either capture or destroy our enemies, Minta."

She shuddered involuntarily, knowing she'd made the right decision to return to *Lydia*. No matter what happened she wanted to be with Brad, to give him one last chance to change his mind or to capture him herself before he risked being killed. "Do you have time to tell me more, Jerry?"

"Five minutes. What do you want to know?"

"What's McMillan doing?"

"He's suspected of selling plans for a super-weapon to the enemy."

"I know that. Why?"

Jerry laughed. "Hell, I don't know. I've read his background and he's only got one blot on it."

"Vietnam?"

He nodded. She protested, "But that was only an allegation."

"I know," he agreed quickly. "But this looks bad, Minta. He's had several meetings with known counteragents."

"I know," she sighed, twisting her hands together. "But there's a chance he's innocent. He told me he contacted the State Department about the men but they wouldn't believe him."

"You've discussed this with McMillan?" Jerry asked, his voice rising in amazement.

She nodded with a slight smile. "I wish I had time to tell you everything so I could watch your expression when you hear where I was most of yesterday and last night."

Jerry grinned. "I can't wait. I've got another minute. Tell me why McMillan is here testing his robot if he knows enemy agents are after it."

"I don't know the answer to that," she admitted. "He seems driven where Hugo's concerned."

"It must be money," said Jerry. "His company is highly successful but it needs to improve its cash flow or its stock will fall. Of course, that's a perfect motive for selling information to our enemies, too."

Things were looking blacker by the minute for Brad. Jerry glanced at his watch and turned to Minta. "Where will you be if I need to reach you?" he said.

"I'll be with Brad," Minta answered.

Jerry's eyebrows lifted imperceptibly. "Are you sure you know what you're doing?" he said.

"Everything's on the tape," she told him, walking to the door.

After she returned to her room she made one last call. To Lydia. "Have you heard from Ted or Brad?" Minta asked casually.

"Yes, Ted called a few minutes ago. I thought you were on the plane to Miami."

"It's been delayed a few minutes," Minta temporized.

"Not because of the storm, I hope. According to

the last reports it's stalled out in the Caribbean. I hate when that happens. The winds get a chance to build. Sometimes they do so much damage."

"Do you have a place to go to if it's bad?" Minta asked. There was something about Lydia that brought out the protective instinct in her, she realized.

"This house is as safe as any. It's over a hundred years old, so it's seen lots of storms. I'm glad you called to say goodbye. I hope you and Brad will visit us again soon."

Lydia appeared to be totally in the dark about Brad's real reasons for being on the island. How about Ted? Until this morning Minta had been certain he had no idea that Brad was dealing with undesirables. But there had been a nervousness about him today that had bothered her. Maybe it was because of the approaching storm. A ship's captain would feel the responsibility for the safety of his ship and crew. "Did Ted say when he and Brad are leaving to search for Hugo?"

"He has to repair the engine first. He got the right part and was on his way back to the ship. I wish they'd just stay in the harbor until the storm's over but Ted says Brad is desperate."

"I sensed that, too. When he rescued me last night...."

"Were you in trouble?" Lydia interrupted.

"You could call it that but I'm fine now," Minta answered quickly. She didn't have time to talk about her kidnapping, but it struck her as strange

Ted hadn't mentioned it to his wife. "Lydia, I'm worried about Brad. Something's bothering him."

"Ted told me I was imagining things when I said that to him. I can't imagine what it could be. He's such a well-known robot expert that he ought to be sitting on top of the world."

"His company's not in over its head financially?"

"We own stock in it, and our shares have dropped recently. I wish I could tell you something more definite."

"You've been helpful," said Minta. "I've got to run now. I'll write."

Minta checked for the small weapon in her purse and then went out into the hall. When she reached the lobby she walked across it briskly and went outside to the taxi stand. As she waited, she scanned the cloud-filled sky. A heavy, humid breeze was blowing that made it seem difficult to breathe, and she could see a crew of men taping the windows on a small gift shop across the street.

When a taxi became available, she climbed in. "To the harbor," she told him. "I'm looking for the section where the fishing boats dock."

He gave her a puzzled look but started the engine. When they arrived at the quay she paid and gave him a generous tip. "This isn't the best area for a woman alone," he told her.

"I know. I can take care of myself," she told him with an appreciative smile.

Ted's ship was still moored at the dock. She

ducked behind a vendor's stall and checked to see who was on the top deck.

A sailor bumped against her. Deliberately, she surmised. Ignoring him, she moved aside as she caught sight of Brad's back. Nervously she moistened her lips as she watched his hands gesturing to one of the crew members.

The sailor continued to stand there, watching her with an insolent stare. An idea popped into her head and she studied his muscular forearms covertly.

Satisfied, she reached in her purse and drew out a large bill. "Is this enough for you to go on board that ship and cause a little trouble? I want everyone on board kept busy long enough for me to slip on without being seen."

CHAPTER NINETEEN

MINTA KEPT OUT OF SIGHT as the sailor she'd paid jumped off the quay onto the deck of *Lydia*. "I've come for the money you owe me," he shouted.

Brad turned, and Minta saw Ted had been standing just in front of him, hidden from her view. Ted stepped forward and faced the sailor. "I think you've made a mistake, mate. Just who do you think you're looking for on my ship?"

Minta took advantage of the fracas to spring across the street and jump down onto the deck of the ship. She kept close to the railing until she reached the ladder leading below deck. The sailor's voice grew louder and she heard Brad joining in, ordering the man to leave the vessel at once.

When she climbed down to the lower deck, she reached in her purse for a credit card and used the small piece of plastic to unlock the door leading into the closet. She crept inside and hid in the room behind several large crates. It was stuffy and hot, and her legs ached in the cramped position she was forced to assume.

The voices above her were muffled now, and gradually she heard them dying away. Minta tried to find a more comfortable position but gave up at length and forced herself to relax in the position she was in. A long wait lay ahead of her and she'd be wise to try to get some sleep. She was confident the motion of the ship, when it finally got underway, would awaken her.

Eventually she slept... fitfully in the beginning with a jumble of dreams, but in the end she slept deeply. When she awoke she felt the wooden flooring under her begin to vibrate and knew the ship was moving out. She attempted to rise from her cramped position and hit her head against one of the shelves. With a moan, she sank back down. The muscles in her legs were aching now and her head was pounding. From lack of food, probably.

She remembered she'd seen a box of candy bars on one of the shelves. Feeling with her hand, she located the string dangling above her. She pulled it and moved quickly when the light came on. After she'd located the box of candy, she selected several and then flipped off the light, not certain if it could be seen beneath the closet door.

After hurriedly eating the candy without enjoying it, she located her purse and secured it on her shoulder. As she maneuvered her way toward the door, she heard the sound of footsteps approaching. They stopped a short distance from her door, and then someone else came up and stopped also.

"Do you have news on the position of the storm?" she heard Brad ask.

"New coordinates will be issued within the hour. I vote we head away from it. We can go over to Brac and wait it out in my house," Ted answered.

"If you're afraid of the storm, Ted, why don't you let down a lifeboat and paddle back to shore? You know I've got to get to Hugo before those bastards do."

The two men started walking away, and Minta strained to hear what they were saying. She recognized Ted's voice saying, "That bunch aren't going to risk taking an expensive yacht like *Omen* out in this storm, Brad. As soon as the storm clears, I promise we'll get to Hugo first."

Brad's tone was stubborn. "We've let the crew go. Now there's only you, Ted. I'm going. . . ."

The voices died away, and Minta pushed open the closet door a crack and peered outside. The lower hallway was deserted. Cautiously she moved outside and crept along it until she reached the ladder.

The sky was much darker than when she'd boarded the ship. She checked her watch and saw that it was still early in the afternoon. As she started up the ladder, she paused on each rung and waited, alert for the least sound. There were none.

When she reached the top of the ladder, she took a quick look around and saw that the two men were in the wheelhouse. Their backs were to her but still she waited, wondering if she should make her appearance when they were farther out to sea. A light mist had begun to fall, cooling her heated body, and she tilted her head back, enjoying the feel of the rain on her face.

The sleep and sugar had energized her in addition to the surge of excitement she always got whenever she faced danger. Totally unworried about the approaching storm, she felt ready to handle whatever happened.

Brad's insistence on reaching Hugo before the spies did left her puzzled. Did he mean he was determined not to let them have his secrets? Or was he only worried they'd steal his ideas without paying for them? Leaning against the rail, she decided that was what she would have to find out before she took any action against him.

BRAD WAS BEWILDERED by Ted's fear of the storm. The man had never reacted like this before. He'd even been guarding the radio so Brad had been forced to insist that he call for the latest weather bulletins.

The storm was bad. No doubt about that. But unless it veered off its present course in the next hour, they'd have time to reach Hugo and either rescue or destroy him before its full force hit them.

He leaned over and shouted above the noise of the engine and wind, "How's the engine doing, Ted?"

"Not too good."

"Sounds perfect to me. I'm getting the strange idea you don't want to rescue Hugo."

Ted glanced up and Brad saw fear in his eyes. "Ted, what's wrong?"

"I'm turning this ship around. I tell you, the storm's too bad, Brad."

"Quit cowering like a whipped dog," Brad shouted. "Hand me that wheel. I'll steer her if you've forgotten how."

He reached for the wheel, angrily elbowing Ted away from it. He'd paid the man top price for the use of this ship, and Ted knew he'd stand good for any damage the storm did. Muttering to himself over his friend's strange behavior, Brad studied the charts before him.

"Hand back that wheel," he heard Ted saying behind him.

There was a menacing tone in the voice that made Brad twist his head around. He stared, disbelievingly, into the barrel of a gun held by Ted.

"You heard me," Ted growled. "This is my ship. It's not going out in this storm."

Brad almost laughed. "Like hell, Ted. I'll buy *Lydia* off of you if that's what it takes to get Hugo."

Ted moved closer and waved the gun at him. "I'm serious about this, Brad. Step away from that wheel."

Brad moved back, not from fear but from bewilderment over Ted's irrational behavior. "What's really bothering you, Ted?" he asked.

Ted kept the gun poised in one hand as he grasped the wheel with the other. "We're turning this ship around. Now, Brad. You're wasting your time asking questions."

From the corner of his eye, Brad saw Minta stride into the wheelhouse, a small weapon held in both her hands. "Drop your gun, Ted," she ordered in a professional voice.

Ted whirled and Minta let go of her weapon with one hand and reached for his in a swift motion. Before Brad could even open his mouth to speak, she had disarmed Ted.

"Minta," he gasped, smiling at her. "It looks as if you're just in time. I think Ted's gone out of his mind."

"You, too, McMillan," Minta said. "Move over beside Ted so I can keep this gun aimed at both of you."

Surprise siphoned the blood from his face. He moved beside Ted, calculating his chances of knocking the gun from Minta's hands. His worst fears were being confirmed. Minta was one of them! Several times he'd thought about the possibility, but until now he hadn't allowed himself to believe it. "So the kidnapping was all a fake?" he said.

She was confused by his odd question but she recovered quickly. "I don't know what's going on in here between you two but I'm in charge now."

"Minta," Ted said, reaching out a hand in a conciliatory gesture.

"Your job is to steer this vessel out to Hugo, Ted," she said coldly.

"And what am I supposed to do?" Brad asked smoothly.

"Keep us on Hugo's trail."

"And then you're going to turn him over to your totalitarian friends?"

Minta kept the gun level with one hand and reached into her purse with the other. With an experienced movement, she grasped her identification card and flipped it out. "Wrong, McMillan. This is an FBI operation and I'm an agent."

"My God," said Brad. "So the State Department did take my call seriously, after all." The relief of knowing he was not all alone in this almost overwhelmed him. Then he realized the full impact of what Minta was telling him. "But, you, Minta," he said in a low voice. "Why didn't you tell me before? You know how worried I've been. Was it all some kind of cruel joke that you kept your true identity from me?"

"I wasn't assigned to this case when I arrived on Grand Cayman," she explained, eyeing Ted when he started to move away. He stopped when he noticed the stern expression on her face and she continued, "In fact, my department isn't even involved with espionage. But gradually I began to realize that you weren't telling me everything, Brad."

"Then came the phone call yesterday morning?"

"Yes, from a friend at the FBI who told me about this case. They told me they suspected you...."

"Me? I'm a suspect? For what?" Not again. A repeat of what had happened in Vietnam. Only it was worse this time. Now the woman he loved was being told lies about him. Even though past experience had taught him it was useless to try to convince people of his innocence, he had to make this effort. Minta meant too much to him. "I've been trying to get away from those bastards since they first contacted me in Austin. They followed me to the Caymans...."

"Why didn't you stop your tests on Hugo for a while?" she demanded.

"The bid. If you're so smart, you must know about the bid Galactia is trying to win. These tests had to be finished before the submission date ran out for us to stand a chance."

"And that bid was worth all this?"

He looked at her briefly. She didn't believe him. He could tell by her sharp questioning. "Galactia's stock has been the subject of a vicious rumor campaign lately. I have a responsibility to a lot of people. Not rich people but ordinary hard-working ones who've invested in my company. I had to make every effort to keep their money for them." Suddenly he turned away and moved over to the window, not caring what Minta did with her weapon. "If I talked myself hoarse, I can see you wouldn't change your mind about my guilt."

Something snapped inside Minta. Brad was telling the truth. She knew it, and she was hurting him deeply by refusing to believe him. "Why were you telling Brad he couldn't find Hugo?" she asked Ted, switching her full attention on him.

"The storm," he said quickly.

She knew he was lying. "It's not that bad," she answered. "We're going after Hugo."

Ted's shoulders began shaking as sobs racked his body. "I'm sorry, Brad," he said. "I never thought I could do something like this. But it was for Lydia. They were blackmailing me. They said if I didn't help them get the robot they'd tell her all about Vietnam."

Brad turned around. "Who, Ted?"

"Andre Mirabeau, the terrorist. He's the middle man in this deal. He's offered to get the technical information and sell it to the agents from the Eastern-bloc countries that have been harassing you."

Brad's face was ashen as he was stunned by another revelation. "You, Ted? You're on their team?" He took a deep breath before continuing. "I should have guessed it. I've known since I arrived something was bothering you. But this?"

Ted's only answer was a sob. "Tie his hands, Brad," Minta said quietly. "Then I hope you know enough about navigation to get us where we're going."

Brad gave her a piercing gaze that made her hands tremble. After a long silence he said, "I assume this means you believe me, Minta."

She nodded. Ted interrupted, snapping the tension between them. "Let me help. I promise I'm on your side now."

"Tie his hands," Minta repeated.

Brad seemed reluctant but he left the wheelhouse,

returning a few minutes later with some rope. Ted held out his hands and Minta directed, "Behind his back."

Brad glanced over at her. She recognized the expression in his eyes. She'd seen it too many times in other men's eyes when she'd performed in a purely professional manner. Although it hurt that Brad was judging her femininity in a new light, she couldn't dwell on it now. Later, when this was over, she'd have to face the fact that Brad may not care for this new side of her. As Brad complied with her instructions, she slipped the gun back in her purse and moved over to the charts.

There was no time for personal conversation the next half hour as they bent their heads over the chart and tried to set a course for Hugo. Minta called for a fresh weather report and traced it on the map. "It's not heading in our exact direction. What do you think, Brad?"

"We'll make it," he said. "If I can only get closer, I have another alternative."

"What's that?"

"I have a control that can cause Hugo to self-destruct."

"But all your work? And the money?"

"I'm not letting our enemies get hold of him."

His quiet determination filled her with a sense of peace. "What good will stealing Hugo do those men? I thought you said that you had the plans in your head."

"I did until the tests yesterday were completed.

Now Hugo's ready to go. He's at the stage now where an expert can decipher most of his secrets. That's why I built in the self-destruct mode.'' He turned back to the ship's wheel.

Ted leaned against the wall in the corner of the room. Several times he interjected some advice, and Minta could see that Brad was eager to listen. ''What happened in Vietnam that could make you a target for blackmail?'' Minta asked him, when things began to run smoothly.

Brad glanced at Ted and nodded his head. ''Tell her, Ted, or I will have to.''

''I don't want Lydia to find out about a baby I fathered over there. We had only been married a couple of months when I went overseas. I was just nineteen. When I got there, I was desperately afraid that I was going to die, so I decided to get all the pleasure I could out of life.''

Minta watched him, silent. Inside she was overwhelmed by sympathy as she watched the tortured expression on his face. Ted continued, ''Anyway, I got this Viet woman pregnant. She was just a kid, and I felt sorry for her. I didn't love her. I couldn't because I still loved Lydia too much. But somehow that made it seem even worse. Like I'd taken advantage of this woman.''

''Tell me what was happening with Lydia during this time,'' Brad said.

Ted lowered his eyes. ''I didn't know it at first, but I'd gotten Lydia pregnant before I left. She had a miscarriage. At first I intended to tell her about this other woman to see if she'd forgive me but then I couldn't. I couldn't even bring my son home when his mother died."

Brad interrupted. "The woman followed Ted everywhere we went. She had a boy and then was killed in the incident where I was accused of passing information on to the enemy."

"Where is your son now?" she asked Ted. The image of Lydia's room prepared and waiting for the child they had never had filled her head, and she had to fight back the tears.

"He's in France. In an orphanage. I've never deserted him. I send money for his support but I don't want Lydia to ever find out about it. I couldn't stand it if she found out I was unfaithful to her when she was carrying our child."

"And Andre Mirabeau found out about this?" Minta asked.

"Evidently. He came to see me, carrying pictures of my son and threatened to tell Lydia unless I fully cooperated."

"What kind of cooperation?"

"I was to help Brad conduct his tests until Hugo was ready. Then I was to prevent Brad from taking him out of the ocean until they had a chance to steal him."

"You should have told me," Brad said. "I'm your friend, Ted. I could have helped you resolve the problem."

"Both of you have forgotten one thing," said Minta. "Lydia should have been told the truth.

She's not a fragile doll. Think how she's going to feel now."

Ted moaned and sank down into his seat. "I ask one thing of you, Minta. If you have any say at all, please let me be allowed to tell her everything myself before she hears it from the FBI."

"I'll try, Ted. Not for you but for Lydia's sake. None of this is her fault," agreed Minta.

Brad's whole face lit up with a smile.

As the minutes ticked by the situation became increasingly desperate. The storm bulletins were coming in more regularly now, and the winds had begun veering in their direction. Brad's knuckles grew white as he held on to the wheel and tried to keep the vessel on course.

Minta made coffee and relieved him at intervals so he could keep an eye on the controls that were zeroed in on Hugo. "If we can only get a few miles closer," he said in a hoarse voice. "I'll never forgive myself if something I've invented falls into such evil hands."

"We'll make it," Minta said. "We're not alone." She explained about her meeting with Jerry Richards earlier that day and about how even now a navy sub was on its way.

"I'm not going to depend on any help," Brad insisted grimly. "I've been down that route before."

Minta went outside into the slanting rain and peered into the ship's telescope. She blinked twice to make sure she'd seen what she thought she had and then ran back to Brad. "*Omen*. It's straight ahead. I saw it through the telescope."

"Damn," he shouted. "Just as we're getting near enough to Hugo to activate his retrieval mode. Are you certain?"

She nodded. "I'm setting the wheel on automatic then," he said. "Grab it if it slips off while I get ready to destroy Hugo."

"No, Brad. Let's wait," pleaded Minta, but it was too late. He was on his way. Minta followed him out, frowning as she watched him through the rain. The waves sloshing against the ship were growing in intensity now, throwing up windswept spray that washed the decks. It whipped Minta's hair as salt spray slashed her face, stinging her lips and tongue.

The sea taunted them, rolling the ship up and then throwing it down with frightening force. The water was foaming in turmoil, reminding her of the approaching storm. Returning inside, Minta found an agitated Ted.

"Let me persuade him not to do it," Ted pleaded. "If you'd let me handle that wheel, I could outmaneuver *Omen*."

Minta hesitated and then untied Ted's hands. "Don't let yourself or Lydia down," she warned him.

When she reached the control room, Brad glanced up. "What's the matter?"

"Ted thinks we have a chance to outrun *Omen*."

"If he was at the controls...."

"He is. What can I do to help in here?"

Brad was suddenly terrified. Not for himself but for Minta. He realized there was a distinct possibility that if he were forced to blow up Hugo, it could destroy their vessel as well.

If it only involved Ted and himself, he wouldn't hesitate. But he loved Minta. He wanted her to live, and he wanted to be with her. He didn't want them both to die now. He knew he had to let her help decide their fate.

"Minta, I love you," he shouted.

She smiled at him. "I love you, too, but why are you telling me this now?"

"I have to. How important is it to you that Mirabeau doesn't get his hands on Hugo?"

Her eyes grew round. "I'd die first."

"You're certain?"

"No doubts. Why?"

"Because destroying Hugo could mean the ship will explode."

She hesitated, letting his words sink in before saying, "And you're willing to do that?"

"For myself, but I can't make that decision for you."

"We'll die together," she shouted above the deafening roar of the storm.

Her words were almost drowned out by a booming voice that came from overhead. Both of them glanced up as it came again. "Ahoy, *Omen*. This is the FBI. You are inside Caymanian territory. Surrender immediately. Either we board you or we will be forced to destroy you."

Minta threw up her arms, shouting, "It's Jerry. He's here with the navy."

Brad pulled her down on the deck as a volley of gunfire erupted from *Omen*'s deck. "That helicopter will be shot out of the sky," he shouted, his mouth close to her ear.

"The navy will destroy that vessel if it doesn't surrender," Minta answered.

When the firing stopped momentarily, they ran for the telescope. Another warning from Jerry threatened immediate action, and then Brad glanced up from the scope, shouting, "They're surrendering. They're hoisting the flag asking to be boarded."

"Let me see," Minta said. She watched as wind tossed lines were lowered from the helicopter. "The storm's too bad. They'll never make it."

Pride filled Brad's voice. "Sure they will. They're a crack navy team."

Brad took over back at the scope and Minta ran to the railing, watching with baited breath until she saw the first of the daring naval men rappeling down the lines. It seemed strange to her that Andre Mirabeau was giving up this easily. She prayed it wasn't a trap.

Brad shouted, "I see two of the men I've met. They're holding guns on another man...."

Minta ran to him and peered through the lens. "Your friends have disarmed Andre Mirabeau. I guess they decided they weren't going to be charged with terrorism along with him."

"Don't ever call them my friends again."

They were still watching as the last man landed on board *Omen*'s deck. The helicopter began moving in their direction, and then they heard Jerry's voice directly above them. "Minta Cordero. Where are you?"

She began waving her arms. Ted and Brad followed and joined in.

"Make room on the diving platform for a landing," Jerry's voice ordered.

They fell back and watched as the pilot attempted to position the helicopter in spite of the heavy winds. Minta had almost given up hope when it finally settled down. She smiled broadly as Jerry Richards stepped from the craft.

"Is everything under control here, Cordero?" he asked.

She looked at Brad and then at Ted and then back at Brad. She recognized his silent plea for her to go easy on his friend. She hesitated for a tense moment and then decided in Ted's favor. "Everything's under control, Jerry. These two men are on our side."

CHAPTER TWENTY

MINTA FIDDLED HALFHEARTEDLY with some paper-work that was already past due. Each time her eyes strayed to the silent phone on her desk she glanced away. She didn't need any more reminders that four days had passed and Brad hadn't called.

She'd run out of excuses for him. At first, she'd reminded herself that after she'd boarded the heli-copter with Jerry and flown back to Grand Cayman, Brad had remained behind on *Lydia* to retrieve Hugo from the sea. It was easy to understand why he couldn't call her until that was finished.

Then Lydia had called two days ago to tell her that both Ted and Brad had arrived back at Brac. The tro-pical storm that had been threatening had changed courses, and the men had been lashed by only the tail end of the massive winds.

The memory of Lydia's call brought a half smile to Minta's lips and she forgot her own troubles momen-tarily. Lydia's gratitude over what she felt Minta had done for them had been effusive. True to the promise Minta had extracted from him, Ted had told his wife the entire story. Lydia admitted she'd suspected part of it for years, but now that it was out in the open she

felt as if they were beginning a whole new life together. She had even hinted that her dream now was
to go to France and meet Ted's son and see if there
was any possibility they could bring him to their
home. Minta was glad this episode had ended happi-
ly. Ted had suffered enough, and she was certain he
had learned a lesson about giving in to blackmailers'
demands.

The phone rang and Minta grabbed for it eagerly,
almost upsetting a mug of cold coffee beside it. She
barely hid her disappointment when she heard Jill's
voice. "Jerry would like you to attend a meeting in
his conference room at ten-thirty today."

Minta flipped over to the correct date on her calen-
dar pad. "No problem," she assured Jill.

"Have you caught up on your sleep?" Jill asked.

"Almost." Since her return she had used fatigue
as an excuse not to accept any of Jill's invitations to
go out together. She couldn't find it in herself to
laugh with friends.

"Stop by my office on your way to the conference
room, and we'll decide when we can go to lunch
together."

"Will do," Minta answered, trying to inject an
upbeat note into her dispirited voice.

She swore softly as she replaced the receiver. It
wasn't her nature to mope around when something
was bothering her. Especially when she'd known all
along that when Brad learned she was an undercover
agent he'd react like this.

Granted she had some cause for disappointment.

She had expected him to call and make a few polite noises about the time they'd spent together. That way she wouldn't feel so totally let down and left hanging.

She grabbed up the phone suddenly, furious with herself for being so passive. It was just as much her right to make the first move as his. She dialed information for Austin, Texas, and got both Galactia's number and Brad's home phone.

Hilda answered at Brad's home. Her strange computer voice brought a rush of tears to Minta's eyes, but she brushed them away angrily. She must be in a bad way to miss a hunk of metal. Hilda announced that Brad wasn't at home. Minta didn't leave a message.

When the switchboard operator at Galactia said Brad wasn't in his office, Minta requested Ron Williams. "What do you wish to discuss with Mr. Williams?" the woman asked.

"On second thought, I've changed my mind. Thanks, anyway," Minta mumbled. As the line went dead in her ear she grabbed up her purse and headed for the powder room. Right now she wasn't fit company for anyone.

The dark circles under her eyes surprised her as she looked at her reflection in the wall-sized mirror in the powder room. She took out some blusher and added more color to her cheeks before brushing her long hair until it shone. For the first time she wondered what kind of conference Jerry was holding this morning. Surely not another wrap-up for the

Cayman case. They'd already dissected each piece of evidence to shreds. Perhaps he had an update on Israel's request to extradite Andre Mirabeau to stand trial for the murder of the ballet dancers in Paris last year.

Jerry might want to discuss Bobby Hall's request to attend a training session at the FBI academy. After her return to Grand Cayman, Minta had called Bobby and invited him to have dinner with her at the hotel. She could still recall the astonishment on his face when she'd told him what had been happening on his tiny island and that she was an agent. She'd had a hard time convincing him that it was better for the Cayman police force not to get involved. Trying to bring charges against the spies for their illegal activities on the island would have been next to impossible. At least he'd called her a few days later to report they'd raided the estate and found the black car and the red-haired woman. She had been deported the same as her co-workers. That's when Bobby had asked to attend the FBI's training program for foreign law-enforcement personnel.

A glance at her watch revealed she only had a short time before she was due at Jerry's meeting, so she smoothed pink gloss on her lips and stood. She hoped it was an informal gathering. The gray linen suit she wore with its lacy camisole was a little less professional than she would have chosen for an interdepartmental meeting but it would have to do, she decided.

Jill jumped up when she came into her office and offered her a cup of coffee. "No, thanks," Minta said. "Have I mentioned how much I appreciate the way you handled my mail and checked on my apartment during my vacation?"

Jill gave her a puzzled look. "Several times, Minta. And you gave me that pair of silver earrings I've been coveting and sent me two tickets to my favorite musical."

Minta gave her a quick smile to hide her embarrassment. "What's on Jerry's agenda today?"

Jill looked down at the appointment book on her desk. "After the meeting this morning, he's having lunch with Ambassador...."

"No," interrupted Minta. "I meant what's going on at ten-thirty."

Jill gave her the wide-eyed innocent look that Minta always found particularly maddening because it meant her friend was hiding something. "Jerry doesn't discuss everything with me, Minta."

Minta laughed mirthlessly. "He doesn't have to. You have such a keen radar you always know what's going on around here."

Jill glanced at the wall clock. "You better get yourself down to that conference room. You're almost late."

"These meetings never get started on time," Minta said, walking over to the window and glancing down at the sidewalk. *The crowds hurrying by seem to all have a purpose,* she thought. *Like I used to have.* She'd only been gone a short time, but it seemed as if everything in her life had changed. And not for the better.

Except here at work, she corrected guiltily. She

was grateful for the change in Al's attitude. They'd had a long discussion the day of her return to D.C. Now they had what she considered a workable truce. He'd even apologized for the strong-arm tactics he'd used on her in the past, adding that he'd had no right to bully her into changing a modus operandi that had been highly effective in her career.

She'd admitted some of her weaknesses also. A tendency to get so involved in a case she didn't rest enough or eat properly. Although she doubted she'd ever have the respect for Al she did for Jerry, she felt good about continuing to work with him now. Especially since he proved how much he'd changed when he had not argued with her after she had insisted on cutting her vacation short to return to work.

"You're five minutes late, Minta," Jill insisted sharply.

Minta turned. "I told you I'm trying to learn to take it easy. Anyway, how about you? I thought you would be taking notes at the meeting."

"I'm waiting for you," Jill answered, flipping a switch on her phone so it would be answered at the main switchboard. She grabbed up her notepad. "Let's go."

Jill pushed open the conference-room door, but then stepped aside for Minta to go in. Minta stopped when she saw the crowd inside. The long conference table had been pushed to the rear of the room. Folding chairs, arranged in even rows, were completely peopled. In the front of the room was a platform and behind it an American flag draped against the wall.

Jerry gave Minta and Jill a sharp glance as he paused in the speech he seemed to be delivering to the audience. Minta slid along the wall with Jill behind her until she located two empty seats. After she was seated she glanced at the person beside her and did a double take. It was Elizabeth Forrester.

Elizabeth leaned over and hugged her and over Elizabeth's shoulder, Minta noticed Wolf and Sarah Larsen. Then she knew what was going on. An honor ceremony. Some kind of commendation for the Cayman case. Nothing else would bring these friends out on a busy Friday morning.

Jerry was speaking again. "As all of you know, the FBI traditionally likes to honor those who participate in ridding our country of the criminal element. Whether it is one of our staff or a civilian, we like to recognize a person who goes above and beyond the call. This morning we're particularly pleased to give this Meritorious Award to a private citizen. Will you please come forward, Brad McMillan?"

A soft gasp escaped Minta's lips as she leaned forward and watched Brad moving with easy strides down the center aisle. When he reached the platform and turned to face the audience she had difficulty breathing. Dressed in a silky gray business suit with his thick dark hair lying smoothly against his neck, he was even more attractive than she remembered.

Jerry continued speaking, "Mr. McMillan is a

private citizen, but he felt a strong sense of duty. When he was approached by enemy agents in Austin, Texas, concerning one of his robotic inventions, he called the State Department and reported it.

"To the shame of all involved, I must admit that the report was lost in one of those unfortunate bureaucratic paper shufflings. Although abandoned by his government, Mr. McMillan then attempted single-handedly to prevent the enemy from stealing his invention as he finished vital tests on his robot in the Cayman Islands.

"It was only through a series of surveillance operations that the CIA and then our own department learned of what was happening and became involved in the case. Not knowing about the call Mr. McMillan had made until we returned to D.C. and did our own checking, we unfortunately mistook Mr. McMillan as our prime suspect.

"I'm happy to report that the enemy was captured. Andre Mirabeau, one of the most vicious terrorists I've ever been involved with, is now on his way to Israel to stand trial for murder. The other spies have had their visas canceled and will no longer be allowed entry into our country. But best of all, Hugo, Mr. McMillan's underwater exploration robot, has been chosen by the navy for one of its long-range projects."

He turned to Brad, "Thanks for not giving up on your country even when it appeared it had deserted you. We in this room are proud to be your fellow citizens."

Minta watched through blurry eyes as Brad accepted the plaque. Brad's voice was steady. "I admit to being outraged by the way a person can be suspected of treason on the basis of circumstantial evidence. This award today restores my faith in our system of justice. I will hang it on my wall proudly."

As he made his way back to his seat, Minta's last hopes were crushed. Brad had to have seen her make her late entrance, but never once had he glanced her way during the entire time he was up front. But his speech had been directed at her, she knew. He was telling her what he thought of the suspicions she had labeled him with. The worst part was she knew she deserved his outrage.

She felt Elizabeth giving her a gentle poke in the ribs, and she glanced up as Al Slessor took Jerry's place. Al's face was ruddier than usual when he started to talk in his gravelly voice. "Today I'm here to present an award to a member of my department. It's hard to stand in front of people and admit you've got egg on your face. But several weeks ago I decided to call an employee in and admonish her to curb her actions. I told this individual she was too zealous, too curious, too dedicated. In fact, I even hinted she was becoming a little unbalanced."

He laughed nervously and glanced over at Minta. She shifted in her seat and wondered what he might say next.

Al continued, "I advised...or should I say suggested strongly...that this agent take a long break from her work. She listened with an open mind and agreed. To make a long story short, she chose the Caymans for this respite. As you've all heard, she stumbled into this terrorist ring there. I'll save the rest of her intriguing story for her to write in her memoirs some day. Minta, please come forward so I can award you with a Commendation for Outstanding Performance.''

Applause broke out in the audience, and Elizabeth pushed Minta to her feet. As she started forward, the audience rose and gave her a standing ovation. When she reached the platform, she stared over the heads of the crowd in an attempt to keep her head held high. And to prevent her from having to see the cynical expression she knew must be on Brad's face.

BRAD STOOD WITH THE REST of the crowd, clapping loudly. He was infinitely pleased to be a part of this moment honoring Minta. Damn, he'd never seen her looking more lovely as she walked onto the platform, head held high, slender body poised and alert and that long, glorious dark hair settling against the length of her straight back.

For four days now he'd been marshaling the arguments he intended to use to convince her their life-styles could mesh. Sure, they were different. They'd never have the kind of marriage where each felt they had the right to make demands on the other. No, both would have to accept that the other was free to leave home for work on a moment's notice.

Even if an emergency arose in one's life, the other would have to understand that the partner might be out of reach. But it would be a good marriage. He knew it would. They loved each other, respected each other and best of all, trusted each other.

He would never forget that moment on the ship when he'd seen Minta's eyes as she'd lowered the gun. He had felt like shouting with triumph. With absolutely no proof to the contrary, Minta had believed in him! She'd known he would never betray his country by selling out to the enemy. If he could have planned a test of love for the woman he wanted to marry, it couldn't have worked out more perfectly. His cynicism about people, his hurt over what had happened to him in Vietnam, had all vanished in the warmth of her love.

But that was his side. While he had no doubts, he still wasn't sure about Minta. She loved him, but was she ready to share her life with someone else? More than anything, he was hoping she wouldn't try to argue that they could have a relationship without committing themselves. While logically it might make sense, it wasn't what he wanted. Maybe he wanted too much, he warned himself grimly, as the ceremony on the stage ended. He groaned silently as Jerry invited everyone to move to the room next door where a reception was being held for the honorees.

He started toward the front of the room and then was beseiged by well-wishers. When Jerry had called the evening before to ask him when he'd be available to come to D.C. to accept his award, he'd explained that he already had a plane reservation for early the next morning. Jerry had told him no reporters would be at the meeting. . .Minta still had too much work to do to risk having her cover blown. He'd tried to convince Jerry that he'd rather receive his award in absentia but Jerry had pleaded with him, saying, "It'll encourage our staff. Sometimes we get the feeling we're engaged in a fight against evil all alone. When we see people like you who help voluntarily, we feel it's all worthwhile."

Brad had agreed and had then tried to get up the nerve to call Minta. But he had given up. What they had to discuss was better done in person. But when, he wondered, as another person shook his hand and congratulated him.

He glanced around and saw Minta across the room, surrounded by a crowd who was busy congratulating her. Slowly he began to inch that way, smiling politely, trying to make himself listen to what each person was saying.

By the time he neared Minta most of the crowd had cleared out. He waited until they were alone in the room. She glanced toward him with a broad smile. "Hi, McMillan. When did you arrive in D.C.?"

SHE VOWED SHE WASN'T GOING to let on that she was melting at the mere sight of him. He was studying her thoughtfully, and she decided to make it easy for him by being casual. "Guess who I was talking to today?" she asked.

He shrugged his shoulders slightly. "I can't imagine."

"Hilda."

The tawny eyes sparkled with amusement. "What did she say?"

"I'll never tell." Minta reached out and hooked her hand in the crook of his elbow. "Everyone's going to come looking for us if we don't show up at our own reception." She felt a muscle in his arm twitch convulsively, and she tilted her head back.

His voice was rough and unsteady as he pulled her into the circle of his arms. "They'll have to wait," he said as hands locked against her spine, clasping her body tightly to his. He lowered his head, whispering against her ear. "I've waited as long as I can."

His tongue traced the soft fullness of her lips before his firm, moist mouth settled gently over hers. They kissed deeply for a long time, and she felt a familiar thrill as she pressed against his masculine contours.

Brad was the first to draw back. "I've been missing you, darling."

She sought to recover her poise. Smoothing down the sides of her skirt, she gave him what she hoped was a cool smile. "Let's go."

He caught her arm. "Not yet."

She started to pull away just as Jill walked into the room. She turned to her friend. "Jill, please tell Jerry to keep everyone busy for a few minutes. Mr. McMillan and I need to discuss something."

Jill's eyes rounded as she surveyed Brad appreciatively. "Gladly, Minta," she answered with a knowing laugh.

Brad chuckled. "So that's Jill."

Minta flushed, remembering the lies she'd told Brad. "I guess you're disgusted with me, Brad."

"That's one emotion that's never entered my mind in connection with you."

"Okay, then angry. I should have leveled with you. I kept meaning to, but . . . ."

"Both of us have a lot to explain," Brad said. "How can I blame you for not telling me everything when I wasn't totally open with you?"

"But weren't you surprised about my job?" she persisted.

He smiled broadly. "Stunned, but I should have caught on when you ran around taking charge of every mysterious event. Would you mind if we saved this discussion until later? I've got something I've got to ask you."

She liked the expression in his eyes. "Oh? What?"

"If you had a choice, would you rather marry in Texas or in Washington, D.C.?"

"Inappropriate question, McMillan. Request further clarification."

"My God, you sound just like Hilda. I'm asking you to marry me, Minta."

"Oh, darling," she said, smiling. "I guessed that. But maybe you better withdraw your proposal. I won't make a very good wife."

He drew her to him and kissed her again, a long, full, intense kiss that left her feeling weak. When he lifted his head he said, "You'll be the best, just like you are at everything you undertake."

"But I won't be with you too much. I don't even know when I'll be ready to give up being an undercover agent. Do you know what my work involves?"

"Every minute I spend with you will be heaven," he murmured sincerely. "I won't let you go, so you might as well say yes."

The words she had given up ever hearing filled her with an infinite amount of tenderness and happiness. She made one last effort to make him understand what to expect from her. "You may change your mind when you see other women taking care of their husbands and their houses."

"I have a housekeeper for that," he protested fervently. "If I wanted another robot I'd invent one."

She laughed from sheer happiness and hugged him tighter. "Let's hope Hilda doesn't decide to join me in my career," she whispered, too low for him to understand.

He drew back and looked down at her. "Did you say yes yet, Minta?"

"A resounding yes. Now we better go next door. We can announce a new chapter in those memoirs is being written today, darling."

EPILOGUE

From the society column of a Texas newspaper:

Mr. and Mrs. Brad McMillan of Galactia Enterprises, celebrated their third anniversary Friday night by throwing a huge bash at their swank new hacienda in Austin, Texas. The guests were delighted as two robots, the well-known Hilda and her efficient companion, Herbert, completely handled all the hosting and hostessing duties at the event. McMillan explained that he believes he has at last made the breakthrough for a generation of affordable household robots.

Minta Cordero McMillan, a dark-haired native American beauty, is an intriguing jet-setter who divides her time between the couple's homes in Washington, D.C. and Austin. She's been reported from time to time popping up in the most unusual places, but she always explains that she's busy selling that fabulous line of silver jewelry she designs herself.

At the end of the evening, Mrs. McMillan popped a surprise on her guests by announcing there will be an addition to the family this fall. The delighted papa-to-be says he's working on plans for a new baby robot that will change diapers and mix formula. Oh, to have a genius for a husband!

ALL THOUGHTS OF HER QUEST MELTED
... PLEASURE OF HIS TOUCH.

**October's other absorbing
HARLEQUIN *SuperRomance* novel**

THROUGH NIGHT AND DAY by Irma Walker

There was a saying that the Pelente men loved only once, and when Mayi Jenners married Laurens Pelente, she knew it would be forever.

They would spend their lives in a fairy-tale village in the high Pyrenees, the Basque country Mayi readily adopted as her own. When the letter came, she saw her dreams shatter.

Laurens didn't want to believe the startling revelation about his wife, but as head of the Pelente household he could not ignore it. So Mayi set out to win back the love—and trust—of her proud husband.

A contemporary love story for the woman of today

These two absorbing titles
will be published in November
by

HARLEQUIN
SuperRomance

COME SPRING by Barbara Kaye

Federal wildlife agent Victoria Bartlett invaded
sheep country to track down the killer of a golden
eagle. She *would* succeed on the job . . . though she
had failed her husband.

Conservationist Grant Mackenzie was the first to
touch her emotionally since the divorce, and his
tender pursuit proved she was indeed desirable. For
Victoria, that was a start.

Too soon Grant wanted more—a woman to fill up
the empty spaces, a commitment. Loving him became oh, so easy, but love hadn't kept her man the
first time. Grant had to show her real men weren't
extinct. . . .

PERFUME AND LACE by Christine Hella Cott

On an urgent cross-Canada blitz to promote her
line of fragrances, Camille Beesley was shadowed
by a vaguely enticing spy. By the time she hit
Toronto, the man had taken definite shape—and
action! Professor Jacob Darleah was like a fine
essence, the first refreshing tang supported by a
lingering sensuous impression. . . .

He was lecturing in ancient remedies; his itinerary
just happened to coincide with hers. He said. Back
home in Vancouver, he was concocting more than
ointment in her lab late at night. . . .

Yet when Camille needed loving, she went to him,
but all she could trust about Jacob were his feelings
for her.